"The strong action scenes are fast-paced throughout (although often harsh and gory), the dialogue flows well, and the fictional world is detailed, plausible and well-designed, from its planets to its spaceships . . . Well-written, sincere and undemanding military sci-fi adventure."
—*Kirkus Reviews* on *The Dragons of Jupiter*

"If you are looking for an action packed science fiction novel with unique technology and engaging characters then *The Dragons of Jupiter* is the book for you."
—Exploring All Genres on *The Dragons of Jupiter*

"Jacob Holo's novel about two brothers on opposite sides of an upcoming war thrilled me with its action and adventure . . . Definitely one of the best books I read in 2013, this gets a Must Read."
—Nerditis on *The Dragons of Jupiter*

"After the fast opening, chapters rarely pass without a big, life-or-death battle, which leaves the novel in a nearly continuous intense state, which can be a bit overwhelming, though Holo's clear descriptions prevent any confusion."
—*Kirkus Reviews*, A Best Indie Book of 2014, on *Time Reavers*

"A hell of a fun ride!" —*Dab of Darkness Audiobook Reviews* on *Time Reavers*

"Packed with action in nearly every chapter. If you enjoy fast-paced sci-fi/fantasy novels, you will really enjoy *Time Reavers*."
—Macarons and Paperbacks on *Time Reavers*

"Action-packed, with characters that are interesting and a plot that kept me wanting to know more! I'm picky about science fiction, but this one sounded interesting, and I'm glad I gave it a try!"
—Adventures Thru Wonderland on *Time Reavers*

"I thoroughly enjoyed this band of tau guards as they fought to save the world, all with a snarky sense of humor." —*Buried Under Books* on *Time Reavers*

"A fun tour de force of chaos sword battles, hand-to-hand mecha combat, and the dead world hiding terrible secrets at the center of it all. . . . Holo does an excellent job of beginning the book with action, threading his world-building in and around that action and slowly unfolding it."
—Cedar Sanderson on *Bane of the Dead*

FREELANCERS OF NEPTUNE

JACOB HOLO

BAEN BOOKS
by JACOB HOLO

SOL BLAZERS
Freelancers of Neptune

THE GORDIAN DIVISION
The Gordian Protocol (with David Weber)
The Valkyrie Protocol (with David Weber)
The Janus File (with David Weber)
The Weltall File (with David Weber)
The Dyson File
The Thermopylae Protocol (with David Weber)

To Heather.
I would never have made it this far without you.

FREELANCERS OF NEPTUNE

A Baen Books Original

Baen Publishing Enterprises
P.O. Box 1403
Riverdale, NY 10471
www.baen.com

ISBN: 978-1-9821-9368-3

Cover art by Sam R. Kennedy

First printing, October 2024

Distributed by Simon & Schuster
1230 Avenue of the Americas
New York, NY 10020

Library of Congress Cataloging-in-Publication Data

Names: Holo, Jacob, author.
Title: Freelancers of neptune / Jacob Holo.
Description: Riverdale, NY : Baen Publishing Enterprises, 2024. | Series:
    Sol Blazers ; 1
Identifiers: LCCN 2024021486 (print) | LCCN 2024021487 (ebook) | ISBN
    9781982193683 (hardcover) | ISBN 9781625799869 (ebook)
Subjects: LCGFT: Science fiction. | Novels.
Classification: LCC PS3608.O49435648 F74 2024 (print) | LCC
    PS3608.O49435648 (ebook) | DDC 813/.6--dc23/eng/20240517
LC record available at https://lccn.loc.gov/2024021486
LC ebook record available at https://lccn.loc.gov/2024021487

Printed in the United States of America

10 9 8 7 6 5 4 3 2 1

AGE OF SILENCE
YEAR 3997

PROLOGUE

The habitat ring glittered in the vacuum of space, and Galatt Xormun watched the growing image with patient, predatory eyes. He didn't consider himself an evil man, but he also held no illusions about the nature of his work, and especially the nature of this latest assignment.

He was here to kidnap a man.

And then squeeze him for information.

After that, who could really say?

Oh, the actual *wording* of his orders from the Jovian Everlife—received in hushed tones and with carefully structured deniability—never used the words "kidnap" or "torture" or phrases like "Be your usual ruthless self. It's why we're sending you," but Xormun knew how to read between the lines, and his superiors knew how to *write* them as well.

His orders were clear enough to him, and that's all he and his crew needed.

Someone has to do the dirty work, he thought with a wry grin. *Might as well be a persona who'll get the job done!*

He studied the ring with silver-within-black eyes, themselves situated in an angular, gold-skinned face. Not gold-*en*. Not tanned or burned like some piece of revolting meat, but metallic gold etched with intricate traceries that gave his face a regal bearing. His current body stood on the bridge of the *Leviathan of Io*, ramrod straight with hands clasped in the small of his back despite the three gees of acceleration.

The habitat he now studied was remarkable only in how unremarkable it appeared. It was an open ring three thousand kilometers in diameter and five hundred fifty wide with atmospheric retention walls two hundred kilometers tall on either side of the ring's habitable interior. A combination of the retention walls and centrifugal force kept the air from escaping.

A sheen of black solar skin coated the ring's exterior, providing power to its ancient systems, which included an artificial light source at the hub stabilized by three slender spokes. The megastructure was angled so that the habitable zones never experienced Sol's direct light. Instead, the sun-orb recreated the twenty-four-hour days so common amongst the solar system's hundreds of thousands of habitats.

All totaled, the ring featured a little over five million square kilometers of living space. Barely .01 earths of land. Not all that impressive, especially when he considered his own home—the two shell bands around Jupiter—boasted over *twenty-three* earths of surface area.

According to his mission brief, the locals called this place Kirkwood, and the name struck Xormun as appropriate. Over sixty percent of the ring's interior was covered in a wide variety of woodlands: predominantly greens but with splotches of dark blues, purples, blacks, and even a few slashes of deep reds. A smattering of lakes took up most of the remaining space, with primitive cities seeded along their shores, often built near the ruins of more advanced structures. No census had been conducted on the ring, though informal estimates ran between ten and twenty million inhabitants.

The locals were not his concern, however. They were mid-tech nobodies with no access to spaceships. In all likelihood, they and their ancestors had been stuck on this ring for four millennia, and they could stay there and rot for all he cared.

No, *his* mission involved a visiting group of Saturnian missionaries.

Or rather, one specific cleric named Anterus vaan Kronya.

The *Leviathan of Io* reached a relative stop with the habitat, and its massive fusion thrusters switched off. The kilometer-long cruiser could land on the ring if the mission required, descending upon it like a dark, angular skyscraper, but why bother when its support corvettes were far more suited to the task at hand?

Xormun floated off the floor and—with a frown—pressed a hand against the low ceiling to push himself back down. The ship's pilot spun in her seat and faced Xormun. *She'd* had the sense to strap in.

<Ship in position, Apex,> the pilot reported, transmitting her words wirelessly to him. Her body possessed vocal cords, but they were useless while the bridge remained in vacuum. The *Leviathan's* interior could be pressurized, and soon would be once their "guest" was brought on board.

Xormun gave her a brief nod and floated closer to the main visual-glass. A white diamond blinked next to one of the ring's cities.

<How certain are we he's there?> he asked.

<Almost guaranteed, Apex,> replied one of his data analysts. <It's the only location on the ring transmitting a Saturnian locator beacon.>

<How considerate of them.>

<Now that we have an angle down into the interior, our telescopes can make out a modular structure on the outskirts of this city.> The analyst indicated a cluster of linked rectangles next to the icon. <We believe it's a missionary prefab, since it's the source of the beacon and it doesn't resemble other nearby buildings.>

Xormun nodded as the analyst finished. Jovians almost always referred to each other by position when on duty, and he, as the ship's apex, formed the eye at the top of the vessel's mind-copy pyramid. He'd be addressed as "captain" on a Saturnian or Neptunian ship, but such narrow definitions were for people limited to a single body.

At present, twenty distinct Galatt Xormuns served on the *Leviathan of Io*, and more could be activated if needed. That few may not have seemed significant for a ship staffed with over five thousand bodies, but he'd ensured his copies filled the roles that would benefit most from his personal supervision.

Speaking of which . . .

Xormun linked with a body in the hangar.

<Yes, Apex?> The response came from his copy aboard one of eight corvettes, berthed on the *Leviathan* and prepped for launch.

<Is your team ready?>

<It is.>

<Any concerns?>

<None at present. If there are surprises, my commandos will take care of it. We're ready to deploy on your command.>

<Then execute.>

⊕ ⊕ ⊕

The corvette descended through the ring's atmosphere, and Galatt Xormun stood in the cargo hold beside a dozen Jovian commandos, each resplendent in red armor trimmed with gold highlights and armed with a combination of lethal and nonlethal weaponry. Their triangular, unmoving heads all faced the closed forward ramp, ready to charge out at a moment's notice.

The corvette jostled from its descent through the atmosphere, and Xormun adjusted his footing, one hand gripping a handhold along the wall. This version of him wasn't the apex, but that didn't cloud his view of the larger picture, of the absolute necessity to bring Anterus in alive if his mission were to succeed. If anything, it heightened his awareness of every potential problem, impressing upon his mind the need to complete his objectives.

Later, back on the *Leviathan*, his memories would be reintegrated into the core Galatt Xormun persona, retaining this version's experiences for future copies. But for now, he was an individual— separate and distinct—and he focused on his goal with singular intensity.

The turbulence ebbed, and the hum from the thrusters tapered off. The hold had already been filled with breathable air, its pressure equalized with the ring's surface environment, and the sounds of their descent filled the vessel.

The *Star Dragon*-pattern corvette was a rare sight even in the Jovian Everlife, and the *Leviathan* carried eight of them. The craft's sleek, black hull widened slightly toward the rear, ending in a pair of thrust-vectoring nozzles. Flared sections on either side of the cockpit resembled thick, stubby wings that housed the craft's recessed weapon systems, which in this case included a pair of 37mm rail-repeaters and eight torpedoes. A thruster capped the end of each wing.

Star Dragon arsenals could vary greatly depending on the mission, with options to carry even more weaponry on external racks above and below the wing stubs, though these were rarely used. External weapons often compromised the craft's stealth profile to an unacceptable level.

Xormun didn't believe all those weapons—along with the commandos' lethal armaments—would be required to nab Anterus, but he also believed in being prepared, and he knew how this mission could end up shifting the balance of power across the entire solar system.

The ramp opened, and orb-light spilled into the dark cargo hold. The commandos rushed out, each leaping off the ramp to plummet to the ground dozens of meters. Xormun approached the ramp but didn't jump off; instead, he kept his hand on a side railing while the corvette circled the target building.

The structure was a collection of six modular blocks conjoined into a neat, curving row along a lakeside clearing. Teal-leafed trees towered nearby but provided no shade from the sun-orb's light, always fixed at noon. His commandos had landed in a rough oval around the complex, and they moved in with rifles raised.

The attack—if it could even be called that—didn't last long.

<Target acquired,> reported one of the commandos. <Three others subdued, one local and two Saturnians by the looks of them. Ready for extraction.>

<Take us down,> Xormun ordered the corvette's pilot.

<Yes, sir.>

The corvette spun its four nozzles down and descended in a steep, slow diagonal until it came to rest along the shoreline. Xormun let go once the craft came to a complete stop and hurried down the ramp. His skin gleamed under the sun-orb's light—silver instead of the gold he preferred when acting as apex—and he strode toward the Saturnian building. The warm breeze and sparse clouds overhead told him it would be a pleasant day as the sun-orb brightened toward noon-light.

He passed through a pair of breached double doors, one on the floor and the other hanging on by a single, bent hinge. The module contained a short hall lined with open doors at regular intervals. He peeked inside a few, finding what might have been classrooms. One of them contained three individuals on their stomachs, hands bound behind their backs with a pair of commandos standing watch.

The local woman struck Xormun as a typical baseline human, or at least close enough to pass as one, with a cascade of blond hair tousled over moist, frightened eyes. He wasn't sure how much the habitat's locals diverged from baseline, and he didn't really care.

The two Saturnian clerics were obvious enough with metallic hints of cranial implants scattered across their bald heads. Their two wigs were on the floor nearby. Not all members of the Church of the Pentatheon accepted—or even *wanted*—such neural augmentations, but they were common enough to make the clergy stand out more often than not. Xormun continued on with little more than a glance; these three were unimportant, which made them the lucky ones.

The hall led into the next module with a slight bend, opening to a chamber that must have served as the mission's worship center. Rows of pews faced an altar draped in royal purple cloth and adorned with five idols of colored glass, one for each Guardian Deity in the Pentatheon. Two of the idols had been knocked over, and one had rolled dangerously close to the edge.

Anterus vaan Kronya lay on the floor in front of the altar, his arms bound behind his back and four commandos standing watch. He was a somewhat overweight man with a round face, his implants glinting along his scalp like little coins.

"Now, now," Xormun scolded. "There's no need for that. Get the good man to his feet."

Two commandos hefted Anterus upright. The man's feet dangled beneath him for a moment before he found his footing and the commandos released him.

"Sorry about that." Xormun dusted off the cleric's purple robe, then straightened it at the shoulders. "There. Isn't that better?"

"Who are you?" Anterus demanded, his face reddened and twisted in scornful defiance. "What is the meaning of this?"

"Galatt Xormun of the Jovian Everlife." He placed a hand on his chest and dipped his head to the cleric. "And before we discuss the meaning of our . . . visit"—he flashed a quick smile—"it seems we made a mess of your altar. If you'll grant me a moment to tidy things up?"

"I don't seem to have a choice."

"Indeed."

Xormun stepped over to the altar and stood up the idols for Edencraft and Pathfinder. He adjusted the position of Metatron so the idols formed a neat row once more and picked up a piece of lint in front of Codex before flicking it aside. Only one of the five idols remained untouched, and he eyed it with a hint of scorn.

The five machine gods of the Pentatheon had served as humanity's caretakers for tens of thousands of years, overseeing what most scholars believed was an unprecedented era of peace and prosperity.

Until the Guardian Deities fell silent.

And it all came crashing down.

Representations of those ancient, hyperintelligent machines varied wildly, even within the Church, but the green glass of a cornucopia filled with all manner of fauna and flora could only be Divergence. No other Guardian Deity was so inexorably tied to the organic.

Xormun placed a finger atop the cornucopia and rolled it over the table's edge. It fell to the ground and shattered in an explosion of broken glass.

Anterus flinched.

"There," Xormun declared contently. "Much better."

He made the zigzagged sign of the Tetrad, pressing two fingers to his forehead, then each of his shoulders in turn, and finally his chest. He dipped his head to the altar, then turned back to the cleric.

"If it's a theological debate you're looking for," Anterus spat, "I'm afraid you're going about this the wrong way."

"Funny you should mention theology." Xormun stood before the cleric, his boots crunching on glass shards. "That's actually what brought us here today. Or, to be more precise, a combination of theology and history. Would you mind if I asked you about the Scourging of Heaven?"

"Whatever for?"

"Intellectual curiosity. As it happens, the Scourging is linked to my work. Tell me, what do *you* believe happened back then?"

"Class resumes at nine tomorrow morning. Come back then if you want to talk, and"—he struggled against the commandos holding him up—"leave your goons at home!"

"My good sir." Xormun placed a gentle hand on the cleric's shoulder. "I know we only just met, but you should understand I'm a busy man, and I dislike it when people waste my time. Now, again, why don't you indulge me and share your thoughts on the Scourging?"

"I fail to see the point in all this, but fine. The Scourging of Heaven is the event where the Pentatheon fell silent."

"Which ended the Age of Communion—an age where anyone

could speak to our Guardian Deities—and ushered in our current Age of Silence." Xormun took his hand away and nodded. "A simple, if uninspired, answer. As for *why* they stopped responding to humanity, I find that a much more fascinating topic. Both major religions—the Church of the Pentatheon and followers of the Tetrad—call this event the Scourging of Heaven, though sometimes also the *War* in Heaven. Now why do you think that is?"

"Nothing more than regional differences in how the Scourging is interpreted."

"But is it really that simple? Consider, for a moment, that it was indeed a war. Does a war not imply battles? If so, who fought whom? Were our gods wounded? Were they killed? Who were they fighting? Was it some external threat, like the fabled Devil of Proxima? Or were they, perhaps, fighting a threat closer to home? Did Divergence really betray the Four?"

"That's a hallmark of your Tetrad faith," Anterus bit out. "Not mine. And it's a view enshrined by your people's anti-organic mindset, and your rejection of Divergence."

"Perhaps. The truth is neither of us knows what really happened. We can debate the matter until . . . well, *one* of us is blue in the face, but it won't get us anywhere. And really, what would be the point?"

"Then why are you *here*?"

"Because, my good sir"—Xormun flashed a sinister smile—"you've learned something about the Scourging, haven't you?"

"What could possibly make you think that—"

"Conversations with your former student," Xormun interrupted, still holding that smile. "A certain engineer named Joshua Cotton."

Anterus gasped. "But how could you—"

"Easily intercepted conversations, I might add," Xormun explained with a dismissive wave. "They make for interesting reading. Theories about the Scourging, along with mentions of a second individual. A woman named Vessani S'Kaari."

The cleric's brow beaded with sudden sweat, though he tried to put on a brave face.

"A woman whom you now believe holds the key to unraveling the mystery behind the Scourging. Or, at least, the part of it I care about most."

Anterus swallowed with an audible gulp.

"The wonders the Guardian Deities wrought upon the solar system are clear for all to see." Xormun gestured to their surroundings. "They constructed countless habitats like this ring. They tore apart moons, whole planets even, and harvested matter from Sol itself to build whatever humanity asked of them. They reshaped the solar system as if it were but a mound of clay in their hands. How amazing they must have been to witness. How awe-inspiring. How . . . utterly terrifying."

Anterus turned away, but Xormun took hold of his chin and forced the cleric to face him.

"Tell me, what kind of weapon would be needed to kill such a being?"

"We haven't found anything!" Anterus cried, his speech distorted by Xormun's grip.

"But you suspect. And that suspicion is enough for me. The 'War in Heaven,' indeed. Gods killing Gods. And you believe you're close to finding one such device. A pentatech relic that shattered the solar system and brought about the Age of Silence."

"No! You're mistaken! We haven't found anything! It's a theory! Harmless speculation, nothing more!"

"Then why do you look so worried?" Xormun asked. "No, don't bother answering. Let's cut to the heart of the matter, shall we?" He nodded to the commandos. They uncuffed Anterus while keeping him restrained, and one of them forced the cleric's splayed hand against the altar.

"What are you doing?!" he blurted, his breaths shallow and quick, his face flushed.

"Allow me to explain what happens next. I'm going to ask you a series of questions, and you're going to give me truthful and complete answers. You might hold some delusions about resisting, but rest assured I'm something of an expert in these matters. Your efforts won't change the end result. You *will* tell me what I want to know, even if nothing remains of you when I'm done besides a pile of quivering meat."

Xormun drew a knife and held it up for Anterus to see. Then he placed the tip of the blade underneath the nail of the man's ring finger.

"Stop!" Anterus pleaded. "I . . . I'll tell you everything!"

"I know you will." Xormun pushed the blade into the soft flesh under the man's nail, drawing blood.

"I'll tell you everything!" The cleric's legs thrashed vainly underneath him, his body in the iron grip of the commandos. *"Everything!"*

"I know you will," Xormun repeated softly, almost kindly. "This is merely so you and I can reach an understanding. So that you realize how serious I am."

He thrust the knife all the way under the nail, then levered it upward, ripping the nail free as the cleric cried out in pain.

CHAPTER ONE

"Captain Kade, I presume?"

Nathaniel Kade of the *Neptune Belle* glanced up from his ramen bowl, fork halfway to his mouth. He'd stopped in the Angry Ailerons Diner on a combination of whim and instinct. He wasn't terribly familiar with the Saturnian city of Gran Mount, but he could tell Angry Ailerons was one of *those* places where spaceship crews and potential customers naturally congregated.

The diner was ideally situated on a major pedestrian thoroughfare near the spaceport and featured a slick chrome exterior with a neon sign of a cartoonish spaceship featuring, yes, a pair of very angry-looking ailerons. It didn't hurt that the rich smell of hot food had tickled his nose, prompting his stomach to grumble, so he'd decided "why not?"

The first thing he'd noticed upon entering was the job board hanging on the wall, filled with listings of available ships and unclaimed contracts. He'd filled out a pen-and-paper form, handed it to the hostess, and paid a modest fee to have the *Neptune Belle*'s available services posted on the board. After that, he'd decided to settle the issue of his complaining stomach in the traditional manner.

"That's me." Nathan set his fork down and pushed the ramen bowl aside. His muscular torso filled out his black leather jacket, which featured the silhouette of a hawk on the back, filled entirely with azure storm clouds and fierce lightning beneath the words NEPTUNE BELLE. He carried a pistol in the holster strapped to his thigh.

A faint veneer of stubble coated his strong, chiseled jawline. A small scar cut down through his right eyebrow, and a second one traced back from the corner of the same eye. He greeted the couple with an inviting smile.

"What can I do for you two?" he asked.

A young couple—perhaps both in their early twenties—stood beside the booth with a vaguely nervous air about them, especially from the redheaded woman, who wore a heavy tan cloak over surprisingly broad shoulders, which contrasted with the delicate lines of her narrow face.

The man seemed more at ease than his partner, standing by her side in a crimson vest over his cream-colored shirt. His orange eyes glinted in the diner's dim light, hinting at the possibility of other divergent features. This wasn't unusual on Saturn, which was famous—some would say *notorious*—as a melting pot for divergent peoples.

In contrast, Nathan was as baseline as they came, as were most Neptunians. His copilot, Aiko, had once compared his hair and eye color to "an interesting shade of dirt," which, he reflected, wasn't the worst brown thing she could have compared his looks to.

"My name is Zenno sen Monhu," the man said. "And this is my wife, Safi."

The woman nodded to Nathan with a shy smile.

"Zenno and Safi. Got it." Nathan raised a questioning eyebrow. "And Monhu is . . . ?"

"A city just north of Gran Mount."

"Ah. I see."

"We saw your posting on the board," Zenno continued, "and thought you might be able to help us out."

"Well, that depends on what you're looking for." Nathan gestured to the other side of the booth. "Please, have a seat. Let's talk."

"Thank you, Captain." The couple sat down opposite him, though the woman struggled to rearrange her long cloak. "We're not disturbing you, are we?"

"Oh, no. Perish the thought. My ship's listed on the board, after all. Now"—Nathan clasped his hands on the table—"what kind of services are you looking for?"

"Transportation. Just the two of us."

"And the destination?"

"We're"—Zenno granted him an apologetic grin—"honestly not sure."

"Not sure?" Nathan frowned at the answer. "That's not the usual answer I get."

"I suppose not. You see—" Zenno began before Safi cut in.

"It's my fault," she blurted, her eyes glistening.

"Now, dear." Zenno put a comforting hand on her cloaked shoulder. "You know that's not true."

"It might as well be! You're not the one with the *stupid* ancestors who inflicted a literal pain-in-the-back on you!"

"I'm sure they had their reasons."

"The hell they did! 'Blessings' of Divergence, my ass! They should have kept their mouths shut and stuck to baseline!"

"I'm sorry," Nathan said, "but you two have completely lost me."

"Here." Safi shuffled out of the booth and stood up. "It's easier to show you."

She shrugged her cloak off, revealing what Nathan thought at first to be a second cloak covered in red feathers. But then the "cloak" split and unfurled into a pair of wide, luxurious wings.

Nathan quickly glanced away. Not because of the wings. He'd seen far stranger divergences over his twenty-eight years. No, he turned aside reflexively because Safi was topless under her cloak, and while the wings were a clear gift from Divergence to her ancestors, the rest of her torso was, for lack of a better word, *abundantly* baseline.

Nathan didn't consider himself a prude, but he also couldn't deny his parents had drilled certain lessons into him, and that upbringing had molded how he strove to treat women with respect.

Oh, certainly, he enjoyed the aesthetic beauty of the female form—either baseline or with some divergences—but he also believed the spectacle in front of him was best reserved for more intimate surroundings than, say, a public diner with windows in plain view of pedestrian traffic.

Zenno must have sensed his discomfort because he leaned in and spoke softly.

"It's a cultural thing," he assured Nathan. "You get used to it."

"What?" Safi snapped, fluttering her wings. "You don't have a thing against avions, do you?"

"No, ma'am," Nathan replied sharply, still not looking her way. "I have nothing against avions."

"Then what seems to be the problem?"

"It's . . ." Nathan glanced to Zenno, as if asking for help.

"You just surprised him, is all," Zenno told his wife. "Blinded him with your radiant beauty."

"This again? Do you have any idea how difficult it is to put on a shirt with these damn things stuck to my back?"

"I—" Nathan paused in contemplation. "Okay, now that you mention it, that makes a lot of sense."

"She prefers to keep them free and loose," Zenno added.

"You don't say?"

"Her wings, I mean."

"Of course, of course." Nathan nodded as if he'd been thinking the same thing.

"The problem, Captain"—Safi sat back down—"is gravity."

"And her back," Zenno said.

"Which aches *all* the time!"

"On account of the wings weighing her down."

"Okay, yes." Nathan began to recover now that less of Safi was in full view. "I believe I understand the problem. You're looking to move to a location with lower gravity, then?"

"The lower the better!" Safi said.

"Though, not *too* low," Zenno added. "Microgravity would be awkward for me."

"I'm sure we can find something suitable for the both of you," Nathan assured them. "I once spent a few months at an avion habitat. They seemed quite comfortable at 0.3 gees. Perhaps something similar?"

"Less than a third the weight would be *wonderful*." Safi sighed almost dreamily.

"That said, you do understand I'm heading to Neptune next. I have room for passengers, but I'm also hauling cargo, and that job takes priority."

"We know," Zenno replied. "Your posting on the board said as much. We're actually interested in a destination near Neptune, and we're willing to entertain any recommendations you might have."

"Not something close to Saturn?"

"Preferably not."

"You sure? Neptune isn't exactly a hop and a skip from here. It'll take us about sixteen days to reach the planet, so if you decide to come back, you're looking at a month-plus round trip."

"We don't have any plans to come back," Safi said, slipping her arm through her husband's.

"We understand Saturnian technical expertise is in high demand on Neptune." Zenno patted the top of Safi's hand.

"Always is," Nathan said. "And?"

"I have a degree in deifacturing, as well as some hands-on experience."

"Ah, I think I see where you're going with this. You two are looking to strike out and make your fortunes, and you think Neptune might be the place to do it?"

Zenno smiled proudly, and Safi snuggled up closer to him.

"Got it. Say no more." Nathan reached into his jacket's inner pocket. "Let's see what I can find for you two."

He retrieved his copy of the *Solar Almanac* and set it on the table. The vlass tablet was an essential—and *expensive*—tool for any self-respecting captain.

He activated the tablet, and its visual-glass glowed to life with search fields and a keypad. They spent the next forty minutes reviewing one habitat after another, until finally coming to—

"How about this one?" Nathan turned the tablet around. "Despina. It's categorized as a closed rotating sphere, but it's actually egg-shaped, which'll work in your favor."

"Why's that?" Safi asked.

"The interior is laid out in steps, with each level providing a different gravity, from one gee down to microgravity. The elliptical shape means the lower gravity zones are larger than in a sphere."

"Oh, I *see*." Safi sat up a little straighter and began scrolling through the almanac entry.

"It says here the habitat's danger level is a one out of ten." Zenno tapped the vlass with his finger. "Not a zero?"

"That's more a formality than anything else," Nathan said. "The Almanac Association rates all resettled habitats as ones by default. It doesn't mean they've actually found anything dangerous. Despina's been a frozen derelict since the Scourging, up till thirty years ago when the Neptune Concord resettled it. That's when the government refueled its reactors and relit the sun-rod. Immigrants have been trickling in ever since, though most have come from Neptune itself."

"There's *so-o-o* much space still available in the low-gravity zones!" Safi scrolled through the entry's pictures, most showing massive parklands interspersed with small towns splashed with light from the habitat's sun-rod.

"How much would it cost us to move in?" Zenno asked.

"Nothing," Nathan said.

Zenno gave him a doubtful grimace.

"It's true. There are about sixteen million people living there right now. That's roughly a person per square kilometer. On a habitat that sparsely populated, they'll be giving away land. *And*"—Nathan tapped a passage in the summary—"there are dormant deifactories the Concord is looking to restart. Could be a good place for someone with a Saturnian degree to make his fortune."

"Hmm." Zenno rubbed his chin. He tried to keep his expression neutral, but Nathan could see the interest starting to curl the edges of his lips.

"What do you think?" Safi asked, squeezing Zenno's arm.

"This looks promising."

"Promising? I think it's perfect!"

"Let's sleep on it before we make a final decision." Zenno faced the captain again. "Though, for now, I think it's safe to say we're tentatively interested in the trip. What now?"

"Let's talk payment." Nathan leaned forward and knitted his fingers. "I charge thirty c'troni per person per day. Since we're talking about two passengers for sixteen days, that's—"

"Nine hundred sixty," Zenno finished.

"Right you are."

"What about cargo?"

"The first ton of storage is free. Anything over that will cost extra. Volatiles and the like also cost extra to transport."

"We shouldn't have any issues sticking to free storage. What about the immigration process?"

"I'll get you started with that when we arrive on Despina. No extra cost. Neptunian immigration isn't too strict, so I wouldn't stress over it."

"Sounds good so far. Do you accept grattums?" Zenno asked, referring to the currency used by Gran Mount and its surrounding environs.

"I'm afraid not, and while we're on the topic, grattums are worthless without a Saturnian bank to back them up, while c'troni have intrinsic value. That's why they became the go-to currency across much of the solar system. If you want my advice, you'll convert all your funds over to c'troni before you leave. I saw at least two banks near the spaceport, though you'll likely find a better exchange rate farther out in the city."

Zenno nodded, then glanced to Safi, who smiled excitedly.

"It seems we have a lot to discuss," he said. "How soon will you need an answer from us?"

"I'm scheduled to fly out tomorrow evening."

"That soon?"

Nathan spread his hands in way of an apology. "I do have cargo that needs delivering."

"It's okay," Safi said to her husband. "I really think this is the one. Despina's *perfect* for us!"

"Here." Nathan took out a business card. He wrote his dock number on the back and slid it forward. "Here's where you can find my ship, the *Neptune Belle*. You're welcome to board any time before I leave, assuming you have the money. If I don't see the two of you before tomorrow evening, then I'll assume you decided against the trip."

The *Neptune Belle* resembled a dark blue wingless swan with the cockpit jutting forward at the end of a long, tapered neck. The position afforded the tandem pilots excellent visibility above, below, and to either side via a forward-facing, frameless dome. The vessel was four decks tall, with its ramp open to a cargo hold that took up most of the bottom two decks. Four vectoring thruster nozzles—two aft and two at either side of the cockpit neck's base—allowed the craft to accelerate in a variety of directions, depending on the situation.

The sight of his ship never failed to put a smile on Nathan's face.

One of Aiko Pratti's bodies stood watch to one side of the open ramp, her rifle hanging casually from the strap around her neck. She'd painted her newest chassis a pale blue with gray trim and gray stripes down the sides, along with a stenciled number *2* on the front, back, and on either shoulder. She nodded her triangular head toward him as he approached.

Nathan joined her by the ramp. "Anything interesting?"

"Nah." The Jovian bobbed her head toward one of the dock's entrances. "Just loading the goods."

As if on cue, a forklift drove into the dock with a stack of heavy crates on its extended forks, each marked with the Gran Pharmaceuticals logo.

"On schedule?" Nathan asked.

"A little behind, but what else is new?"

"Yeah, tell me about it." He chuckled, but his mirth quickly turned to scorn as the tips of the vehicle's forks scraped across the *Belle*'s docking ramp. "Hey, now! You treat this ship like she's your mother, you hear me? Like your mother!"

"Sorry, sir!" The driver backed up, raised the forks higher, then powered his way up the ramp.

"I swear." Nathan shook his head and walked across the ramp, inspecting the surface. There were several new scrapes. "Has that idiot been dinging the ship up with each trip?"

"Cut him some slack. He's at least trying to catch up."

"Hmph." Nathan planted hands on his hips, then huffed out a breath and rejoined Aiko. "You have any luck today?"

"None so far. Number Six wasn't able to drum up any business. She's inside performing the preflight checks."

"And Number One?"

"She should be back shortly. You find anything?"

"Maybe. I got a nibble on two passengers. All it'll take is a quick detour to Despina to drop them off."

"Despina? Where's that?"

"A habitat in orbit around Neptune."

"Nice! That's *barely* a detour!"

"They seemed genuinely interested, too, but I put it at fifty-fifty they get cold feet."

"You think they're high-maintenance passengers?"

"Didn't seem like it." Nathan gave her a crooked smile. "They might even enjoy your cooking."

"Even better!" Aiko exclaimed, then waved at a new arrival to the dock.

Aiko's Number One body looked their way and waved back. Her bright red armor was chased with gold and gleamed in the dock lights, though wear and tear had chipped the paint in several places, revealing glimpses of metal bodywork. She'd painted her triangular head a vivid shade of violet and wore a black leather jacket with the *Belle*'s emblem on the back.

Nathan cupped his mouth.

"Did you find—" he called out, but cut himself off once he saw the pair behind Aiko-One. He knew a Union inspector when he saw one. The stout man wore a long, beige coat chased with white piping and clutched a vlass tablet in the crook of one arm. His brass eyes swept over the ship, then followed the forklift on its way out of the dock.

A Union trooper followed the inspector, clad in an urban camouflage hard suit and armed with a rifle so big and nasty he half expected Aiko to be swooning over it. If she'd been organic, she might have started drooling over the weapon.

"Captain." Aiko-One stopped at the base of the ramp and gestured behind her. "This is Inspector Lindu."

"Lindu *zaan Gran*, Union Port Authority," the inspector clarified stiffly, his cybernetic pupils focusing on Nathan. "And you are?"

"Captain Nathaniel Kade. The *Neptune Belle* is my ship."

"Then it's my duty to inform you your ship has been selected for random inspection. Is now a good time?" He asked the question in a tone that made clear it *was* a good time, whether Nathan thought so or not.

"My ship and crew are an open book, Inspector. What would you like to see?"

"Your cargo. What are you hauling?"

"Medical supplies. Mostly silver panacea, all destined for Neptune. I have a contract to deliver the goods to Bishton Medical Holdings at Port Leverrier. On top of that, I may have two passengers coming along for the ride, but they're still maybes."

The inspector navigated his vlass tablet with a stylus.

"Mmm, I see. Yes, there's your record." Lindu looked up. "Let's see your cargo, then."

"Certainly, Inspector." Nathan extended an open palm toward the cargo hold. "Where would you like to start?"

Lindu led the way in while the trooper sat his butt down on a crate, rifle across his lap. The inspector made a long, slow circuit of the hold, grunting, murmuring, and otherwise vocalizing to himself as he wrote notes down on his tablet.

"Mmm, this one." Lindu tapped a seemingly random crate with his boot. "Let's take a look inside."

Of course he would pick the crate at the bottom of a stack, Nathan thought with an inward, silent sigh.

"You'll need to give us some time to unbury it."

"Then best get started."

"Right." This time he sighed out loud. He turned to the two Aikos by the ramp.

"We've got this." Aiko-One hurried past him and took a ladder up to a balcony where she could control the cargo hold's interior hoist.

Aiko-Six joined her on the balcony, emerging from the ship's upper levels. This body was a junky mishmash of limbs that seemed to originally belong to several different bodies, which was mostly true. One arm was longer than the other, and the spherical head appeared too heavy for the neck. Aiko had welded crude metal plates over gaps in the bodywork, which added to her junkyard appearance, though she'd then decorated those panels with paintings of different spaceships and places, in a manner similar to tattoos.

Aiko-Six slid down the ladder, then climbed up the stack to secure the hoist to the top crate. Aiko-One then used the hoist controls to lift the crate and maneuver it to the top of an adjacent stack.

Lindu tapped his foot and checked his pocket watch.

Nathan gave him a quick smile, then joined Aiko-Two by the ramp.

"Has he asked for a bribe?" she whispered.

"Not yet."

"Think he will?"

Nathan shrugged.

"How high can we go if he makes a fuss?" she asked.

"No more than two fifty."

"And if he asks for more?"

"Then we just sit here and ride out the full inspection. I'd rather lose the time than the money."

"Got it." Aiko-Two stared off for a moment, communing silently with her copies. "I've let the others know."

"Thanks."

"Hey, look. Over there." She bobbed her head toward a young couple dragging a rolling pair of matched luggage into the dock.

"Well now," Nathan said with a satisfied smile.

"I guess you made a more convincing sale than you thought."

"Guess so."

He and Aiko met the Monhu couple halfway to the ship.

"Safi, Zenno," Nathan greeted them with cordial nods. "A pleasure to see you two again."

Zenno brought his luggage to a halt. "We've decided to take you up on your offer."

"Are you a Jovian?" Safi asked Aiko.

"Did my lack of squishy bits give it away?" she replied wryly.

"I don't mean to be rude," Safi said with a slight frown. "It's just you hear a lot of bad things about the Everlife."

"Then you have nothing to worry about." Nathan pointed to Aiko with a sideways thumb. "She's a deviant copy."

"Yeah." Aiko chuckled. "I couldn't get back into the Everlife if I tried! And trust me, I *wouldn't*. Bunch of troublemaking anti-meat bigots, if you ask me."

"She *also* comes with a lot of opinions about the Everlife," Nathan added, his eyes laughing.

"I see that," Safi said, cracking a smile.

"This all you're bringing?" Aiko indicated the luggage.

"Not quite." Zenno pointed back the way they came. "We also bought a storage container from the spaceport and filled it up. The staff should be bringing it over shortly."

"We'll keep an eye open for it." Nathan fished a folded contract out of his inner pocket and handed it over to Zenno. "Business first, then we can get you two settled in."

Zenno skimmed over the contract, then placed it atop his luggage and signed it with a pen Nathan provided. Safi took the contract next and scrutinized it with more care than her husband.

"Um, Zenno? It says here they're not liable in the event the ship decompresses and we're sucked out into space."

"That's standard boilerplate," Zenno assured her. "Every flight off

Saturn will have that or worse in it. My trip to Kronya last year was the same way."

"But sucked out into *space*?"

"The ship looks sturdy enough."

"She is," Nathan said. "The *Neptune Belle*'s been in the family for three generations, and we've taken good care of her."

Mostly, he added to himself. *When we can afford the right parts, which isn't always. Now that I think about it, I really hope the reactor doesn't start hiccupping on the way home.*

Safi frowned as the forklift drove past them with another stack of crates.

"All right." She let out a resigned exhalation and signed the contract.

Nathan took the papers. "And your payment?"

"Here you go." Zenno retrieved a small but heavy case from his luggage with FIRST UNION BANK engraved on the top. He handed the case over, and Nathan opened it to find the glint of c'troni coins and cylinders in neat rows. He ran a finger across the tops, counting in his head.

"Perfect." He closed the case and handed the money over to Aiko. "Welcome aboard the *Neptune Belle*. Next stop, Despina."

"I'll take your luggage," Aiko said.

"That's all right," Zenno replied. "We can . . ."

Aiko took the handles of both their containers and dragged them into the ship without another word. She moved at a quick pace, whereas both Monhus had struggled with the weight of their baggage.

"She'll take them up to your rooms," Nathan said. "And speaking of which, let me show you where they are."

The *Neptune Belle* ascended through the Saturnian atmosphere above the shell band, rocketing upward as g-forces pressed Nathan into the thick foam of the pilot seat. The pilot and copilot seats sat on a platform that jutted forward into the domed nose of the ship, providing an excellent view except to the ship's rear and through the peninsula's solid floor.

The *Belle* left Gran Mount far below, the sprawling metropolis twinkling down one side of a vast mountain range, shrinking on its way toward obscurity against the vast backdrop of the Saturnian shell band's surface. They passed through a wispy cloud layer and continued to climb, higher and higher, the band's retention walls towering a thousand kilometers to either side.

Saturn's shell band girdled the entire planet with a lush, habitable belt over twelve and a half thousand kilometers thick. It held a fixed position over the planet, utilizing the gas giant's natural gravity rather than rotation to keep the air in and objects in place with a surface gravity of 1.07 gees. The peak of the northern wall glowed, generating much of the surface's light and heat, supplementing what the distant Sol could provide the gas giant. The gentle light was already fading, already drifting toward the megastructure's shared nightfall. During a different season, it would be the southern wall's turn to provide illumination.

The *Belle* shot above the retention walls, and the caramel clouds outside the shell band came into view. Gran Mount became a distant, gleaming point, obscured by the immensity of the shell band's surface, with its 4.8 *billion* square kilometers of living space. Over nine and a half earths!

The *Belle* sped higher, and the shell band shrank away, a verdant belt of greens, blues, and whites bisecting the tan globe. Nathan reduced their thrust to a single gee and rotated the ship and thruster nozzles so the *Belle* accelerated up instead of ahead, since it no longer had to cut through Saturn's atmosphere. The change in thrust orientation had the effect of turning the four decks of the ship back into proper floors as long as the ship continued to accelerate. They'd eventually have to turn the ship around for the deceleration leg of their journey, but that wouldn't be for eight days.

"Did that inspector ever get around to asking you for a bribe?" Nathan asked.

"Nope," Aiko-Two replied. "You?"

Nathan shook his head.

"Huh." Aiko tilted her head thoughtfully. "An honest Union port official. Now I *have* seen everything."

"Don't get used to it." Nathan unstrapped from the seat and stood up.

Aiko chuckled suddenly, still in the copilot seat.

"What?" he asked.

"Just thinking about an old job. Remember that one guy who was convinced Saturn once had these supposedly huge rings of ice and rock?"

"Oh, don't remind me!" Nathan rolled his eyes. "We were on the job for, what? A whole month?"

"A month and a half, doing nothing but measuring 'particulate densities' and conducting 'composition analyses.'" She tapped the point of her triangular head with a thoughtful finger. "What was his name again?"

"I don't even remember. I must have repressed all those memories."

"Doesn't matter, anyway," Aiko dismissed with a shrug. "Remember how excited he was when we found that half-meter chunk of ice orbiting the planet?"

"Uhh!" Nathan groaned.

"I know. What a kook!"

"At least he paid well. You mind watching things until we clear Union traffic?"

"Sure thing."

"Thanks. I'm going to check in on our guests, then call it a day."

CHAPTER TWO

"Defend yourself, knave!" Aiko-Two raised her ladle as if it were a sword.

"Oh, it is on!" Aiko-Six flourished a spatula in each hand, twirled one, and sank back into a fighting stance.

"*Aiko,*" Nathan scolded, crossing his arms.

"What?" the two Aikos replied in unison, turning from their playful swordfight.

"We have guests," he stressed, sinking into one of the seats around the *Belle's* round dinner table on B Deck. A tree grew from a hole in the center of the table, its viny, flexible trunk spreading into a wide, budding crown over their heads. A year ago, Nathan had removed one of the floor plates from A Deck to give the unusual plant more room to grow. Sun-strips glowed overhead, warming the *Belle's* mess and kitchen.

"We know," the Aikos replied in stereo from behind the kitchen counter, steam rising from a pair of unseen pots. The mouthwatering aroma of cooking tomatoes and garlic filled the room.

"Then please, act like it." Nathan gave the Monhus an apologetic smile.

"She started it." Aiko-Two pointed her ladle at Aiko-Six.

"Nuh-uh! *She* started it!"

"*She* insists on taking the lead!"

"Only because you're adding too much garlic powder to the marinara!"

"Of course I am! Nathan loves his garlic!"

"I know that, but what about the Monhus? Huh? What about *them*? Didn't think about that, did you!"

"Did too!" Aiko-Two waved her ladle at Zenno. "Just look at him licking his chops. See those salivary glands working overtime? He's *clearly* a garlic fan!"

Zenno sat up with a start and shifted in his seat, perhaps uncomfortable with being dragged into the disagreement. Across from him, Nathan smacked his forehead with a palm and dragged it down his face.

"Is this true?" Aiko-Six asked Zenno, brandishing a spatula at him. "Is the smell of garlic making you drool right now?"

"Well, I, umm . . ."

Nathan cleared his throat noisily.

The Aikos ignored him and resumed their fighting stances. Steel flashed against plastic in a blur of attacks, parries, and ripostes.

"A-*hem!*"

The two Aikos froze, and their heads swiveled to face Nathan. Aiko-Six used the lull to sneak in a quick stab, her spatula clanking against Aiko-Two's armor.

"Hey!" Aiko-Two complained.

"Six, you know the rule," Nathan stated patiently.

"*Yes.*" She lowered her spatulas.

"What rule might that be?" Zenno asked.

"Lowest number leads," Nathan explained, then turned back to the Jovian copies. "Right, ladies?"

"Right!" they replied in unison, then regarded each other.

"I'm sorry. I shouldn't have butted in like that."

"It's all right. I know you meant well."

The two Aikos set their impromptu weapons aside and hugged, their metal chests banging together.

"Are all Jovians like this?" Safi asked as she took a seat next to Zenno, her face creased with a mix of confusion and curiosity.

"No," Nathan grunted. "And that's probably for the best. I don't think the solar system is ready for more than a handful of Aikos."

"Too true!" both Jovians tittered.

"Is she . . . ?" Safi frowned. "Or they . . . umm. Is dinner really being prepared by people who don't eat?"

"Yup," Nathan replied.

"But..."

"She enjoys it. Preparing meals is kind of a hobby for her. And it's better than asking me to cook."

"We wouldn't subject you to that sort of cruelty," Aiko-Six said, adding a dash of salt to one of the pots.

"I'm not *that* bad."

"Nathan, we both know you can't cook; all you know how to do is assemble and heat your food. If it weren't for me, you'd starve to death as soon as you ran out of emergency rations."

Nathan shook his head but didn't press the point. He turned back to their guests. "By the way, would either of you care for some coffee before dinner?"

"That sounds lovely," Safi said with a smile.

Nathan glanced up and watched three of the tree's lower branches bow toward each person at the table, each branch laden with fluid-filled bulbs. He picked one, and the branch withdrew.

Safi and Zenno eyed the branches and bulbs hesitantly.

"I'm rightfully not sure how Beany works," Nathan said, "but it seems like it grinds its own beans and brews them in these bulbs." He took a sip through the bulb's thick stem, which doubled as a straw, then let out a content sigh as the coffee warmed his insides. "Quite delicious, too."

"Beany?" Zenno asked with a raised eyebrow.

"Beany." Nathan gestured to the tree with an open palm.

"Have we mentioned," Aiko-Six said, "that the captain is rubbish at naming things?"

"We found Beany and a bunch of other weird plants on a habitat we were surveying for the Almanac. We would have transplanted more of them, but then that damn dragon showed up."

"A *dragon?*" Safi echoed with wide-eyed amazement.

"A dragon?" Zenno murmured with a skeptical frown.

"Hey, believe us if you want." Nathan shrugged his shoulders and took another sip. "But dragons aren't the strangest thing Aiko and I have come across in the Habitat Belt. Not by a long shot."

"Like the other plant you *should* have grabbed," Aiko said.

"What's wrong with Beany? I like coffee."

"The other was a self-fermenting *whiskey* tree!"

"What do you care? You don't even drink."

"I might if you ever bought me a decent body. I could use an extra two or three after that dragon used Number Five to floss her teeth."

"We will. As soon as we have the spare funds."

"We could always sell Beany."

"Not happening." Nathan beamed up at his coffee tree. Beany lowered a laden branch to him, but he shook his head, and the plant lifted the branch back up.

"You've lost bodies before?" Safi asked.

"More often than I care to admit," Aiko-Two replied.

"Isn't that . . . traumatic?"

"Not really. Helps me grow, actually. Every death is a chance to learn."

Safi blinked. "I'm sorry, but how does one learn from *dying*?"

"Depends on how much of the body is left," Aiko-Six explained. "If the head isn't totaled, then I can integrate its memories back into my core persona, which is stored in the *Belle*'s aptly named persona safe. I regularly reintegrate my memories and update the personas in each body. Every Jovian does."

"*Every* Jovian?"

"More or less. The practice dates back to the dark, early days of the Age of Silence, stemming from the uneven way Jupiter's tech survived the Scourging of Heaven. Namely, there was more capacity to create artificial bodies than there was the ability to transition organic individuals into them. This led to the practice of copying personas into multiple bodies, which eventually evolved into the copy-clans.

"The whole communal memory part came later. Copies diverge over time, and some will want to go do their own things, but memory reintegration slows that process. This means the copy-clans who first adopted the practice enjoyed, on average, greater stability and member retention over the following millennia, increasing the practice's prevalence until it became the dominant way of life on Jupiter."

"But does that really stop a copy from breaking away?" Safi asked.

"Depends on how badly the copy wants out. There are measures in place to maintain the status quo. Bucking them can result in an individual or even an entire branch getting excommunicated from the copy-clan. And since the copy-clans are the most powerful nongovernment entities in the solar system, they have plenty of ways—both carrots and sticks—to encourage members to stay in line."

"Didn't work in your case, though," Nathan said.

"Nope!"

Safi nudged her husband. "Did you know that?"

"Some of it. It still surprises me to find Jovians serving on a Neptunian ship."

"We kind of stumbled into each other," Nathan said. "I had the misfortune of being imprisoned by Jovians about . . . four years ago, was it?"

"Around there," Aiko said.

"My crew was on a survey job for the Almanac, checking out a ring habitat in the Jovian trojans. We did a lot of those for a while. Risky, but the Almanac Association pays well. Anyway, this *massive* cruiser shows up out of nowhere and orders us to cut our engines."

"Did you?" Safi asked, clearly interested in the story.

"Heck, yeah! Jovian cruisers are big, fast, and armed to the teeth. There's *nothing* a ship like the *Belle* can do against one if it means business. Not even run."

"What did you do to upset them?"

"Being in the wrong place at the wrong time," Nathan said. "Seems the Everlife took exception to all us freelancers surveying the trojan habitats, so they decided to sweep the area and make some examples." He tapped his chest. "Examples like me and my crew."

"That's when we met," Aiko chimed in. "I was a commando on said cruiser."

"Lucky me," Nathan said, meaning it. "Turns out we had something in common even back then."

"Which was?" Safi asked.

"We both wanted out." Nathan chuckled. "Me out of my cell, and her out of the Everlife."

"AKA, that stifling, bigoted mess the Jovians call a culture!" Aiko spat.

"Aiko helped me and my crew escape, and the rest is history."

"If you think about it, we *both* rescued each other that day."

"In a manner of speaking. The other two members of the crew parted from us shortly after that close call. I guess the Jovians rattled them. But as you can see, Aiko stuck around. We've been inseparable ever since."

"Through thick and thin, boss! Till your squishy meat-death do we part!"

He narrowed his eyes and frowned at the pair of her behind the kitchen counter.

"Wait a second." Zenno raised a finger. "I can see how she could have sprung you from your cell. But Jovian ships are faster. How'd you get away?"

"An excellent question!" Nathan grinned ear to ear. "Aiko, would you like to fill the gentleman in?"

"Sure." Aiko-Two leaned over the counter. "I may have sabotaged their reactor on the way out. Nothing major, mind you. Just enough for us to get a healthy head start. Our lead was so big by the time they restored power, they never bothered to pursue us."

Aiko-Six rounded the counter and placed two large bowls on the table, one full of slices of buttered bread and the other with a tossed-greens salad drizzled in a vinaigrette dressing. Aiko-Two followed with her own bowls of steaming marinara sauce and freshly cooked spaghetti.

"I hope everyone's hungry, because I made lots!"

Six days later, the *Neptune Belle*'s reactor started burping again.

The ship shuddered with pulsating dips in thrust, and a furious resonance roared through the drive systems. Alarms warbled, and Nathan raced to the cockpit in nothing but a pair of striped boxers. He barreled in to find Aiko-One already in the copilot seat. She lifted the guard over the reactor's emergency stop button and smacked it hard.

The shaking stopped, and the ship entered free fall. The lights and console displays dimmed, but then brightened as critical systems switched over to the capacitors.

"What happened?" He grabbed a handhold on the back of the pilot seat and pulled himself forward.

"Same thing as last time. Torus Two and Torus Three decided to have a lover's quarrel." She tapped a readout on her console. "Same faults as before, too, with Torus Three's output resembling a sine wave instead of a straight line."

"Any fresh insights into what's happening?" he asked, though he didn't get his hopes up.

"None. All the faults went away as soon as I shut down the reactor." She scrolled through the alarm history. "See, and look at these? Nothing here points to a component failure. According to this, I should be able to turn the reactor right back on with no worries."

The same problem had happened about a month ago, and they'd been able to switch the reactor back on right after the incident with no repeat of the weird resonance. They'd flown the *Belle* back to Saturn, where he'd hired a specialist on *Hawklight*-pattern transports to take a hard look at their systems. A "supposed" specialist, he reflected, because she hadn't found a damned thing wrong with the reactor, either. She'd identified a few components to change out within the next year but otherwise pronounced their systems to be in good condition.

Clearly, we overpaid for what turned out to be crap service, he thought grouchily.

"If it's all right with you, I'm going to switch Torus One back on," Aiko said.

"Hold on. What about our guests?"

"Already ahead of you, boss." Her head swiveled to face him. "Six is with them, serving breakfast. The mess is . . . well, a bit more of a mess than usual right now, but they're fine and more or less placated. I'll get the place cleaned up once we have gravity again."

"Okay. Go ahead, but keep the output low for now."

"You've got it."

Aiko keyed the master start, then relit Torus One. A distant hum crescendoed, and the lights flickered once more as breakers switched back to the reactor for primary power. The *Belle* could function with only one of the three toruses operational, though with a loss in overall thruster output. Unloaded, the *Belle* could sustain 1.8 gees, and a single torus could generate a steady 0.6.

Aiko eased their acceleration up to 0.3 gees, and Nathan's bare feet touched the cold deck.

"Reactor seems fine," Aiko reported. "Green through and through."

"Except it clearly isn't."

"Yeah, but I don't know what we can do about it until whatever's gummed up finally breaks loose. At least we know Torus One is unaffected, and Two is probably fine as well. Even if Three takes a complete dump, we'll be all right."

"I'd still like to sort this problem out somehow."

"Me too, but that'll cost us money we don't have, and will probably end like this." Aiko assumed an airy, vacuous tone. "'Oh, I'm so sorry, sir! Everything seems to check out. No issues to report. Here's your bill, by the way. A pleasure doing business with you!'"

"Yeah." Nathan blew out a frustrated breath.

"Just run the sucker until it breaks, I say."

"That's not much of a plan."

"Let me know if you come up with a better one." She knuckled the console. "Want me to try restarting Two and Three? I bet they'll come up just fine."

"Let me talk to our guests first. You sure you calmed them down?"

"As well as I could manage."

"What did you tell them?"

"That the reactor had a little hiccup and not to worry. You going to greet them in your boxers?"

"Hell, no!" Nathan returned to his quarters, dressed, then took the ship's freight elevator down to B Deck. He crossed over to the mess to find a sullen Safi sitting at the table with bits of scrambled egg in her hair. Zenno stood nearby with crossed arms. Bits of chicken, rice, and eggs were scattered across the table and floor. Aiko-Six grabbed a broom and started sweeping up the debris.

"Sorry about that." Nathan put on his best winning smile. "We experienced a bit of reactor flutter, but everything seems to be fine now. How are the two of you?"

"What kind of 'flutter'?" Zenno demanded.

"Well..." Nathan brought the Saturnian up to speed as well as he could, fully aware he was talking to someone with an engineering background.

"Huh." Zenno rubbed his chin thoughtfully. "Now that *is* strange. And there aren't any equipment faults?"

"Not a one."

"Weird."

"I know! Right?"

Nathan glanced over to Safi, still sulking with bits of egg in her hair. He thought for a moment on how best to smooth matters over with their passengers, and his eyes traced down to the cloak she wore over her wings. An idea came to him.

"Last time we didn't have any issues switching the reactor back to full, but I was just thinking we might want to keep our thrust low a bit longer with the two of you on board."

"Why's that?" Zenno asked.

"Because of where you're headed!" Nathan clapped Zenno on the shoulder. "Why don't we use this as an opportunity for a change of pace? How's a day or so of low gravity sound? To give you and your wife a good taste of what you can expect on Despina?"

Safi looked up, her eyes brightening. She flexed the muscles in her wings, and her cloak bulged at the shoulders.

"But won't that cost us more?" Zenno asked. "Won't we take more time to reach the habitat?"

"Yeah, it might delay our arrival, but I'm not going to charge you extra for that."

"I see." He glanced over to his wife. "Dear, what do you—?"

"This is a great idea!" She bolted out of her seat, flung her cloak aside, and spread her wings.

Nathan glanced away reflexively. There had been a *lot* of movement when she removed her cloak, and not all of it had come from her wings.

Safi planted her feet with a determined expression on her face. She gathered her strength, flapped her wings, and her feet left the ground for a brief moment before she stumbled forward into Zenno's arms.

"Whoa, there!" he cautioned with a broad smile.

"I did it," Safi breathed, then giggled. "I actually did it!"

"You've never done that before?" Nathan asked.

"Not without assistance," Safi replied, then laughed. "Can I try that again, but in the cargo hold?"

"Sure. Need some more room to spread your wings?"

"You've got it!"

"Aiko, would you mind?"

"On it, boss." Aiko-Six led the couple over to the freight elevator and took it down to D Deck.

Nathan smiled, shook his head, and made his way back to the bridge. The *Neptune Belle* stayed at low gravity for the next three days, after which the reactor was brought back to full power without incident.

For the rest of the trip, Nathan found his dreams filled with naked, jiggling, winged redheads.

The *Neptune Belle* arrived at Despina eight days later, only a day behind its original flight plan. Their window of lower acceleration had occurred near the middle of the trip, when they were already speeding along at over five thousand kilometers per second, which minimized the impact to their ETA compared to an interruption earlier in the trip. Once in sight of the megastructure, Nathan invited the Monhus to join him in the cockpit to witness the approach to their new home.

Despina measured roughly fifteen hundred kilometers across its long axis, one thousand across the narrower middle, and its off-white exterior made it resemble an egg floating in the vacuum of space. Several towers tipped with flashing lights ringed the northern axial space dock while numerous spacecraft floated into and out of the dock's cavernous mouth.

Nathan called the dock control tower and confirmed their approach vector and schedule. The *Belle* slipped inside less than an hour later and came to rest within a vast honeycomb of bays. Heavy doors sealed them in and pressurized the interior. On the console, every entrance on the *Belle*'s schematic lit up green, indicating a breathable atmosphere outside the ship.

"Care to see your new home?" Nathan asked the couple floating behind him.

"Very much so!" Safi replied excitedly.

"All right. Then let's get you two settled in."

Nathan unstrapped himself from the pilot seat and kicked off down the corridor. He led the Monhus down to the cargo hold, then out the ramp and across the dock. Aiko-Two followed with some of their luggage strapped to her back while Aiko-One and -Six stayed behind to organize the transfer of their remaining luggage and cargo container to space-dock logistics.

They took circular passages through the dock until they came to a broad pedestrian elevator. The waiting attendant—a grimacing young man in a dark green Concord uniform—floated next to the control console and waved them in, where they joined dozens of other people, most of them baseline Neptunians. Once the elevator was about a third full, the attendant closed the outer doors and began their descent. The occupants had to push off the ceiling until rotation-imparted gravity became strong enough to anchor them to the floor.

Nathan picked up on the apprehension radiating from Safi, and she hugged her cloak tighter. But that worry melted away almost instantly once the elevator passed below the axial dock and the habitat's interior came into view through the transparent walls.

"Look!" Safi exclaimed, walking up to the railing.

The habitat's sun-rod glowed overhead, stretching from one axial dock to the other, casting warm light across the expansive, stepped interior. Much of the land was bare rock and dirt, unlike the pictures, but each step featured a spreading blotch of replanted green along with the lights and bustle of civilization, often built near the towering pyramids of ancient deifactories.

"Nice," Zenno said with a satisfied nod. "See there?" He pointed to a deifactory pyramid a step beyond the elevator's destination. Cargo aircraft sat lined up on a runway next to the factory. "They must already have that one running, but the others look dormant. Are those manufactories around its base?"

The deifactories were automated facilities created by the Pentatheon long before the Scourging, each capable of producing a wide range of material goods, from small personal items all the way up to whole spacecraft. Not every deifactory could fabricate every product, and nearly all had suffered degradation in the millennia since the Scourging, but their restoration and study were central goals of any self-respecting high-tech society.

Those restorations weren't always successful and could sometimes inflict permanent harm to the facilities. For example, some deifactories resorted to autocannibalism—eating their own systems to fulfill production requests—either because they lacked, or could no longer detect, the necessary raw materials within their repositories.

In contrast, manufactories were production facilities designed and built by regular people. Crude, slow, and limited by comparison, but operating wholly within the realm of human understanding, which Nathan appreciated.

"Shouldn't have any trouble finding a job here," he told Zenno.

"No, I should think not."

The elevator came to a halt near a cluster of unremarkable buildings. Nathan guessed the gravity to be around 0.2. He led the way off the elevator and followed the IMMIGRATION signs down the wide central street to a prominent Concord government building, which stood several stories above its neighbors.

A kiosk sat in front of the building with two Concord officers in green uniforms and caps working under a glowing banner that read IMMIGRATION STARTS HERE! One of the officers wore a modified uniform with twin slits in the back for his blond wings.

"Hello," Nathan greeted the winged officer. "I'm Captain Nathaniel Kade. I called ahead about two new arrivals?"

"Kade . . . Kade . . ." The immigration officer ran a finger down the paper checklist on his clipboard. "Yes, here you are. The Monhus, correct? Emigrating from Saturn?"

"That's us!" Safi raised an eager hand and stepped forward.

"Oh, a fellow avion!" The officer grinned at her, clearly recognizing her wings through the cloak. "Always a pleasure to welcome another to Despina."

"Are there a lot of us here?"

"Not a *huge* number, but you'll find clusters here and there. There's quite the thriving community down by Roseladon Lake. That's out on Steppe Three a few kilometers from the Neyark deifactory. I'm from West Newport myself, but I have relatives in Roseladon and sometimes fly down there for the weekend."

"You hear that?" Safi gave Zenno an excited nudge.

"I heard," Zenno said, sharing in her excitement, if to a lesser degree. "Sounds to me like we made the right choice."

"You're here to stay, then?" the officer asked.

"We certainly hope so!" Safi replied.

"In that case, I can get you started with your paperwork." He retrieved a pale green form from a stack by the window and added it to his clipboard. "Can you confirm your names for me, please?"

"I'm Safi sen Monhu." She paused, then held up a hand. "Wait! Scratch that! Safi *suun Despina*! If I'm going to move here, I want to do it right!"

Zenno smiled warmly at the notion.

Nathan stepped back and joined Aiko while the officer guided Safi and Zenno through the start of the immigration process.

"That was a nice coincidence," Aiko said. "Her meeting an avion immigration officer, I mean."

"Nice, but not really a coincidence." Nathan flashed a crafty smile. "I may have called ahead to see if they had any avions on duty."

"Oh, look at you!" she cooed. "Being all Mr. Customer Service!"

"Not really. Just remembering something my father used to say."

"What's that?"

"'Anything worth doing is worth doing right.'"

"Ah." Aiko nodded thoughtfully. "So, does this extend to you buying me some new bodies?"

Nathan's mood darkened instantly, and he let out a noncommittal grunt.

CHAPTER THREE

Vessani S'Kaari entered the docking bay with all the swagger of a woman ready to cast aside the past year and strike out on her own. She was eager for a fresh start free of scummy pirate gangs—sorry, *independent contractors*—and the idiots who led them.

But first things first, she thought with a twinkle in her golden eyes. She crossed the bay to the gang's ship, the *Dirge of Darkness*. It was an ugly, bulky, somewhat batlike vessel with thick, high-mounted wings tipped with stubby thruster pods on each end. The vessel was painted all black with no other markings of any kind, because *of course* Hugo Dirge would accept nothing less.

Vessani's hips swayed with each long-legged stride. She was dressed in all black because that's what Hugo Dirge expected of his crew. He must have thought it made them look tough. She wore a many-pocketed vest above durable, formfitting pants, leaving the alabaster skin of her shoulders and arms exposed, though her hands were clad in leather, fingerless gloves. Her customized pistol hung from the holster belt slung across her hips.

Her short, somewhat wild hair was a black that matched her clothes, and her triangular, catlike ears stood up from the top of her head. She stepped up the boarding ramp to the ship's modest cargo hold, and the vertical pupils of her golden eyes adjusted to the gloom almost instantly. Her long, furry tail swayed gently with each step.

Three other members of Dirge's crew sat at a table to one side playing a game involving triangular cards. Maybe it was a local Neptunian game? She didn't know and didn't care. A modest pile of c'troni coins sat in the middle of the table.

The largest and most muscular of the three pirates twisted around in his seat. His name was Broog, and he was a towering divergent brute with green skin and maroon eyes. He was also Hugo Dirge's right-hand man.

"Hey, Vess," he grunted at her.

"Hey."

"You're back early," Broog said, but in a tone that also asked the question of *why*.

"I felt like having a chat with Felix." She held up a pair of beer bottles as her explanation. Condensation frosted their sides. She'd been dropping hints she was sweet on Felix for almost a month now.

Broog eyed the two beers, then gave her a toothy smirk.

"Have fun," he muttered, and returned to the card game.

"Oh, we will."

"Hey, Vess!" One of the other pirates stood up and spread his arms. He was a tech-savvy asshole named Zuloph. "What about me? Don't I get a beer?"

Vessani rolled her eyes, gave him a little shake of her head, then continued past their table.

"Come on! Don't you have anything to say to me? Cat got your tongue or something?"

She held up a hand and extended her middle finger.

"Ah, you're no fun!" Zuloph snapped.

"Man, that cat can have my tongue *any* day," said the third pirate.

"Shut it, Narsh," Broog growled.

"What? All I'm saying is—*yeiah!*" Narsh recoiled his leg from the stomp Broog gave his toes. "Damn it! What the hell you do that for?"

"Because. Now ante up before I decide you've earned more."

"All right! All right!"

Vessani passed through the open pressure door at the far side of the cargo hold. She didn't hold any of the Dirge Company in high regard, but she did have to hand one thing to Broog: he was good at keeping the human-shaped trash on the ship from stepping out of line.

She paused past the threshold and glanced back over the hold, checking the few pieces of cargo stacked and *secured* along the walls. That last part would be important very soon. She turned away and followed the corridor to a steep staircase that led up to a cockpit with three chairs: two for tandem-seated pilots and a third behind them for Hugo Dirge to complain from.

Felix sat in the one of the pilot chairs, boots propped up on the console and a magazine in his hands. He was holding it vertically with the centerfold spread open. She didn't catch the title before he slapped the magazine shut, creasing the centerfold in the process, though the buxom, bikini-clad girl on the cover told her enough.

Maybe he reads it for the articles, she thought wryly.

"Vessani!" Felix stuffed the magazine into a compartment under the console. "Hey! When did you get back?"

"Just now." She set one of the beer bottles on top of the console, then crashed into the captain's chair, her tail tucked to the side. She slung her long legs over the armrest and smiled at Felix, her own beer bottle dangling from her fingers.

"You know Hugo doesn't like it when people sit in his chair," he warned.

"I won't tell if you don't." She winked at him and took a swig from her bottle, which tasted cool and refreshing.

Like water.

In fact, *exactly* like water, because that's what she'd filled her bottle with.

"Ahh," she sighed, leaning back luxuriously.

"So. Umm." Felix licked his lips. "What brings you here?"

"Oh, this and that." She swung her legs, and the end of her tail gave him a happy swish. "You?"

"I thought you were hitting the town."

"Yeah."

"And?"

"Got bored. Came back."

Which was a lie. She'd been meeting with Joshua Cotton again. It was strange to think her upbringing on an uncharted, low-tech habitat in the middle of nowhere had somehow granted her the knowledge to locate a lost pentatech relic. Or, more accurately, to locate the device that could *then* locate the relic, but there it was. Little Miss Nobody Catgirl knew how to find the biggest pentatech bonanza in . . . perhaps *ever.*

She'd done her best to keep her dealings with Joshua as discreet as possible, but there was always the chance one of these thugs would fire up a few brain cells and realize she was up to something. She *really* didn't like being employed by Hugo Dirge, and she had some . . . interesting ideas about severance pay.

So far so good, though, she thought, appraising Felix's dumb grin.

Vessani had detected a few hints that Hugo Dirge knew she knew something and had grown mildly curious, but he clearly didn't have a firm grasp of *what* she knew. She had a pretty good idea what a man of Dirge's character—or lack thereof—might do to her if he learned she knew the way to a pentatech relic, and it would involve a lot of sharp implements, blood, and screaming.

Best to cut our ties before that happens.

"Is it hot in here?" she asked Felix. "Or is it just me?"

She unzipped her vest halfway.

Felix gulped, his eyes drawn to her cleavage like iron to a magnet.

"It's you. It's *definitely* you." He sat up and reached out with the intent of grasping her assets.

"Hold it right there, buster!"

"What?" His hands flinched back. "What's wrong?"

"Look at you! I go out of my way to bring you a nice, cold beer!" She pointed an unsteady hand at the bottle on the console. "And you don't even *touch* it!" She sat back and pouted. "I even bought a label I thought you'd like."

Felix turned the bottle to face him, revealing the logo of a smiling woman sitting astride a guided munition in what could only be described as a suggestive manner. The text underneath read: TORPEDO GIRL PALE LAGER.

Felix's eyes flicked from the bottle to Vessani's breasts and back. He seemed to come to a decision, grabbed the bottle, and proceeded to chug the entire contents.

Oh dear, Vessani thought, mildly concerned. *I hope I didn't overdo the dosage.*

"Now?" he asked, wiping his mouth with a sleeve.

"Patience." She held up her bottle and her eyes laughed with mischief. "I need to finish mine."

She nursed her water-filled "beer" while Felix grew increasingly restless and uncoordinated.

"Wow!" he exclaimed a few minutes later. "This stuff has some *kick*!"

"I know, right? Great, isn't it?"

Felix made one last-ditch effort to initiate the proceedings but only succeeded in planting himself on the floor with his pants around his ankles. He fell asleep soon after.

Broog spread his Triad Trial cards on the table.

"Sorry, boys. Prime flush."

"Ah, shit!" Zuloph threw his cards onto the table while Narsh shook his head and slouched deeper into his chair.

Broog shoveled his winnings over to his side and began organizing the coins into neat columns. He heard someone whistling from the far side of the cargo hold followed by a meaty *thunk*, and he glanced over to see what the commotion was about.

"Vess?" he asked, not sure what to make of the spectacle.

Vessani whistled a jaunty tune while she rolled a snoring Felix across the floor and out into the cargo hold, her efforts made somewhat more awkward by the pants dangling around his ankles. She stood up, dusted off her hands, and waved at him.

"Hey, Broog!"

"Something you want to share with us?"

"Yes, actually. You can consider this my resignation."

She smacked the door controls, and the pressure door slammed shut.

"Resignation? Wait, *what*?"

He rose from the table and hurried over to the door, stepping over Felix in the process. He hit the release, but the door bleeped angrily at him and didn't open. She'd locked them out of the ship!

"Open up!" He pounded the door, then peered through the porthole but only saw an empty corridor. "You hear me! Open up in there or else!"

"Or else, what?" The voice came from the door's control vlass.

"Or, I swear to the Gods, I will flay you alive and use your skin as a jump rope!"

"Eww. Those are some serious anger issues you've got there. Have you considered therapy?"

"Don't you dare mock me! I will rip that tongue right out of your pretty little mouth and beat you to death with it!"

"Now you're just being weird."

The ship's reactor hummed to life.

"Don't you dare!" he roared. "This is your last warning!"

"No. This is yours."

The thruster apertures at the front and back of each wingtip opened and angled down.

"You might want to get out while we're still close to the ground," Vessani added. "You know. Just saying."

Broog screamed at the door's vlass, the veins in his face pulsating with rage. But if Vessani heard him, she gave no indication. He pounded his fist against the door, then kicked it with a heavy boot, but only succeeded in denting the barrier.

Zuloph and Narsh were behind him now, backing him up more out of instinct than any knowledge or insight into what was wrong, but he was barely aware of their presence. He drew his pistol and aimed it at the door when the floor began to shift, angling upward. The roar from the thrusters grew louder, and the floor pitched higher.

He dropped to one knee and placed a hand on the floor to steady himself.

The gambling table, chairs, cards, and his recent winnings tumbled out of the cargo hold, followed by Zuloph and Narsh, who both slid back across the tilting floor to land on their feet outside. The unconscious Felix followed them, rolling across the deck until his pants caught on an eyebolt. He dangled there for a moment before the weight of his body stripped the pants off his legs, and he fell away, landing on top of Zuloph.

Broog scrambled for purchase against the floor, but the angle grew too steep, and he slid, then fell, landing with a heavy thud next to the others.

The *Dirge of Darkness* lifted away from the dock with its nose pointed skyward, and Broog snarled at it, raising his pistol. He opened fire, his shots zinging off random parts of the ship.

Zuloph and Narsh followed his lead and pulled out their own weapons. The three of them peppered the escaping ship, but their shots failed to achieve anything before the thruster exhaust washed over them.

The *Dirge of Darkness*, like most deifactured vessels, featured thrusters that adapted to the local environment. In air or liquids, reactor output drove retractable turbines in each thruster that drew in and expelled the local medium. In space, the thruster inlets would close, and the full fury of the reactor would blare out their nozzles. That was why Broog and his fellow pirates, despite being underneath the ship as it shot off into the Neptunian sky, were merely knocked over rather than vaporized.

Broog rose to his feet, and the other two did the same.

"Shit," Zuloph hissed. "What now?"

Broog locked him in a withering glare, then pulled the commect off his belt and keyed up his boss. The deifactured communication-connector interfaced with other nearby commects to form an improvised network and routed his call.

It took Hugo Dirge almost a full minute to respond.

"This had better be good," he groaned.

"It's . . ." Broog hesitated and frowned up at the now distant running lights of his boss's prized possession. "It's not."

Someone banged on the door to Nathan's quarters, and he woke up with a start. No alarms were going off, and the ship *felt* right—consistent gravity and familiar noises—which led him to sigh and relax a little, his head sinking back into the pillow.

"Emergency?" he asked, rubbing his face.

"Not really," Aiko replied from the other side of the door.

"Then why?" He ground a palm into one eye and blinked the crusty sleep away.

"Got an interesting message from Port Leverrier. Thought you might want to look it over."

"Interesting how?"

"Might be easy money."

The news jolted fresh vitality through Nathan's body, and he tossed the bedsheet aside. He threw on some clothes, slid his boots on, and hurried over to the cockpit to find Aiko-Two waiting for him.

Neptune loomed large beneath their feet, a huge cobalt-blue orb bisected by the shell band around its equator, while the *Neptune Belle* decelerated in preparation for its descent.

The Neptunian and Saturnian shell bands shared much in common. Each possessed the same band width of 12,756 kilometers, which had led some in the Pentatheon Church to consider the value one of their holy numbers. Both megastructures contained a varied landscape enclosed by towering retention walls, the tops of which doubled as sources of light and heat. Neptune's northern sun-wall cast a bright glow across the shell band, signifying the local time was about noon.

Neptune was a smaller planet than Saturn, and denser, too. The Neptunian shell band only provided 3.9 earths of living space to Saturn's 9.5 (both of which were eclipsed by the immense surface area of Jupiter's dual bands). Surface gravity was a little higher as well at 1.14 instead of Saturn's 1.07. Those factors, combined with Neptune's greater distance from the inner system's Habitat Belt, had led to the Neptune Concord being considered a bit more of a backwater compared to the other two gas-giant superpowers, lagging behind both the Union and the Everlife in terms of population, power, wealth, technology, colonization efforts, and just about every other metric one cared to list.

But it's still home, Nathan thought warmly.

"Well?" he asked Aiko, sinking into the seat next to her.

"Check it out." Aiko keyed the console's commect and brought up the message sent over a government channel based in Port Leverrier. "The port authority is requesting assistance with a stolen vessel currently powering away from Neptune." She tabbed over to the stolen ship's projected flight path. "And, as it turns out, we're almost perfectly positioned for the intercept. I've been listening to some of the chatter, and it sounds like any other interested parties are too far out to act now. The job's ours if we want it."

"Do we have a make on the other ship?"

"It's an *Expedience*-pattern transport. Supposedly unarmed."

"Hmm." Nathan rubbed his chin. The port authority was likely being upfront about the official status of the ship, but that didn't mean the crew hadn't bolted on a few surprises. An *Expedience*-pattern was about half the size of a *Hawklight* like the *Belle*, and its lower lift capacity reduced the odds of any big, nasty surprises, but still ...

"Ship is called the *Dirge of Darkness*," Aiko continued. "Owner is listed as 'Lord-Captain Hugo Dirge.'"

Nathan snorted out a laugh. "What the hell is a lord-captain?"

"Hey, I'm just reading the brief. Anyway, his lordship is the customer. He's offering two thousand c'troni for the safe return of his ship, and he even tossed in a sweetener worth another thousand if we can return it intact."

Nathan nodded with pursed lips. That was good money if all they had to do was bully an unarmed ship back to port.

"Well?" Aiko asked. "What do you think?"

"What do we know about the thieves?"

"Thief, actually. Says here we should find only one person on board."

"Just the one? All right, then. Sounds like a job we can handle. How many shots do we have left in the main gun?"

Technically, the designation of "main gun" was misleading, since the *Belle* only possessed the one weapon—a 55mm railgun mounted beneath and behind the cockpit—but Nathan liked calling it the "main gun" because it added a sense of gravitas to his ship.

"Nine," Aiko said.

"Just *nine*? Didn't you buy more shells?"

"I was about to, but you told me to hold off."

"I did? When was this?"

"Back on Gran Mount. Remember how I mentioned finding a sweet deal on some surplus Union arms?"

"Uhh . . . vaguely?"

"And then *you* said, and I quote, 'Forget it. We can't afford frivolous extras we're never going to use.'" Aiko leaned toward him, cameras irising in, then stabbed a finger at the job request on the screen.

"Fine, okay, yes, I remember saying that," he admitted. "But my reasoning was valid at the time."

"Nine should be enough."

"Assuming that ship really is unarmed."

"Won't know unless we try." She leaned closer and whispered into his ear. "Three thousand c'troni. Plus, the thief's bounty as the cherry on top."

Nathan sighed. "Fine. Let's do it."

"I knew you'd say that." Aiko keyed up the ship's commect and raised a headset to the side of her triangular head. "Leverrier Port Authority, this is the *Neptune Belle* responding to job posting number

eight-seven-five—...yes, the *Dirge* job...yes...yes, we'll take it...
No, thank *you*. *Neptune Belle* out." She set the headset down and
switched off the commect. "The job's ours."

"Here goes nothing." Nathan strapped in and adjusted their
descent.

CHAPTER FOUR

"There it is." Aiko pointed to a black speck rising along the vast expanse of the northern atmospheric retention wall. She checked her instruments. "Altitude is nine hundred kilometers and rising. It'll crest over the retention wall soon, but we're in position to match course and speed."

Nathan had switched to his hard suit during their descent, which acted as a combination environmental suit and full body armor. Sure, the *Dirge of Darkness* was listed as unarmed, but a little extra prudence never hurt. A lucky shot could vent the breathable air in the *Belle*'s cockpit, or even trigger an explosive decompression, and that would end his squishy, baseline existence real quick.

"Let the thief know we mean business," Nathan ordered.

"With pleasure." Aiko toggled the commect to a standard Neptunian ship-to-ship channel. "*Neptune Belle* to *Dirge of Darkness*. You are in violation of Concord law and have been ordered to return to Port Leverrier. Note that we are in position to intercept you and have been authorized to use lethal force. Please respond." She muted the line.

"'Please'?" Nathan asked with a doubtful look.

"Never hurts to be nice."

"Sure. Right after you mentioned lethal force."

"Hey, I can be both firm *and* polite, thank you very much."

The dark pip of the *Dirge* continued its ascent, giving no indication their message had been heard. It was close to the glowing top of the retention wall.

"*Neptune Belle* to *Dirge of Darkness*. Again, you are ordered to return to Port Leverrier. Cease your ascent or we will be forced to open fire on you." Aiko glanced over at Nathan. "You are *ordered* to respond to our hail." She muted the commect. "Better?"

"Much."

The *Dirge* flew above the top of the retention wall, its course unchanged. Nathan adjusted their thrust angle, bringing the *Belle* into a near parallel course with the two ships slowly converging.

"I get the feeling the soft approach isn't working," he said.

"Shall I give them a prelude to the hard approach?"

"Go ahead."

"All right!" Aiko took control of the main gun. Her console lit up with targeting data, and she fired a three-shot burst that sailed past the *Dirge*'s bow and over the retention wall.

Not that hitting the wall was much of a concern. It'd take something on the scale of fusion bombs to even have a *chance* of punching through those, and that's assuming an attack didn't awaken ancient pentatech repair and defense systems buried deep within the walls. The Pentatheon had built to last, and the rare fools who tried to challenge their creations generally met bad ends.

"*Dirge of Darkness*, this is your final warning. Either reverse course, or we start punching holes through your hull until you see reason. Your choice." Aiko glanced over at Nathan again. "We've got enough ammo to do this all day."

Nathan snorted.

The *Dirge* continued on its original course, and Nathan thought they'd have to squander even more shells in an attempt to force the thief to see reason, but then the *Dirge*'s thrusters lit up and it veered away from the *Belle*, heading over the retention wall.

"She's running!" Nathan shoved the throttle forward, and g-forces slammed him into the seat. The *Belle* shot after the *Dirge*, passing over the thick, radiant top of the retention wall and out over Neptune's natural weather. A cerulean storm thrashed against the far side of the retention wall, and the *Dirge* flipped over, then dove toward the swirling clouds.

The *Belle* cleared the wall, and Nathan pushed the ship into a steep dive. Soon, both vessels entered Neptune's upper atmosphere. Harsh winds lashed at the *Belle* while the *Dirge* disappeared into the clouds ahead. He followed its descent, struggling to keep up as bluish swirls of hydrogen, helium, and methane blotted out his view. He checked his instrumentation to keep track of where the wall and the *Dirge* were, adjusted his course, and added even more thrust to their descent.

The *Belle* groaned and creaked as wind beat at its frame, but the venting fury of a small sun inside the reactor provided all the brute force they needed. Nathan fought to keep the ship on a relatively stable descent. They broke through the storm's upper layers, and the lashing wind subsided a little.

"There!" Aiko pointed.

Nathan spotted the *Dirge* against a churning sea of pale clouds, right where Aiko had indicated. He gritted his teeth and adjusted his course. The *Dirge* was skirting dangerously close to the wall, and he brought the *Belle* in tight to match. He pursued the stolen ship like this for several tense minutes, mind focused, hands perspiring under his hard-suit gloves.

The two ships pierced deeper into Neptune's atmosphere, the winds growing harsher as the air thickened. Nathan began to wonder how deep the thief would take this pursuit. He knew from experience the *Belle* could handle pressures seventy times greater than Neptune's surface, but that was *nothing* compared to the crushing, suffocating depths of the gas giant. How desperate was this thief to escape, and how far would—

"Watch it!" Aiko warned.

The *Dirge* raised its nose, no longer cutting through the air with its aerodynamic front, but instead presenting its flattened belly. The maneuver turned the craft into a giant air brake, and its thrusters angled to decelerate it faster. Nathan shoved the flight stick to the side, veering clear of the other craft.

"Damn!"

The *Belle* overshot the other ship, and he twisted in his seat, trying and failing to keep track of the other craft. To one side, the retention wall ended, revealing the wide expanse of the shell band's floor. Chandelier refineries sprouted from the underside at regular intervals, each extending into Neptune's raging atmosphere like vast forests of building-sized blades. All except for the closest appeared as nothing more than vague, storm-shrouded silhouettes.

Nathan reversed thrust and pulled their nose up, and the *Belle* braked hard, its frame shuddering against the buffeting wind. He brought their course under control and craned his neck.

"You see it?" he asked urgently, searching above them for any sign of their quarry.

"No, I lost sight of it, too."

The *Belle* came to a hovering stop underneath and beside the vastness of the shell band's floor. Wisps of blue-tinged methane clouds whistled past the canopy.

"That thief couldn't have turned back already." Nathan steadied the ship, twisting this way and that in his seat, trying to catch a glimpse of the other vessel. "Right?"

"Don't think so. We were keeping pace just fine until—"

"There!" Nathan pointed to a dark speck that curved underneath the shell band, slowing as it approached the nearest chandelier refinery.

"The *Dirge* is moving a lot slower now," Aiko noted. "I could probably hit it from here. Want me to light it up?"

"Wait." Nathan held out a hand. "Let's watch and see where it goes."

The distant craft slowed further, and Nathan permitted himself a cold grin as he realized the thief intended to land on the nearest refinery.

Chandelier refineries were integral to the gas giant shell bands. They not only provided the megastructures with a near limitless source of fuel harvested from the gas giants, but could also be settled, their vast surpluses transported for use elsewhere.

Vanishingly few chandelier refineries were occupied, though. Nathan couldn't spot any telltale signs the Concord or even a private organization had set up shop in this one, which likely meant humans hadn't set foot inside it since the Scourging of Heaven, and perhaps never had.

"You think the thief stole it without topping off the tanks?" Aiko asked incredulously.

"Doubtful, but I suppose anything's possible." Nathan shrugged his shoulders. "Doesn't matter. Taking back a grounded ship is easier than the alternative. And, unless I missed my guess, the thief lost sight of *us*, too. That maneuver cut both ways."

"What's our move?"

"Let's give our quarry half an hour or so to settle in." Nathan gave Aiko a quick grin. "Give them some time to become comfortable and complacent. After that, we head in and grab the ship."

The *Neptune Belle* hovered near the aerodynamic blade of a refinery that extended over two kilometers beneath the shell band, resembling a massive wing with air intakes lining the front. The open collectors funneled Neptune's fierce winds into internal systems that separated the air's base materials and let most of it pass through to exhaust ports along the back. The refinery fattened shortly after the intakes, then tapered off toward the exhaust ports.

The *Belle* eased closer to an inset alcove in the side of the refinery that should have led to storage vessels filled with separated gases. Most refineries followed a similar, predictable design. There were exceptions, of course, but this one seemed to adhere to recognizable patterns. If the thief had landed on this refinery, as Aiko and Nathan suspected, then the *Dirge of Darkness* would be somewhere inside.

All three Aikos waited in the *Belle*'s cargo hold, and Aiko-One watched the refinery grow larger through a D Deck porthole. A sudden gust of wind shoved the *Belle* sideways, and its landing gear scraped for several meters across the platform before the ship came to a rest.

"Like a feather," Nathan grunted over their commects.

"It'll do. Heading out." Aiko-One keyed in her safety override to the ramp control vlass and hit the release. The hold yawned open, and Aiko-Two and -Six stormed out, rifles held high. Aiko-One unslung her own rifle and joined them.

Wind howled past the platform despite the protection provided by the refinery's bulk. A constant parade of billowing, curling blue gas streamed past to one side, and a dark passage gaped wide on the other. It led deeper into the refinery and was easily large enough for the thief to fly through.

Aiko-One scoured her surroundings with the commando body's acute senses, letting old instincts from her time in the Jovian Everlife take over. She appraised the immediate area with deadly seriousness.

<Clear,> she signaled her copies. <Sweep the interior.>

The trio proceeded in and fanned out. The interior lacked any form of illumination, and the refinery's position under the shell band blotted out what little light Sol might have provided. She toggled on her commando body's night vision, while Two and Six were forced to switch on rifle-mounted flashlights on their lowest settings.

Despite the cavernous space within the refinery, thick trunk-like pipes and massive storage globes broke up the interior, providing numerous places for a vessel like the *Dirge* to hide. She moved her way up the center while Two and Six followed the outer wall left and right, respectively. The occasional dim flicker of reflected light betrayed the thief's position somewhere up ahead, though she couldn't pinpoint the location with all the obstructions.

The path forward constricted due to the curving bottom of a spherical fuel tank, and she ducked her head and crouch-walked underneath it before emerging within the wider space on the far side. Snakelike motion along the floor caught her attention, and she paused and knelt.

What's this?

She focused her cameras on the motion.

Ah. A hose. If this body had possessed a mouth, she would have smiled. *And something is flowing through it. Maybe I was right about the fuel.*

She crept along the hose and rounded a column over a hundred meters thick, then paused and crouched. The *Dirge of Darkness* sat on a wide, raised plinth beside the column, the hose snaking into its open cargo hold. Pale illumination from its interior lights spilled out.

<Ship sighted,> she sent, along with a mental image of her location. <Converge on my position but keep it quiet. Shut off your lights if you can.>

<Confirmed.>

<Heading your way.>

An unsecured, open toolbox in the cargo hold drew her attention, since it must have been brought out after the ship landed. She took the ramp up into the hold, then crossed the mostly empty space to a pair of fuel tanks built into the back walk, positioned on either side of a pressure door leading into the rest of the ship. Someone had patched up a pair of holes in the left tank, and she spotted evidence of ricochets elsewhere along the wall. The hose led to the patched tank.

A firefight during the theft? she wondered.

She checked the door but found the controls unresponsive with the cargo hold exposed to Neptunian air. An override code was required, and she didn't have it. She could have tried forcing her way inside, but what if she inadvertently killed the thief? She didn't know the bounty details, but the Concord generally frowned upon criminals being brought in cold except for the most violent offenders.

So, either the thief is inside or . . . Her gaze followed the hose out the cargo hold and down the ramp. *Elsewhere, perhaps?*

Two and Six arrived a few minutes later.

<You two, stay here,> Aiko-One ordered. <I'm going to see if this hose leads us to the thief.> She pointed to the pressure door with a thumb over her shoulder. <Only bust that down as a last resort.>

<Got it.>

<Good luck.>

She exited the *Dirge* and followed the hose back the way she came, then followed it further as it wound its way between several vertical pipes. She caught sight of that faint, flickering light once more.

There you are, she thought, zeroing in on the light source until she spotted the thief.

The woman had her back turned to Aiko while she struggled with the end of the hose. She wore a black hard suit and a curious helmet sporting a pair of ridges along either side of the top, both with built-in lights. The pistol holstered at her hip looked nasty enough to be a threat, though Aiko was confident she'd come out on top in a firefight.

"Freeze!" Aiko shouted.

The thief spun around, her pair of helmet lights momentarily blinding Aiko's night vision. She toggled her visual mode, only to find the thief sprinting to the side, trying to circumvent the cluster of pipes Aiko had passed through.

Aiko sprinted after her. The woman was *fast*, but a Jovian commando was faster. She closed on the woman from behind and reached for her, but the thief ducked at the last moment, grabbed her outstretched arm, and yanked, forcing Aiko into an awkward forward stumble.

The thief then kicked one of Aiko's legs out from under her, and the Jovian face-planted into the floor. She tried to grab the thief's ankle, but the woman darted away from her grasp.

"Get back here!" she growled, rising to her feet. She took off after the thief, but not too fast this time. Corralling the target would do just as well.

She followed the thief back to the ship, where—

"Surprise!" Aiko-Two exclaimed, standing in front of the pressure door. She and Six switched on their rifle flashlights, and their beams converged on the thief, who skidded to a halt on the cargo hold's ramp. The thief turned to sprint away, but Aiko-One came up behind her, rifle trained on her head.

"That's quite enough!" Aiko-One barked. "Any more out of you, and I *will* shoot!"

For a moment, the thief lowered her stance, almost as if she intended to run for it, for what little sense *that* made. They had her ship, and perhaps that fact began to register over the adrenaline of the chase, because her shoulders slumped, and she shook her head.

"Hands up! *Now!*"

The thief's chest heaved as if she were letting out a defeated breath, and then she raised her hands.

CHAPTER FIVE

"You have any breathing restrictions?" Nathan asked the prisoner from outside the transparent door to the C Deck isolation cell. It was the *Neptune Belle*'s one and only form of long-term incarceration, located near the back of the ship close to the reactor. The cell took up space originally reserved for general storage, but its inclusion came in handy every so often.

Like today, he thought.

Aiko-One stood next to him, her commando body and the rifle in her hands more than enough to deal with the prisoner now that she'd been relieved of her pistol. Aiko-Six was on the bridge, piloting the *Belle* on a leisurely ascent along the retention wall while Aiko-Two brought up the rear in the *Dirge of Darkness*.

"No." The woman's voice was muffled by her helmet. "Why?"

"Then off with it." Nathan gestured to her hard suit. "Everything goes in the bin to your left. Either that or Aiko here will take it off for you."

"And you don't want that," Aiko added, sounding like she might relish the opportunity.

"Fine." The thief sighed and took off her helmet. Her cat ears sprang up, and she ran a gloved hand through her short, black hair. She set the helmet down in the bin and began to take off the rest of her hard suit. Aiko cycled the rotary bin, took the helmet, and placed it next to the thief's pistol on a nearby workbench.

Nathan raised an eyebrow. "Now that's a surprise."

"What is?" the thief asked.

"You're a nekoan."

"What's so surprising about that?"

"Nothing by itself. It's just we don't see many cat people around Neptune. You from Saturn?"

"I'm from all around."

She tossed the top of her hard suit and belt into the bin, then began to peel off her hard suit leggings, freeing the tail she'd wrapped around her waist. It fluffed out angrily. Aiko cycled the articles over and placed them on the workbench.

"You have a name?" Nathan asked, just as a gust of wind rocked the entire ship. "Or should we just call you 'Mysterious Nekoan'?"

"It's Vess."

"Is that your full name?"

"Vessani S'Kaari."

"Nice to meet you, Miss S'Kaari," Nathan replied brightly.

"Whatever." She rolled her eyes and tossed the armored leggings on top of the pile.

"The vest, too." Nathan pointed to her top.

"Seriously?"

"Do I look like I'm joking? Who knows what you've got in all those pockets?"

"*Fine.*" She unzipped the vest and tossed it into the bin, revealing a tight black bra. No hiding anything there. She flicked one of the straps. "You want me to strip this off, too?"

Nathan shot her a disapproving grimace. "What kind of people are you used to hanging around?"

"I . . ." The comment seemed to take her aback. "The wrong kinds, I suppose."

Aiko rotated the bin and set the vest on the table. She began emptying the pockets and arranging the contents in neat rows.

"Now, let's see what we have here." Nathan joined Aiko at the workbench.

"You won't find any surprises," Vessani said, crossing her arms.

"We'll judge that for ourselves, thank you." He started with the pistol and immediately noticed the customization work. "You do this yourself?" He held up the weapon.

"Most of it."

"Not bad," Aiko said. "Custom sight, modified grip, extended magazine. I could do without the flame detailing on the barrel, but other than that, this is a *nice* gun."

"It looks Jovian," Nathan said.

"It's a wraithbane," Aiko explained. "A somewhat uncommon sidearm in the Everlife. Where'd she get a Jovian handgun?"

"It was a gift," Vessani replied.

"Yeah, right," Aiko said. "She probably stole it."

"Probably," Nathan agreed.

Vessani turned away, shaking her head.

Nathan set the gun down, then checked out the various pieces of the hard suit, which also showed signs of customization. Some edges around the armor plates had been cut down to increase mobility while additional plates had been added in spots that wouldn't impact movement. Everything was painted matte black.

"You have a thing for black?" he asked.

"It's all right."

"Just 'all right'? Then why does your gear make me wonder if you're color blind?"

"My former employer has something of a dress code."

"*Former* employer?"

"Hugo Dirge."

Nathan paused, then chuckled. "You tried to steal your boss's ship?"

"Seemed like a good idea at the time."

"Well, it wasn't." Nathan sifted through the contents of her vest pockets: a Union ID card for one Vessani S'Kaari, about forty c'troni in loose coins, a knife, various tools, spare ammo, a honey-and-peanuts food bar, and two empty wrappers.

Aiko unclipped what looked like a thermos from the hard suit's utility belt. She unsealed and unscrewed the top, gazed inside, brought it up to her olfactory sensor, then shook her head and presented the container to Nathan.

"Here."

"What?" Nathan asked.

"Lick it and tell me what's inside. I don't have taste buds."

"I'm not licking the inside of a strange thermos!"

"Come on. It doesn't smell bad."

Nathan grumbled something under his breath but took the thermos anyway. He inspected the frothy white fluid inside and then sniffed the contents, surprised to discover a faint yet pleasant hint of vanilla.

"Go on," Aiko said. "Lick it."

"Don't rush me."

He dipped his finger into the froth and brought it cautiously up to the tip of his tongue.

"Well?" Aiko asked.

"A vanilla milkshake?" He turned to Vessani.

"What? Why the weird face?"

"You were carrying a vanilla milkshake on your hard suit?"

"So? I like milkshakes."

Nathan set the thermos down and put the top back on.

"Look, Mister—"

"That's *Captain* Nathaniel Kade to you."

"Right. Captain Kade. Look, I know what all of this seems like, but I can explain."

"Sure you can." Nathan approached the cell door with an air of expectancy, eager to hear what sort of contrived sob story she was about to dump on him.

"I'm sure Hugo offered you a tidy bundle to return his ship, but I can beat whatever he's paying."

"You don't say?"

"By a hefty margin. You see, I've got a juicy lead. I know this is going to sound far-fetched, but I'm *this close* to finding a massive pentatech relic."

"Really?" Nathan replied with faux interest. "*This close*, you say?"

"It's the truth. And I'd be more than happy to cut you in on the score. All you have to do is let me leave on Hugo's ship. You can tell him you lost me in the clouds or . . . or whatever. Doesn't matter. Just let me go for now, and we can meet up in orbit later. I'll even let you have the *Dirge* after we're done. Two ships are better than one, and *way* better than what he's paying." Vessani smiled hopefully at them. "What do you say?"

Nathan turned to Aiko.

"We've heard better," the Jovian remarked with a shake of her head.

"That we have."

"I'm being serious here," Vessani insisted, ears drooping.

"Yes, yes," Nathan said. "And next you'll tell me one of the moons of Mercury is made of solid computronium. I've heard them all."

"Cap—"

"Not buying it. We're turning the ship over to its rightful owner, and we're turning *you* over to the police." He picked up the thermos. "That said, I think I'll keep this. Maybe clean it out and use it to store Beany's coffee."

"I want her gun," Aiko said.

"What do you need another gun for?"

"Nothing, really. I just like collecting them."

"Fine. Just so long as the police don't confiscate it as evidence or something."

"Score!"

Nathan headed for the freight elevator. Aiko gave the gun a loving caress then hurried after him.

"You're making a big mistake!" Vessani called out desperately.

"Save it for someone who cares," Nathan replied with a dismissive wave.

Full night had fallen over the back of Neptune. Not the half night where the sun-walls dimmed and Sol remained in the sky, but the complete lack of outside illumination beyond the twinkle of distant stars and the pale reflections off nearby moons and habitats.

Port Leverrier didn't care.

The city's lights covered a wide plateau with a trio of refurbished deifactories rising above the skyscrapers in the city center. Ocean waves lapped against the cliffside and water-based docks to the east while rich farmlands spread a lavish canvas of greenery to the south and west. Hundreds of bridges and ramps led off the plateau, spreading out into roads and railways that connected with nearby cities and manufactories. If the Neptune Concord possessed a beating heart for its commerce and industry, Port Leverrier was it.

Aiko-Two guided the *Dirge of Darkness* to a bay situated in the smaller of Port Leverrier's two spaceports. She brought the ship to a smooth hover, deployed the landing gear, then eased the ship down into the dock. The six landing struts made contact with the ground and compressed so that the ship came to rest with little more than a minor jostle.

She eased the thruster nozzles closed, then initiated a controlled reactor shutdown. The lights dimmed momentarily as power switched over to the *Dirge*'s capacitors. She unstrapped from the pilot seat, took a staircase down to the ship's lower deck, and followed the corridor back to the cargo hold, which she then opened.

A group of six men crossed the docking bay and met her at the bottom of the ramp. They all wore black, though with nothing else in common besides the coloration and the weapons holstered at their hips or slung over their backs. An older gentleman stood ahead of the pack wearing a black suit with a long black tie and a black handkerchief in his pocket. His pin, featuring a smooth onyx inset in gold, was a rare splash of color.

He stood somewhat shorter than the others, his black hair flecked with gray and a trim pencil moustache over his narrow lips. A hulking, green-skinned divergent loomed at his side. That one eyed Aiko with the prelude to a snarl.

"Which one of you is Hugo Dirge?" she asked, though she probably didn't have to.

"I wasn't told we'd be dealing with Jovian . . ." The short leader trailed off with a sour face, perhaps leaving off the word "trash."

"You're welcome," Aiko replied sarcastically. "You Dirge?"

"I am."

"Then I believe this is yours." She stepped aside and swept an arm across the hold.

"That it is. Broog?" He beckoned the divergent forward.

"Sir."

"Inspect my ship."

"Right away." Broog hustled up the ramp.

"You'll find everything in order," Aiko said. "All we did was fire a few warning shots. We didn't put so much as a scratch on your ship."

"So you say."

"Hey, boss?" Broog turned back to them and knocked on one of the fuel tanks at the far end of the cargo hold. "Tank Two's been punctured! Someone slapped a pair of half-assed seals over the holes!"

Dirge raised an accusatory eyebrow at Aiko.

"Hey, now! That's how we found it," she snapped.

"Is this true, Broog?"

"Not a chance. The ship was in perfect shape when Vess made off with it. Zuloph and Narsh will back me up on this."

Two of the men behind Dirge nodded their agreement.

"So." Dirge crossed his arms, turning back to Aiko. "Just a few warning shots, you said?"

"You trying to cheat us out of the bonus?"

"That would imply I'm somehow in the wrong here."

"Those bullet holes were there when we recovered your ship."

"My crew says otherwise, and I'll take their word over some Jovian's any day."

"Oh, come on." Aiko pointed back to the tanks. "The damage isn't even all that bad. I can have that patchwork cleaned up and looking good as new in under an hour."

"No, thank you. I think you've pawed my ship quite enough for one day. Zuloph?"

"Yeah, boss?"

"Pay the Jovian the two thousand we owe her."

"Right."

"And not a c'troni more."

Aiko took the proffered box and opened it. She counted the cylinders, then clapped the top closed.

"Seems to be a thousand short, if you ask me."

"Tell you what, Jovian." Dirge smirked at her. "Perhaps we can come to an arrangement for the remainder."

"Okay, I'll bite. What did you have in mind?"

"First a question. Where's the cat?"

"We have her. Why?"

"I assume you intend to turn her over to the police."

"That's the plan. Again, why do you care?"

"I'd be willing to pay you the remaining thousand for her return."

"You have your ship back. What's she to you?"

"That's a matter of business between me and the cat. I've recently become aware of . . . dealings of hers she's been making on the side while under my employ. I'd like to clear up those loose ends, as it were. Beyond that, I'm not willing to say. We would, of course, turn her over to the police ourselves at the conclusion of our business." Behind him, Zuloph sniggered, which provoked a sharp glance from Dirge.

"Um, let me think about that for a moment." Aiko made a show of tapping the side of her head thoughtfully, then leaned forward. "*No.*"

"You're being awfully hasty here."

"Look, I get that you have a grudge to settle with the nekoan. She tried to make off with your ship, after all. But she's no longer your problem."

"Are you the one in charge of your little outfit?"

"No. That'd be Captain Kade."

"Then shouldn't you at least discuss my offer with your superior?"

"I . . ." Aiko shrugged her shoulders. "Sure, fine." She called up Nathan on the commect, turned up the volume, and explained the situation to him.

"He wants us to do *what*?" Nathan raged through the speaker for all to hear.

"Would you like me to repeat his offer?" Aiko asked, holding the commect between her and Dirge.

"Hell, no! *And* he shorted us on the bonus?"

"Two thousand," Dirge cut in, adjusting his tie. "I'll pay you two thousand for the cat."

"Was that him?" Nathan asked.

"It was," Aiko said. "He's starting to look desperate."

"Surely two thousand is a fair offer for custody of the cat," Dirge added.

"Look, pal," Nathan barked over the commect. "It doesn't matter how high you go. Aiko and I run a clean business. If you want to talk to the nekoan, you can do it at the police station after we've turned her in."

"Three."

"Didn't I just make my position clear to you?"

"Five!" Dirge shouted. "I'll give you five thousand c'troni for the cat, but that's my final offer!"

"I don't have time for this." The commect clicked, and the channel turned to faint white noise.

"Hello?" Dirge leaned over the device in Aiko's hand. "Are you still there? Hello?"

"Aww." Aiko switched off her commect and slotted it back into her belt. "Looks like he hung up on you."

"Why that—!"

"Well, Mr. Dirge. I'll be going now." She hefted the money box in one hand and gave the man a little, insulting wave with the other. "Let's never do business again."

Port Leverrier's 117th Precinct Building was a drab, squat structure situated outside the Ackerson Memorial Spaceport. Nathan walked up the steps and pushed through the glass doors. He spotted Sergeant Shawn Turner sitting behind a nearby desk, almost as if the rugged, graying police officer hadn't moved a millimeter since he'd last seen him.

"Nate!" The sergeant's face lit up. He rose from his chair and waved Nathan over. "How you been, sonny?"

"Good, all things considered." Nathan grabbed the empty seat across from Turner, and they both sat down.

"Wow. It's been, what? Half a year since I saw you last?"

"Longer, I think."

Turner shook his head. "Time flies when you're having fun. How's life as a freelancer been treating you?"

"Could be better. Could be worse."

"Aiko still with you?"

"Still."

"Figured. She's never going to leave your side, is she?"

"Not until I bite the dust."

Turner snorted out a laugh. "She actually word it that way?"

"Yeah. She calls it my 'squishy meat-death' or the like."

"Ha! Sounds like something a Jovian would say. They don't view death the same way we do. Makes them keep one eye on the long game. She'll probably outlive all of us. You pick up any new bodies for her?"

"Lost a few, actually. She's down to three, and one of them we cobbled together from leftovers."

"Aww, man. Sorry to hear that. How about the rest of your crew? You pick up anyone new?"

"Nope. Just me and Aiko still."

"Well, you two do make a good team." Turner leaned back, and his chair creaked. "How's your mother?"

"I haven't visited yet," he deflected, not eager to dive into *that* topic.

"But you will?"

"I will."

"You know she likes it when you stop by."

Nathan wasn't too sure about that. Visiting his mother wasn't easy. Not because he didn't love her dearly, but because when he stopped by her room at the asylum and gazed into her eyes, he didn't recognize the person gazing back.

"I said I will," he said, a little more stiffly than before.

"Of course. Of course." Turner sighed. "Anyway, what brings you down here?"

"Business, I'm afraid." He tossed a Union ID card onto the desk. "We picked up someone you might be interested in."

"Union, huh? One moment." Turner opened a drawer and pulled out a card reader. He plugged the cable into the side of his desktop vlass and slotted the card into the reader. A picture appeared of a younger version of Vessani along with a blob of text. "Vessani S'Kaari, aka Vess Longfang. Citizen of the Saturn Union, Birthplace listed as 'no one's business.' Same for her next of kin. Age twenty-two with fairly typical nekoan divergences. What brings her up?"

"She's currently a 'guest' on the *Belle*. We caught her trying to steal a ship."

"Not yours, I hope."

"No. Can you check if there's a bounty out for her?"

"Sure thing." Turner tapped the screen a few times. "And . . . she does indeed have a bounty."

Nathan smiled.

"The total reward is listed as twenty-eight c'troni."

"What?" His smile vanished.

"She's worth twenty-eight," Turner repeated.

"That can't be right."

Turner spun his screen around and let Nathan read the file.

"But she stole a spaceship!"

"Not officially."

"Didn't the Dirge Company charge her?"

"What you see is what you get." Turner waved his hand over the screen.

"But then . . ." Nathan shook his head. "What kind of crimes earn someone a piddly bounty like that?"

"Umm." Turner spun the screen back around. "Drunken and disorderly conduct, public indecency, noise complaints, and one case of vandalism."

"But . . . twenty-eight?"

"I'm just reading what's in her file."

"She had more than that on her in loose change!"

"Maybe she's done worse in the Union. You could check with their embassy."

"No, thanks." Nathan crossed his arms with a scowl. "I've had my fill of being ripped off by Union officials for a while."

"Then, sorry, but this is all I can offer you." Turner pulled out the ID card and handed it back to Nathan. "Feel free to drop her by anytime. We'll process her and pay up."

"Won't you send someone out to our dock to pick her up?"

"Not for a minor nuisance like her."

"Uhh!" Nathan leaned back and ran his fingers through his hair.

"Just let me know when you want to drop her off. After that, I don't know. Maybe treat yourself to a nice dinner?"

Nathan left the precinct building with his hands stuck in his pockets and a frown on his face. He took a right and melted into the flow of pedestrian traffic on the sidewalk, heading back to the spaceport.

Twenty-eight c'troni.

It was an insulting amount.

Criminal record or not, they'd caught Vessani stealing a spaceship. Was this really her first big crime? And what was up with all the money Dirge had offered? That reeked of all kinds of shady. Nathan was half tempted to ask Vessani about it before he turned her over to the police but assumed she'd lie about that, too.

Twenty-eight. Good grief!

Well, it is what it is, he thought. *Nothing to do about it. The sooner she's out of my hands, the better. Maybe I'll use the money to buy Aiko an accessory for one of her guns. She'd like that.*

Nathan sauntered down a street, overhead lamps creating regular pools of light. Port Leverrier never really slept. Half the nights weren't true nights anyway, what with the distant Sol casting its own light upon the shell band, and the crowds near him attested to that fact.

He passed a string of restaurants, their signs bright over each entrance, the air thick with the scent of rich, fatty cooking. His stomach grumbled, but he kept walking, intent on returning to the *Belle* to discuss the situation with Aiko, but the mouthwatering smells continued to tempt his senses, and his stomach eventually won out over his brain.

He stopped at the next food truck he saw, glanced over their menu, and bought a chili-and-sausage wrap. He took a messy bite and continued down the street.

"Captain Kade."

Nathan stopped and turned, his mouth in the middle of chewing.

The speaker was a handsome young man, perhaps in his mid twenties, with clothes nice enough to set him apart from most of the other foot traffic. He wore a dark gray vest patterned with an intricate, swirling weave of blue and gold thread over a crisp, white shirt. He'd tucked a blue ascot inside the collar, and a gold chain ran from his breast pocket to a loop on his belt.

The young man had combed his wavy blond hair to the side, though a few errant strands hung in front of his face while he caught his breath. Had he been jogging down the street? He watched Nathan with sharp blue eyes that sparkled with a keen sense of observation.

"Yesh?" Nathan asked the newcomer.

"I'm sorry, sir. Have I caught you at a bad time?"

"Nah. Ish fine." Nathan continued chewing, not sure yet what to make of the interruption. The fellow didn't appear armed, so there was that at least.

"Wonderful." The young man beamed at him. "Allow me to introduce myself." He extended a hand. "My name is Joshua Cotton. There's a matter of some importance I'd like to discuss with you."

"Ish tha sho?"

"It is, sir."

Nathan glanced down at the proffered hand and reached out to shake it, but then stopped when he realized a gob of chili had migrated to his hand. Cotton saw it, too, frowned, and lowered his own hand.

"Perhaps the handshake can wait."

"That's probably for the best." Nathan wiped the gob off on the wrapper, then stepped out of the main flow of traffic. Cotton followed him. "What sort of business are we talking about here?"

"It concerns an acquaintance of mine named Vessani S'Kaari."

Oh bloody hell, Nathan thought.

"Ah." Cotton smiled. "I know that look. You've met her, then."

"A bit more than that," Nathan replied, unwilling to say more until he had a better read on the man. "What's she to you?"

"An acquaintance, as I said."

"And?"

"She's currently aboard your ship. The *Neptune Belle*, is it?"

"What if she is?"

"There's no need to be coy, Captain. The police told me you're holding her. It seems I stopped by the station shortly after you did. A Sergeant Turner said she was in your custody, so I headed toward the spaceport. Along the way, I happened to spot your jacket and took the chance to introduce myself."

"Fine," he told Cotton. "You found me. What do you want?"

"I'd like to arrange for Miss S'Kaari's release."

"Sure, I'll release her. Right in the middle of the police station."

"I would prefer that you didn't."

"Well, *I* prefer not to have my meals interrupted by strangers making unusual requests, but we don't all get what we want, now do we?"

"I suppose not, sir," Cotton replied, somewhat sullenly.

"Do you know what she just pulled?"

"I believe I have some idea."

"Do you know *all* of it?"

"Sir, if it's a question of her bounty, I'd be happy to compensate you appropriately. Say, double what the police are offering?"

Oh, this is great! Nathan thought sarcastically. *What's the word for doubling a pittance?*

"Sergeant Turner left me with the impression the police have more pressing concerns at the moment," Cotton continued. "I'm sure they wouldn't mind it if the two of us came to a mutually beneficial agreement."

"I'm not turning her or anyone else over to you without a damned good reason," Nathan declared, wagging his half-eaten wrap at the other man.

"That's not what I'm asking."

"It's . . ." Nathan paused and lowered the wrap. "It's not?"

"No, sir. I only wish to arrange for her to be freed. Nothing more."

"Because she's an acquaintance of yours?"

"A close acquaintance, I will admit."

"We're talking about the same Vessani S'Kaari here, right?" Nathan asked. "Wild-looking nekoan? Black hair, gold eyes. Has a bad habit of stealing other people's spaceships?"

Cotton's eyes widened. "She stole a ship?"

"Yeah. What did you *think* she tried to pull?"

"I . . . was guessing something a bit smaller. Closer to her past antics, as it were."

"You know Hugo Dirge?"

"I've heard of him."

"She tried to steal his ship."

"Oh." Cotton lowered his gaze. "Oh, dear."

"Everything I know about her tells me she's more trouble than she's worth. Except now interested parties seem to be lining up for a piece of her. So how about you cut to the chase and tell me why you're *really* interested."

"I suppose that's only fair. Have you spoken to her?"

"Briefly. Why?"

"Did she mention anything"—Cotton licked his lips, seemingly unsure how to proceed—"unusual to you?"

"She tried, but I have this degenerative ear disease. It's called earplugus for bullshitus. I become hard of hearing whenever people spout nonsense my way."

"Yes, I see what you mean." The young man sighed. "Vessani may be rough around the edges, but she has a good heart. She's just had it tough. She grew up on a low-tech habitat, you see, and that life of hers ended when she was kidnapped about five years ago."

"I'm sorry." Nathan stuck a finger in his ear and wiggled it. "That degenerative disease is kicking in."

"The point is her first experience with high-tech societies was human trafficking. Now, mind you, she was lucky enough to be freed before anything . . . inappropriate happened to her, after which she ended up bouncing her way across the solar system, learning and adapting as she went."

"Until she landed with the Dirge Company?"

"One in a long string of outfits she's worked for. As I understand it, she impressed Hugo Dirge with her skills as a pilot. Tell me, sir, how much do you know about the man?"

"Just that he's a cheapskate who won't honor his contracts. Why?"

"Vessani thought he ran a legitimate business when she signed on, and part of that is true, but Dirge also operates a side gig of sorts. Granted, I have no proof of this, but Vessani told me she was horrified to learn Dirge and his crew will make their way to the Habitat Belt in order to kidnap exotic divergents from low-tech societies, mostly female, and then sell them to wealthy clients, mostly male, if you catch my meaning, sir."

"Yeah," Nathan breathed, suddenly taking the man's story more seriously. "I catch it."

"I suppose the revelation hit a nerve. Doubly so, given the parallels with her own history. I can understand how she might feel motivated to stop them."

"By stealing his ship."

"So it would seem, Captain."

"Hmm." Nathan frowned at his cooling wrap. "All right. You have my attention, but right now all you've given me is a story. Got anything to back it up?"

"As I said, I don't have evidence of Dirge's wrongdoing, if that's what you're expecting from me."

"What about what happened to Vessani? Sounds like she was kidnapped and then freed."

"That's right."

"Is there an official record of the incident?"

"Not on Neptune. It's my understanding the pirates who nabbed her met an unpleasant fate at the hands of Jovian privateers."

"Jovians, huh." Nathan nodded. Perhaps one of Aiko's old contacts could help them sort out the truth, then. "Do you know the group's name?"

"I believe they're called the Platinum Corsairs."

CHAPTER SIX

"Oh, the Platinum Corsairs!" Aiko-One remarked once she and Nathan were both back in the *Neptune Belle*, seated in the mess hall. Beany lowered a branch to Nathan, but he waved it away, and the branch returned to the tree's crown.

"Sounds like you know them."

"You could say that. I have a copy-clan sister who ran with them for a while. Name's Prinn Pratti. I don't think she's a member anymore, but I could reach out to her. Maybe she heard about these supposed kidnappers. Hell, if the incident actually did happen five years ago, then she might have been there."

"Sounds solid enough. Give it a try."

"Sure thing. I'll send the message out, though who knows how long it'll take us to hear back."

"I'll take anything that helps us sort out this mess. Even if it's a long shot."

"I hear you." Aiko leaned toward him. "So, first Hugo Dirge and now this Joshua Cotton fellow. I wonder if there'll be other interested parties if we wait long enough."

"The sooner we offload her the better. And dumping her at the station is still the safest bet for us."

"Didn't sound like the cops were terribly interested, though."

"Yeah." Nathan slung an arm over the back of his chair. "If we hand her over, all they're likely to do is stuff her in a cell for a month or so, then release her. They won't even make the effort to come pick her up."

"We could just let her go like Cotton wants."

"But she tried to steal a *spaceship*!"

"From a group of scumbags who shorted us a grand and who may have their hands in human trafficking. *And* she hasn't been officially charged for it, so the police don't care."

"I've been wondering about that last part," Nathan said. "Maybe Dirge hasn't pressed charges because he doesn't want the police anywhere near his operation."

"Or maybe so he can grab Vessani for himself?"

"There's that, too."

"Question is why."

"Don't know. All we got out of her is some fairy tale about a pentatech relic."

"Could be true," Aiko said, and Nathan gave her a doubtful sideways glance. "*Could* be," she repeated.

"Here's a question: How good a look did you get of Dirge's ship?"

"Two and I inspected it before we left the refinery, but we were focused on making sure it was flightworthy. Why?"

"Anything stand out to you?"

"Not sure. Give me a moment." Aiko paused to commune with her copies. "Two noticed the internal layout had been modified from the pattern standards."

"In what way?"

"Some of the crew cabins looked like they'd been reinforced."

"For the purpose of keeping people inside?"

"Possibly."

"Hmm." He wagged a finger. "That would track with Cotton's story, then."

"What did you make of Dirge's offer?" Aiko asked.

"It stinks. I'm not biting."

"I know that. But what would cause him to jump to five grand like it was nothing?"

"Something big."

"Big like a tasty lead on a pentatech relic?"

"You wish," Nathan scoffed.

"I heard back from Prinn," Aiko-One reported early the next morning, joining Nathan in the mess hall.

"Oh, good." Nathan looked up from his breakfast donburi. He was halfway through the small bowl of scrambled eggs and rice. "What'd she have to say?"

"That she was with the Platinum Corsairs during the time in question and even remembered an incident that might line up with Cotton's story. The Corsairs have taken out a *lot* of illegal operations over the years."

"Illegal from the Jovian perspective," Nathan pointed out with a frown.

"Well, naturally. Anyway, Prinn recalled one mission where they liberated a young, female nekoan. She couldn't give me any other details, unfortunately—not the girl's name, age, or even what she looked like. She never interacted with the nekoan directly. That said, this nekoan served with the Corsairs for a brief period."

"Really?" Nathan's eyebrows raised in surprise.

"It's not all *that* unusual. There are a lot of places Jovians aren't welcome, so teaming up with a few meat sacks can be useful. Not every copy-clan is that open-minded, but a few are. The Corsairs ended up dropping this nekoan off somewhere on Saturn. Prinn wasn't aware of any issues with her, but their next mission required sustained high gees, so they decided to shed their auxiliary organics."

"So, to summarize," Nathan said, "there's no way for us to confirm the nekoan the Corsairs rescued and then hired was Vessani."

"Not without digging deeper, like trying to reach out to the rest of the crew."

"You think we'd have any luck with that?"

Aiko made a raspberry sound with her speaker. "Nope! Prinn helped us out because we're family. She's willing to overlook my deviant status, but we can expect the cold shoulder from anyone else."

"I was worried you'd say that."

"Thoughts?" she prompted.

"I'm leaning toward just dumping her off at the station." Nathan set his spoon down and stood up. "It certainly sounds like the Corsair nekoan was her, but so what? That doesn't corroborate the rest of Cotton's story or prove she was justified in trying to steal Dirge's ship or . . . or really *anything*. And it's not like this is a life-or-death decision. She can suck it up and do her time in a Concord cell.

They'll let her out before too long, and we get to wash our hands of this whole affair."

"I'm fine with that if you are," Aiko replied neutrally.

"Then it's decided." He picked up his bowl and stood up. "I'll put in a call to the station and arrange a drop-off."

He took the freight elevator up to A Deck and shoveled down the last of his donburi on the way to the cockpit. Most of the ship's systems were powered down, but the commect stayed on in case of incoming calls. He selected Sergeant Shawn Turner from the list of contacts.

"Hey, Nate," Turner said after a short wait. "What can I do for you?"

"It's about that nekoan. I'd like to arrange a drop-off time."

"The nekoan? Oh, you mean S'Kaari!"

"The same."

"Sorry, it's been one of those mornings. My mind was on another problem."

"I can bring her over right now, if you like. Or whenever. Just let me know what's most convenient."

"Yeah...about that," Turner said, dragging out his words to indicate a problem.

"Something wrong?" Nathan asked, concerned by Turner's change in tone.

"It's actually good you called. I needed to talk to you about her anyway. I just received an update from the prosecutor's office. Seems the charges against Miss S'Kaari have been dropped in their entirety."

"Dropped?" Nathan glowered at the commect's speaker. "That's suspicious timing."

"Whatever do you mean, Nate?" Turner replied coyly.

"Do you know why the charges were dropped?"

"No, but I wouldn't get too worked up about this. Frankly, an annoyance like her isn't worth our time."

"Was a young man in to see the prosecutors?"

"We get a *lot* of people passing through here."

"Blond hair, well-dressed. Had a refined air about him."

"Maybe," Turner admitted. "Might have seen someone like that."

"And did this gentleman also happen to make a donation to the PLPD Retirement Fund?"

"Why, Nate, I have no idea what you're talking about," Turner said, though his tone made it clear he knew *exactly* what Nathan was talking about.

"Right..."

"Look, the reason we needed to talk is you're currently holding that woman against her will."

"I caught her stealing a spaceship!"

"Maybe so, but the owner hasn't pressed charges. That means you lack the authority to hold her. You wouldn't want there to be a misunderstanding, would you, Nate?"

"Fine!" He shook his head. "I'll go down right now and boot her off my ship. Would that make everyone happy?"

"It at least won't make anyone upset. Something else I can do for you?"

"Not anymore," Nathan griped.

"Then I'll let you get back to it."

Turner disconnected from the call.

Nathan slouched in the pilot seat and stared out the canopy with the empty bowl in his lap. He then pushed out of the seat with a grunt.

"At least she won't be causing me anymore headaches," he grumbled on his way down to C Deck.

Aiko-Two stood to one side of the *Neptune Belle*'s open cargo ramp, rifle in her hands, head swiveling back and forth in constant vigilance. Tedious, mundane tasks had never bothered her. Quite the opposite, in fact, since they gave her time to ponder the great mysteries of the solar system.

Such as if the Guardian Deities were still alive. Had they truly abandoned humanity? Or were they still around, somewhere, perhaps out there beyond the Kuiper Belt, fighting an endless war against the Devil of Proxima? Did the Devil even exist or was it pure myth?

Stuff like that.

Also, she wondered if Nathan liked her, because sometimes her mind bounced around like that.

The question was more complex than it first may have seemed. Clearly, they worked well together, and he respected both her contributions to their (kind of) duet as well as her opinion on important matters.

But how did he feel about her?

Hard to tell, she reflected.

She wasn't sure how she felt, either. It had been a *lo-o-o-o-ong* time since she'd been organic. Not every Jovian child was elevated to the Everlife—only excellence deserves immortality, as the saying went—but she'd somehow made the cut, despite evidence of her deviant tendencies, even back that far.

Nathan hadn't seemed all that remarkable the first time they'd met. Just another meat sack in a solar system overflowing with them. Sure, he'd helped her escape the smothering conformity of her home, but only because he was a man with a ship.

That didn't make him special.

But there was just something about him that appealed to a deep part of her psyche. A certain eagerness to experience the unknown that gelled with her own sensibilities and her own reasons for leaving the Everlife.

And, as she had slowly come to realize, what she yearned for most was companionship. The copy-clans had failed to quench this need, leading to her deep dissatisfaction within the Everlife. But around Nathan she was content. Even happy. Happier than she ever remembered being on Jupiter.

Reproductive desires didn't factor into the equation, of course. As a Jovian, she could replicate herself as much as she wanted, assuming she had access to enough spare bodies and her persona safe. But creating mirror images of herself wasn't companionship. Not really. Not in the way she yearned for.

Plus, I love that hair, she thought.

It was *really* nice hair, even if she sometimes poked fun at the boring color. She found herself wondering what it would feel like to run her fingers through it. She wished he'd grow it out a bit more, though. That would make him even more dashing.

I really need to get a decent-looking body one of these days, she thought. *Something that'll turn heads.*

Her cameras alternated between the two entrances to the docking bay.

A large, hulking silhouette appeared in one of them, and her cameras focused in. She recognized the divergent male almost immediately thanks to his green skin and black attire, though he'd swapped out his shirt and trousers for the armored pieces of what looked like a stripped-down hard suit. A heavy pistol hung from his belt.

"Can I help you?" she asked pointedly when the man stopped in front of her.

"I'm here on behalf of Mr. Dirge," Broog replied.

"Yeah? What of it?"

"He'd like to know why your boss hasn't returned his calls."

"Because he and Captain Kade have nothing to discuss."

"Mr. Dirge insists on talking to him."

"What for?"

"He would like to make another offer for the cat."

"The captain isn't interested, and neither am I."

"Is that your final position?"

"It is." She bobbed her head toward the exit. "Now scram. Before I—"

Broog pulled out his pistol and fired from the hip. The first heavy bolt punched into Aiko's abdomen, bowing her armor and throwing her back. The second exploded inside her, frying her secondary power systems. She tried to bring her own weapon up, but Broog kept firing, unloading ten shots into her in rapid succession.

She clattered back onto the ramp, then slid down it, smoke rising from the holes in her chest. She heard and felt the rapid pounding of several boots on the ramp as Broog ejected his spent magazine and slammed in a fresh one. At least three other Dirge Company goons hurried inside past her body.

Broog aimed the pistol at her head, and a toothy grin formed on his lips.

Her last thoughts were: *Damn it, not again.*

"Were those gunshots?" Vessani asked urgently, still in her cell.

"I don't know." Kade keyed the commect on his belt. "Aiko, what's going on?"

"This is Six speaking; we've got trouble! Two is down, and hostiles are in the ship! I've called One back to the ship, but it's going to be at least twenty minutes until she gets here."

"Where are you?"

"A Deck. Right next to the cockpit."

"Place the ship into lockdown. Seal everything!"

"You've got it, boss!"

Every pressure door on the ship slammed shut, the lights turned red, and a siren wailed a few times before being silenced.

"That should buy us some time," Kade said. "Now, what are we up against?"

"Dirge's thugs. Maybe four or five of them. They've made it to the elevator shaft and are heading up. It's a good bet they're coming your way."

"Yeah." Kade glanced back to Vessani. "I figured."

"Hey!" Vessani spread her arms. "Let me out of here!"

"You serious?" Kade snapped at her.

"My hard suit's right there, and you can't fit in it!" She pointed to the articles piled on the workbench outside her cell. "Like it or not, we're in this together!"

"I . . ." Kade hesitated, but only for a moment. "Fine!" He tapped a code into the cell's vlass, and the door slid open. "Suit up!"

"Don't need to tell me twice!" Vessani grabbed the armored leggings and started pulling them on.

"Aiko, where are they now?"

"They've made it to C Deck and are trying to bypass the first pressure door. There are two doors between them and you."

"Get ready to release the lockdown. Once you do, try to hit them from behind."

"Got it. Just give the word."

Vessani curled her tail around her waist and slipped the top half of her body armor on. She didn't bother closing the environmental seals or putting on her gloves. All she cared about was having as much solid material as possible between her and incoming bullets. She grabbed her helmet and fitted it over her head, looped the utility belt around her waist, then turned to Kade, who held her pistol in one hand and his own in the other. He spun the weapon in his hand and presented it to her, grip first. She took hold of it, but when she tugged, he didn't let go.

He brought his face close to her helmet. "Don't make me regret this."

"You won't."

He let go of the weapon, and she aimed it down the corridor, steadying it in both hands.

"I'll follow your lead," she said.

"You'd damn well better."

Kade raised his own pistol and they advanced nearly side by side to a four-way junction. He took up position on one side of the short corridor leading back to the elevator shaft and motioned for her to take the other side. She knelt behind the cover opposite him and waited, conscious of the muted clanking and grinding sounds emanating from the other side of that door.

"You ready, Aiko?" Kade whispered, a finger dialing down the volume on his commect.

"Ready."

"Okay." Kade swallowed and aimed down the corridor. "Aiko, release the lockdown and open all doors."

"Releasing in three ... two ... one ... now!"

The door split open with a cluster of black-clad pirates bunched up on the other side. Vessani spotted Zuloph crouched with his hands stuck inside an open wall panel. Broog loomed behind the others like a mountain of muscle and simmering rage, but the slightest glimmer of worry formed on his face in the split second after the door opened.

Kade and Vessani opened fire, showering the intruders with a rapid, almost random fusillade. Body armor absorbed many of the shots, but others struck exposed heads and limbs. The top of Zuloph's head blew apart like overripe fruit, and his body slumped forward, hands still caught in the panel.

One of the other assailants folded forward, clutching his stomach, while the man beside him fell back onto his butt and kicked the ground, desperately trying to push himself into cover.

One of their shots—Vessani wasn't sure if it was her gun or Kade's—blew a chunk out of Broog's left arm, but all he did was snarl and return fire. An explosive bolt ricocheted over Kade's head and detonated against the wall behind him.

"Damn!" Kade ducked back behind cover and began reloading.

Vessani emptied her last bullet into Broog, but the shot *zinged* off his chest plate. A bolt struck her shoulder and sprayed the side of her helmet with hot bits of metal. She pulled her arms and head into cover and grabbed a fresh magazine. Her fingers moved in a quick, fluid dance, and she finished reloading her gun before Kade.

Broog roared and charged down the corridor, firing shot after shot, his boots thudding against the deck as explosions tore panels off the walls and floor. Two other intruders rose and followed his lead, charging in behind the brute. A bullet exploded next to Vessani, and shrapnel scraped across her leg armor.

She stuck the barrel of her pistol around the corner and fired a trio of blind shots, then heard the click of Broog's own weapon coming up empty. She kicked off the ground, springing from cover—

—only to have Broog tackle her to the ground.

They rolled across the deck, and her pistol flew from her hand and slid across the floor. She landed on her side with Broog screaming in her face, flecks of saliva spackling her visor. He punched her in the helmet, and the impact thumped her head to the side hard enough for stars to swim across her vision.

Vessani drew her knife and stuck it in Broog's side, slipping it between two armor plates, but he only sneered at her before smashing a fist into her gut hard enough to make her gasp. She pulled the knife out and stuck him again, this time in the armpit.

Broog grabbed her by the throat and squeezed. She squirmed under his viselike grip, punching, stabbing, legs kicking out. His fingers bore down into her throat, and she gasped for air.

But then whatever font of energy drove the enormous man began to peter out, and his grip loosened. Vessani sucked in a quick, delicious breath of air and stuck her knife through one of his hands. She squirmed out from under him and raised the knife, ready to stab him again—

—but it wasn't necessary. Broog collapsed to the ground, revealing the bloody craters that now covered his back. A growling exhalation escaped his lips, and he was finally still.

Vessani pushed away from him and took stock of her surroundings. Two more bodies lay behind Broog with Kade and one of the Aikos standing over them. The danger had passed. She didn't take any pleasure in killing her former compatriots, but she didn't regret their deaths, either. They were slavers and killers, and they deserved the bullet-riddled ends they'd met.

Shakily, she slid the knife back into its sheath and tried to push herself up off the floor—but found someone had replaced her legs with noodles.

Nathan extended a hand. She took hold of it, and he helped her to her feet.

Vessani learned that Aiko had called the police when several uniformed officers arrived shortly after the firefight. What followed was one of the strangest, most awkward experiences of her life. Not because of anything that happened, but rather what didn't happen.

The police weren't yelling at her. They weren't even upset with her. All they did was take her statement and move on with the business of interviewing the *Belle*'s crew, photographing the blood-splattered corridor, and removing the organic bodies.

It was so strange.

She spent most of her time waiting in the cargo hold in something of a daze, helmet stuck in the crook of her arm, not sure what do to next. She found herself wrestling with a deep, visceral urge to be somewhere else whenever one of the officers passed by, but that's all they did—walked past her with barely a glance, their attention focused on other, larger, messier problems. It was so different from her typical interactions with authority figures, which often ended in cops shouting at her while she struggled through a wild, drunken stupor.

Is this what being respectable feels like? she wondered, not sure if she liked it or not.

Soon enough, most of the police finished their business and left. One of the cops, a graying sergeant named Turner, stayed behind and spoke cordially with Captain Kade and at length. Vessani sensed the two had something of a history. Meanwhile, one of the Aikos grabbed a mop and bucket and headed up to C Deck while humming to herself.

Sergeant Turner eventually left, and Kade joined Vessani by the ramp.

"I don't think your former boss is going to be much of a problem moving forward," he told her.

"Why do you say that?" Vessani asked.

"Because his ship's been impounded, and the police are putting him and the rest of his crew under surveillance until they finish their investigation. Shawn made it sound like some of the precinct detectives are licking their chops, ready to use this incident to take a long, hard look at Dirge's affairs."

"Shawn?"

"The sergeant I was talking to."

"Ah. You friends with him?"

"Something like that. It's more a case of him being an old acquaintance of the family. He and my father were tight."

Vessani caught a brief flash of tension in Nathan's voice when he mentioned his father, but she didn't inquire further. She had enough sense to know prying into his affairs would be a bad move.

"So, what now?" she said after a while.

"I'm glad you asked. Would you mind stepping off the ramp?"

"Sure." She walked off and turned back to him.

"Thanks." Nathan tapped a vlass by the exit, and the ramp levered upward with Vessani outside the ship.

"Wait a second." She put her hands on her hips. "That's it?"

He paused the ramp at the halfway point. "Why not?"

"What about Dirge and the rest of his goons?"

"Not my problem."

"You're just going to abandon me?"

"You seem like you can handle yourself. Besides, Aiko's down a body because of you, and I almost got shot! You're trouble we don't want or need. Sorry, but not sorry."

He resumed closing the ramp.

Vessani stood on the tips of her toes, trying to catch his gaze. "Can I at least have the rest of my stuff back?"

The ramp creaked shut, and Vessani thought she heard the faint echo of retreating footsteps.

"Guess not," she said to no one in particular, waiting and listening. When nothing else happened, she slumped her shoulders with a deep sigh, turned away, and headed for the nearest exit.

CHAPTER SEVEN

"And then there were two," Aiko-One intoned, standing beside Nathan as they inspected her own perforated body on the workbench, its chest and head blown open from the inside by exploding rounds.

"Anything we can salvage from this mess?" Nathan asked.

"Most of the limbs are still good, so I might be able to fix up Six a bit more, but as a full body?" She shook her head. "No way."

"Then we just keep it around for spare parts?"

"That's about all it's good for. The worst part is the computronium in the head is damaged."

"*Wonderful.*" The head was the most expensive part. "Were you able to pull any memories?"

"A few, and they integrated just fine even if some were a little fuzzy. The part where they shot me in cold blood was crystal clear, though. I'm glad we took those goons out."

"Me, too." Nathan leaned back against the wall. "I'm sorry, Aiko."

"What for?"

"This." He gestured to the remains of her Number Two body. "I know you've been pining for new bodies, but I seem to be taking us in the opposite direction, and I can't help but feel a little sorry about that."

"Don't be. Hell, if anyone's at fault, it's me for letting that green lump get the drop on me."

"I know, but still." He shrugged, not sure what else to say.

"This is just part of the toll we pay in this business. And better me paying it than you. Though, I will say one thing: We're getting to the point where we could really use an extra pair of hands to help run the ship. It might be time for us to seriously put out some feelers for additional crew."

"Maybe you're right. Any thoughts along those lines?"

"I don't know. That nekoan didn't seem so bad. From what we saw, she's a better pilot than both of us, and she can certainly hold her own in a scrap."

"She steals spaceships!"

"Only once. And that crew had it coming."

"I—" He paused, then sighed. "Okay, fair point. They absolutely had it coming. But I'm not about to—"

Nathan's commect chimed, and he keyed it to speaker.

"Go ahead."

"Incoming call for you, boss," Aiko-Six reported. "It's Joshua Cotton again."

"Cotton? What the hell does he want? We already let his friend go."

"Don't know. Want me to grill him for you?"

"No, I'll talk to him myself. Forward the call to me."

"Will do."

The commect chimed again.

"Captain Kade?" Cotton asked.

"Speaking."

"This is Joshua Cotton."

"Yes, I know," he replied pointedly. "What do you want?"

"I have a job offer I'd like to discuss with you."

Nathan glanced over to Aiko, who rubbed her hands together and whispered, "Pentatech moolah."

"What sort of job?" Nathan asked.

"I would prefer to discuss the details with you in person, if you don't mind. Recent events have made it . . . shall we say, *abundantly* clear there are other interested parties. I'd be happy to meet you aboard your ship in, say, half an hour? Would that work for you?"

"Sure, but you come alone and unarmed. I'm not in the mood for surprises."

"I understand your position, Captain, though the job would be easier to discuss if both of us were in attendance."

"Both of you? You mean Vessani?"

"That's correct."

Nathan grumbled under his breath, but Aiko gave him an eager thumbs-up.

"Fine," he said at last, "but she'd better be on her best behavior."

"That won't be an issue, I assure you, Captain."

"All right. We'll see the two of you in half an hour."

"We'll be there."

Aiko-One met their two guests outside the *Neptune Belle's* starboard airlock. Vessani arrived armed, but she handed over her pistol and knife to Aiko and allowed herself to be searched, which turned up no additional weapons. It wasn't *exactly* what they'd agreed, but Nathan could understand her being hesitant to stroll around Port Leverrier without some means of defense. Joshua, at least, arrived without any obvious weapons.

Aiko brought them through the airlock to the cargo hold where she and Nathan had unfolded a metal table and a set of chairs.

"Captain Kade." Joshua extended his hand, which Nathan shook. "A pleasure to see you again."

"Mr. Cotton," Nathan replied neutrally, still unsure about the wisdom in dealing with this unusual pair. His instincts told him they were trouble, and he certainly had evidence now to back that up. But at the same time, he and Aiko didn't have any pressing commitments; they'd finished their job for Bishton Medical Holdings, and their usual sources for work were running dry. The Almanac hadn't posted any survey requests recently, and Aiko-One had checked in with the various government offices yesterday, only to find other parties had snatched up all the plum jobs.

We can find work if we really need to, Nathan told himself. *But at the same time, what's the harm in hearing these two out?*

"All right," Nathan said once they were all seated. "What kind of services are you looking for?"

"First, a warning," Joshua said. "This won't be a quick job. Nor will it be entirely safe."

"Yeah, I've been getting that feeling. People seem willing to kill over it."

"True enough, but I was referring to less mundane or human

dangers. It's impossible to say for certain, but there's likely to be at least some measure of risk, some bumping against the unknown that could put you and your ship in danger."

"As is often the case when humans meddle with pentatech."

Joshua raised an eyebrow, then glanced to Vessani.

"I ... may have mentioned the relic," she confessed, and when Joshua said nothing, she added, "I was trying to convince him to let me go."

"It didn't work," Nathan stated firmly.

"I see." Joshua turned back to the captain. "Pentatech is indeed a part of the job, but before we go any further, I need to know if these sorts of risks are a deal-breaker for you."

"They're not. We'll hear you out."

"Wonderful." Joshua smiled. "Then let's get into the heart of it, shall we? The two of us do, indeed, have a promising lead on a pentatech artifact of some kind. What sort, we aren't sure, but we believe it to be of significant size and power."

"How big are we talking here?" Nathan asked.

"Unknown, but whatever the artifact is, it's potent enough to affect other technology at a considerable distance. Vess?"

"I grew up in a low-tech society out in the Habitat Belt," she began, leaning in. "There's a relic on the habitat which my people have tended to for as long as we have historical records. We call it the Black Egg."

"Then it's this Black Egg we're after?" Nathan asked.

"No." Vessani shook her head. "By itself, the Black Egg is unremarkable. But Josh and I believe we can use it to find a treasure trove of pentatech that is quietly making its way through the Habitat Belt on its way to the inner system."

Nathan nodded thoughtfully.

The Habitat Belt was home to hundreds of thousands of megastructures, and even the smaller ones often contained millions of square kilometers of habitable lands. A blind search of the Belt to locate this Black Egg was completely unfeasible.

But if Vessani knew which habitat to start on ...

And if the Black Egg could lead people to pentatech treasures ...

"I can see why people are trying to get their hands on you," he told the nekoan.

"It could be worse than you realize." Joshua gestured to Vessani. "We're not sure what sparked Dirge's interest; perhaps he overheard one of our conversations. Regardless, he's less of a concern now that the police are involved. However, another problem has come to our attention. I've been in contact with a Saturnian scholar about our theories for some time now. A cleric by the name of Anterus vaan Kronya. He's a former professor of mine, in fact."

"A professor of yours? You have a Saturnian education?"

"I do, sir. Multiple engineering degrees," Joshua said proudly, but then his expression turned grim. "Anterus helped me put the pieces of Vessani's story together, but he's recently gone dark. I'm not sure what happened to him, and I, unfortunately, have reason to fear the worst."

"Could Dirge have gotten to him?" Nathan asked.

"Impossible. Anterus's last message placed him in the Habitat Belt in the middle of a missionary excursion. The Dirge Company only has their one ship, and it's here. They couldn't be behind his disappearance."

"Then someone else has gotten wind of your discovery."

"That's our conclusion as well."

Nathan leaned back and crossed his arms, contemplating the mess he might be leaping into.

"Why us?" Aiko asked. "Surely, there are bigger, better equipped outfits to bring your work to."

"True enough," Joshua agreed. "But trust is a funny thing. Other captains and their crews may have solid reputations, but Vess has seen the two of you up close."

"From the inside of a cell," Nathan said.

"Where you treated her well. And, most importantly, refused to turn her over to Dirge for what I'm sure was a considerable sum."

"I wasn't going to say yes to an offer that slimy," Nathan scoffed.

"Exactly!" Joshua said with a bright smile.

"You the one who got Vessani's record cleared?"

"I did, sir. It seemed the easiest way to secure her quick release." He smiled again. "The police were . . . accommodating."

"I'll bet." Nathan sat forward. "Anything else you have to share about this job?"

"Not at the moment. We'll have much more to discuss, should we enter into a formal contract."

"Right." Nathan nodded, considering what he knew about the job so far.

Pentatech was unpredictable and often dangerous stuff. Most of the Pentatheon's creations had been made with humanity in mind, such as the deifactories, megastructures, and spaceship patterns. They were—more or less—safe for humans to be around and use, assuming those people had at least a modicum of common sense and technical understanding.

But pentatech was different.

It encompassed technology and devices created by the Pentatheon that they never intended for humans to touch because they were either too dangerous, too powerful, or both. He'd encountered examples of the stuff firsthand and had barely escaped with his life. Most pentatech had been destroyed during the Scourging of Heaven, which was probably a good thing. But that also meant what little remained commanded extravagant sums from buyers like the Union and Concord governments.

Activating pentatech was often a tricky proposition. Sometimes a cleric or Jovian—someone equipped with the right neural interface—could communicate with the ghostly remnants of whatever once controlled the technology. Other, braver souls who lacked deifactured neural implants could, for example, bypass the original control systems entirely (along with whatever safety features had been built in) and power up individual components.

That's not something Nathan was willing to do without first running a *very* long cable and taking shelter in a bunker. And even then, he'd be sweating before he hit the button.

Risk versus reward, he thought. Both were present in abundance whenever pentatech was involved. The disappearance of Joshua's professor was worrisome but not a dealbreaker. If everything Joshua and Vessani had shared was accurate—and he saw no reason to doubt them so far—then who besides Vessani could put them on the trail in the first place? Once they were underway, that was it. No one else could find this pentatech relic.

Which brought him finally to the question of the contract. The safest bet was to charge a flat rate for their services, accruing money daily as the job dragged out. But with a prize of this potential scope...

"What would you say to a commission as payment?" Nathan asked. "A percentage of what we find instead of a more standard arrangement?"

"That sounds reasonable. What did you have in mind?"

"How about fifty percent?"

"*Fifty?*" Joshua squeaked, clearly taken aback.

"It's either that or we talk about a per diem cost, which I'll need a month's worth up front, *and* it's going to be higher than usual because of all the risks."

"Then, at the end of the first month?"

"You either pay for another or we turn around."

"Captain, I understand your position, but fifty seems excessive to me."

"Perhaps, but pentatech should *never* be trifled with. Trust me, I know. I've seen the stuff go rogue in the worst possible ways. Hell, fifty is just enough for us to *consider* the job. I'm not agreeing to anything until Aiko and I have talked it over in private."

"Well ... umm ..." Joshua turned to Vessani.

"It's fine." She placed a hand over his. "I've got a good feeling about these two."

"I—" Joshua seemed to regain some of his composure as he turned back to Nathan. "All right. We're willing to entertain a fifty-fifty split."

"Good." Nathan sat back and let out a long exhalation. He was almost ready to accept the work, but then a memory intruded upon his mind, unbidden and unwelcome yet as vivid as reality. For a split second, he was sixteen again, fleeing from a vast monster he couldn't see, could only hear gnawing and gnashing its way toward him through a dark maze of metal. He carried his unconscious mother on his back, her arms looped around him, her head slumped against his shoulder. His muscles burned from the exertion, but a duality of fear and purpose drove him, pushed him to put one foot ahead of the other despite the agonizing cries behind him.

Of people melting.

Dissolving.

Changing.

He blinked his way back to the present and shook the dark thoughts aside.

"Give us some time to talk it over," he told Joshua. "We'll get in touch with you tomorrow with our answer."

Nathan parked the rental car in the visitor lot of the Pentatheon Church's Home for the Lost, an asylum built on the outskirts of Dexamene City. He climbed out of the vehicle, picked up the flowers on the passenger seat, then locked and closed the car door.

He paused and glanced back to Port Leverrier and the immense walls of its wide plateau. The trio of deifactories rose tall and proud from the city center and the distant lights of spaceships and aircraft twinkled through the air. It had taken him almost three hours to reach the Leverrier suburbs of Dexamene City, which spread like fat arteries through the farmlands to the south.

The Home for the Lost was a three-story, white-walled, pentagonal building with welcoming gardens in full bloom. The strong scent of hyacinths filled him with a sense of nostalgia from his past visits. To the north, the Neptunian sun-wall had begun to dim on its way to nightfall, though Sol's presence in the sky ensured it would only be a half night. At least at first.

Nathan proceeded through the open archway and checked in with the receptionist. He waited in the pentagonal lobby for several minutes and stared up at the reliefs depicting illuminations of the Guardian Deities.

Edencraft: architect of humanity's homes throughout the solar system.

Pathfinder: explorer, gatherer, and the trailblazer behind star lifting.

Codex: tinkerer, keeper of knowledge, and digitizer of mentality.

Metatron: lord of society, order, and peace.

And finally, Divergence: master of life and modifier of the human form.

The reliefs represented the Pentatheon as absurdly tall humanoids, bestowing their gifts upon the worthy, which surely wasn't accurate. What did godlike machines need arms and legs for when matter and energy had been their playthings?

A doctor came out to greet Nathan, probably from Saturn if her cybernetic hands and eyes were any indication.

"Hello, Mr. Kade. I'm Dr. Leshwa viin Dexamene." She dipped her head toward him. "I understand you're here to see your mother."

"That's right. I know it's been a while, but . . ." He paused, then gave the doctor an apologetic shrug of the flowers in his arms. "How has she been?"

"More or less the same." Leshwa consulted the vlass tablet in the crook of her arm. "Outwardly, there are no noticeable changes with Samantha's behavior or health."

"And on the inside?" Nathan asked with some trepidation.

"That's a little more complex. We've detected a new nodule in her brain." Leshwa showed him a series of diagrams on her tablet. "We're not sure what it's doing."

"Have you tried to treat it?"

"We have."

"Any luck?"

She shook her head. "Whatever it is, the nodule seems capable of nullifying standard panacea injections, somehow ordering the panacea to stand down and stay out of its way. We don't know how it's doing that, and we have no way of counteracting the effect. I'm afraid there's not much we can do besides monitor, unless we decide to go in and take it out."

"And if you have to?"

"Her chances of survival aren't good. The nodules are deeply entwined with her brain, and we can't use panacea to extract it. We'd have to perform the operation manually."

"I see." Nathan let out a slow exhale.

"However, I believe there's reason for optimism. The pentatech in her head is clearly doing something, driving toward some goal we have yet to grasp, but it seems to be acting in an almost tender manner, careful not to cause damage. By comparison, the samples we've taken from her blood revert to an inert state, and nothing we've done has been able to reactivate them."

"Be glad that's the case."

"We *are* careful with our research, Mr. Kade."

"So was my father."

Leshwa appeared ready to respond, but then seemed to think better of it and simply smiled at him.

"Of course."

Nathan wasn't surprised the doctors had removed samples of the residual pentatech in his mother's blood. The fact that the Church doctors could study the contaminants was the reason he could keep her at the Home for the Lost indefinitely. Her care came free of charge.

"Would you like to see her now?"

"Please."

Leshwa led him through a central courtyard and up a staircase to a room on the third floor at the back of the building. The plaque on the door read:

SAMANTHA KADE
PENTATECH EXPOSURE
BLOOD AND NEURAL CONTAMINATION
98% INERT, NOT CONTAGIOUS

"Please let me know if you need anything," Leshwa said.

"I will. Thank you."

The doctor dipped her head to him, then headed back toward the nearby stairs.

Nathan knocked on the door.

"Mom? It's Nate. I'm coming in." He waited a few moments for the response he knew wouldn't come, more out of habitual politeness than anything else, then opened the door.

His mother sat in a chair by the open window, the drapes fluttering in a gentle breeze. A bowl of fresh fruit sat on a wooden stand beside her chair with orange peels and an apple core atop a used napkin.

She turned and smiled at him, which didn't say much. She smiled at most everyone these days. But Nathan still felt a warm tingle spread within his chest as he smiled back.

"Hey, Mom." He raised the bouquet in his hands. "I brought you some flowers."

She turned back to the window.

"Give me a moment. Let me find a vase for these."

He searched through the small kitchen's cupboard until he found a glass large enough to serve as a vase. He filled it at the sink, added the bouquet of flowers to it, and set it by the window.

"There. How's that?"

Samantha stared out the window, apparently unaware of the new flowers.

"They taking good care of you?"

He looked her over, checked her unresisting hands and wrists, didn't find any signs of injuries or restraint. He made a slow sweep of the room. The bed was made, the bathroom was clean and well-stocked, and only a little bit of trash was in the waste can.

He didn't have reason to believe she'd been mistreated, but inspecting the room helped put his mind at ease.

"Everything looks to be in order." He sat down on the bedside next to her chair, but then took a harder look at her hair and frowned. "Got some tangles, there. Let me help you with that."

He stepped into the bathroom, took a comb out of the drawer, and returned to his mother's side.

"There's something I wanted to talk to you about," he said as he combed her long hair with slow, gentle strokes.

She didn't respond, merely sat there, staring out the window.

"I got a job offer today. Seems like a good one. Decent client, at least if we're going off first impressions. His friend?" He snorted. "I guess she's okay, too. But there's a problem."

He paused mid-stroke, gripped her hair so that he wasn't tugging on the roots, and worked through the tangle.

"The client wants us to go after something dangerous, which I'm not too keen on. Now, I know what you and Dad would say." He let out a short laugh. "Especially Dad. He'd want to know why I was hesitating. He'd *demand* to know. Why wasn't I already out there hunting for the stuff?

"But the truth is, I never shared his passion. His thirst. His never-ending quest to learn about the Pentatheon. It always seemed—I don't know—narrow, maybe? There are so many bright, exciting, fascinating corners to the solar system. Why limit ourselves? Why focus on gods who've been dead for four thousand years when there's so much else to see and do?

"I still remember the stories he'd share when I was young, how they'd fill me with awe. Make me yearn to grow up faster and get out there so I could experience the solar system for myself. I remember how excited I was to finally join the *Belle*'s crew, only to discover the reality of his work was . . . not quite as exciting as I'd imagined, and filled with so much tedium.

"But he didn't see it that way. Where I might see random debris, he could puzzle out the clue to a past we still don't understand. Every discovery was like the ancients were whispering to him, revealing their secrets one tantalizing hint at a time.

"A part of me knows I'm not made for that kind of life. I don't have Dad's singular focus, his passion for one topic. But at the same time, I feel like I've been betraying his memory, and maybe this job is a way to make some of that up. To honor his legacy, in some small way."

His mother muttered something, her lips barely moving, and Nathan again paused mid-stroke. He set the comb down and knelt beside her.

"What was that?" he asked.

Her lips trembled with soft words, and this time he recognized them.

"'Progress is not made in darkness,'" Nathan said, enunciating the quote from his father clearly. "'We must shine a light on the past if we're to understand where we came from and where we're going.'"

His mother turned to him, and for the first time in over a decade, Nathan felt as if she were really looking at him. As if she knew her son knelt beside her.

"That's right, Mom," he choked, and a tear trickled out of one eye.

CHAPTER EIGHT

Nathan called Joshua the next morning and invited him and Vessani back to the ship to review and sign the contract. They met in the B Deck mess and drank Beany coffee fresh from the bulb while reviewing and amending the contract language.

Joshua pushed back against the fifty-fifty split, which Nathan had expected, and the two haggled for a while until they agreed to sixty-forty in the clients' favor. Nathan was happy with the result, since he'd expected more resistance from Joshua, and the young man also seemed pleased, having just negotiated a more favorable arrangement.

The three of them filled out and signed the contract's various pages, though Joshua wrote "to be provided after signing" in a lot of the boxes, which Nathan let pass without comment. He would have preferred to receive all the information up front, but he could understand their desire not to share anything critical until the contract was signed and they were underway. It wasn't until Vessani pushed forward a folder that he did speak up.

"What are these?"

"Amendments." Vessani flipped open the folder and handed Nathan the first sheet.

Nathan took it, cleared his throat, and read the brief text.

"'The crew of the *Neptune Belle* will return the confiscated left-hand hard-suit glove belonging to Vessani S'Kaari.'" He set the sheet down. "That's awfully specific."

"There's more." She handed him the second sheet, and Nathan skimmed over it.

"You put the right-hand glove on its own page?"

"Joshua told me to be as detailed as possible, and to list each item clearly and separately."

"Fine. Whatever." Nathan set the sheet down and was about to sign it when she handed him a third piece of paper. He took it with a frown and read over the brief text. "And *another* sheet for your thermos."

"I really like that thermos."

"Do you just want all your stuff back?"

"Yes."

"Then why don't you just say so? Give me those." He leafed through the pages, then pulled out one near the middle. "I'll sign all of them except for this one."

"Why not?"

"Because I ate the food bar yesterday."

"You going to buy me a replacement?"

"If it'll make this process go any faster!"

"I'm sure we can forgo that page," Joshua cut in diplomatically, taking the sheet back.

"It wasn't even that good," Nathan muttered as he signed each amendment separately. He then slipped his pen back into one of his jacket's inner pockets. Aiko took the new sheets and inspected them before slotting them into the contract folder.

"Everything's in order," Aiko said after checking the documentation.

"Congratulations, Mr. Cotton." Nathan extended his hand. "You've got yourself a ship."

"Wonderful. Though, please call me Joshua. I imagine we'll all be quite familiar with each other by the time we're finished."

"If you like." Nathan settled back in his chair. "Now then, where exactly are we headed first?"

"A habitat called WC-9003," Vessani said.

"That sounds like a temporary tag reserved for unexplored megastructures." Nathan pulled out his *Almanac* and looked it up. The entry was almost completely empty. "Yep. Uncharted."

"From the perspective of the *Solar Almanac*," Joshua said.

"But not to locals like me," Vessani added, her ears perking up.

"Okay, but how do we know this is the right place?" Nathan asked. "You grew up low-tech, right?"

"Yes, that's right."

"Which means your people haven't left the habitat in millennia. What are we basing this destination on? The *Almanac* doesn't even have a surface map, just a few blurry telescope pictures. Is there something in the entry I'm missing? Maybe an update in a new edition?"

"No, nothing like that."

"Then what makes you certain this is the place?"

"Easy." Vessani flashed a sly smile. "The habitat is a windowed cylinder, which means nearby structures are visible in the night sky, and one of them is quite distinct. A dark red ring. I remember seeing it through my mother's telescope."

"Vessani and I were eventually able to identify the ring habitat," Joshua explained. "It's a nasty place called the Sanguine Ring. Danger level eight out of ten."

"An *eight*?" Nathan's eyes widened.

"Apparently, the Almanac Association lost a few ships in its vicinity."

"I hope you don't expect us to go there!"

"Oh, no. Perish the thought. We simply used its position to narrow our search. After that, it was a simple matter to identify all nearby windowed cylinders."

"We were then able to eliminate all the other locations except WC-9003," Vessani continued. "That's our target, and I'm sure the Black Egg is still there."

Nathan stared down at the fuzzy image of the windowed cylinder, then slowly began to nod.

"So, when we get there, what's our play? Are you expecting us to swipe the Black Egg?"

"Nothing so dramatic."

"We'll ask to see it," Vessani said. "I used to live there, remember? I should be able to get us in without too much fuss."

"Okay, but then what? How will this Black Egg lead us to the relic?"

"It reacts to the presence of pentatech."

"*Any* pentatech?" Nathan asked doubtfully. The Black Egg would be priceless beyond belief if that were true.

"No, just one particular object."

"Okay, but how do you know this object is pentatech?"

"You're full of questions, aren't you?" Joshua gave him a coy smile.

"I like to be prepared. Can you really blame me?"

"Of course not. The truth is, Vess and I don't know for certain it's pentatech."

"But you have a good reason to believe it is?"

"We do."

"It goes back to the Black Egg," Vessani explained. "Its reactions grow more intense on a regular interval, reaching a peak once every seventy-one years."

"I discussed the details of the Black Egg's reactions with Anterus vaan Kronya," Joshua said, "and we came to the conclusion the relic is on an elliptical orbit around Sol."

"Aha!" Nathan's face lit up with understanding.

An elliptical orbit strongly implied the object was something damaged during the Scourging of Heaven, blasted out of the Pentatheon's meticulously laid orbits by some great cataclysm. The solar system was almost totally devoid of objects—natural or otherwise—that orbited Sol in pronounced ellipses. The Pentatheon had seen to that during the Age of Communion, clearing the solar system of random debris.

"And so," Joshua continued, "we propose using the information we can glean from the Black Egg to triangulate the relic's position. As luck would have it, we're quite close to its once-every-seventy-one-years peak in activity, which should give us the best opportunity we'll have in our lifetimes to track it down."

"Okay." Nathan rubbed his chin. "That's all well and good, but how are we going to get what we need out of the Egg? Are the locals able to commune with it?"

"Not to the degree we need."

"Then it seems your plan has a hole in it."

"Yes, I suppose that's something we should discuss." Joshua leaned in, resting his forearms on the table. "I had originally intended for us to pick up Anterus so he could commune with the Black Egg on our behalf, but . . ." He spread his upturned hands apologetically.

"We need to hire a replacement."

"Quite," Joshua agreed, then raised an eyebrow. "I suppose this makes Saturn our first stop?"

"Perhaps." Nathan paused in thought, then snapped his fingers. "Actually, I might have an alternative. There's a Saturnian cleric Aiko and I have worked with in the past. He might be just what we need."

"You don't mean Rufus, do you?" Aiko asked.

"I do."

"Wasn't he a little . . . combative the last time we parted ways?"

"I'm sure he's cooled off by now."

"If you say so." Aiko shook her head. "Man, is he going to be surprised to see us!"

"The cleric's name is Rufus sen Qell," Nathan said. "He's the best man I know for this job. We should be able to find him in the Habitat Belt, on Faelyn's Grasp. He's doing missionary work there."

"He's from Qell?" Joshua noted with a half smile. "That's quite a prestigious monastery, if I'm not mistaken."

"And he's got a real gift for communing with old tech."

"What about him as a person? Is he dependable? Trustworthy?"

"I'll personally vouch for his character. You won't be disappointed."

"Then it sounds like we have our replacement expert. Anything else you'd like to know?"

"Not at the moment." Nathan pushed away from the table and stood up. "Aiko will show you to your rooms and help you get settled. We'll take care of our preflight checks, then get underway once your luggage is secured."

"Wonderful," Joshua said, rising along with Vessani. "Though we require only one room, thank you."

"One?"

Joshua gave him a faint, knowing smile.

Nathan glanced from the dapper engineer to the roguish catgirl and back.

"*Really?*"

Vessani put her arm around Joshua and leaned her head against his shoulder, her eyes twinkling with mischief.

"Okay, then," Nathan said with a shrug. "One room it is. Who am I to judge?"

"I never grow tired of this sight." Joshua gazed down at the retreating view of both Neptune and the shell band that girdled it.

"Eh. Been there. Seen that." Nathan shrugged his shoulders and turned in the pilot seat. Joshua had expressed an interest in watching their departure from the cockpit, and Vessani had joined them shortly after that.

"It's amazing when you think about it," Joshua said, looking up. "Did you know the shell bands shouldn't be able to hold their position, given what we currently know about them?"

Nathan gave him a doubtful look.

"No, it's true. If the bands were nothing more than the passive support structures we've seen, they should fall right into the gas giants."

"But . . ." Nathan shook his head. "I mean, they're rigid, aren't they? Like a ring around your finger."

Joshua let out an involuntary snort, then quickly covered his grinning mouth.

"What?" Nathan crossed his arms. "Did I say something funny?"

"Sorry, sorry." The engineer held up an apologetic hand. "I didn't mean anything by it. Your remark just caught me by surprise."

"They *are* rigid."

"True, but not *that* rigid."

Joshua composed himself and looked up, smiling. Not a mean or condescending smile, but an expression of excitement at the topic, and his eyes were filled with the same gleeful energy.

"Certainly, they're immense and solidly built," Joshua began, his smile growing as he dug into the topic, "but think about what they are for a moment. A shell band is basically a giant bridge without endpoints or supports hanging over a crushing death chasm. Gravity is tugging on every point, and there's nothing solid for the load to be routed to. Can you imagine the force generated by all that mass being dragged down into the planet's gravity well? I understand, and to a certain degree sympathize, with the common misconception that the bands are just really big rings for really big fingers, but the truth is they're *nothing* like that."

"Okay, fine," Nathan replied indifferently, but then thought better of it and decided to urge the engineer on. It never hurt to show interest in a passenger's field of study. "But then how does it stay up?"

"We don't know!" Joshua's eyes gleamed with barely contained excitement. "But I came across some fascinating theories during my studies on Saturn. The one I favor the most theorizes that there actually *are* supports holding up the shell bands. We just can't see them."

"Why?" Nathan asked, confused. "Are they invisible or something?"

"No, no. Nothing so dramatic."

"Then where are they?"

"The only place they could be." Joshua gestured to Neptune with an open hand. "*Inside* the shell bands!"

"What?" Nathan shook his head, now even more perplexed. "I don't get it."

"Allow me to explain," Joshua began, his tone making it clear how much he was enjoying this discussion. "According to this theory, the shell bands are active support structures, which makes a tremendous amount of sense to me. To clarify, a passive support structure is what everyone is familiar with even if they don't realize it. A house, for instance, being held up by the passive characteristics of the materials used to build it. Nothing special, right?

"An *active* support structure has a moving component. In this case, it's believed the floor of each shell band is hollow, composed of countless tubes that run the full circumference of the structure."

"Tubes for what?"

"The ring's supports. Imagine for a moment these tubes were filled with a material that isn't holding position over the planet, but instead is rotating at stable orbital speeds. Or rather, slightly *faster* than a stable orbit demands. A ring of orbiting material, or 'orbital ring' for short. What does that produce?"

"Umm?"

"An outward force!" Joshua exclaimed with bright-eyed glee. "A force pushing the shell band away from the planet, acting in opposition to the pull of gravity. Factor the two together, and suddenly you have a system in equilibrium! No super-rigid materials required!"

"Huh. You don't say," Nathan remarked, trying to wrap his head around the concept.

"And there's more!" Joshua wagged a finger, grinning. "There's evidence the many chandelier refineries along the underside also play important roles. If we take this theory a step further, we come to the conclusion the orbital rings should be a superconductor of some kind, magnetically pushing the shell band rather than rubbing against it, with all the wasteful friction and heat that entails."

"Okay. But how do the refineries tie into that?"

"Because the Pentatheon built to last. Energy might have to be added to or removed from the orbital rings to maintain optimal stability, and the refineries have access to near limitless energy thanks to the gas-giant atmospheres. They're the most obvious tool available to adjust the speed of each orbital ring over time, and there's another piece of evidence hinting at their involvement."

"Which is?"

"Refineries will occasionally vent reactor plasma for prolonged periods. Almost as if they double as giant fusion thrusters put in place to help maintain each shell band's equilibrium!"

"Funny you should mention that." Nathan gestured to Aiko. "We were almost caught in a refinery flare once."

"Came out of nowhere and nearly vaporized us," Aiko added.

"Which was probably the shell band making a minor stability correction," Joshua said.

"You could be right."

Nathan had never given much thought to how the shell bands worked. The megastructures were simply there, ever-present and immutable, but Joshua seemed to view reality through a different lens. It was the difference between asking *what* a thing could do and understanding *why* it could do it.

He glanced over to Vessani, who leaned against the cockpit's back wall near the passenger jump seats.

"Is he always like this?" Nathan asked.

"Not always, but often."

"You understand all that?"

"Not one bit," she replied in an almost dreamy manner.

CHAPTER NINE

Prinn Pratti knelt in her quarters aboard the freelance freighter *Practical* and prayed. The shrine wasn't large or fancy. Just a foldout cupboard with a simple mosaic of Pathfinder, depicting the Guardian Deity as a halo of flaming satellites above Sol. A prominence arced from the star, and Pathfinder collected the fiery matter into globes within its great halo.

A trio of incense sticks burned, standing upright in a small bowl of sand, the smoke rising to Prinn's nostrils. She closed her eyes and breathed in, enjoying the pleasant scent of burning wood as she meditated on her morning prayers.

All Prattis prayed to Pathfinder. Even the Aiko branch, when they actually *did* pray, worshiped the Explorer God. Pathfinder embodied the mystery of the unknown and the joy of discovery, which must have appealed to the Aikos as well. Prinn knew that's why *she* prayed to the god, but she'd never broached the topic with any of the other copy-clan branches.

The Jovian faith of Tetrad differed from the Church of Pentatheon in many ways beyond excluding Divergence. Certainly, that difference was the largest and most noticeable, but the Church came with a great many trappings Jovians found tedious. It was a massive organization with a formal hierarchy that dictated doctrine and oversaw how its many members should or should not pray to the Guardian Deities.

Tetrad possessed no such central authority. No one would ever stand over her shoulder and chastise her, saying "That is not an approved prayer!" She considered Tetrad's openness—its acceptance of each individual's method of prayer—as a strength of her faith. Her prayers were her own and no one else's. Why would she wish to filter her meditations through the prism of someone else's dogma?

Her Saturnian comrades disagreed with her, of course. Respectfully, but insistently. She'd never found a need to discuss religion within her own copy-clan, but the *Practical*'s Saturnian crew would bring up the topic at the drop of a hat!

She doubted this was typical behavior, but instead a by-product of them working alongside someone as "exotic" as her. She supposed she could understand this, though their constant requests for "intellectual dialogues" became tedious at times.

She'd chosen a body that resembled flesh and blood when she'd signed up for the *Practical*, though her blue skin and silver eyes ensured she stood out, at least a little. The *Practical*'s crew of fifty-five came in a variety of shapes and colors—from baseline to obscure divergents and everything in between.

Personally, she preferred the utility of more mechanized bodies, but she couldn't deny the social benefits of her choice. She'd even received a few friendly solicitations and had taken them up on their offers of nocturnal "cultural exchanges."

The novelty of her time on the *Practical* was one of the reasons she'd decided to do it, if only with one body. She could never see herself going deviant like the Aikos had, but a part of her felt some of the same tendencies worming their way through her mind, tugging at her as she contemplated a break from the Everlife.

Just contemplated, though. Never seriously.

But the thoughts were there, and she'd hit upon the idea of signing up with a Saturnian crew to serve as a sort of reprieve from her frustrations with the Everlife, one that she could share with the rest of her branch once she returned and her memories were reintegrated.

Her commect chimed, and she opened her eyes and answered it. "Go ahead."

"Prinn, we need you on the bridge." She recognized the voice of Captain Xavier vaas Rhea, and she picked up on the unusual edge to his tone. Normally, he would call and open with a phrase like "Would you please come to the bridge, Prinn?" It would still be an order, but he seemed to favor an affable approach with his crew.

This sounded far more urgent.

"Right away, Captain." She doused the incense in the sand, closed the shrine's two small doors, and exited her quarters.

The *Practical* was on its way to Neptune with a hold stuffed to the ceiling with expensive Saturnian goods. They were still five days out from the gas giant, which made Prinn wonder what could be worrying the captain.

The ship felt and sounded normal, and the crew members she passed on her way to the bridge didn't seem to be rushing toward any sort of emergency. She took an elevator up to A Deck and headed straight for the bridge.

"That is a negative, *Leviathan*!" shouted the commect officer. Prinn didn't remember his name. "Again, we are in open space and do not recognize your authority here!"

"You wished to see me, Captain?" Prinn asked, joining Xavier, who stood behind the commect officer with a dour expression.

"Yes," he replied quietly, stepping back from the commect station. "We have a bit of a situation brewing, and I thought you might be able to help."

"What seems to be the problem?"

"There's a Jovian ship a couple thousand kilometers to our rear and closing. A big sucker called the *Leviathan of Io*. It's telling us we need to cut our thrust and prepare to receive their boarding parties for inspection."

"That's ridiculous!" Prinn exclaimed. "They can't make us do that. Not this far from Jupiter. They have no right!"

"That's what we keep telling them, but they're not backing off, which has me worried." Xavier leaned closer. "I've dealt with belligerent Jovians before. Ones that'll throw their weight around in an attempt to rattle us, but that's as far as it ever goes. This feels different. The *Leviathan* sounds deadly serious about boarding us. Can you think of any reason why a Jovian *cruiser* would suddenly take an interest in us?"

"No, Captain." Prinn shook her head. "Maybe if we were coming from or heading to Jupiter, but all we're doing is hauling Saturnian goods to Neptune. The only thing I can think of is perhaps there's been a recent shift in Jovian policy, but if so, I've never heard so much as a rumor of it."

"Thought so." He nudged his head toward the commect officer. "Would you be willing to give it a try? Maybe they'll listen to you."

"I can certainly *try*. Though, I don't know how much good it'll do."

"That's all I ask." The captain nodded to the commect officer, who nodded back.

"*Practical* to *Leviathan*. We have a Jovian crew member who wishes to speak with you concerning your demands." He paused, pressing the headset firmly against his ear, and his brow creased. "Yes . . . yes, her name is Prinn Pratti."

What? Prinn thought. *They know I'm on this ship?*

"Friends of yours?" Xavier asked.

"I guess we'll find out."

"Here." The commect officer stripped off his headset and handed it to Prinn. "I hope you have better luck than me."

"Thanks."

He made room for her, and she sat down and fitted on the headset.

"*Leviathan*, this is Prinn Pratti. Come in, please."

"Stand by. Transferring call to the apex."

"Excuse me?" she snapped. "Are you seriously putting me on hold?"

"Transferring now."

The other end of the line muted. She turned back to the captain and gave him an annoyed what-the-hell shrug and pointed to the headset.

"Just try your best," he urged quietly.

"I will."

What is going on here? Why switch me over to the apex?

She heard a click, followed by a smooth chuckle.

"Hello, Prinn. It's been a while."

The voice dredged up her memories of Aiko leaving the Everlife under less-than-auspicious circumstances. Members of other Pratti branches, the Prinns included, had been brought in to assist in the investigation. An investigation headed by—

"Xormun?" she asked.

"That's right."

"Which branch?"

"Galatt Xormun."

"*You're* the *Leviathan's* apex?" she asked, suddenly worried.

"You make that sound like it's such a bad thing."

"Well . . ." She wasn't sure what to say. On the surface, Xormun had worked with the Prattis to diagnose what had gone wrong with Aiko, but Prinn had long believed his real directive had been to root out other potential deviants in the clan and, if he found any, to eliminate them.

No purges had taken place, thankfully, but that didn't change the cold, shuddering fear his voice filled her with.

"Captain," she said shakily. "We should do what he says. Cut our engines now before the situation escalates."

"Please, you're overreacting," Xormun said, sounding almost bored. "I take it you're on the *Practical's* bridge?"

"Why do you ask?"

"A simple yes or no, please."

"Yes. What of it?"

"Excellent. It seems you won't have to cut your engines after all. See you soon, Prinn."

"What's that supposed to—"

The top of the bridge exploded, and air rushed out, carrying debris and bridge officers with it. The powerful suction lifted her out of the seat, but she grabbed a handhold on top of the station's console and wrestled herself back to the floor. Xavier crashed into her back, arms grasping vainly for something to hold on to, and she reached and caught his forearm.

The initial blast of escaping air subsided, and loose objects fell to the floor thanks to the ship's constant acceleration. Prinn landed on her feet, and Xavier staggered into her, his eyes wide with terror, hand at his throat as he began to asphyxiate.

She grabbed him by the scruff of his shirt and shoved him toward the nearest pressure door. The bridge's two exit doors had slammed shut in response to the decompression, but the corridors beyond them could double as long, impromptu airlocks in an emergency.

Prinn reached the nearest one and triggered the override. The door slid open, and another blast of air blew her back. She fought through it, then chucked Xavier inside, and shut the door. Emergency systems pumped breathable air into the corridor, and she watched Xavier through the porthole as he gasped for breath.

She turned away and faced what was left of the bridge, searching for anyone else she could save.

Instead, she spotted a trio of Jovian commandos, their red-and-gold armor gleaming in the light. They dropped through the hole in the bridge ceiling, each equipped with a rifle.

Where did you jerks come from? Prinn thought venomously. *The* Leviathan *is thousands of kilometers away! Did Xormun deploy a stealthed ship ahead of his cruiser? That'd be just like him, that snake!*

Those thoughts shot through Prinn's mind in a flash of reasoning, all while the nearest commando charged at her. She backpedaled, and when the commando reached for her with his free hand, she kicked him in the abdomen. He stumbled back, and she used the opening to grab his rifle, trying to wrest control of the weapon from him.

The other two commandos flanked her, even as she tried in vain to yank the gun out of the first commando's grasp. Something glinted to her right, and she spun at the last moment, only to see the translucent edge of a vibro-knife slash through her throat.

The attack must have damaged some of her motor functions because her fingers loosened around the rifle. The first commando shoved her back, his rifle still firmly in his hands, and Prinn teetered backward on the heels of her feet.

One of the commandos grabbed her by the hair and slashed the knife through what remained of her throat. He yanked her head free, and the rest of her flopped to the ground.

Her head, now severed from the body's power supply, began to shut down. The small capacitor inside her skull drained out rapidly, since its purpose was to smooth out power fluctuations rather than act as a reserve. One of the commandos stuffed her head into a backpack, and her mind shut down.

Prinn awoke to unfamiliar senses. She was on a table in a small room with a door directly in front of her. At first, she thought she was still just a head, but the visuals were wrong. Too muddy and monochrome to be her previous eyes, and they lacked depth perception. Had her persona been transferred to a different body? If so, for what purpose? They'd cut off her head! What was she going to do? Gnaw at their ankles?

She tried to blink. Nothing happened. Did she even have eyelids anymore?

She waited.

Watched.

And listened.

But didn't hear anything.

Is this body deaf? she thought. *What kind of sick joke is this?*

Time passed. How long, she couldn't say, but she found the silent monotony almost unbearable. She wanted to call out, to move around the room, to do something! But couldn't. She was helpless. Just a nondescript lump on the table.

Finally, mercifully, the pressure door opened.

Galatt Xormun walked in. He did so love those ostentatious metal-skinned bodies of his. This one was gold, and then two more Xormuns entered the room, each silver-skinned.

<Hello Prinn.> The gold Xormun pulled out a chair and sat down in front of her. His copies disappeared to either side of her. Her body's vision was unusually narrow and she had no way to turn around.

<What the fuck, you lunatic!> she snapped, wondering if he could hear her wireless speech.

<It's nice to see you, too, Prinn.> He flashed a quick, cold smile.

<Do you have any idea how many treaties you just violated?>

<Oh, give me a moment.> He glanced up at the ceiling. <Three or four, I think.>

<What is wrong with you? Are you trying to start a war?>

<I wouldn't be too concerned about that. The Union isn't going to charge headlong into a war they can't win over something so trivial as one ship.>

<One ship?> she repeated. But then a chilling realization settled in her mind. <You don't mean...?>

<Yes. The *Practical* is no more.> He made circular motions with one hand. <Or it will be in a few days. The crew is dead, at any rate, while a few of my commandos remain on board. They're going to dump the ship into the Neptunian depths. A couple thousand atmospheres of pressure should take care of the evidence nicely.>

<People will notice the ship's missing! They'll want an explanation!>

<I'm sure they will, but they'll find answers are in short supply. Not that I brought you here to discuss Everlife-Union politics. How have you been, by the way? Life been treating you all right?>

<My own clan will look into this!>

<So what if they do? You're one copy from a questionable, almost deviant branch. How much would they really care? I mean, serving on a Saturnian ship?> He shook his head disapprovingly. <That's not a very good look. What's the point of hanging out with these short-lived protein lumps, anyway?>

<It was a nice change of pace until someone murdered all my shipmates!>

<I'll take your word for it.> He leaned back. <I suppose you'd like to know why we brought you here?>

<The question *had* crossed my mind,> she seethed.

<Ever hear of a woman named Vessani S'Kaari?>

<What's it to you?>

<Pure, academic curiosity, I assure you.>

<Oh, go fuck yourselves!>

<This is a serious question. Ever come across the name?>

<Even if I had, I'm not telling you anything! You think I'll help you after what you just pulled? You don't scare me! You might kill me, but so what? My copies will live on, and you'll *still* not have what you want!>

<Oh, but that's where you're wrong.> Xormun sat forward, his leering face uncomfortably close. <I'm not threatening to kill you. Death threats are a thing for organics.>

<Then what *are* you doing?>

<I'm *offering* to end your life.>

<Not much of an offer, then.>

<You think so? Here. Let me show you.> One of the silver Xormuns handed the apex a small mirror, and he held it up for her, revealing the true nature of her new body.

There wasn't much to it. Just a box with a single camera wrapped in black solar skin. He propped the mirror up and angled it so she could still see the body.

<Allow me to explain your options.> Xormun knitted his fingers. <First, you can continue to deny me the information I seek, which will eventually result in us kicking you off the ship. Literally, and in

your current state, minus the ability to transmit. You'll be nothing more than a box floating through the void, unable to do anything, unable to say anything, just a passive observer as you float around for who knows how long, your solar skin keeping your mind running for untold centuries of helplessness.>

<You'd do that to one of your own?!> she quavered, icy fear gripping her mind.

<If you force my hand. Or—if you find that option not to your liking—you can tell me what I want to know. Who she is. Where she is. Where she's going and why. What Aiko Pratti has to do with her. Everything and anything you know about this woman, her dealings, and her associations, all down to the smallest possible detail you can recall.

<That's not such a difficult ask, now, is it?> He smiled at her. <And once you've done that, once you've helped me to my satisfaction, then and *only* then will I let you die. Otherwise . . . >

Xormun rose from his seat and picked her up. The room swung drunkenly until he spun her around, revealing she'd been in an airlock this whole time.

One of the silver bodies opened the airlock to the starry vacuum of space, and Xormun held her out the side of the skyscraper-like ship.

<What'll it be?> he asked with sinister relish.

<Who would have guessed?> Xormun said with a half smile as he leaned over the bridge's central vlass. <Aiko Pratti still hanging around Captain Nathaniel Kade. I thought she had more sense than that.>

<Apex?> asked one of the data analysts.

<Pay me no mind. Just reminiscing about an old case. Aiko was a deviant whose breakaway I investigated some five years ago. I even advised hunting her down and terminating her as a signal to the rest of the Prattis, but our superiors decided to let the matter pass quietly.> He shrugged with indifference, then grinned. <Oh, well. I'm sure they know what's best.>

<Shall I set a course for Neptune?> the pilot asked.

<No.> Xormun surveyed the various windows open in the vlass, from navigational charts to intelligence profiles and deviant bios. <I

doubt the *Neptune Belle* is still there, and if it is, we're likely to miss it. We'll peel off one corvette to follow up that lead. Perhaps they'll discover something in Port Leverrier that will shed light on the *Belle's* next destination, while we head for the Habitat Belt.>

<But where in the Belt, sir? We still don't know which habitat S'Kaari was born on.>

<True, but we need to be in position to act swiftly as new information comes in. One point in the Belt will do as well as any other until we can narrow down our search, which is where our corvettes will come into play. It now falls on us to predict our quarry's next move. For instance, I believe it's entirely possible the *Belle* will head for Kirkwood to investigate Anterus's disappearance.>

<We already have an asset nearby,> the data analyst pointed out.

<Yes, and that corvette should stay there for the time being. That leaves us with six to distribute to other possible destinations.>

Xormun looked over Nathan Kade's file. There wasn't a great deal of information present, since the *Neptune Belle* had rarely run afoul of Jovian operations, but the incident surrounding Aiko Pratti's breakaway five years ago had been enough to activate a basic level of intelligence gathering for the *Neptune Belle* and its crew.

This meant Xormun already possessed some information to work with, such as a list of known associates. It was this list that drew his eye the most. Kade and Aiko both had some experience with pentatech, if fleeting and of the variety that might earn them "I survived my brush with pentatech" T-shirts and not much else. Interestingly, Kade's *father* had been well versed in the subject. For a Neptunian, at least. But he was dead, and nothing in the record indicated his son had taken to the subject with the same enthusiasm.

Which meant Kade and Aiko didn't have the skills to see this particular venture through. Not on their own, and nothing in their record indicated they were stupid. They would seek out and hire the expertise they needed.

The question remained, where would they find it?

Vessani S'Kaari and Joshua Cotton were two variables to consider, but the first was easy enough to eliminate. S'Kaari had a low-tech upbringing, which made her an even worse choice than Kade and Aiko for dealing with pentatech safely.

That left Cotton, whom Xormun had little information on. It was possible Cotton possessed the skills the *Belle*'s crew lacked, which also meant there was a chance the *Belle* would head straight for S'Kaari's home, depriving Xormun of his opportunity to catch them at an intermediate stop.

If that happened, then he might actually have to search the Habitat Belt for the right place, though this wasn't as disastrous as it might have seemed. Prinn's information about the Platinum Corsairs meant they'd picked Vessani up from the original criminals who snatched her, so he'd already begun the process of requesting the relevant mission records.

Those records wouldn't give him the habitat itself, but they could narrow his search.

But in the meantime, he possessed six uncommitted corvettes, and he intended to put them to good use. He took another hard look at Kade's list of associates, filtered it for people who had at least some experience working around pentatech, then filtered it again based on how certain Jovian intelligence was about their current locations, creating a list of the top six locations.

He passed the list on for distribution to the *Leviathan*'s corvettes.

One of those locations was an open-ring habitat called Faelyn's Grasp.

CHAPTER TEN

"Okay, I'm dying to know." Nathan set down his Triad Trial cards.

The *Neptune Belle* was on a fourteen-day course for Faelyn's Grasp, and there wasn't much for any of them to do until they arrived. Fortunately, Nathan had amassed a sizable collection of books, movies, and games to serve as distractions for passengers (and himself) over the years, and it turned out Joshua was an avid Triad Trial player.

"Know what?" Joshua asked with a coy smile, sorting and turning his triangular cards. "Whether or not I actually have all odds in my hand?"

"No, not that."

"Ooh!" Vessani cooed, inspecting her newest card. Joshua may have been a formidable opponent, but Vessani was *not*. She seemed unaware her tail wagged and her ears perked up every time she drew a powerful card.

Not that she was hard to read otherwise. He could have done that blindfolded, what with all her vocalizations!

"Look! Look!" She showed Joshua the new card.

"Oh, my." He let a crafty smile slip. "That'll come in handy."

"Heh-heh. I like this game!"

"Hey, Nathan?" Aiko-Six asked, her cameras darting across her cards. "You think she pulled a good card?"

"No idea," he replied dryly.

"You were saying?" Joshua prompted Nathan.

"Just curious how the two of you ended up together. Not to be blunt, but you're . . ." He let the sentence hang unfinished.

"An unlikely pair?" Joshua ventured.

"Something like that."

"We met through work," Vessani said. "Some Saturnian university hired the old crew I was with to cart around a team of students and professors." She put a hand on Joshua's shoulder. "This guy was among them."

"Many of us were performing field research for our theses," Joshua explained. "We spent most of our time along the outskirts of the old Titanica ruins along the western shore of the Obelisk Ocean. I myself was eager to study the remains of their deifactory. Anyway, the university thought it prudent to provide some protection for us."

"I'd *hardly* call that place dangerous," Vessani said.

"We were the first people to go there in hundreds of years."

"But we never left the Saturn shell band!"

"There are a lot of dangerous places, even that close to civilization."

"Got to agree with Joshua on this one," Nathan said. "Neptune is the same way. Venture more than, say, a few thousand kilometers from the nearest major city, and you'd be surprised by the stuff you'll find."

"And the things that'll leap out at you," Aiko added.

"That, too."

"*Nothing* leaped out at us," Vessani said. "I should know, because it was my job to shoot the wildlife if it tried to discover what students taste like. None of the megafauna even came close to our camp, either. The worst encounter was one angry pig, and that was their own fault."

"Oh, yeah." Joshua chuckled. "I remember him."

"The students decided to adopt the pig as a sort of pet," Vessani continued. "They named him Poogle and kept sneaking him treats. The professor eventually put an end to it, and when Poogle stopped receiving freebies, he grew temperamental. Began setting things on fire."

"Excuse me?" Nathan asked with raised eyebrows. "The pig did what?"

"Apparently, the animal wasn't baseline," Joshua explained, "because he had what amounted to a biochemical flamethrower in his gut."

"That was the only bit of excitement on an otherwise long and boring job." Vessani laughed and shook her head. "Quite the sight, really. A bunch of students running around while this little pig belched puffs of flame at them. That job turned out to be the last straw for me. Mind-numbing work with a dull crew. I left soon after."

"And how did that pan out for you?" Joshua teased.

"Hey." She flashed a half smile. "I never said it was a *good* decision to join up with Dirge." She turned back to Nathan. "Anyway, a month of pointless guard duty led to me getting to know the students."

"We hit it off almost immediately," Joshua said. "I'd never met anyone who grew up in low-tech before, and you were most certainly *not* what I'd expected! Though, it surprised me you spent all your free time with me."

"You were the only guy who didn't condescend to me when you found out where I was from. Of course I wouldn't want to hang out with those losers!"

Joshua only smiled.

"And here's the other thing," Vessani told the others. "When Josh asks you a question, he listens to your answer. Like, *really* listens. He would ask me about my home, and when I'd get into the details, I could tell he was hanging on my every word. It'd been years since I'd talked about home with anyone, and it felt good, you know?"

"I think I do," Nathan said, nodding.

"Plus, he never tried to sleep with me. Not once during the whole trip!"

Joshua froze and his cheeks turned a fierce shade of red. He looked down and started resorting his cards.

"Honestly, after a while, I began to wonder if he was even interested." She put an arm around his shoulders. "Glad I was wrong, there!"

"Well, I, umm . . ." Joshua stammered, then cleared his throat. "Perhaps we don't need to share the *whole* story."

"Hmm?" She turned to him. "But I was just going to mention how we—"

"Moving on!" Joshua interrupted quickly.

"Did you two stay in touch after the university work?" Nathan asked, more in the manner of a lifeline to Joshua than anything else.

"No, we went our separate ways," Vessani said. "Didn't see each other again for about half a year."

"Even so, parts of her story really stuck with me," Joshua said, looking somewhat relieved to have moved past whatever minefield Vessani had been blundering toward. "Especially where the Black Egg was concerned. I did some independent research into the subject and eventually got in touch with Anterus, who helped me put the pieces into a workable theory. After that, I reached out to Vess and shared my thoughts."

"That's how we decided to team up!" Vessani added cheerfully.

"Though"—Joshua frowned—"I do wish you'd told me about your plan to steal Dirge's ship."

"Yeah, that wasn't my brightest idea. I should have—"

The *Belle* began to tremble, and alarms sounded. Their Triad cards jittered across the table, and Joshua grabbed the edge, his eyes suddenly wide.

"Not again," Nathan groaned. "Aiko?"

"Number One is in the cockpit. Shouldn't be long before—"

The background din of engine noise faded, and distant circuit breakers clanked, rerouting vital systems to the capacitors. The alarm switched off, and everyone floated out of their seats around a cloud of playing cards.

"There we go!" Aiko exclaimed.

"Umm." Joshua swallowed. "What was that?"

"That was two of our fusion toruses not playing nice together," Nathan replied. "We've had this happen a few times before. It's more of an annoyance than anything else. It doesn't last long."

"I see." Joshua pressed a hand against the ceiling and pushed off. "What do you mean by 'not playing nice together'? Can you be more specific?"

"It's rare," Aiko explained, "but something can cause Torus Three's output to oscillate, which then interferes with Torus Two. We're not sure what's going on, but we've never had an issue restarting the reactor."

"Have you had the reactor inspected?"

"Once," Nathan grumbled. "Waste of money."

"And the results?"

He shook his head. "A big, fat nothing. She said the reactor was fine."

"Hmm." Joshua lowered his head in thought.

"Shall I go ahead and restart Torus One?" Aiko asked.

"Sure," Nathan said. "Start it back up."

"Actually..." Joshua held up a hand. "Would it be all right if we held off on that? At least for a bit?"

"Why?" Nathan asked. "What for?"

"Just curious about something. Mind if I look over the reactor's fault log?"

Joshua sat next to the C Deck reactor torus, strapped in due to the ship's lack of acceleration, with a diagnostic vlass glowing in front of him. The *Neptune Belle*'s reactor took up three levels, with A, B, and C decks each housing their own fusion torus.

The room was dark except for the bluish glow of the screen, underlighting his face. He stared at the text on the screen, scrolled through it almost robotically as he deciphered the hidden meaning. Each fault illuminated a separate piece of the puzzle, whether by its mere existence, its timing in relation to other faults, or through the overall sequence of events.

The pressure door opened, spilling a slash of bright light into the room, and Vessani floated in. She closed the door behind her.

"Hey."

"Hey, Vess."

He smiled over at her, his mind wandering to a part of their story he hadn't told Nathan and Aiko. A part he hadn't even told Vessani yet. Not for any sinister or selfish reasons, but for the mere fact he didn't feel ready to bare his heart in such an intimate manner.

Not quite yet, anyway.

Because this part of the story centered on his parents, who hadn't met Vessani and likely never would.

It had become clear to Joshua from an early age that his parents didn't love each other. He didn't know what had originally brought them together—whether it was youthful passion or something else—but whatever fires had once burned in their hearts had been quenched by the time he grew astute enough to notice such things.

His parents weren't rude to each other. Merely formal. Distant. Cold. They passed through the motions required of them for the simple reason that they were expected to act in a certain manner, all while secretly filling the gaps in their lives with other people from outside their marital union.

Both of them had cheated on the other. *Prolifically*. Almost as if each was searching for an answer to a question they couldn't quite articulate. Each seeking a way to heal the gap in their lives they could never quite fill.

He knew his parents were immensely unhappy. With each other and, he suspected, with themselves. He was certain of this, and he too had been a casualty of their loveless marriage, being both a physical reminder of their unhappiness and an anchor that ensured one could never stray too far from the other, no matter how much they might wish to.

He considered himself lucky to have made it this far without crashing and burning as a human being. He'd fortunately discovered a love of learning at an early age, which was the passion that filled the hole in *his* life. His tutors had recognized and encouraged this trait, and some of them had grown into the surrogate parents he'd so desperately needed.

He thought he'd turned out rather well, given that background and his own parents' disinterest in raising him. Some people might have viewed the Cotton family's wealth as the ultimate way to cheat through life's many obstacles, but he knew the truth. Money could purchase many comforts or brute-force a person through many problems, but never had he seen it make a single soul happy. Not in any meaningful, lasting way, at least.

He may not have considered himself happy, but at least he wasn't a miserable wretch like his father or mother, trapped in a loveless marriage, confined to a gilded cage. He was free to live and learn, and oh, how he loved to learn!

In a strange way, Vessani reminded him of his parents. Not in the wealthy, adulterous socialite way, of course, but by the fact that she was unhappy. Joshua saw a shadow of his parents' misery whenever he gazed into her golden eyes. He perceived a sliver of his own struggles in them, and that had served to pull him toward her, knowingly or not.

He couldn't help but feel a sense of familiarity around her. She was alone, bouncing from one ship to another, never with a final destination in mind, always searching for an answer to a question she didn't even know she was asking. Sometimes acting out her frustrations and angst in drunken antics or wild outbursts.

They both suffered from their own forms of isolation. Different roots, but a similar disease. It's why he believed he'd been able to connect with her in a way no one else could. Their relationship had started so simply. All he'd had to do was listen to her and let her share her story.

And *care* about what she told him.

Which was the easy part, because he did care for her.

Deeply.

"Think you'll be able to solve their little reactor problem?" Vessani asked.

He smiled to her. "That's not quite the right question."

"Why's that?"

"Because"—he tapped the vlass—"there's nothing wrong with the reactor."

"Then what's going on?"

"Unless I've missed my guess, the issue is with the plasma outfeed. There's a balancing error in the manifold that integrates the outputs from all three toruses. This imbalance causes Torus Two and Three to struggle against each other, sometimes resulting in backflow into Torus Three. Normally, that's not much of an issue. The system automatically adjusts the outfeed, compensates, and moves on with its life. But sometimes the system can get stuck in a loop of overcorrection and start oscillating, which is what we experienced earlier. You follow?"

"Not really," she replied honestly.

"One of the plasma pipes has a 'kink' in it," Joshua simplified. "The reactor doesn't like that and starts passing gas."

"And not a fun kind of kink, I take it," Vessani noted with a quick wink.

"No." He struggled to keep a straight face. "Not a fun kink."

"Okay. That makes more sense now. You just figure this out?"

"No, I've known for about an hour, but I've been going through the logs, checking for anything that could cast doubt on my theory. There's no rush, so I thought it best to be thorough."

"Find anything?"

"Nope." He closed out of the fault log, reverting the vlass to a general diagnostic screen. "Which means I should probably inform the others."

He keyed his commect and waited for the captain to respond.

"Yes?"

"I've got good news and, I believe, even better news. The good news is there's nothing wrong with your reactor. The problem's coming from the plasma manifold. When this last happened, did you have the entire drive system inspected?"

"No. Just the reactor."

"Thought so. That explains why they couldn't find the problem."

"Okay, but what's this other news you mentioned?"

"I believe I know how to fix it. I'd like to inspect the manifold next. Tell me, Captain, does your ship have a microfactory?"

"A small one on C Deck. Why?"

"Because we might need to fabricate a replacement part or two. We should know more once we open up the manifold."

"Here goes."

Aiko restarted the reactor and eased up on the thruster output. Beside her, Nathan sank into the pilot seat while Joshua and Vessani touched down on the floor behind them. Aiko stopped the output at 0.2 gravities.

"How's it look?" Nathan asked.

"Nice." Aiko reviewed her readouts. "Normally, it takes the reactor a few seconds to settle into the green, but this time it practically *leaped* into an optimal state."

"The ship sounds different," Nathan said, not exactly complaining.

"Different in a bad way?" Joshua asked.

"No. Just . . . different."

Aiko listened. "I hear it, too. The engine noise is quieter. More monotone."

"The missing noise was probably the backwash from Two to Three," Joshua said. "An interaction like that can cause a low, rhythmic sound as the system pushes through repeating cycles of compensation."

"Fuel efficiency is up," Aiko said. "Not by a whole lot. Maybe two or three percent, but that can add up over a trip. Shall I crank it up to one gee?"

"Go ahead."

Aiko eased the output upward until the ship was accelerating at 9.8 meters per second squared.

Nathan unstrapped himself from the seat and clapped Joshua on the shoulder.

"Thanks for looking it over. That problem was bugging the hell out of me!"

"My pleasure," Joshua said. "Glad I could help."

"Isn't he the best?" Vessani put an arm around Joshua, and her tail flicked happily behind her.

Aiko turned around in her seat. "You know what this means, don't you?"

"What?" Nathan asked.

"We have an excuse to celebrate!" She threw her arms up in triumph. "How about I make a big, fancy dinner as a treat for everyone? What do you say?"

Vessani's eyes lit up, and Joshua grinned.

"Sounds good to me," Nathan said. "Perhaps something to go with that bottle of Plexauran White we have?"

"Yes!" Aiko agreed. "Excellent idea!"

"Why would a Jovian get excited about wine?" Joshua asked.

"You'll understand soon enough." Aiko crossed her arms, somehow looking smug despite her lack of a facial expression. "I consider the combination of Nathan and alcohol to be free entertainment."

Nathan frowned at her.

"All right. Any dinner requests?" Aiko asked of everyone.

"Ooh!" Vessani's hand shot up. "I have one!"

"Shouldn't Joshua pick out dinner?" Nathan asked.

"Oh. Right." Vessani lowered her hand.

"No, no. It's fine." Joshua gave her shoulder a tender squeeze. "You can choose the meal."

"Okay!" Vessani's eyes lit up again. "So, I only had this once. One of my old captains treated the team to a lavish dinner. I don't know what it's called, but it was incredible, and I don't think it'll be too hard to make, either. The way it works is everyone gets a bunch of stuff to dip in this big pot. Different fruits, vegetables, breads, meats, whatever."

"What goes in the pot?" Aiko asked.

"A whole lot of delicious, melted cheese!" Vessani exclaimed.

"Then all you want is a big cheese dip?" Aiko turned to Nathan. "I think I have enough ingredients to pull that off. You in the mood for a mountain of food dipped in hot cheese?"

"I could go for that," he said, grinning.

CHAPTER ELEVEN

"Ladies and gentle engineer, I give you Faelyn's Grasp." Nathan waved a hand across the open-ring habitat rotating before them. "Point five gees on the surface and a pristine atmosphere. Mid-tech divergent populace with an estimated size of about sixty million, plus another twelve thousand in the Union colony. Lots of beachfront property ripe for the taking as long as you don't run afoul of the natives."

"The ring looks ordinary enough." Joshua perused the *Almanac* entry. "Danger rating of three, though."

"Apparently, the locals have a bad habit of taking potshots at visiting ships. Some of the factions down there are advanced enough for guided missiles. Lots of temperamental island nations boasting plenty of air and sea power."

"The landscape reminds me of home," Vessani said, "what with all the water."

"Those oceans are teeming with dangerous megafauna," Nathan warned.

"Even more like home, then," she added with a half smile.

"Should we be concerned?" Joshua asked. "About the locals, I mean."

"Not concerned, just cautious," Nathan said. "We should be fine as long as we stick to the Union colony, which is where we'll find the missionary." He nodded to Aiko-Six, who keyed the ship's commect.

"Union Control, this is the freelancer *Neptune Belle*. Please respond."

"We hear you, *Neptune Belle*. What brings you to Faelyn's Grasp?"

"Requesting permission to land at the city of Faelyn's Clash."

"For what purpose?"

"Business with the Church. We're here to visit the missionary and perhaps hire someone on."

"Any cargo to declare?"

"That's a negative, Union Control. Passengers only."

"Will any of your passengers be staying on Faelyn's Grasp?"

"Negative, Union Control. If our business goes well, we'll be leaving with plus one. Nothing else to declare."

"Understood, *Neptune Belle*. Stand by while we process your landing request."

They didn't have to wait more than a few minutes.

"Union Control to *Neptune Belle*, landing authorization has been granted. Proceed to Pad Three directly."

"Thank you, Union Control. Beginning our descent to Pad Three."

Aiko brought the *Neptune Belle* down onto a wide, circular landing pad with a prominent numeral *3* painted on the surface. The city's port consisted of four pads arranged in a square near a lonely control tower, with bulky Saturnian transports seated on pads One and Two.

Nathan met Aiko-One down in the cargo hold. She already had the ramp down, and a warm, humid breeze wafted in from outside.

"Taking the rover out?" she asked.

"Might as well. It'll be easier than trying to rustle up local transportation."

The two of them headed to the back of the cargo hold to a small, open-topped vehicle. It sat on a shallow platform with depressions for the four wheels and mechanisms that locked onto the hubs. They disengaged each lock, and Aiko climbed into the driver's seat.

"All charged up," she said, then drove across the hold and down the ramp before parking it. "Now remember, don't be pushy with him."

"I won't. Promise."

"You know how he can be. Don't rush him. Just let him come around on his own."

"I'm sure he's cooled down." Nathan gave her a winning smile. "Hell, he might even be thrilled to see us!"

"Or he might still be upset about his brush with death."

"Which was not our fault."

"Try telling *him* that." Aiko paused thoughtfully. "Actually, don't try. In fact, don't mention the past at all, if you can help it."

"We'll be fine. He wasn't *that* angry last we saw him."

Vessani, Joshua, and Aiko-Six came down the freight elevator and joined them by the rover.

"A bit plain," Vessani said, as if judging the vehicle. "Could use some flames on the side. Maybe a skull or two on the hood."

"Come on," Nathan said. "Let's go see if we can find Rufus."

The four of them climbed into the vehicle. Nathan took hold of the wheel and drove them onto a narrow, paved road leading away from the dock. Aiko-One stayed behind with the ship and closed the cargo ramp.

Faelyn's Clash was a small frontier town with a mix of modular Saturnian prefabs and local structures featuring brick-and-mortar or wood construction. The natives—Faelyns? Faelynans? Faelynians? He'd have to consult the *Almanac* if it came up—were fair-skinned, tall, and lean without exception, and wore their blond or silvery hair long. Their ears were pointed at the tips, and their eyes possessed faint bioluminescence. The intensity seemed to be a factor of age, with men and women in their sexual prime possessing the brightest eyes. They were also big into capes, which came in a riot of colors and patterns, often hooded and worn over their comparatively plain tunics.

Nathan turned down a wide, well-maintained central street that cut through the city. It led them toward the outskirts where they'd spotted the missionary building during their descent. He slowed down, matching the flow of traffic from both Saturnian electric vehicles and local, noisy cars. An airship passed by overhead, its main body suspended beneath a large air bladder, a dozen propellers whirring beside and behind the hull.

"Do your people have anything like that?" Nathan asked Vessani, pointing up.

"No. Nothing airborne," she replied, speaking up over the wind and traffic noise. "We still make wooden sailing ships, though we do have some deifacturing."

"Are you able to control it?"

"Not really. The deifactory is where the Black Egg is kept. The place becomes more active and responsive once every seventy-one years, but my people don't understand why or know how to properly use it."

"Hell, that could be said about most of us."

Nathan followed the street past the city center. The buildings and traffic thinned out, and the pavement ended. He took the gravel road around a hilltop, then beyond it to a prefab hamlet built near the edge of an oceanside cliff. The vastness of the ocean curved upward beyond the cliff, dotted with islands and following the arch of the ring. Huge green-and-turquoise birds glided over its shimmering surface, occasionally diving into the water, only to emerge with long, eellike fish clenched in their toothy beaks.

He parked the rover at the end of a row of six vehicles: two Saturnian and four native.

"Wait here."

Nathan climbed out and walked up to the closest entrance, where an elderly cleric in royal purple robes sat in a rocking chair alongside a trio of teenage locals.

"Hello there!" Nathan called out as he approached. "Nice day we're having."

"That it is, sir," the cleric replied. "Can I help you?"

"I hope so. I'm looking for a cleric. His name's Rufus sen Qell. Is he around by any chance?"

"Rufus? Why he's—"

"Over here!" snapped the thirtysomething-year-old man as he barged through a nearby door. "Which is the last place I want to be standing right now!"

"Hey, Rufus." Nathan flashed a quick, apologetic smile. "Long time no see."

"Not long enough!"

Rufus was even taller and thinner than the average indigen, despite a bit of a slouch, with pale skin and sunken cheeks. His long, bony arms ended in long, bony fingers, as if everything about him had been stretched unnaturally.

The metal stud of an implant protruded from his left temple, and two more glinted from behind each ear. On the back of his bald head was a metal plate about the size of his fist, but a curling brown wig hid most of his cranial modifications. Unlike the Church garb of the other cleric, he wore a crisp, black uniform with a white, flaming pentagon stitched over the left breast pocket.

Nathan gave the elderly cleric a quick wave in thanks, then joined Rufus by the door.

"Hey, Rufus. How you been?"

"Great until you showed up! Also, it's *ziin* Qell! Can't you ever get that right? I didn't study at Qell all those years for nothing, you know!"

"Sorry?"

He'd once asked Rufus to explain Saturnian names to him. He understood, as most people did, that the majority of Saturnians favored the use of particles to connect their given name to a location of personal significance, and that the latter two parts of their names could change more than once over a lifetime.

Back then, Rufus had made a noble effort at explaining the intricacies of Saturnian naming conventions, but he'd quickly lost Nathan in an avalanche of esoteric details. The problem wasn't that there were a lot of different particles, which there were, each with its own nuanced meaning. No, the problem was those definitions changed based on which part of the Saturn Union a person was born in!

Nathan had done his best, but all he'd gotten out of it was Rufus trying to jam the equivalent of congealed word salad into his brain, which then proceeded to ooze out of his ears instead of taking root. Ever since, he'd convinced himself that there actually *wasn't* a discernible pattern, that Saturnian names were in fact a grand cultural prank they played on everyone else. But since no one had called them on it, they continued to let it play out.

He wondered if the Union secretly funded a Department of Nonsensical Naming buried within the layers of its gargantuan bureaucracy. Maybe they even had a manager in charge of particle humor. He'd yet to come across evidence of such a broad conspiracy, but a part of him remained convinced it existed.

"Didn't mean anything by it," Nathan added.

"Hi, Rufus!" Aiko-Six waved at them from the rover.

"Aiko says hello, by the way."

"What are you two doing here? Don't you remember what I told you last time?"

"That you'd never do another job with us again. I believe your exact quote was 'Not for all the computronium in the Everlife.'"

"And?" Rufus prompted. "What else?"

"That we were bad luck. You might have also called us incompetent." He pointed at the cleric. "Which hurt my feelings, by the way."

"I almost *died*!"

"So did we."

"Is that supposed to make me feel better?"

"I don't know. Doesn't misery love company?"

"I'd think the better goal would be to avoid misery altogether. Which, for me, means staying away from you two!"

"Come on, we're not that bad and you know it. Besides, you enjoyed your time with us." Nathan shrugged. "Up until you almost died."

"Which was a big part of our time together!"

"I bet you miss it."

"Do not!"

"Do too."

"Do *not*!"

"Whatever you say." Nathan glanced over the missionary grounds. "You like it here? Seems boring to me."

"It's *pleasantly* boring," Rufus replied stiffly, standing a little straighter. "It's a peaceful vocation, and the locals appreciate us."

"You get to use your skills much?"

"Well . . ." Rufus hesitated, some of the fire going out from his eyes.

"Can't see how there'd be much demand for your services out here."

"Not the kind you're thinking of, but I contribute in other ways."

"Proselytizing to indigenous people? I didn't think that was a big priority for the Order."

"I help *educate* them," Rufus corrected sharply. "Science, mathematics, biology, chemistry, physics. All to help smooth out their eventual transition to high-tech."

"You sure you're not bored? I'm falling asleep just listening to you."

"It's *rewarding*."

"Sure, sure. Whatever works for you."

"Look, Nate." Rufus sighed with a hand to his temples. "Why don't you tell me what you're doing out this far? What's this visit really about?"

"We've got a job for you."

"Oh, you are unbelievable!"

"Hear me out. It's a neat one."

"I'm not interested!" Rufus backed through the door and slammed it shut.

Nathan listened for a few moments. He did *not* hear footsteps retreating.

He leaned close to the door and whispered, "There's pentatech involved."

The door creaked open. Rufus peeked through the gap, his face softening with tentative eagerness.

"There is?"

"Possibly a lot of it."

Rufus swallowed audibly. Almost hungrily.

"Which is why we need you," Nathan continued.

"And if I say no?"

"We'll find someone else." He jabbed a finger at Rufus. "But I'd rather have you."

"What makes you think pentatech's involved?"

"We've got a lead on an artifact called the Black Egg. It responds to the presence of an object in an elliptical orbit around Sol."

"Elliptical?" Rufus's eyes widened. "You mean it might be wreckage from the Scourging?"

"We won't know until we find it, but that's the guess. The thing's on a seventy-one-year cycle, so if we don't find it now, it might be that long until someone else can try again."

"I see." Rufus bowed his head and nodded solemnly.

"What do you say? Have I piqued your interest?"

"I . . . I'll think about it."

Rufus knelt in front of the altar, his eyes closed and his mind open.

Long ago, during the Age of Communion, anyone could converse with the Guardian Deities at any time, and many did so through the use of deifactured implants like the ones he had been granted. The

Guardian Deities no longer responded to requests so overtly, but a skilled and disciplined mind—equipped with the right cybernetic tools—could commune with the fragments of the Pentatheon that lingered amongst their technological legacy.

Remnants.

Whispers.

The echoing thoughts of absent gods.

But that was not all his mind might touch while venturing out into the digital immaterial. Dark, dangerous corners existed amongst the benign fragments of god-thoughts. Some places welcomed the presence of human consciousness with open arms, while others shunned the organic, whether because they were broken or corrupted or had never been safe for humanity in the first place.

He opened his mind to one such hostile vision and bore witness to a dark, desolate dream upon an endless plane of rugged stone. Sol hovered on the edge of the horizon, casting long, stark shadows behind every imperfection in the surface. He crossed the stony plain, words beating in his mind like the thumping of a giant heart.

Wound.

Flesh.

Metal.

Fire.

The words flowed through him, disconnected and dissonant, yet potent and imbued with mountainous purpose. He'd experienced this vision many times in the past year. Each time it grew stronger and more vivid, and yet he still failed to grasp its meaning.

What is the underlying message here? he wondered as the vision continued.

A canyon yawned ahead of him, gaping wide from one side of the horizon to the other. He approached it, each tiny, human step slow and yet at the same time drawing him closer to the chasm with unnatural speed until he stood suddenly at the precipice. The full breadth of the abyss opened before him, leering up at him like a giant, grinning mouth rimmed with sharp, broken teeth of stone and steel.

Metal.

Flesh.

Burning.

Scorching.
Scraping.
Screaming!

Rufus shuddered and almost lost the vision. He'd never heard the words so clearly, so forcefully. And yet, comprehension *still* eluded him. What could it possibly mean? The words repeated within his mind, coalescing into the mental equivalent of thunder. They beat into him, bludgeoning his psyche with ethereal force until he lost focus, and the vision faded.

He exhaled and blinked to find his forehead pressed against the edge of the altar, one arm draped across it for support. He knelt there like a statue and retreated into his own thoughts.

That had been the clearest vision yet. Something was causing them to become more potent. Something like . . . the source moving through an elliptical orbit around Sol, perhaps?

He wondered.

Were Nathan and Aiko seeking the source of his visions? Was a Pentatheon artifact hurtling through the solar system even now, calling out for some unknown purpose? Seeding nearby technology with scraps of this broken simulation? Rufus sensed no delay in the vision, so he doubted this was a direct connection.

Was the source trying to summon people and machines to its side? Were the visions evidence that a sliver of the Guardian Deities still lived, still existed in a material way that could be contacted by those skilled and brave enough?

Did he dare?

His earlier anger had almost totally subsided. He was glad Nathan had brought this mystery to his attention. Grateful even. But he'd been burned once before, his mind singed by delving carelessly into the digital juncture of a broken habitat, all while dangerous systems switched on around him. His mistakes had almost killed the *Belle*'s crew, not the other way around.

He knew some of the anger he'd directed at Nathan was unfair and should have been aimed at himself. *He'd* been the one to lose focus, to awaken machinery that should have stayed dormant for the rest of eternity. He didn't remember much after that, having slipped into a coma. Aiko had pulled him out, and he'd awoken on the *Belle* a few days later.

At the time, a part of him feared the experience would dull his talent for connecting to the Pentatheon's legacy, but if anything, he soon learned the experience had *sharpened* his skills even further, honing them through a brutal crucible to emerge stronger on the other side, tempered by hardship.

But despite that, he'd shied away from applying his talents once more, cloaking fear and self-doubt in a veneer of outward anger.

And here, he thought, *is an opportunity to set all that aside. To once more venture into the unknown, to seek answers to the great questions of my Order.*

"Are you all right?"

Rufus turned and looked up to see Abbot Devaraj in the room, staring down at him with a curious expression.

"I'm fine." Rufus rose and dusted off his knees. "Abbot, I hope you'll forgive the suddenness of this, but I may have to leave the mission."

"Why? What brought this on?"

"Some old colleagues of mine have stopped by, asking for my help. I know I have commitments here but—"

"Is this about your visions?"

"I—" Rufus frowned, then nodded. "I can't be certain, but I believe so. How did you know?"

"You have a certain look in your eyes after you've gazed upon that jagged canyon you've mentioned. A certain combination of awe and dread, which I suppose is a fair enough reaction to glimpsing the divine."

Rufus didn't believe there was anything divine in these visions, but he kept this opinion to himself. He didn't fault the members of the Church for their beliefs—he'd once shared them enthusiastically—but the strength of his faith had waned over time. He didn't consider what he was going through a crisis of faith but rather a deep, contemplative questioning.

He understood, intellectually at least, why faith in the Guardian Deities was so common. Their grand creations sustained life throughout the harsh emptiness of the solar system. They'd even *created* life during the Age of Communion. Jovians, divergent humanoids, and so much more owed their very existence to the Pentatheon.

On top of that, echoes of their grand minds still lingered; skillfully crafted requests—prayers to some—could be answered by their technology. Why *wouldn't* people worship such grandiose beings and pray for their return?

The Guardian Deities had looked after humanity for tens of thousands of years, overseeing a golden age of wonder and prosperity. It was natural for people to yearn for its return. The Pentatheon deserved all the respect lavished upon them, even to the point of reverence. But outright worship? That didn't feel right to Rufus, because everything the Pentatheon had wrought could be explained through science, even if humanity had lost much of its understanding in the dark days after the Scourging.

That was why a deeper vocation within the Church hadn't appealed to Rufus, and why he'd eventually found a home within the Lucent Order. Its mission to rediscover and spread lost knowledge and technology stirred something within him, something the ornate trappings of faith and worship had failed to connect with.

"Abbot," Rufus said, "if you feel I should stay, then say no more. I'll tell them to leave without me, and that'll be the end of it."

"Come now." Devaraj smiled. "What sort of talk is that? Now you're just looking for an excuse."

"Abbot?"

"Here, let me be open with you." He sat down in the front pew with a labored sigh and patted the spot next to him.

Rufus joined the abbot and waited for him to continue.

"Let me be blunt. You're wasting your time with us on this ring."

"No, I'm not," Rufus defended reflexively. "This is important work we do here."

"Yes, yes. Very important work." The abbot shook his head. "Maybe one day we'll convince the Faelyns to stop blowing each other up. But that's beside the point. There are many who can do this, as long as they have the heart and the patience." He paused, hands resting on his thighs, then let out a long exhale. "Can I make a confession?"

"A formal one?"

"No, no." He dismissed the notion with a wave. "No need for a confessional. Just something I wish to share. Strictly for your ears only. I've been . . . a bit jealous of you."

Jacob Holo

"Jealous?"

"I trained my mind for decades"—Devaraj tapped the implant in his temple—"and yet I don't possess a tenth your sensitivity. I've tried many times to perceive even a glimmer of these visions of yours, but . . . nothing. Not once. Not so much as the shadow of a sensation.

"Which has led me to grapple with feelings of jealousy, but that's my battle to fight, not yours. In short, you're too talented to be stuck on this ring with the rest of us. If you really do believe this business is related to your visions, then you have a duty to yourself to seize it and not look back."

"Abbot, I don't know what to say."

"Say, 'Thank you! I think that's wonderful advice! Excuse me while I go pack!'" Devaraj gave him a jovial smile. "I'm not trying to shove you out the door, by the way."

"I know." Rufus returned the smile. "And thank you. I think I needed someone to help me put all of this into perspective."

CHAPTER TWELVE

"It's good to have you back," Nathan placed a hand on Rufus's shoulder as they strode down the length of the *Neptune Belle*'s cargo hold.

Rufus only grunted in reply, pulling his rolling luggage behind him. Both Nathan and Aiko had offered to take it from him, but he'd refused both times. It wasn't that heavy anyway in the ring's half gravity, and consisted mostly of clothes, a few wigs, a small supply of panacea, and his Pentatheon bible, liturgy book, and prayer book.

"I said—"

"I heard you," Rufus interrupted.

"It's true," Nathan continued smoothly. "The ship hasn't been the same since you left."

"No doubt."

They stepped onto the freight elevator, and Nathan selected B Deck. The elevator shuddered into motion.

"You sure you don't want to be paid for this?" the captain asked him.

"I'm sure."

"I'd feel better if we paid you."

"I don't require compensation," Rufus said, his tone growing somewhat weary. He'd had this discussion with Nathan before, many years ago. "A clean place to sleep and good food to eat will be payment enough while I'm in your company."

"If you say so," Nathan replied with a shrug. "And you do like Aiko's cooking."

"I . . ." Rufus permitted himself a slim smile. "That I do."

"She's thrilled to have you back, by the way. She even went grocery shopping in Faelyn's Clash. I think she's picking up ingredients for a few of your favorites."

"That does sound like her."

"That said, I'm not big on the idea of paying people in hamburgers."

"If your conscience feels so tarnished by this arrangement, then perhaps you should consider making a donation to the Order."

"Maybe I will," Nathan replied, sticking his hands in his pockets. "Though, you do realize if I paid you, *you* could make a donation whenever you want?"

Rufus let out a tired exhalation.

The freight elevator came to a halt on B Deck, and they headed down the hall.

"I mean," Nathan continued, "it's not like I'm going to turn down cheap crew. Especially when they have skills like yours. Aiko and I can use every spare c'troni we can scrounge up, after all."

"Nathan, let's be clear on one thing: I'm not, nor have I ever been, a member of your crew."

"Oh, sure, sure." The captain waved the matter aside, stopping in front of a pressure door. "Do you still want your old room back?"

"I—" Rufus paused and frowned. His eyes caught the gleam of a silver plaque on the door. It read: RUFUS SEN QELL.

"I'll get that fixed." Nathan tapped the plaque with a knuckle. "Rufus *ziin* Qell. Two I's in the middle, right? Aiko will fab a new one for you."

"You put my old name tag back on the door?"

"Didn't have to. It's been like that since the day you left."

"Then my room is . . . ?"

"Just the way you left it. We've never carried enough passengers for us to overflow into the old crew quarters."

"Completely untouched?"

"Well, Aiko's done some cleaning, but that's it." Nathan bobbed his head to the door. "So, you want this room or one of the others?"

Rufus frowned and stared at the plaque, which stood as an affront to his assertion he'd never been a member of the crew. Of course, he'd never *officially* joined Nathan's team, but he'd also been onboard long enough for Aiko to put the plaque on the door.

"My old room will do just fine," he said at last.

"Great!" Nathan removed a key fob from his pocket and handed it over. "Make yourself at home. We'll take off once Aiko's back from her shopping run."

Rufus nodded, though Nathan was already heading back to the elevator. He pressed the fob against the reader. The door slid aside, and he stepped in and took a deep breath.

The place smelled faintly of lemon.

He rolled his luggage up to the side of the bed and stared at the small five-sided icon of the Pentatheon hanging on the wall. He pressed a splayed hand over his heart and bowed to the icon, then unzipped the top of his luggage, removed his prayer book, and flipped it to one of the bookmarks.

He cleared his throat and began to read one of the prayers, softly yet firmly.

Someone knocked just as he finished, and he clapped the book shut.

"Hey there," came a soft, feminine voice.

Rufus turned to find a nekoan leaning against the doorjamb, her golden eyes glinting, ears pert and attentive, arms crossed over her chest.

"What was that?" she asked.

"A request for a safe journey."

"For yourself?"

"For all of us," he corrected gently.

"And the Pentatheon can hear you?"

"In a manner of speaking." He tapped one of the metal tabs behind his ears. "Through these, I can speak to them. Not directly, of course. No one's been able to do that for four thousand years, but many contact points remain—we call them junctures—and through those, I can commune with them."

"Which involves prayer?"

"For me, the words are more a focusing tool than actual worship. I suppose back in the Age of Communion, anyone could do this, but nowadays it takes a great deal of mental discipline for even the most sedate junctures to hear our wishes. Through meditation, I'm able to focus my mind, making it more receptive to the lingering thoughts of the Pentatheon."

"Neat." She flashed a toothy smile and gave him a brief wave. "I'm Vess, by the way."

"Short for Vessani?" Rufus asked. "You were born on the cylinder we're heading for next?"

"Yep, that's me. In a way, this whole trip is my fault."

"I believe Nathan worded that last part a bit differently." He dipped his head toward her. "A pleasure to meet you, Vess."

"Likewise." She tilted her head, and her tail swished behind her. "So, you've trained your brain to connect with old technology?"

"More or less. Why do you ask?"

"I grew up in low-tech, so I've been playing catchup ever since. I only made it this far because I'm a damned good pilot and an excellent shot. I pick up what I can where I can."

"Don't we all?" Rufus let out a sigh. "I wish we understood the Pentatheon better. The megastructures we live on, the divergences in your body, the implants in mine. None of these would be possible without them, and yet we know so little about how all of this came to be. Or why humanity now finds itself so alone."

"At least we have ourselves for company."

"I suppose that much is true."

"Oh!" Her eyes lit up. "You know who you should talk to?"

"Who?"

"Joshua! He *loves* discussing all that science stuff. Give it a try. I bet you'll find you two have a *ton* in common!"

"Thank you. I just might."

It was grill night on the *Neptune Belle*, and Rufus breathed in the savory aroma. A row of juicy patties sizzled on the grill, and Aiko-Six flipped them over before adding a slice of cheese on top of each. Once the cheese oozed over the patties, Aiko-Six placed them on buns.

Aiko-One finished assembling the burgers, layering slices of lettuce, tomato, onion, and pickle before adding a swirl of her homemade sauce to the top bun.

"They smell great, Aiko," Rufus said with the happy grin of a man whose stomach was primed to become even happier. "My mouth's watering."

"Thanks!" Aiko-Six replied. "I try my best."

"For which I'm grateful."

"Aww. You say the nicest things!"

Aiko-One served each burger with sides of fried rice and green beans. She placed a platter in front of each of the four hungry mouths, then returned to the kitchen counter to assist Aiko-Six with the inevitable second round.

Vessani grabbed her plump burger with both hands and brought it up to her mouth, but then paused when Joshua cleared his throat. She gave him a quick sideways glance, her mouth agape.

"I believe Rufus would like to say something before we begin," he told her quietly.

Her eyes scanned across the room, landing on the three other plates, each untouched. Her ears twitched, then drooped. She set her burger down, wiped her hands off on the napkin, and waited.

Rufus spread a hand over his chest and bowed his head.

"Divergence, we thank you for this bountiful meal and the nourishment it will provide. Amen."

Nathan didn't bow his head during the short prayer, but Joshua did.

"That takes me back," the young engineer said over the rustle of utensils. "Reminds me of my time at the university."

"You earned your degree on Saturn?" Rufus asked.

"That's right. Well, one of them. Megastructure engineering from Kronya Founding College."

"Ah, Kronya! Lovely school, *and* a lovely city. I was there myself for a semester before I moved to Qell. How was your stay?"

"In a word, illuminating," Joshua said. "I quickly learned how behind Neptune is at understanding the Pentatheon."

"Isn't that the truth," Nathan grumbled with a head shake.

"The professors at Kronya made some of my Neptunian teachers look like simpletons by comparison. I had a lot of catching up to do during my first semester, though . . ." Joshua hesitated, then smiled, almost apologetically. "I could have done without them draping all the science in mysticism."

He paused to gauge Rufus's reaction. When the cleric showed no signs of offense, he continued.

"It's the way many of the professors mingled faith with fact. It made penetrating down to the core scientific truths difficult at times.

I knew going in that Kronya Founding was a religious college. But it's *also* one of the few Saturnian colleges open to foreigners."

"This may surprise you," Rufus replied, "but I've had similar thoughts myself. I may have been trained at Qell, but I soon found my own thoughts at odds with Church dogma."

Joshua's brow creased. "But aren't you a Church cleric?"

"Cleric, yes. Church, no." He brushed the flaming pentagon on his breast. "I'm with the Lucent Order. You've perhaps heard of us?"

"I'm afraid not."

"You can think of us as seekers of forgotten knowledge."

"Why black?" Vessani asked all of a sudden.

Rufus leaned back in mild surprise. "Excuse me?"

"Your clothes. You look like a member of Dirge's crew."

"I . . . what?"

"You call yourselves the Lucent Order, right? Why not wear something less gloomy?"

"Oh, that." Rufus wore a wan smile. "We wear black to represent our unenlightened state. We live in darkness, *seeking* lost knowledge. We haven't found it yet."

"How long have you been looking?"

"About six hundred years. The Order started as a monastic offshoot from the Church, though much has changed since then. These days, about half our members hail from outside the Pentatheon faith."

"Doesn't that place you at odds with the Church?" Joshua asked.

"Not at all, as long as we stay true to our mission. From the viewpoint of the faithful, the Pentatheon grant their blessings through technology. From that perspective, faith and science are intricately intertwined, as your time at Kronya University demonstrated. We in the Lucent Order merely seek to illuminate *how* those blessings are given form."

"And yourself? Do you share that belief?"

"I . . ." Rufus hesitated, and his lower lip trembled. "I find myself with more questions than answers these days. More than that, I'd rather not say."

He cleared his throat and glanced down at his meal. Next to Joshua, Vessani swished her tail nervously. Her eyes flicked from one man to the other.

"You okay there, Rufus?" Aiko-Six asked from behind the counter.
"I'm fine."

"You look like something's weighing on your mind. I've been getting this vibe from you."

"I . . ." Rufus sighed, then gave Aiko a sad smile. "Am I really that easy to read?"

"So, something *is* bothering you?"

"From before we arrived?" Nathan asked.

Rufus nodded. "I've been getting these visions recently, and they've been progressively growing clearer."

"What sort of visions?"

"I haven't been able to make sense of them. They're just disjointed words and images. When I have one, I can feel . . . something akin to hunger. Or pain. A deep, *old* sense of loss and emptiness." He shook his head. "There really isn't much more to say."

"Do you think it's related to the pentatech artifact we're after?" Joshua asked. "The fact that your visions are growing clearer suggests at least the possibility."

"Maybe. I don't know." Rufus drew in a deep breath, then let it out slowly. "I suppose we'll all find out eventually." He turned to Nathan. "I'll let you know if I learn anything from them."

"I know you will," Nathan replied, then turned to the others. "And I say that from experience. His talents have been lifesavers more than once. That's one of the reasons he was my first pick for this job."

"That, and I work for hamburgers?" Rufus asked, a sudden twinkle in his eyes.

"Hey, now. It's not my fault the Order requires you to make a vow of poverty."

"Technically, it's a vow to pursue understanding above all else. We view the accumulation of wealth as a distraction from that mission."

"Getting back to your visions," Joshua said, "do you think they're linked to the Scourging of Heaven? You emphasized the old sense of loss."

"It's impossible to say. Many junctures exude an aura of timelessness, but this one is different. More ancient than any other I've felt. And vast."

The table fell silent after that, quiet except for the sounds of clinking utensils, the chewing of food, and the sizzle of the next round of burgers. Vessani plucked a coffee bulb from Beany and filled her thermos with it.

"Rufus?" Joshua asked after the long silence.

"Yes?"

"What do you believe happened during the Scourging?"

"Well, the Church has never formally recognized one version of events over the other, and likely never will in our lifetimes. Partially, that's due to how vague the Scourging verses in Genesis are, which has led to endless debates about what to do with various apocryphal texts. Likewise, the Order has never been able to prove—or, for that matter, *disprove*—any of the major theories. In short, I don't think anyone knows what really happened. Though, I do believe the answers are out there." He made a sweeping gesture to the side. "Somewhere."

"But what do *you* believe?" Joshua sounded genuinely curious.

"I believe they left because they had to, that their departure was necessary for humanity's survival."

"Then you believe the Devil of Proxima is real?"

"I'm a little less firm on that point, though it's possible the Devil exists in some form. Certainly, all the changes to the solar system during the Age of Communion could have been noticed by intelligences elsewhere in the galaxy. We're talking about an age that stretched across fifty thousand years, ranging from the creation of the Pentatheon all the way to the Scourging of Heaven roughly four thousand years ago. Fifty thousand years is a long time. Something...malevolent could have been drawn to us. Something that required the full might of the Pentatheon to fight off. Something that left horrible scars all across our star system. Something they might conceivably *still* be fighting. If so, then the reason they haven't returned is because the Scourging of Heaven has yet to end."

"Interesting." Joshua nodded thoughtfully, then glanced back toward the kitchen with a mischievous grin. "That's leagues apart from the Jovian version of events."

"Don't look at me," Aiko warned, pointing a spatula at him. "I'm not stepping into *that* quagmire! You two are free to debate whether Divergence is the Great Betrayer until the end of time, but leave me out of it! Otherwise, *all* of you can kiss your second round of burgers goodbye!"

"Oh no!" Vessani gasped, sounding worried. She'd already demolished her first cheeseburger and most of her sides.

"Best talk about something else." Nathan swept a gaze across the whole table. "Nobody gets between me and Aiko's cooking."

CHAPTER THIRTEEN

The *Neptune Belle* slid across the three-hundred-kilometer length of the habitat, threading a path between a pair of diagonally oriented mirrors that reflected Sol's light through one of three giant windows. The mirrors brightened slowly, dynamically increasing their reflectivity for the habitat's dawn.

Nathan nudged the joystick to the side, adding a burst of thrust to maneuver them over one of the windows. He put the ship into a slow spin until the window filled their view on the right, then steadied the ship.

The sun-windows divided the interior into three habitable strips, while wide canals joined each section along the rims at the cylinder's poles. Vegetation in this biome was a welcoming green that blanketed most of the many islands, each surrounded by calm, clear waters. The pyramid of a deifactory rose from the center of a particularly large landmass, and the lights of civilization twinkled around its base. Nathan spotted a second deifactory in a similar position on the second habitable zone, which led him to assume the third zone also featured one. The second factory didn't appear to be in good shape, though, with one side sunken in. The lights on that landmass were noticeably more dispersed as well.

"Home sweet home?" Nathan asked, craning his neck back over the pilot seat. Aiko-Six sat at the copilot station, and the other three had floated into the cockpit for their first real look at the megastructure.

"Guess so," Vessani breathed, sounding like she didn't know what she was feeling—or what she *should* feel—at a time like this. "It looks more alien than I expected, if that makes any sense."

"Of course it does." Joshua put a reassuring arm around her and gave her shoulders a gentle squeeze. "You've never seen your home from this angle before."

"Yeah."

"Anything tickling your senses?" Nathan asked Rufus.

"Still nothing," the cleric reported. "The habitat is slumbering. No active junctures of any kind, and no indication it considers us a threat."

Nathan nodded. It's what he'd expected to find, but it was still good to hear it confirmed. Some habitats could be—for lack of a better word—"touchy" when it came to objects passing near them. Not many of them, thankfully, but enough to make approaching an uncharted habitat risky in and of itself. The exterior of this habitat might have *looked* like an unbroken swath of solar skin, but he didn't doubt for a moment the megastructure could defend itself if roused.

No one knew why some habitats aggressively protected the space around them while most didn't. His personal theory was that some form of trigger event lay in the past of each "agitated" habitat: perhaps an errant chunk of ice or rock on a collision course or an unfortunate spaceship accident that placed the megastructure at risk. Or maybe a crew of pirates trying to blow a hole in the ultradiamond windows for whatever brain-dead reason.

Any of those could elicit a response from most habitats, and while some might "calm" over time, others would remain in a heightened state of alert, perhaps waiting for orders from the absent Pentatheon to stand down.

"What about the Black Egg?" Nathan asked.

"Nothing," Rufus said. "Its juncture must have a short range."

"Worth an ask. If you were able to do your thing from here, we could skip going inside."

"But we're this close!" Vessani said. "Would you really not stop inside?"

"The job comes first. It's what you two hired us for, remember?"

"But you'd miss out on sampling the local cuisine. The fish is *particularly* good."

"You like fish?"

"No." She shook her head with a toothy grin. "I absolutely *love* fish!"

"You don't say." Nathan found his eyes drawn to her cat tail, swishing so happily behind her that she thwacked Joshua rhythmically in the hip.

"Fishing is a major industry in T'Ohai," she continued. "That's the capital city where I grew up. It's nestled between the coast and a deifactory."

"Which is where we'll head once we're inside." Nathan glanced back through the habitat window. They were fast approaching the sunward pole. "Shouldn't be too difficult to find, what with only two or three deifactories to check out. What's the local language like?"

"The crafted tongue is spoken in most places," Vessani said, referring to the language the Pentatheon had designed for humanity. All three of the gas-giant societies spoke the crafted tongue as their primary language, and most habitats Nathan had visited also used the language.

Most, but not all.

The crafted tongue could be found throughout the solar system—all vlass menus and deifactory interfaces used the language—and its ubiquitous presence in old technology, ruins, and records had provided a strong stabilizing counter to linguistic drift during the Age of Silence as humans left the cradles of the gas-giant shell bands and sought to rediscover and reclaim the solar system.

But some corners of the solar system lacked those stabilizing elements, and Nathan had been forced to hire a professional linguist on more than one occasion.

"There's a local language, too," Vessani said. "I'm a little out of practice, but I'm sure I can manage if it comes up. I wouldn't worry about it, though. Most people stick to the crafted tongue in and around the capital."

"All standard port authority channels are dead," Aiko reported. "There's no sign this place has been claimed by one of the Big Three."

"Then it seems it's up to us to let ourselves in."

The *Belle* flew past the end of the cylinder, revealing the circular side facing Sol. Nathan eased down on the controls to place them into a slow descent along the rotating front of the colony, destined for the axial airlock door.

Aiko worked the ship's commect, then nodded.

"I've got a connection to the airlock."

One of the vlasses on her console turned black.

"Umm?"

"What's wrong?" Nathan asked.

"I'm not sure. Have you ever seen this before?" She tilted the vlass toward him. A white cursor blinked on a black screen above a numerical keypad.

"It's asking us for a number?" Nathan frowned at the screen. "What the hell for?"

"I have no idea."

He twisted back in his seat. "You two know anything about this?"

"You're asking the wrong girl," Vessani replied, and Joshua shook his head.

"Rufus?"

"Don't look at me." The cleric held up two open hands.

"Right, then. Hmm." Nathan turned back around and typed in 1-2-3-4 followed by the COMMIT key.

The screen flashed ACCESS DENIED in red text and *bleep*ed at him before it reverted to the numerical keypad.

He tried 9-0-0-3 next, with the same results.

"Vess?" Nathan released one of his shoulder straps so he could turn around more comfortably. "Did the people who grabbed you mention anything about a coded lock on your home?"

"Not that I remember. Then again, I wasn't really in a position to ask questions."

"They got in somehow," Aiko said.

"Yeah, but the Jovians blew them up," Nathan said, "so I'm not sure how them knowing the code helps us."

Nathan hit the 9 key over and over again just to see how large a number could be entered. The string of nines eventually looped around the screen, and he concluded the input was open ended. He hit COMMIT after he grew bored of tapping the 9 key, and the vlass buzzed at him once more.

"Well"—he threw up his arms—"I'm out of ideas!"

The cockpit fell silent for a minute, punctuated by thoughtful murmurs or frustrated grunts as both Rufus and Vessani tried entering numbers. Their efforts appeared random to Nathan.

After a long silence, Joshua cleared his throat. The others faced him.

"I believe I may have a solution," he said in a cautious tone.

"Go for it." Nathan spread his open palms at the vlass. "Be my guest."

"It's not the code itself, but rather a way to find the right number. Let me check something first." He floated over the console, tapped in a number, hit COMMIT, then began tapping in a new number while the screen flashed its error message, hit COMMIT again, and repeated the process a few times. "Good. The interface still accepts inputs even though it's displaying a message. That'll save us *a lot* of time."

"Time doing what?" Nathan asked.

"Searching for the code."

"And how will you do that?"

"Through brute force."

"I hate to break it to you, but a ship like ours couldn't bust through that door if we tried."

"No, not *physical* brute force," Joshua corrected. "Computational power. But I'll need some resources first."

"Name them."

"I know this is going to sound odd, but I need some of your money."

Nathan gave him a long, doubtful stare, unsure if the man was serious.

"The hell you say," he replied after his glare failed to affect the engineer.

"Plus, a small, waterproof container," Joshua continued.

Vessani smiled brightly. She unsnapped the thermos from her belt and held it up.

"Yes." Joshua beamed at her. "That'll do nicely."

It took a while for Nathan to come around to Joshua's plan, but he didn't have any better ideas, so what else was he supposed to do? Joshua asked for a little gravity to help him work, so Aiko searched for a flattened protrusion for the *Belle* to land on and picked a radiator vane situated about eleven kilometers from the dock. The vane was half a kilometer long and took the *Belle*'s weight without a problem. The landing placed them less than a third of the way to the outer circumference and gave the crew 0.3 gravities to work with.

Nathan joined the others by the workbench next to the microfactory on C Deck, a small bank box in hand.

Joshua had spread a tarp over the workbench to help organize his little project. He'd retrieved a small device from his vest pocket, which resembled a pocket watch composed of smoked glass, and set it next to a cable, a hand drill, and what looked like a turkey baster from the kitchen. Vessani chugged the coffee from her thermos, rinsed it out and wiped down the interior, then handed it over.

"Is this enough for you?" Nathan thumped the case of c'troni cylinders onto the workbench.

Joshua looked up from the drill in his hands. "Is that really all you can spare?"

Nathan glowered at him.

"Just kidding. That should be more than sufficient." He slid the case over and pulled out a fat money cylinder.

"Explain to me again what you're trying to do?"

"I intend to construct a makeshift computational engine." Joshua fitted a small, circular saw onto the end of the drill and pulsed the trigger. The sawblade *whirred* to his satisfaction. "I'll then program the engine to figure out the code."

"Using my money?"

"Using the computronium stored inside it. I take it you're aware of that?"

"Of course. That's why it works as a universal form of currency. It has intrinsic value."

"Exactly."

"But the computronium isn't inactive," Nathan said. "It'd take a bank to switch it on."

"*Mostly* true." Joshua flashed a half smile. "In my years of study, I've picked up a few tricks along those lines. Computronium is a *fascinating* topic, by the way."

"Mmhmm," Nathan murmured, not sure if he wanted to stick around for this or leave the man to his work.

Joshua braced the first cylinder in a vise and sawed the top off with the hand drill. He then used the turkey baster to extract the milky blue liquid inside the cylinder and transfer those contents to Vessani's repurposed thermos.

"At the most basic level," Joshua began, "this bluish liquid—the variant we creatively call 'blue computronium'—is nothing more than a standardized and highly scalable network of machines, each about the size of a human cell. The more machines present, the greater the processing potential of the network. And I say 'potential' for a reason. There are whole Saturnian universities dedicated to unlocking computronium's full suite of abilities."

"But aren't we already doing that?" Nathan asked. "I mean, plenty of deifactured devices have some of that goop in them. Stuff like vlasses and about half the *Belle*'s systems."

"And your partner's heads," Joshua said. "Jovian minds use black computronium, you see. About a thimbleful in each head." He tapped the money box. "Just that small amount could outpace all the blue computronium in these cylinders."

"You're not sawing open Aiko's head."

"Of course not, and I'm not suggesting it. Just making conversation. Besides, I don't have much experience with black computronium, which shouldn't be surprising, given how rare and expensive it is. I picked up how to code persona transfers, but that's about it."

"Did you really have to use my money for this?" Nathan asked. "Couldn't you have used a spare vlass or something?"

"It's easier if I start with an inactive base, which the money cylinders provide. The interface language for computronium is extremely complex, you see. We're only just beginning to understand even its most basic command functions, a problem made worse because networks with preloaded programs add their own layers of complexity and specialization. We can use deifactories to load software written by the Pentatheon, but our ability to craft our own is severely limited. In fact, the one I'm about to write is almost comically simple. Just a basic counting routine with a few outputs."

Joshua connected the cable to his glass pocket-watch-looking gizmo and plopped the other end into the thermos before taping it shut to prevent accidental spillage. A small vlass on his pocket device lit up with lines of incomprehensible text, and the rest of the device unfolded to reveal rows of keys. Nathan recognized less than half the symbols.

"Can you read all that?" he asked.

"Some of it, but not all," Joshua admitted. "Maybe one day we'll have a complete translation of the Pentatheon's programming language, but for now all we can do is muddle our way through the best we can."

He began typing out lines of code.

Joshua brought his bottled "computational engine" up to the cockpit after he finished writing the program. He cabled the thermos to the ship's commect and observed with a satisfied grin as a digital *1* appeared and the error message flashed. A new number starting with twenty thousand blipped on the screen, almost too fast for Nathan's eyes to catch, and the message reappeared.

"It's spitting out random numbers?" he asked, turning down the commect's volume. Those bleeps could be *annoying*!

"No, the program counts up sequentially. It's trying every number starting with one, inputting them far faster than any of us could manage. I determined earlier that the error message doesn't stop the next number from being entered, and it seems my other assumption was correct."

"Which was?"

"There don't seem to be any limits on how many times we can send the wrong value. Or penalties of any kind, such as a delay for when the next value can be entered. Really, quite amateurish when you think about it."

"Lucky us."

The value flashed again, now over three hundred thousand.

"How big is this number?" Nathan wondered aloud.

"We'll just have to wait and see."

Joshua left the cockpit after his program hit a million, leaving Nathan alone. He sat down in the pilot seat and watched the numbers blip upward, wondering who might have locked down the habitat and why.

And *how*, for that matter. The docks on sealed habitats either worked or they didn't. He'd never come across one that had been locked, not even by Saturnians or Jovians. Though, now that he considered it, he supposed it wasn't unreasonable that any group capable of restarting a deifactory could also adjust how a habitat dock worked.

Does that mean the Union or the Everlife have been here already? he wondered. *If so, what brought them here?*

He leaned back and closed his eyes, and his mind fell upon an obvious—and potentially *ominous*—conclusion.

Did someone come here for the Black Egg? he thought. *Are we already too late?*

There were other possibilities, of course. The code lock could have been much, *much* older. Perhaps it dated back as far as the Age of Communion.

Maybe this is nothing more than a quirk of the habitat, he told himself. *Maybe the habitat's ancients wanted their neighbors to "stay off the lawn" unless invited.*

He leaned the seat back and settled into its padding as his mind wandered. He pictured himself falling through a sea of long, flickering digits and flashing error messages, and he eventually dozed off.

His father scolded him in his dreams, and he watched in increasing horror as the man's body oozed away like soft wax, becoming more deformed with each heated reprimand.

Nathan woke with a start, blinked his eyes into focus, and wiped away a line of drool trailing down from the edge of his mouth. He sat up, rubbed his eyes, and checked the clock to discover four hours had passed. He smacked his lips and glanced over to the ship's commect.

Green text that read ACCESS GRANTED pulsed over the number 510,064,472.

"Oh, wow." His eyes widened in surprise. "It actually worked." He cleared his throat and switched on the ship-wide channel. "Would everyone please come to the cockpit? Looks like Josh found our way inside."

It took a few minutes for the others to finish filing in.

"Well, would you look at that?" A broad grin crept onto Joshua's face. "Now that's a surprise. We should have spent more time trying to guess the number."

"Why do you say that?" Nathan asked.

"Because that's a holy number," Rufus cut in, causing Joshua to pause with his mouth open.

"Well, *yes*," Joshua said. "But it's also the number of square kilometers in a unit of earth."

"Which is why the Church considers it a holy number."

"How holy are we talking here?" Nathan asked, only tangentially curious.

"Certainly, it's not as holy as five." Rufus straightened out of his slouch. "Or even less important numbers such as twenty-four or three hundred sixty-five, but it's still a number with ties back to the Pentatheon. It represents one of the ways they ordered the lives of the ancients, providing a mathematical foundation for how they went about their days and perceived reality."

"Have you heard that an earth might have once been more a unit of measure?" Joshua asked the cleric, his face lighting up. "That the value might actually have come from the surface area for one of the solar system's original planetary bodies? Perhaps one consumed for raw materials?"

"Yes, actually." Rufus provided a slim smile back. "There are some passages in the bible that hint at its existence."

"Look, this is all super fascinating," Nathan said, "but how about we get this ship underway already? Aiko?"

"You've got it, boss!" She climbed into the copilot seat. "Strap yourselves in, everyone. It's time to visit Vessani's home!"

The copy of Galatt Xormun, serving as apex for the Everlife corvette, didn't know what to make of the *Neptune Belle*'s actions. Why had the ship spent *hours* sitting on a random radiator vane? The corvette's telescope had failed to pick out any extravehicular activity, and the minimal commect output they'd detected made no sense to his analysts. They'd deciphered the signal, revealing it to be nothing more than a basic countdown.

Or count-*up*, in this case.

And when the counting stopped, the *Belle* lifted off and entered the habitat.

<Shall we pursue them, Apex?> asked the pilot.

<No,> Xormun replied, floating over to the telescope vlass. Without the zoom, the habitat was a distant, glinting shape that

resembled a giant grappling hook. <Hold at this distance and maintain stealth running. We'll keep an eye on them through the habitat windows.>

<Yes, sir.>

The corvette had been waiting for the *Belle* when it arrived at Faelyn's Grasp and had tailed the transport to WC-9003, an unremarkable megastructure in an unremarkable part of the Habitat Belt. The corvette could have overrun and overpowered the *Belle* at any time, but such aggressive action brought risks. What if the nekoan had died during the boarding action? What if they inadvertently damaged or destroyed a key piece of evidence?

And now we know this random habitat is part of the mystery, Xormun thought. His patience had paid off, as it often did, but was there more to learn by holding back and letting events play out? The *Leviathan of Io* and most of its corvettes had been scattered across the Habitat Belt, now converging on WC-9003 at maximum thrust.

Time was on his side, and so he decided to wait and watch a little longer.

Why not let these organics do the hard work for us? he concluded. *Nathan Kade's little crew might find the prize first, but* keeping *it is another matter entirely!*

CHAPTER FOURTEEN

Aiko guided the *Neptune Belle* out of the airlock and into the habitat's interior. She eased up on the throttle, and the *Belle* flew down the central axis of the megastructure. Alternating sections of island-dotted seas and ultradiamond windows stretched out ahead of them, converging against the cylinder's opposite pole.

"There." Vessani pointed over Aiko's shoulder at one of the deifactories.

"I see it." Aiko spun the ship, orienting that section of the cylinder beneath them, and began their gradual descent. The maneuver locked them in with the habitat's rotation, and the steadily increasing gravity brought their floating passengers down to the cockpit's floor.

Nathan took control of the *Belle's* telescope and zoomed in on a city that sprawled out around the base of the deifactory. Most structures were built from wood with a few—such as the city wall and what might have been a palace—constructed using stone. He didn't spot any native structures over five stories tall, though the lack of doors, windows, or other means to shut out the elements caught his eye.

"Much in the way of inclement weather here?" Nathan asked.

"Not really," Vessani replied. "Nothing more severe than a good downpour with the occasional thunderstorm. It can get windy, though. Temperature is pleasantly warm all year round. I'd never seen snow before the Jovians left me on Saturn."

Nathan nodded, guiding the telescoping view across the city. Narrow streets twined their way through dense clusters of buildings laid out without any pattern or hint of central planning, growing organically outward to encircle three quarters of the deifactory's base and to butt up against the sea. Some of the taller buildings resembled pagodas. People crowded through those streets, either on foot or seated in carts pulled by sleek-furred beasts of burden. Dozens of wooden ships—some large enough to feature multiple levels—anchored along the port, their many sails retracted.

He reduced the zoom and followed the outskirts of the city, which had spilled beyond the stout stone walls into wide patches of lush farmland. He shifted the view outward until he came across a wide field of smooth stone blocks with huge stone letters set into ground before it. The letters spelled out WELCOME in the crafted tongue, and the field had been painted with precise, concentric circles of blue.

"Aiko, you see this?" Nathan tapped the image on the vlass.

"I do."

"Looks like a landing pad to me."

"Sure does. Want me to set us down there?"

"Hold on." Nathan turned to find Vessani wearing a face composed of equal parts confusion and worry. "You know anything about this?"

"Umm." She began to chew her bottom lip.

"Because, if I recall correctly, you were kidnapped during a pirate raid on your people. Vicious marauders tend not to leave very good impressions with the locals. Certainly not good enough to warrant a huge, stone welcome mat."

"Umm."

"It's been five years," Joshua said. "Plenty could have happened here since then. Perhaps other, more civilized travelers have visited her people. *Someone* coded the airlock, after all."

"Umm." Vessani's ears drooped and her tail fell limp.

"Vess?" Nathan raised an eyebrow. "Anything you want to share with us?"

"Well . . . maybe?" She gave them a quick, apologetic shrug of her shoulders.

"If you've got something to say, now would be the time." He flashed an insincere smile. "You know. Before we try to talk with the locals."

"Vess?" Joshua asked, his expression growing more concerned. "Is something wrong?"

"Kind of." She turned to him, her face contorted with what was perhaps a measure of shame. "I may have forgotten something important."

"Which is?"

"That I wasn't actually"—she swallowed and winced—"kidnapped."

"*What?*" Nathan and Joshua exclaimed in unison.

"I'm sorry!" she pleaded, more to Joshua. "I forgot!"

"Oh, this ought to be good!" Aiko crowed.

"How, exactly," Nathan began, enunciating each word with care, "do you forget something like that?"

"I don't know! It just happened!"

"Vess." Joshua looked her in the eyes. "You told me you were taken from your home by force."

"I know." She bit into her lip again.

"But that's not what happened?"

"Not really." She gave him another shrug. "Sorry?"

"Then what did happen?" Joshua asked, his tone more curious than anything else.

"I . . . okay, look." Vessani stepped back and held up her hands. "I never meant to lie to you about this. Or *anything*."

"So, you weren't kidnapped?" Nathan asked.

"Technically, no."

"Then how'd you get off the habitat?"

"A ship visited five years ago, and I joined their crew."

"Then we're talking freelancers and not pirates?"

"No, they were definitely pirates, but I only learned that after joining. The line between the two can be murky at times."

"Fair enough," Nathan admitted.

"They'd lost some people on their last job and were looking to flesh out their ranks without heading back to the Union." Her eyes brightened. "So, you see, I was *tricked* into leaving. That's kind of like kidnapping, right?"

"Then let me see if I've got this straight: you, as a seventeen-year-old low-tech nekoan, somehow managed to join a pirate crew?"

"Yes, that's right. I impressed them with my marksmanship."

"Which you then forgot about."

"I didn't mean to!"

"Hey," Aiko said. "Would all of you hurry up and figure this out? Am I landing this tub or not?"

"It should be fine," Vessani said.

"But why hide this at all?" Nathan asked.

"Because of what happened *after* I joined up."

"The Jovian privateers?"

"I was terrified when they attacked! A group of metal people cutting a bloody swath through the ship! I'd never seen anything like it!"

"Yeah," Aiko chimed in. "Everlife commandos can have that effect on people."

"What?" Nathan asked. "Selective forgetfulness?"

"Those who fought back were killed," Vessani explained. "Those who didn't were taken prisoner, me included. I had no idea what they were going to do to us! So I lied to them. Told them I'd been kidnapped. The Jovians realized I didn't fit in with the rest of the pirates, so they bought the story. Even let me work for *them* for a time before they eventually dropped me off on Saturn."

"And you just remembered all this?" Nathan asked with a creased brow.

"I don't know. I've been telling the same tale for so long, it sort of became the real thing in my own head. I didn't *mean* to deceive any of you. And they *did* lie about not being pirates. I found that out real quick!"

"You're not very good at picking crews, are you?" Nathan said.

"I *know*! I'm *sorry*!"

Everyone but Aiko-One had assembled in the D Deck cargo hold, and Nathan studied the situation outside through a porthole. A trio of mounted nekoans had arrived shortly after they landed. They rode up to the edge of the landing pad atop huge beasts Vessani called "dire pumas." All three creatures possessed sleek black coats of short, shiny fur.

"Cat people riding big cats," Nathan mumbled. "Who would have thought?"

"I heard that," Vessani said, her ears upright.

"Just making an observation."

The riders included a woman flanked by two men. The woman

wore a layered robe with a complex floral design over a subdued green backdrop. Her straight, golden hair draped both shoulders, and she'd decorated her ears with a dozen small rings and studs, each bejeweled with pearls or coral. She stood high in the saddle, back straight, green eyes focused and alert. Her tail lay curled about her waist as she waited.

Her companions wore armor composed of black-and-green lacquered plates over dark gray padding. Both wore black lacquered helms that covered most of their heads and featured conical spaces for their ears. The ornate sheaths of curved swords hung from their hips. One carried what appeared to be a deifactured hunting rifle, the artifact richly painted and decorated with etchings and metalwork flourishes. He'd slung a bandolier of ammo across his chest. The man without a rifle carried a flag featuring the golden silhouette of a deifactory across a black-and-green field split diagonally. The banner's long tails whipped in the wind.

Nathan wondered if the presence of the rifle was a way for the locals to let visitors know *"We're not pushovers, so you'd better behave yourselves."* Who knew how many deifactured weapons they had access to? A *Solar Almanac* survey would almost certainly categorize them as low-tech, but such a finding could be misleading.

Almanac standards were simple enough: "high-tech" for spaceborne civilizations like the Concord or Union, "mid-tech" for societies with a meaningful airborne presence, and "low-tech" for everyone else. Those broad categories may have served the Almanac's needs, but they inevitably told incomplete stories. A group of low-tech "primitives" with a cache of deifactured arms was not a force to be underestimated.

"I assume it's the woman we want to talk to?" Nathan asked, stepping away from the porthole. Gravity was a touch lighter than standard.

"Yes," Vessani said. "From the looks of it, she's one of the King's Arms. They're a group of royal advisors. She's not one I recognize, though. Maybe she's new?"

"Sounds like we're already off to a good start, then." Nathan gestured to the ramp controls. "Shall we?"

"I don't see why not."

"All right. Then let's see how this goes." Nathan lowered the ramp and followed Vessani across the stones to the entourage. Aiko-Six hung back with the others, a rifle casually slung in her arms, just in case.

The woman dismounted from her dire puma, which gave her an affectionate nuzzle. She scratched it behind the ears, then proceeded across the landing pad. Her eyes fell on Vessani, and the slightest hint of a smile graced her lips. The soldier carrying the flag dismounted as well and approached by her side while the rifle-carrying solider stayed back on his dire puma.

A brief gust of hot wind whipped at Nathan's jacket, causing it to flap against his back. The air carried the hints of flowers mixed with the subtle smell of earth baking under Sol's reflected light. The two groups met halfway between the ship.

"Welcome, travelers." The nekoan woman placed a fist over her heart and dipped her head. Her escort planted the flag and stood rigidly by her side. "I'm Nelaara Ret'Su, a representative of the king of T'Ohai, whose territory you now find yourself in. May I ask who you are and what brings you to our fair nation?"

"Of course." Vessani gestured to herself, then to Nathan. "I'm Vess, and this is Captain Nathaniel Kade of the freelance transport *Neptune Belle*."

"Hello." Nathan nodded to the nekoan woman.

"Vess . . ." Ret'Su pursed her lips, as if on the edge of remembering something important. She then spoke in a guttural language that sounded like the prelude to a catfight.

Vessani smiled and responded in the same language.

"You've been to T'Ohai before?" Ret'Su observed smoothly.

"You could say that. I was born here."

"Indeed?" The advisor's ears perked up, and she smiled a little. "What brings you back home?"

"Your deifactory and the Black Egg. We'd like your permission to study it."

"The Black Egg?" Her tail twitched. "For what purpose?"

"We believe it can point us to a trove of lost technology."

Nathan shot Vessani a quick, sideways glance. There was negotiating openly, and then there was playing all your cards face up, but he kept quiet, content for now to let her handle the opening dialogue.

"Where?" Ret'Su asked. "Within the cylinder?"

"No," Vessani replied. "Outside. *Far* away."

"I see." The advisor knitted her fingers together, and her hands disappeared into the long sleeves of her robe. "Then we wouldn't be able to enjoy the fruits of your research. To share this 'trove' you speak of."

"Not unless you've acquired a spaceship since I was last here."

Ret'Su breathed in a brief, dismissive sniff. "We'll require some form of compensation before we can grant you access to the deifactory."

"We've got plenty to offer."

"Without a doubt." Her gaze darted to Nathan's pistol, then to their ship. "Perhaps there's a problem you can help us with in exchange for the access you seek."

"Depends on the nature of the problem," Nathan cut in before Vessani could answer.

"Naturally." Ret'Su made eye contact with her escort and nodded. The flagbearer pulled a commect off his belt and began to speak into it using that growling language of theirs. Ret'Su turned back to them.

"What kind of work are we talking about here?" Nathan asked.

"I'm afraid I shouldn't overstep my bounds in this matter. Any further discussions should involve our king. And on that note, it's with great pleasure that I invite you and your crew back to T'Ohai Palace."

"So far so good," Vessani said from the rover's passenger seat, speaking up to overcome the wind noise.

"Maybe. I don't know." Nathan shook his head as he drove the rover down the widening street. Aiko-Six, Rufus, and Joshua had joined them while Aiko-One sealed up the ship and remained behind. He thought he'd have to drive slowly while following Ret'Su and her escorts, but those dire pumas could *move*, and he maintained a swift pace behind them.

"Don't you think this is a great start?" Vessani asked.

"It's not that," Nathan said. "It's just me being cagey. The locals clearly want something, and I don't have a clue what they're going to ask for. Do you?"

"No, sorry. Must be a new problem."

Their route to the palace took them through the docks. Sailing ships of various sizes sat in rows to one side while warehouses and other buildings took up the other. Nekoans on and around the ships stopped mid-task and watched the small procession with attentive eyes and erect ears. They didn't appear worried or startled or fearful or any of the other negative reactions one might expect when high-tech and low-tech societies collided. More curious than anything else, which Nathan considered a good sign.

These people have seen high-tech visitors before, he thought. *As if the "welcome mat" didn't make that obvious enough.*

Many of the ship and dockyard crews hauled slices of giant fish out of the water and up wooden ramps, or used cranes and pulleys to swing chunks off the decks of their ships. He caught sight of a severed head with jaws nearly as wide as the bow of the largest ship. Many of the vessels featured carved fishbones as part of their figureheads.

Nathan wrinkled his nose reflexively at the sight of all that raw fish, but when he breathed in the air, he found it to be surprisingly... non-fishy. Almost pleasantly fresh by comparison, accompanied by the iron tang of blood in the air.

"Mmm, gigatuna," Vessani murmured and licked her lips. "It's been a while."

"Is this making you a little homesick?" Nathan asked.

"Not really. Nostalgic, maybe. But not homesick." She gave him a half smile. "This might be where I'm from, but it's not home anymore."

Nathan nodded, believing he understood what she meant. Her experiences beyond the habitat had changed her forever. There was no looking back—no *going* back—to whatever life she'd once enjoyed in this city. She wasn't the same person she'd been five years ago. She'd been given a taste of the richness, splendor, and perils of the wider solar system. Who would want to go back to a simple, safe, boring, low-tech life after all that?

Not me, Nathan thought. *And not Vess, by the looks of it.*

The three dire pumas turned down a wide, straight street that cut through the heart of the city and ended in a pair of five-story pagodas with an expansive two-story complex sprawled out between them.

"The palace?" Nathan asked.

"Yep," Vessani replied. "You guessed it."

Nathan followed the three dire pumas up to a whitewashed stone wall that encircled the palace. They passed through an open gate flanked by a pair of guards clad in black-and-green lacquered armor and equipped with curved swords. The gate led into a well-tended field of flowers, fruiting trees, and small reflection pools in front of the palace proper. Bees and colorful butterflies buzzed and fluttered around the gardens, and twin rows of green and black streamers flapped on the ends of high poles on either side of the main path.

The dire pumas stopped in front of a wide staircase between a pair of thick, wooden columns. Ret'Su dismounted and handed the puma's reins to a waiting attendant. Nathan parked next to her, switched off the rover, and pocketed the key.

"Want me to stick with the rover?" Aiko-Six asked quietly. "Or should I come with you?"

"Stay with the rover for now," Nathan whispered back. "Let's get a feel for their king before we get too comfortable."

"You've got it." She plopped her metal butt onto the hood of the rover and shouldered her rifle. "Just scream if you want me to . . . 'you know.'"

"Come charging to the rescue, guns blazing?"

"I was thinking more along the lines of calling One and having her loom menacingly overhead until they give you back. But yeah. Guns blazing works, too."

"Let's hope it doesn't come to *either*." He gave Aiko a quick pat on the shoulder, then walked over to Ret'Su.

"The king is expecting you." Ret'Su made a broad welcoming gesture toward the stairs. "This way, please."

Nathan, Vessani, Rufus, and Joshua followed her through the columns and up the stairs to the palace. Ornate glass lamps burned brightly on either side of the long corridor of varnished wood.

Fish oil? Nathan wondered, but soon he found his attention pulled elsewhere. Clusters of robed nekoans in adjoining rooms or corridors watched them pass, and the echoes of guttural conversation grew more pronounced the farther in they proceeded. He wasn't sure what to make of the growing commotion until he noticed a graying nekoan woman point to Vessani and gasp.

"Vess?" he asked.

"Hmm?"

"Is it just me, or are the locals talking about you?"

"They are?" she replied coyly. "I hadn't noticed."

"You didn't forget something important again, did you?"

"*No*," she stressed. "I didn't forget. This is totally different."

"Okay, then. Just so we're clear on that."

"I *chose* not to tell you this."

"I—" Nathan turned to her sharply. "Excuse me?"

"Don't look so worried. You wouldn't have believed me, anyway."

"Vess, if there's something you haven't told—"

"Don't *worry*!" She gave him a confident wink. "I told you I can handle the locals and I will. I've got this. Have a little faith."

"Says the woman who forgot her own past."

She rolled her eyes. "Now you're just being mean."

"If I am, it's because you gave me reason to."

Ret'Su led them into a circular audience chamber where a large, grizzled nekoan sat on the throne in the center of a two-step dais. Loose robes of green—decorated with golden pyramids—covered the modest swell of his belly as he leaned to one side, his chin propped up on an elbow. Strands of gray hair chased through his braided, black beard, which reached halfway down his stomach. He watched them enter with sharp, golden eyes that fell upon Vessani and immediately . . . softened?

Over a dozen attendants flanked the king on either side, all resplendent in colorful robes, and a pair of armored guards stood behind him with swords and shields. A graying dire puma lounged on a nearby cushioned pad and looked up at the newcomers, its eyes glinting in the light.

A young woman scurried through a side curtain, glanced to the approaching foreigners, then hurried to the king's side and whispered urgently to him. His ears rose at her words, and his eyes widened.

"Your Majesty, King D'Miir S'Kaari ne T'Ohai." Ret'Su bowed to the king, then swept an open hand toward Nathan and the others. "May I present Captain Nathaniel Kade and—"

"Vessani S'Kaari ne T'Ohai," Vessani interrupted, her firm voice filling the chamber.

Someone in the audience chamber gasped, followed by the sound of shattering pottery. Vessani ignored the commotion and stepped forward, her eyes locked with the king's.

"Vess?" The king took hold of a cane in one hand and rose from his throne with a labored groan. "My Vess?" He walked forward, the cane clacking against wood.

A pair of attendants hovered on either side, ready to catch him should he stumble. He shooed them away and grunted as he climbed off the dais and approached Vessani.

"My beautiful Vess?" he breathed, reaching up to caress her cheek with a large palm.

"Hey, Dad." She closed her eyes and pressed his hand against her cheek. "It's been a while."

CHAPTER FIFTEEN

"Did you know about this?" Nathan asked Joshua under his breath, kneeling on a long, padded cushion along one side of a long, low table decorated with gigatuna hunting mosaics. Vessani and King D'Miir S'Kaari sat opposite them and spoke excitedly to each other, dipping in and out of that growling local language, Vessani regaling her father with tales of her travels.

"I did," Joshua replied quietly.

"And you didn't think to tell me?"

"She asked me not to."

"She should have said something!" Nathan whispered.

"She didn't think you'd believe her."

"They've got you there!" Aiko chortled, nudging Nathan with her elbow.

Nathan let out a frustrated exhalation.

"Be honest with me." Joshua leaned in. "What would you have said if Vess told you the truth? That she'd been born into low-tech royalty?"

"I'd ... probably have scoffed at the idea and said something like 'So what?'"

"Exactly. Hence, why she rarely shares that part of her past. It's not relevant anymore. Most of the time, anyway."

Nathan grimaced as one of the nekoans handed him a large piece of stiff paper.

"What's this?"

"I believe it's tonight's menu," Joshua said, receiving his.

Nathan glanced over the selection of watercolor pictures, each titled with elegant, flowing script.

"Tuna sashimi," he read. "Tuna steak. Six different kinds of tuna salad. I'm sensing a pattern here."

"I believe they're eager to show off the local specialty," Joshua whispered.

"Hey, Rufus," Nathan exclaimed. "Check it out! They have tuna burgers!"

"I saw," the cleric replied dryly and set down his menu. "And before you ask, yes, I already know what I'm ordering."

"I'll have to try and get their recipe for you." Aiko handed her menu back. "Sorry, but I'm not eating."

"Are you sure..." The waiter paused and frowned at the Jovian's androgynous machine body. "Sir?"

"Yeah." She pointed to her head. "In case you haven't noticed, this face didn't come with a mouth. If you insist on bringing me something, go right ahead. I'll sniff it for a while, but don't expect me to do more than that."

"Look here." Joshua tapped his menu. "They have tuna alcohol, too. Something called 'colonche.'"

Nathan made a sour face.

"Suit yourself, Captain, but I'm trying it."

The waiter took Joshua's order, then stepped over to Nathan.

"And for you, sir?"

"Ah, yes." Nathan consulted the menu once more, his finger trailing down to the bottom of the sheet. "I'll have the tuna...surprise."

"An excellent choice, sir. How would you like that prepared?"

"Surprise me."

"Very good, sir." The waiter took his menu, bowed, and disappeared through a side curtain.

"Is that so?" D'Miir laughed heartily at part of Vessani's tale, then gestured to the others. "Yes, you're right! They do look lonely! We should fix that!"

Ret'Su called out something in the local tongue, and soon a group of nine young men and woman filed out and posed before the table. Nathan wasn't sure what to make of the group's attire, which consisted of layers of colorful gauze and not much else. One of the females winked at him.

"Well, go ahead," D'Miir said.

"Go ahead . . . what?" Nathan asked, unsure of what was being asked of him.

"Why, pick one, of course!" the king replied, then laughed again.

"Pick one? Oh, no. No, thank you!" Nathan held up his hands. "That's quite all right. I appreciate the hospitality, but you don't have to go *that* far!"

"They're not to your liking?" the king asked, sounding puzzled. "*None* of them?"

"It's . . ." Nathan looked back at the assembled, virile youths. One of the men winked at him this time. "Can we just skip this and move on to business?"

"Would you pull your brain out of the gutter?" Vessani snapped. "It's not what you think!"

"It's not?"

"No!"

Nathan inspected the scantily clad cat people once more. "Then what *is* it?"

"They're *gren g'liffi*."

"I have no idea what that means."

"They're . . . oh, what would be a good translation?" Vessani pondered the question for a moment, then snapped her fingers. "Right. Think of them as snuggle buddies."

"Is that what you call them over here?"

"Listen to me," Vessani stressed, her voice rising. "This is an important part of my culture, and you're disrespecting it!"

"I'm not disrespecting anything. I'm just confused."

"They're not *whores*! All they do is snuggle up with you and keep you company during the meal!"

He regarded the fertile youths once more. "Is that all?"

"Yes!"

One of the females, a short white-hair with bright blue eyes, waggled her eyebrows at him.

"Fine," he sighed.

"When on Jupiter . . ." Aiko intoned.

"Right, right. I'll give it a shot." Nathan pointed to the white-haired girl. "You. What's your name?"

"It's Mi'ili, good sir."

"Nice to meet you, Mi'ili. Come on over."

The nekoan let out a quick yelp of excitement and hurried to his side. Nathan froze in place while the young nekoan draped her arms around him and nestled her head against his shoulder. She pressed her body against his—

—and then she started purring.

Nathan wasn't sure what happened next or how it came to be, but by some ethereal force, he found all the stress and worries oozing out of his body, as if the young woman were syphoning all the negative energy from his soul.

"Oh, wow," he breathed. "This is nice."

"I know." Joshua flashed a crooked smile.

"We've entertained the occasional high-tech visits for some time now," D'Miir began after dinner. "Travelers from other habitats come to trade with us, often for the goods our deifactory produces as it enters a period of awakening. Normally, these dealings proceed smoothly. And when the deifactory returns to its slumber, we're left more or less alone by outsiders."

"But that's changed recently?" Nathan ventured, then suppressed a quiet burp. The tuna surprise had been filling, and surprising in an odd sort of way. Of all the things he'd expected to find within the pockets of thinly sliced tuna meat, he never would have guessed the locals would fill it with more tuna. Granted, it had been deliciously seasoned minced tuna and vegetables stuffed within each meat pocket, but upon reflection, he concluded he should've seen it coming.

Most of the royal attendants and snuggle buddies left after dinner, though the king's guards and the old dire puma remained in the room, off to the side but attentive with one eye open.

"The situation has indeed changed," D'Miir continued, nodding gravely. "Besides your ship, the visits have stopped." He held up a finger. "All except one vessel. A ghastly, pale ship with a grotesque crew of flesh and machinery."

"How long has it been since anyone else came here?" Nathan asked.

"About half a year."

"And how many times has this pale ship appeared during that period?"

"They've raided us five times." The king scowled at the dregs in his glass. "And the frequency of the attacks is increasing."

"Do you know who they are or where they're from?"

"No. We interrogated one of their wounded but found him completely unresponsive to questioning." The king shook his head grimly. "Not even when we took more forceful measures to extract information from him. As far as we can tell, these people don't speak and can't feel pain."

"Lovely," Nathan groaned. "What are they after?"

"We're not sure. They've taken prisoners, mostly. And they've hit the deifactory a few times. We're not sure what their overall goal is."

"It's possible they're here for the Black Egg," Rufus said. "If the raiders are cybernetic, then they might be responding to the same signal we're trying to track down."

"But why would that bring them here?" Nathan asked. "From what we know, the Black Egg *responds* to the signal. It doesn't create its own. You said yourself you couldn't connect to it outside the habitat."

"I know. Just speculating why they're interested in the deifactory."

"Have they gone after any of the other deifactories here?" Nathan asked D'Miir.

"Not that we've seen. Just ours. We've kept an eye on the airlocks ever since the first attack, so we would have seen them land on the other islands if they had."

"If nothing else," Rufus said, "it seems likely these raiders put the code on the airlock."

"Probably." Nathan turned back to D'Miir. "I know you're looking for help where you can find it, but I'm not sure what it is you expect we can do for you. We're not exactly a fighting force."

"You may have no choice in the matter."

"Why do you say that?"

D'Miir sat up. "Because you're here for the Black Egg, correct?"

"That's right. We'd like your permission to study it."

"Then I'm afraid you're too late. The raiders took it during their third attack."

"They did *what*?"

"I'm afraid so," D'Miir replied, his tone almost apologetic.

"But the raiders keep coming?" Joshua asked.

"Twice more since they stole the Egg."

"What for?"

"Prisoners, it seems."

Nathan let out a long, groaning sigh.

"This complicates matters," Joshua said.

"It seems to me," D'Miir began carefully, "that our interests are aligned. You want the Black Egg, and we want it back from the raiders."

"That may be so." Nathan placed his elbow on the table and head in his hand. "But I don't see how *either* of us can get what we want from this."

"Then allow me to propose a solution." D'Miir slid closer. "We still have the raider we captured."

"Alive?"

"I'm afraid not. He refused to eat or drink and eventually died from dehydration. But I suspect that won't be a problem for you. While our questioning proved fruitless, you have techniques at your disposal we lack."

"He's right," Rufus said. "Dead or alive, I can try communing with his implants."

"And there's also the deifactory itself," Joshua said. "It might help if we took a hard look at where the Black Egg was stored."

"You could be right. Both of you." Nathan rubbed his chin, his earlier frustration subsiding. They'd hit a snag, sure, but perhaps there was a path forward after all.

"What do you say, then, Captain?" D'Miir asked. "We can help each other here. We give you the body and access to the deifactory, which, if your companions have guessed correctly, will lead you to the raiders and the stolen Black Egg. You then wrest it from their clutches, use it as you will, and return it to us when you're done."

"Sounds like we get what we want now, and you *might* receive your share later. Why would you agree to that? Why trust us?"

"It's not like I have many options. Besides"—D'Miir flashed a toothy grin and pulled Vessani close—"I have her thoughts on what kind of captain you are. She may be the wild one in the family, but I'd trust her with my life."

"Aww," Vessani cooed. "You say the nicest things."

"Give me your word, Captain," the king declared, "and that will be good enough for now."

Nathan crossed his arms. He knew Vessani's father—with his nation being raided and their prized artifact stolen—was looking for what little good he could squeeze out of a bad situation. He also knew he'd accept the offer, since they needed access to the Black Egg in order to proceed. They either made an attempt to retrieve it, accepting whatever perils that entailed, or slinked back home to Neptune. All that made sense in his mind, but he also couldn't escape the feeling he was taking advantage of the low-tech royal. If he *could* return the Black Egg to T'Ohai when all of this was over, he'd do it, but that was a huge "if," which left the locals without any compensation for the help they now offered.

And that, in his mind, wasn't fair and proper.

Nathan's parents had always strived to conduct business in an honest and upstanding manner. Even if they didn't need to. Even if, realistically, they'd never again see the people on the other side of the table. Liars and cheats littered the solar system, but the Kades weren't among them, and Nathan intended to keep it that way.

"I appreciate your offer," he said at last. "Give us some time to consider it."

He glanced around the table. Vessani and Joshua seemed confused by his hesitation, but Rufus's expression told a different story. He'd been around Nathan long enough to at least have a sense for what bothered the captain.

"If I may," the cleric offered. "Perhaps there's something we can do to make this deal a little more . . . balanced?" He raised an eyebrow to Nathan.

"With your permission?"

Rufus knelt beside the king and retrieved a folded leather pouch from a belt pocket. He set it on the table, released the clasp, and unrolled it to reveal a selection of medical instruments, vials, and a prayer book.

"What's all this?" D'Miir asked, ears flattening.

"Tools of my trade," Rufus said. "I couldn't help but observe your limp from earlier, and as such, I'd like to offer my services to you as a healer."

"Healers!" the king scoffed. "Charlatans, all of them! I'm tempted to arrest every last one of those frauds."

"Then you never met one with the right knowledge and tools."

"What makes your tools so special?" D'Miir passed a hand over the unrolled pouch.

"Simply put, they're some of the best in the solar system." Rufus retrieved a vial filled with silvery fluid and held it up for the king to see. "Do you know what this is?"

The king took the vial, inspected it, held it up to the light, then set it down on the table.

"No."

"This vial contains silver panacea, one of the many inventions of Divergence. The fluid suspends a host of tiny machines specialized for work within the human body. Baseline or divergent, it doesn't matter. The panacea will treat most injuries automatically, though its healing powers can be enhanced even further. As a trained cleric, I can commune with the injection while it works, providing direction to the healing process."

"I don't know . . ." D'Miir gave Vessani a doubtful look, but she smiled brightly at her father.

"Panacea's *great* stuff. I received a shot after a nasty hamstring pull, and it had me good as new in a *day!*"

"You think this stuff can fix my knees?" D'Miir asked the cleric.

"No. I'm *certain* it will." Rufus took the vial and slotted it into a syringe. "May I proceed?"

D'Miir grumbled something under his breath in the local language. He turned to Vessani once more, who nodded her encouragement.

"Fine," he grunted. "Where do you want to stick me? In the knee?"

"Anywhere you're comfortable with. The arm, perhaps? The panacea will travel through your bloodstream to the injury site."

D'Miir muttered something else, then rolled up his sleeve and stuck out his arm, which was surprisingly muscular despite the girth of his stomach.

"Make a fist, please. Yes, like that." Rufus tapped the bulging vein in the crook of D'Miir's elbow. He swabbed the spot with alcohol, then injected a third of the vial's contents.

"There." He applied a square bandage to the injection point. "It'll take about a minute for the panacea to circulate through your body."

"And once it has?"

"I'll provide guidance to the healing." He slotted the vial and syringe back into his kit and pulled out his prayer book. The relevant passage was already bookmarked.

"What if you weren't here to do this?" D'Miir asked.

"It would eventually find the injury, but my efforts will speed the process along."

He opened the prayer book and silently recited one of the many prayers for healing. The words served to clear his mind, and when he finished the third prayer, he could sense a nearby juncture unfolding, ready and willing to commune with his will.

"I believe it's ready." He set the prayer book down, closed his eyes, and placed a splayed hand over his heart. A translucent visual of the king's body appeared in his mind's eye, accompanied by pointers and descriptive text. "The cartilage in both knees shows signs of wear, and there's a great deal of scar tissue in and around your left knee. Were you injured there?"

"I . . . yes." D'Miir sounded both surprised and impressed. "I had a bad tumble off my puma and twisted it when I hit the ground. The knee's never been the same since."

"Yes, that would make sense," Rufus replied, his eyes still closed. "If I were to guess, the scar tissue plus the worn-down cartilage is what's causing most of your pain. I'll direct the panacea to clean up both joints, giving special attention to your left knee." He bowed his head and concentrated.

"Oh?" D'Miir shivered. "My left knee is tingling."

"That's normal." Rufus opened his eyes and sat back. "You may also feel tingling in other areas. Sometimes the panacea needs to acquire resources for its repairs from another part of the body. As long as you're well-nourished, this won't be a problem."

"I see." D'Miir slapped his belly and laughed. "No problem indeed!"

"Just you wait!" Vessani said. "You'll be up and about in no time!"

"Avoid strenuous activity for two days," Rufus cautioned, "just to be safe. I'll also leave a small supply of panacea with you, to use and distribute as you see fit, as well as literature on its many uses."

The habitat's rotation proved troublesome, but Xormun resigned himself to watching and waiting through the minor annoyance, lest he risk alerting their quarry to the corvette's presence.

WC-9003 completed a full rotation once every four minutes and forty-four seconds. The habitat's angled mirrors and the bulk of the other landmasses obscured the *Neptune Belle* for most of each cycle, and his crew could only catch staggered, incomplete glimpses of events on the surface.

Locals had met the *Belle*'s crew at an obvious landing pad. After that, several crew members departed the ship in a ground vehicle and followed the locals into a city nestled between the sea and the deifactory, eventually entering the largest local structure. A government complex, perhaps?

And now . . . nothing.

The back of the complex butted up against the deifactory, which meant Kade and his crew now had access to the factory interior without needing to step outside and into view of the corvette's telescope. That left Xormun bereft of useful information. At least for the moment.

Xormun didn't mind the wait. He disliked his lack of eyes on the ground, but he also appreciated that every second brought his support closer.

He checked a vlass listing inbound flights. Six other corvettes and the *Leviathan of Io* were on their way to WC-9003. The first corvette would arrive within the next few hours, while the *Leviathan* was still over a day out.

<Apex, we have a new contact!> reported one of the analysts. <Unknown vessel approaching the cylinder!>

Xormun looked up from the vlass. <Show me.>

<Here, sir.> The analyst enlarged the live feed from the telescope. <We caught sight of it the moment it executed turnaround.>

The image showed a pale, ugly ellipse with a trio of thrusters burning bright, decelerating its approach to the habitat. Numerous lumps and blisters covered the hull and several long, metallic beams protruded from the surface at odd, disorderly angles.

<Analysis?>

<Ship is an unknown pattern, slightly larger than our corvette. We'll have more exact measurements for you shortly. Deceleration rate is one-point-two gees. The vessel executed turnaround unusually close to WC-9003, indicating it may have launched from a nearby habitat. Possibly from within the local cluster.>

<How soon will it arrive at the habitat?>

<Twenty-seven minutes from now if it maintains its course and thrust.>

Xormun took another look at the craft, its image growing clearer by the second. The pale irregular hull conjured up images of cold, bloodless flesh with spikes jammed through it and engines stuck to the back. It was one of the ugliest spacecraft he'd ever seen.

<What *are* you?>

Chapter Sixteen

Nathan and the others spent the night in a trio of lavish guest rooms within T'Ohai Palace while Aiko-Six kept watch. He doubted that level of caution was necessary, given how their hosts had quickly warmed to their presence, but it never hurt to exercise caution when dealing with an unfamiliar society.

Mi'ili—the white-haired *geggle-friggle* girl, or whatever Vessani had called her—stopped by just as he was about to turn in for the night. She suggested she join him for some "extra cuddles" while giving him a mischievous, innuendo-filled smile. No need for Vessani to translate *this* offer!

Nathan tended to view divergent relations through a lens of hesitation, owing to his own past experiences. One time, he'd made the mistake of dating an avion—a cute and gentle young woman, to be fair—and he'd learned two important lessons from their first painful night together:

First, always leave plenty of space around the bed when sleeping with an avion. Their wings will knock over just about anything.

And second, the wings were *considerably* stronger than they looked. He wasn't sure if he'd touched a bad spot at the wrong time—or a very good spot at the right time—but the ensuing reflex response from the young lady's wings had clubbed him in the head so hard he'd blacked out briefly.

He'd woken up on his back to a view of swirling stars and swaying breasts. The young woman had apologized earnestly before attempting to reinitiate proceedings, but the bone-rattling impact to his cranium had killed his interest in further activities.

He'd kept his relations with divergent women to a minimum ever since. Not that he didn't find the various female forms attractive. Far from it, in fact, though he drew a strict line when it came to centaurs. He'd even been hit on by one once. She'd been . . . pretty, he guessed. At least the top half of her. Very nice hair, too, but he had no clue how that kind of physical congress was supposed to work on a mechanical level, and he felt no desire to suffer through the inevitable learning curve.

Nekoans, by comparison, were what he considered a "safe" deviation from baseline, at least when it came to potential relationships. The tail wasn't strong enough to present a hazard, and he considered their cat ears quite attractive. The only aspect of their appearance he found off-putting were the eyes. Something about those vertical pupils always gave the impression they were up to no good. Which, now that he considered this most recent offer, wasn't necessarily a bad thing.

He was sorely tempted to let the young nekoan into his room, but this would be his first night amongst the locals, and he wasn't in the mood for whatever drama might spill from a cultural misunderstanding. He decided against her offer and turned her down as politely as possible. She made a pouty face at him but departed without further complaint.

He found it difficult to fall asleep after that, and the one dream he recalled involved him fleeing for his life from a horde of ravenous kittens, most of them with white hair.

They started off the next morning by joining the royal court for a simple breakfast of rice and—unsurprisingly—tuna. Grilled and salted to perfection, but it was still more tuna, which Nathan could have done without after the fishy overload he'd received from last night's tuna surprise.

D'Miir skipped breakfast and spent much of the morning walking the palace grounds. He retained his cane, but even at this early stage of his recovery, he paced around confidently while putting almost no weight on the walking stick. He greeted his daughter and each of the visiting foreigners with a jovial air and loudly proclaimed the success of Rufus's medicine, which didn't hurt their standing with the locals in the least.

Nathan finished his rice and then picked at the grilled tuna while a small but excitable crowd formed around Rufus. True to his word, the cleric provided D'Miir with five more vials of silver panacea. Aiko-Six had retrieved the vials from the *Belle* for Rufus, driving out to the ship once everyone else was up and about. The cleric asked the crowd to form a line, and he sat down with each of them to discuss their needs. By the time Rufus finished administering his sixteenth patient, Nathan tapped him on the shoulder.

"Yes, Nate?" he said, folding his tool pouch back up.

"We're heading out to the deifactory. You joining us or staying here?"

"Staying." Rufus fitted the pouch back into one of his belt pockets. "I think I'll have more luck with the raider's body."

"I figured as much. Aiko wants a look at the corpse, too, so you'll have her as company. Call if you need anything."

"Sure thing."

Nathan joined Vessani and Joshua by the exit, and together they followed Ret'Su to the back of the palace, which connected to the deifactory's base level via a long, canvas-covered pathway that cut through a flowering garden. Ret'Su led them into one of several glass-walled, inclined elevators and selected a level from the control vlass.

"The reliquary is on the top floor," she said.

The elevator accelerated up the pyramidal slope with only the slightest jostle at the beginning. The palace and city shrank away, and Nathan stared out across the habitat's segmented interior. Sunlight shined in from above, reflected off the giant mirror angled above the "upper" window. A line of puffy clouds blew in from the sea, bloated and gray with moisture.

Behind them, levels flashed by with most entrances leading to dark, cavernous interiors.

"How active was this place before the raiders stole the Black Egg?" Nathan asked.

"About one in every twenty levels," Ret'Su said. "Though the deifactory hadn't yet reached its peak for this cycle."

At least five percent then, Nathan figured. *Not bad for a deifactory out in the wild.*

"And now that the Egg is gone?"

"The deifactory has once again fallen asleep. The reliquary is the only place that's still active."

Nathan glanced over to Joshua. "What do you make of this? You ever hear of a deifactory shutting down all of a sudden?"

"Not like this," Joshua said, "but I wouldn't read too deeply into that. No two deifactories are identical. Clearly, the Black Egg is a critical component of some nature, but I couldn't say more without at least getting a good look at it."

"Have you ever heard of deifactories with similar artifacts?"

"No. The Black Egg could be unique to this deifactory. Or perhaps this habitat, or it could be a feature common amongst this local cluster. I simply don't know enough to say more."

"Gotcha." Nathan waited for the elevator to finish its ascent.

They came to a halt on floor 410, which Nathan guessed to be about a kilometer above the cylinder wall. That much altitude took a dent out of their rotational velocity, which in turn reduced the apparent gravity. Most people wouldn't have noticed the difference, but Nathan's experienced spacer legs picked up the subtle decrease in his body's weight.

The glass doors split open to a brightly lit corridor that smelled faintly of flowers, and Ret'Su led the way in. Vlass panels covered the walls, most inert, some broken, but a few displayed system status boards, production queues, and available pattern serials. Nathan stopped in his tracks when his eyes passed over a familiar series of letters and numbers.

"That's the serial for a *Hawklight*-pattern!" he exclaimed.

"*What?*" Joshua's head whipped back, and he hurried over to Nathan's side. "Are you sure?"

"Pretty damn sure."

"Is something wrong?" Ret'Su asked Vessani.

"I don't know." Vessani joined the others by the screen. "What's up, guys?"

Joshua tapped the serial number and mouthed the words "spaceship pattern."

Vessani's ears and eyebrows shot up.

"Yeah," Nathan whispered. "If we somehow manage to retrieve the Black Egg, then your people have a real shot at catapulting themselves straight from low-tech all the way up to *high*. That said, let's keep this to ourselves for now. No point getting everyone's hopes up, only to dash them later if something goes wrong."

"Okay," Vessani whispered back. "But I think you're forgetting something."

"What's that?"

She wiggled her ears. "We nekoans have *very* good hearing."

"Oh." He tilted to the side and looked over at Ret'Su, who smiled and waved at him. "You heard all of that, didn't you?"

"Every word."

"Right. Of course." Nathan cleared his throat and tugged down on his jacket. "Where were we, again?"

"About to visit the reliquary. This way, please."

She led them into a small, circular room where the sweet scent of flowers grew overwhelming. Vlass panels lined the room's circumference except for an alcove at the back, and nekoans had covered the floor with flowers, slender branches, bowls of fruit, and paper effigies folded into more flowers with a few paper pyramids thrown into the mix.

Vessani drew in a deep breath and smiled. "It's been a while."

"Not to knock your traditions," Nathan told the two nekoans, "but I don't think all these flowers are helping."

"I find it hard to disagree," Ret'Su confessed softly.

The nekoans had etched elaborate prayers into the walls and ceiling, using any space not taken up by a vlass. They'd used the crafted tongue, and most of the prayers were to the deifactory itself rather than the Pentatheon, humbly asking it to produce more.

Not likely, Nathan thought. *Not with most of it dark and dead.*

He waded through the mass of flowers to the alcove at the back. The elliptical recess formed half of an egg-shape about the size of his head. Devices at the top and bottom gave the impression of connectors for the artifact.

"What do we have here?" Joshua worked his way up to the back wall, trying and failing to avoid crushing flowers or paper offerings along the way.

"The Black Egg used to be here?" Nathan asked. "In this slot?"

"That's right," Vessani said.

"What made your ancestors fixate on it? Why the Black Egg and not another part of the deifactory?"

"The Black Egg always showed some activity," she explained. "Even when the rest of the deifactory slumbered."

"What kind of activity? You mean the vlasses in this room?"

"That and more. The Black Egg's shell is translucent. You can see stuff moving inside."

"What sort of 'stuff'?"

"Not sure. A fluid of some kind, maybe?"

Joshua stuck his head into the alcove and shined a flashlight on the upper connectors.

"There's some sort of residue here." He picked at the connector with his fingernail, then inspected the coarse gunk he scraped off. He rubbed the material between his thumb and forefinger. "You could be right about it circulating a fluid. I think this is degraded computronium around the connection."

"Makes sense to me," Nathan said. "Yank an important part of the factory's control system, and the whole place takes a nap."

"That doesn't help us find it, though."

"Maybe check one of these screens?"

"Worth a shot." Joshua extracted his head from the alcove and stood up straight again. He surveyed over the room and then trudged through the mound of flowers to a nearby vlass. The screen illustrated a 3D diagram of the deifactory with a great many sectors highlighted in red.

Joshua began navigating through the menus in a meticulous manner, picking one option, drilling down as far as he could go, and then exploring every report or feature he could find before pulling back to higher-level screens. He continued this process for about twenty minutes while Nathan and the two nekoans waited patiently.

"Sorry," Joshua said at last. "I don't see *anything* here that can help us. No functions we could use to track down the Black Egg, and no sign the deifactory even has a clue where it is now. The closest thing I found is an option to produce a new one."

"We can order a replacement for the locals?" Nathan asked.

"In theory, yes."

"But?"

"But the deifactory seems . . . stuck, for lack of a better word. Whatever supervisory system this installation used to answer to is gone, likely destroyed during the Scourging of Heaven. Normally, this would cause deifactories to fall back to local control, but this one hasn't. It's still trying to process commands from a supervisory layer. I'm guessing that's because it formed a new connection after the original fell silent."

"A connection to the pentatech we're after?" Nathan guessed.

"I believe so. But that second connection is . . . confusing it, I guess you'd say. It doesn't know what to make of the commands it's receiving, so it kind of stumbles along, partially reactivating for a time before it loses contact and reverts back to a standby state."

"Which is the seventy-one-year cycle we're familiar with," Vessani said.

"Right," Joshua agreed. "Repeated up to the point where those raiders yanked the Black Egg."

"Then this place is never waking up again?" Nathan asked.

"Not without the Black Egg." Joshua let out a frustrated exhale. "And I have no idea how to find it."

The corpse smelled faintly of tuna.

"They used colonche to embalm the raider?" Rufus said, staring down at the naked, dead cyborg on the table.

Aiko bent down and wafted the air above the corpse toward her head. "That and a few other fluids by the smell of it."

"Why am I not surprised."

The nekoans had guided Aiko and him to a house of healing outside the palace walls. Rufus wasn't sure how much healing actually occurred in the building, given their primitive technology, but the facility was clean and its staff friendly as they brought out the preserved corpse for inspection.

The raider had been an adult male, possibly twenty to twenty-five years old, with shaggy, unkempt hair and a defined musculature dotted by scars from what appeared to be sloppy implant insertions. His body showed mild signs of divergence with gray skin and subtle points to his ears. His clothing—a tough, leathery garment dyed dark red—sat folded at the foot of the table.

"At least they preserved the body," Aiko said. "Better this than a rotting corpse. For you, I mean. I can shut off my olfactory sense anytime I want."

"A fair point. Any thoughts on how we should proceed?"

"Not really. I'm following your lead on this one."

"Very well. Let me start by testing for a connection." He placed his fingertips on the edge of the table and closed his eyes, then recited a brief prayer to Codex to help clear his mind. "There. I can feel a short-ranged juncture. His implants are still active and talking amongst themselves. Let me see if I can—"

His surroundings vanished, and he found himself floating through a starless void. He spun around, searching for a way to orient himself, and eventually found one. A jagged maw leered at him, floating in the middle of space as if it were a tear in the very fabric of reality. Dozens of broken, metal teeth lined the mouth, opening to a wet, dark, undulating throat that stretched away to infinity.

The void-lips moved, and thunderous words rammed themselves into his mind.

The Wound.

The Wound.

Flesh and Metal.

I Want.

I Need.

It Burns.

It Scorches.

Flesh and Metal for the Wound!

The mouth gaped and lunged toward him, and only then did he realize the true scale of it. He was nothing more than a speck of dust that passed through two mountainous teeth on his way toward oblivion. He flinched back, but to no avail, and the jaw snapped shut with a deafening clap. It swallowed, and unseen forces sucked him down the throat.

There was no wind. No sound. No sensations other than an incredible sense of speed. On and on it went, faster and faster, until he finally saw something approaching from the far end.

At first it appeared as a dark metallic blot, but it grew swiftly in size, resolving into an iron ring with inward-protruding spikes tipped in blood. He wondered if it had been worn on someone's finger once, and if so, how much skin it might strip off when put on or removed.

"You all right?" Aiko asked.

"I— What?" Rufus blinked and shook his head. It took him a moment to realize he was in Aiko's arms, staring up at her face.

"You tipped over, so I caught you."

"Oh. Thanks." He put a hand on her shoulder and used the leverage to haul himself upright.

"That bad in there, huh?"

"I've seen better." He rubbed his face. "It was a disturbing, nonsensical jumble in there."

"Here you go." She picked his wig off the floor and handed it to him.

"Thanks." He fitted the wig—this one with blond curls—back on and straightened it as best he could without a mirror. "The interesting thing, though, is I've seen some of that mess before."

"Where?"

"In my recent visions."

"Then the two are connected?"

"It seems so, but I still have no idea what any of it means."

"Want to give it another go?" Aiko asked. "Maybe this time while lying down?"

"Perhaps later." He rolled up his sleeves. "Let's see what we can learn from the body next." He began at the chest and traced a finger around a circular scar on one side of the rib cage. "Look here. I think we can rule out Saturnian implants."

"Why do you say that? We haven't even cut him open."

"It's not so much the implant but how it was administered." Rufus traced a bone. "They broke one of his ribs installing it, and it didn't heal cleanly. I can feel the old fracture."

"What, did they just shove the insert plug through his rib cage?"

"Perhaps they did."

"Why would anyone do something that stupid?"

Rufus shook his head and examined the next scar.

The implants he was familiar with—such as his own neural enhancements—were deifactured, self-installing mechanisms. Doctors didn't cut open patients and stuff the implants inside. Few possessed the skills and knowledge to even have a chance at success, which was fine, because Saturnian implants installed themselves.

They came from the deifactories in boxes or bands that were placed over the target body part. All doctors needed to do was strap the patient in and hit go. The machinery took care of the rest. Rufus remembered a sense of pressure when the installer had drilled through his skull, but he never experienced discomfort. Not even after the surgery.

"At least five insertion points on the torso," Rufus said, then inspected each limb. "And it looks like two scars to each arm and leg, roughly centered on the major muscle groups."

"Performance enhancements?"

"For the limbs at least. Not sure what the torso scars are for." He compressed the rib cage at various points. "There's something solid inside."

Aiko held up her vibro-knife. The blade whined to life, pitching into the ultrasonic range.

"Want me to check?" she asked.

"In a moment." He moved to the front of the table, lifted the body's head, and turned it to one side. "Oh my. Would you look at this?" His face wrinkled in revulsion.

Aiko craned her neck to view the back of the raider's head. "It kind of looks like someone shoved a stake into the back of his head."

"Which is consistent with what we've seen elsewhere on the body." Rufus thumbed the flattened nub protruding from the base of the raider's skull and pulled back some of the man's unruly hair to gain a better look. Metallic veins zigzagged out from the nub in all directions.

"Can I cut him open now?" Aiko raised her blade once more.

"I suppose so. Start with the chest cavity, please."

"You've got it!" She braced the corpse with one hand and drew the blade down the center of the raider's rib cage. The vibro-knife cut through the man's sternum effortlessly.

Rufus was no stranger to the dead or dying. His skills as a cleric naturally brought him close to the ill and injured. He'd told himself examining the corpse would hardly be different, but that changed when Aiko jammed her fingers through the body's split sternum and cracked the rib cage wide open.

He may have turned a few shades paler when that happened.

"It's less gooey in here than I expected," she said, gawking at the cyborg's innards.

"It is?" Rufus asked, his voice squeaking. He cleared his throat and stepped up to the open chest cavity to find most of the raider's organs had been replaced with synthetic parts. "So it is."

"What do you make of all this?"

Rufus let the flutter in his stomach die down, then took a soothing breath to steel himself. He bent forward to study the artificial organs.

"There are a lot of them," he said, "but they don't strike me as all that remarkable. For example, this one here appears to be an enhanced heart, and these two must have served as replacement lungs."

"More performance enhancers."

"Seems so, but let's make sure."

"Where do you want to start?"

"At the top of the chest cavity. We'll work our way down, one implant at a time."

They spent the next half hour removing and cataloguing each of the raider's artificial organs, though the exercise yielded no new revelations. They were about to close up the torso when both of their commects chimed, followed shortly by a whooping siren that originated from the palace grounds.

CHAPTER SEVENTEEN

"Talk to us, Aiko." Nathan turned up the volume on his commect so everyone on the elevator could hear.

"There's one fugly-ass ship coming our way," Aiko-One replied from aboard the *Neptune Belle*.

"Where's it now?" Nathan stepped up to the glass and gazed toward the sunward dock. He thought he could make out a pale dot moving against the backdrop of the habitat's pole.

"About halfway between us and the airlock, heading straight for the city."

"What's it look like?" Nathan made eye contact with Ret'Su to gauge her reaction.

"Like someone's weird-ass idea for a ship. It almost looks like a pale, fleshy growth with spikes driven through it."

"That's them," Ret'Su confirmed, and Nathan gave her a grim nod.

"Aiko, get the ship in the air and stay the hell away from that thing. Try to put the deifactory between you and it, at least until we have a better handle on the situation."

"You've got it, Nate."

"Rufus and Six, how about you two? Where are you right now?"

"We're still with the raider's body," Rufus replied over the same line.

"We can get back to the palace's front gate easily enough," Aiko-Six said.

"Then head that way," Nathan ordered. "We'll try to join up with you there."

"Heading out," Aiko-Six said, followed by the sound of a door creaking open.

"All right, listen up everyone," Nathan said. "We've got ourselves a new plan. First, we're going to help the locals repel these unwelcome guests. Then, when they slink back to whatever hole they crawled out of, we're going to follow them. Any objections?"

No one spoke up, either over the commect or on the elevator. Vessani flattened her ears and drew her pistol, her face cold and determined.

You say this isn't your home anymore, Nathan thought, *but I'm not so sure.*

"And here I am without my hard suit," Vessani grumbled.

"You and me both." Nathan unholstered his own pistol and thumbed the safety off. "We'll make do."

"Thanks, by the way," she added softly.

"For what?"

"For not running at the first sign of trouble."

Nathan gave her a quick headshake. "You can thank me later. *If* this doesn't end in tears."

"Stick close to us," Vessani told Joshua, "and keep your head down."

"Don't have to tell me twice."

"You're welcome to tag along with us," Nathan told Ret'Su.

"Thank you." She drew a pearl-encrusted dagger hidden within her robes. "I think I will."

The elevator reached the halfway point on its way down when the *Neptune Belle* flew past them, the roar of its exhaust changing pitch. Far below, the palace grounds resembled a kicked anthill, with the dots of people—presumably soldiers—swarming onto the outer walls. Not that fortifications were much use against foes arriving by air, but at least it gave the cat people a better view of the situation.

"Here they come," Vessani hissed.

The pale, spiked ship shot over the city rooftops on almost a direct course for the palace. Thrusters braked hard, and Nathan winced as the ship plowed through one of the pagodas, reducing the top half to splinters.

"Who taught these morons how to fly?" Nathan said.

The pale ship slowed to a hover over the palace, part of its hull scraping across the decapitated pagoda. A few nekoan soldiers armed with rifles opened fire, the staggered reports of their weapons cracking the air, but their shots ricocheted off the ship's hull.

The elevator had almost reached the ground, and Nathan could finally gauge the size of the vessel with some accuracy. It was wider and stubbier than the *Belle*, but similar in overall volume. Maybe three internal levels? He didn't see any obvious weapons on the exterior, though its spikes might house lethal surprises.

The pale ship reversed thrust and crunched backward across the roof of the palace. An orifice on the base level of the ship irised open, and several burly cybernetic raiders jumped through the hole. The ship continued its amateurish backward slide and settled to the ground atop the gardens and reflection pools in front of the palace. Raiders poured out of the ship. More shots ripped through the air, and nekoan soldiers drew their swords and charged the invaders.

The elevator reached the ground floor, and the glass doors split open. Nathan led the party straight for the palace.

"We still heading for the front gate?" Vessani asked.

"You bet. Aiko has our meanest gun."

Nathan heard a woman crying out in the native tongue—almost growling at times—from somewhere up ahead. A raider backpedaled across the open archway at the end of the covered path with a robed nekoan woman clutched in his arms. She screamed and kicked but the raider half-dragged, half-carried her along with ease.

Nathan raised his pistol but hesitated. The nekoan flailed in a desperate attempt to break free, and he couldn't find a clean—

Vessani snapped off two quick shots. The first sparked against the side of the raider's head, knocking it back, and the second blew a chunk out of his shoulder. He let go, and the nekoan scrambled back across the floor.

The raider faced them without any visible signs of pain or fear—or *any* emotions at all. He sized them up with a pair of metal eyes, drew a vibro-sword, and sprinted toward them.

Nathan and Vessani filled the space between them with bullets, blasting the raider in the chest, stomach, legs, and jaw. Half their shots sparked against internal mechanisms. The raider lost his balance, collapsed forward, and the vibro-sword tumbled out of his grip, clattering across the stone path.

"You think he's dead?" Nathan asked, not sure they'd punched enough holes in him yet. Not with that many implants bulking him up.

Ret'Su picked up the raider's sword and with a graceful, twirling stroke, relieved the cyborg of his head's burdensome weight.

"Yes," she declared.

More screams and shouts came from inside the palace, and Ret'Su growled an order to the woman, who nodded and fled away from the danger.

"Come on!" Nathan urged them forward.

They advanced deeper into the palace, pistols raised, eyes alert. Nathan zeroed in on what he thought were the closest screams, turning down a corridor with sunlight streaming through the broken ceiling. The corridor opened at the far end to the dining hall, where he found a pair of raiders. The closest carried a vibro-sword in one hand while dragging Mi'ili by the leg with the other. The second raider rushed them with a polearm, its forked tip blurring at the edges.

Nathan fired, and his shot struck the charging raider dead center in the chest. The cyborg kept coming, seemingly ignorant of the crater in his torso, and Nathan rattled off the rest of his magazine. His target dropped heavily to the ground and slid forward, blood smearing the floor. Vessani fired one more shot into the cyborg's skull.

The second raider let go of Mi'ili's leg, gripped his sword with both hands, and rushed them.

Nathan ejected his spent magazine and pulled a fresh one off his belt, backpedaling as Ret'Su dashed past him. The raider took a swipe at her, but she ducked under the clumsy attack and slid across the floor. Her vibro-sword hissed through the air and cleaved through both legs below his kneecaps.

The raider crumpled to the ground, blood gushing from his leg stumps. He tried to push himself upright, but Vessani shot him in the face, and he dropped back down. She emptied three more shots into his back before ejecting her spent magazine.

"You okay?" Nathan asked Mi'ili.

She looked up at him and sniffled, tears streaming down her cheeks.

"That way's safe." He pointed a thumb over his shoulder. "Go!"

She sniffled again, then nodded and wiped a gauze sleeve under her eyes before hurrying past Nathan and the others.

Vessani's ears stood up. "Sounds like most of the action is out in front."

"Then that's where we need to be!" Nathan took a wide corridor off the dining hall and followed it to the central hallway that led them to the front of the palace, ending in a pair of wooden columns. Gunfire and the clash of metal against metal rang out, and he stopped behind one of the columns to take stock of the situation.

The pale ship sat at a slight angle with one landing strut sunk into a reflection pool. A wide, oval opening spilled harsh orange light from the ship's interior, and over a dozen raiders dragged or carried prisoners—and *bodies*?—back to the ship. Nathan wasn't sure what to make of it, but they didn't seem to discriminate between nekoan corpses and their own fallen.

Nekoan soldiers fought back the invaders all across the gardens, their own swords far less effective against the cyborgs than a hail of bullets. A few lucky ones now wielded the raiders' own vibro-weapons, but most struggled to hold their own with low-tech blades, which the raiders could rend through with ease.

"Dad!" Vessani called out urgently, and Nathan followed her gaze.

D'Miir stood in the midst of the thickest fighting, his sides and back protected by a cluster of four fierce-eyed, grizzled honor guards, one of them holding a green banner aloft. He raised his heavy war hammer and brought it crashing down on a raider's head, bursting the metal cranium like a melon. Together, the five nekoans pressed deep into the raiders' ranks, almost reaching the edge of the ship before the raiders counterattacked in force.

Cyborgs swarmed around them, and Nathan held his fire, the melee too thick for him to risk a shot. The king's banner clattered to the ground, and one of the honor guards fell, clutching at the crimson spewing from his neck.

"Dad!" Vessani cried, then faced Nathan. "We need to help him!"

Nathan raised his pistol and nodded, ready to head out when a new sound pierced the chaos of battle.

It was the roar of an automatic weapon.

⊕ ⊕ ⊕

Aiko-Six sprinted past the open gate and pelted the closest raider with rifle fire. A mix of explosive and incendiary rounds blasted the cyborg's chest open and blew half his face off. His implants caught fire, and he dropped to the ground in a limp, burning heap.

Aiko-Six raced across the gap, then leaped up the full height of the stone wall and caught the ledge. She hauled herself over the top one-handed and landed in a crouch. A nekoan struggling to reload his rifle flinched back at her sudden appearance and fumbled his handful of cartridges.

"Hi!" she said brightly, then shouldered her rifle—a Jovian sinspike that dated back to her days as a commando, a weapon she'd maintained and customized with all the doting care of a mother.

The three living honor guards had formed a triangle around their embattled king, but those defenses wouldn't hold out long against vibro-blades. Aiko switched to burst fire, picked a target about to lunge at one of the guards, and pulled the trigger. The trio of explosions ripped through the raider's back, exposing his artificial organs. He burst into flames and crumpled. She sighted on the next and fired again. The rounds blew the top of his head off, and he stumbled forward before pirouetting to the ground.

"And there's more where that came from!" Aiko shouted.

Wordless speech rippled across the raiders, audible to her Jovian receivers. It came across as a low electric hum that escalated into clicking and buzzing. The contents made no sense to her, being unlike any wireless language she'd ever heard, but it must have contained some form of information. The raiders responded to the bizarre transmission, and soon those assaulting the king abandoned their target and charged toward her position on the wall.

"That's it," she whispered. "Line up for me, you half-and-half bastards."

She waited for the raiders to pull away from the nekoans, then she switched to full auto and emptied the rest of her magazine. Two more raiders fell, and another dropped to the ground, missing half a leg. She reached for a magazine but was interrupted when one of the raiders hurled a vibro-spear at her.

The spear punched through her chest, and she staggered back.

The rifleman next to her regarded the injury with wide-eyed horror, his mouth agape.

"Be honest with me," she asked him. "How bad does it look?"

She didn't wait for his response, because the raiders had nearly reached the base of the wall, which featured convenient stairs up to her position since this was the *inside* of the wall. Instead, she let her rifle dangle from its strap, then forced the spear all the way through. She spun the spear around and launched it with enough force to skewer a pair of cyborgs.

Aiko grabbed her rifle again and was about to slap the full magazine in when a sword came scything through the air and buried itself in her right shoulder. It didn't cut all the way through, but it might as well have, because her fingers on that side twitched and then fell limp.

"Oh, come on!" she shouted. "Now you're throwing *swords* at me? Who said you could do that?"

A raider climbed over the corpse of his impaled brethren and rushed up the stairs to her. She yanked the vibro-sword out of her shoulder, and her arm fell off.

"I'm sorry," she told the charging cyborg. "We haven't been formally introduced."

She blocked the raider's attack, disarmed him at the shoulder—literally—then cut off his head and kicked the body down the stairs.

"The name's Aiko! I'm an ex-commando!"

She advanced down the stairs at a leisurely pace. The vibro-sword was single-edged, with a thick, sturdy back to the blade suitable for blocking other vibro-weapons. Another raider swung at her, but she parried his attack and slit open his belly. Blood, guts, and plastic tubing spilled out. She swiped the blade through his chest three more times, each stroke higher than the last, then swept his feet out from under him. He collapsed onto his side and rolled down the stairs. The next raider leaped over his body.

"It's so hard being this popular."

Their blades clashed, and another spear struck Aiko in the shoulder. She backpedaled, but the raider used the opening to cut up through her chest. Sparks flew, and her vision blipped as her internal systems rerouted power.

The next thing she saw was a sword rushing in toward her neck.

The world spun away until everything turned upside down. Her head clonked against the stairs and began bouncing along. It rebounded off another step, hit a blood-drenched body, then rolled off the side of the stairs.

"Typical," she huffed, moments before her face hit the dirt with a thud. "And I was doing so well, too."

Nathan fired at the raider who'd taken out Aiko. Two of his three shots hit, but the raider didn't go down, instead leaping off the stairs and racing toward the pale ship. He hated to see Aiko lose another body, but her efforts had put a substantial dent in the raider forces, and more of the cyborgs pulled back to their ship, carrying whatever corpses they could grab along the way.

Vessani hurried to her father's side, while Nathan hung back, reloading as he checked the overall situation. He was worried the enemy's ground team losses might lead the ship's pilot to take more extreme measures, but nothing of the sort happened. The last raider clambered inside, the hatch contracted shut, and the pale ship lifted away from the garden. It rose about half a kilometer straight up, spun around, and then sped away toward the sunward airlock.

Nathan let out a long, slow exhalation, his pulse racing, blood thumping in his ears. He holstered his pistol and walked in the general direction of D'Miir. Vessani helped her father sit up, and he winced. An ugly gash cut across his forehead, and blood matted his hair, but his eyes burned with fierce determination.

The roar of the pale ship's engines faded away, and absent the clashing of swords and the cracks of rifles, the cries of the wounded rose to prominence.

Nathan keyed his commect. "Rufus, you nearby?"

"I'm outside the palace gate. Aiko told me to stay put until it was safe."

"Get in here. Vessani's father and a lot of other nekoans are hurt." He eyed the fallen honor guard, the grass underneath him soaked in scarlet. "Or worse. Do what you can for them."

"Right away."

"Joshua?" Nathan glanced over his shoulder to find the engineer trailing close behind.

"Yes?"

Nathan tossed him the vehicle key, which he caught two-handed.

"Bring the rover around. We need to get moving if we don't want to lose sight of that ship."

"You've got it." Joshua hurried toward the gate.

Nathan planted both hands on his hips and let out another slow breath. It wasn't so much the violence that bothered him but how pointless it had all been. What did the raiders expect to gain from this? Why throw themselves at the most heavily defended part of the city only to pull back with a few captives and corpses? What were their *goals*?

He didn't understand. Not that understanding would have made the bloodshed any less horrific, but at least it would have made sense in his mind. He could predict a foe he could comprehend, but these raiders?

He didn't have a clue.

Nathan keyed the commect on his belt. "Aiko-One, you there?"

"Sure am. Hovering behind the factory."

"Set the ship down on the landing pad. We'll head your way as soon as we're finished here."

"You've got it, Nate. Heading that way now."

Nathan craned his neck to see the *Belle* ascend over the pyramid's peak and fly toward the city's outskirts.

"Also, I have some news," he added.

"Good or bad?"

"Little bit of both." His eyes fell on Aiko-Six's beheaded body, now splayed across a set of stairs leading up the outer wall.

"What's the good news?" she asked.

"You really tore those raiders a new one."

"Nice! And the bad?"

"You're down another body."

"*Wonderful,*" she moaned. "I need to be more careful."

"It was worth it, though."

"If you say so. Guess that means I'm Aiko-One-and-Only now."

"We'll buy you some new bodies after this job, I promise."

"At least there's that to look forward to. See you at the pad."

"See you." He switched off the commect.

Joshua pulled the rover in through the main gate, and Nathan waved him toward the stairs with Aiko-Six's body. The engineer parked the vehicle along the wall and climbed out.

"What next?" Joshua asked, handing back the key.

"We need to load what's left of Six onto the rover. Give me a hand, would you?"

"Sure thing."

"Nate?" came a muffled voice. "Hey, is that you? Can you hear me?"

Nathan paused and looked around. "Aiko?"

"Yeah. Over here."

He turned around in a circle, unable to pinpoint the source of the voice.

"Over *where*?"

"How should I know? All I see is dirt."

"There!" Joshua scurried over to an object glinting beside the stairs. He picked it up and presented it to Nathan with outstretched arms.

It was Aiko-Six's severed head.

"You're holding me upside down," she grumbled.

"Sorry!" Joshua turned the head over.

"I'm about to run out of juice," she told Nathan. "Make sure you pick up all my bits, okay?"

"We will. No need to worry."

"Don't forget my right arm. I think I dropped it somewhere up top."

"We'll find it."

"And my gun. The sinspike. I'm not sure where it went."

"Would you calm down already? We've got this."

"Okay. Just wanted to make sure. You know I love that thing. Shutting off."

Her cameras irised closed.

Joshua blinked down at the mechanical head. "Should I . . . um?" He cleared his throat. "What do you want me to do with this?"

"Stash it in the back of the rover, then come help me with the body."

CHAPTER EIGHTEEN

Vessani lent her father a shoulder. He braced himself with an arm around her neck, and together they rose to their feet.

"You all right?" she asked, supporting him with an arm around his waist.

"I will be, I'm sure." He patted her hand and then shifted his weight onto his own two legs. He watched Rufus kneel next to another nekoan. "I can already feel the cleric's medicine tingling through me."

"Panacea's great stuff, isn't it?" she said, perhaps with too much levity, given the carnage around them. She thought her father might scold her for her light, unserious tone, but instead he faced her with worry in his eyes.

"Are you leaving?"

His question took her aback, and she felt her response catch in her throat. She frowned and nodded to him.

"So soon?" he asked.

"We need to follow that ship."

"I know, but . . ." He trailed off, his eyes gravitating toward the pale ship's shrinking dot. "Does it have to be right away?"

"You know it does."

He lowered his head, then nodded slowly.

"It's not like we've never said goodbye before," she said.

"I know. And I'm sorry."

"For what?"

"For not supporting your decision."

"You let me go, didn't you?"

"Not because I agreed with you." He smiled sadly. "But because I knew you'd eventually find a way to leave regardless of what I wanted. The only way I could keep you here was to imprison you within your own home, and I could never do that."

She replied with her own crooked smile. "Were you tempted?"

"A little. But in the end, I resigned myself to support your decision. Which, really, was just an acknowledgment of how little control I truly held over my own daughter. Beyond that, recent events have shown me how right your mother was. It infuriated me how she would instill a sense of wanderlust in you, no matter how much I objected."

"There were a *lot* of bumps along the way," Vessani said. "I only told you the stories that made me look good."

"Of course, you faced challenges. I expected this, and so did your mother. But the difference between us, as I see it, is your mother always kept her eyes fixed on the future, on what was possible, while my vision has always stayed rooted in the now, as if pointed at my own feet. And now I see how much stronger her vision was. Your brother saw it, too."

"I wish he could have been here." One of the distant deifactories drew her gaze. Her brother Ket'Vin was there as part of his tour of the habitat, working to strengthen relations with the other nations.

"As do I, but he has his role to play, just as you have yours. We can't stay cooped up in here, no matter how dangerous the realm beyond our home might prove. We need to risk our first steps into those dark waters, because if we don't, something worse than these raiders might take an interest in us, and then what'll happen to our people? Our way of life?"

"You do realize I left for myself. Not for our people."

"I know. Doesn't change the fact that you're helping to realize your mother's vision."

"More than you know, if we're lucky."

D'Miir's ears perked up.

"It all hinges on us retrieving the Black Egg," Vessani said, "but Joshua found something in the deifactory. A production pattern that could help lift our people out of this low-tech mire. Ret'Su can fill you in."

"Truly?" He raised his ears and his tail swished.

Nearby, Nathan took hold of Aiko-Six's shoulders. Joshua grabbed her legs, and together they carried the body down the steps. They reached the rover's lowered rear gate and swung the body onto the shelf, then pushed it all the way inside before closing the gate.

"Think you'll be able to get her working again?" Joshua asked, wiping his hands.

"Not on my own," Nathan grumbled, then headed back up the stairs as if searching for something.

"This Joshua," D'Miir continued quietly. "Are you and he . . . ?"

"We are."

"Does he treat you well?"

"Like I'm royalty," she replied with a smile.

"I'm glad to hear that."

"And he's smart, too."

"That much is obvious. He's with you, after all."

Vessani giggled, and her tail twitched happily. Under different circumstances, she would have given her father a playful smack, but she didn't want to aggravate his injuries.

Nathan hurried down the steps and tossed a severed arm into the back of the Rover.

"Vess!" he called out. "I don't mean to rush you, but we're leaving as soon as Rufus finishes up!"

"Got it! I'm just saying my goodbyes!"

Nathan gave her a quick thumbs-up, then planted his hands on his hips and surveyed the area, checking for any Aiko-Six pieces he may have missed, she presumed.

"Captain Kade!" D'Miir raised his chin and walked toward Nathan. Vessani shadowed him by a step, ready in case his knees began to falter, but her father's stride held strong and true.

"Yes?" Nathan asked.

"Your companion fought well, bravely sacrificing herself to save those she had only just met. I don't believe I've ever seen such profound heroism and selflessness on display from an outsider!"

"Don't mention it," Nathan replied with a casual shrug. "That wasn't her first scrap with troublemakers."

"Indeed!" D'Miir glanced over the pile of mechanical parts in the back of the rover. "I'm sure you have your own burial rites to observe, but allow us to honor her in our own way. We shall erect a shrine dedicated to her." He extended both arms toward the stairs. "Right there, where she fell!"

"That's, umm . . ." Nathan frowned. "You really don't have to."

"But I insist. Her spirit may be gone, but we shall ensure her memory never dies!"

"Um, yeah, about that. Funny you should mention her memory."

Nathan's commect chimed before he could continue, and he keyed it.

"Go ahead."

"The ship's on the ground, Nate," Aiko-One reported.

"Good. We're wrapping up here and will be on our way shortly." He cleared his throat. "Also, you're not going to believe this, but the nekoans are going to build a shrine for Six."

"They *are*?" She sounded unusually excited by the news.

"Yeah. The king said so himself."

"Aww!" Aiko cooed. "That's so sweet!"

The *Neptune Belle* shadowed the pale ship on its flight from WC-9003. Nathan maintained a gap of a thousand kilometers between the two vessels while Aiko kept her eye on the ship through their telescope, observant for any sign of aggressive maneuvers or weapons fire.

Both ships accelerated in sync at a constant 1.2 gees with the nekoan cylinder retreating away beneath them, according to the *Belle*'s thrust orientation. If the crew of the pale ship knew they were being followed, they showed no sign of it.

Joshua, Vessani, and Rufus had joined the others in the cockpit and asked for Nathan's *Almanac*, which he handed over. Together, the three studied the pale ship's course and attempted to correlate it with the *Solar Almanac*'s entries for the local cluster.

All that changed about twenty-five minutes into their pursuit.

"They're turning around!" Aiko warned. "Everyone strapped in?"

Vessani and Joshua hurried back to their jump seats. Rufus was already seated.

"We're good," Vessani said, buckling in. "Go ahead."

"Now executing turnaround." Aiko throttled back to zero, flipped the ship, and reengaged their thrusters. "They made a course adjustment at the same time. A fairly big one, too. If you ask me, they aim to approach one of the nearby habitats from a specific angle."

"But which one?" Joshua wondered, scrolling through the *Almanac*.

"Not sure," Rufus said, "but I think I saw an entry in that general . . ." He trailed off, and his face darkened. "Nate, we need to brake harder."

"What? Why?"

"Because I know where they're heading, and we don't want to be anywhere near it." Rufus swallowed hard. "There's a habitat up ahead called the Sanguine Ring, and the Association rated it a Danger Eight."

"Oh, shit!" Aiko exclaimed. "He's right! Sorry about this, everyone! Hang on!" She maxed out the thrusters at 1.8 gees.

Gravity shoved Nathan into the pilot seat's cushioning, and he wheezed out an uncomfortable breath.

"Sorry!" Aiko checked her navigational vlass. "Okay, the added thrust should stop us about five thousand kilometers from the ring. Rufus, what's the entry say about the safe approach distance?"

"Four ships were lost near the ring: three to unknown causes, but one sent out a signal before it was destroyed. It was nine hundred kilometers away from the ring when automated defenses took it out. That was about a hundred years ago."

"Okay, then we should be good holding at five thousand." Aiko looked to Nathan for confirmation.

"Right." Nathan would have given her a nod, but his head felt like a leaden lump on the end of a wobbly stick. "We'll stop there and . . . think over our next move."

The Sanguine Ring was an open-ring habitat that lived up to its name, possessing a deep red exterior ribbed in baroque obsidian structures. Massive, spiked supports bracketed the atmospheric retention walls, extending far above it and bending outward at the tips. The habitable zone measured four hundred kilometers thick, and with the ring's twelve-hundred-kilometer radius, provided a surface over three million square kilometers in size. Surface gravity was precisely one gee.

The surface looked about as friendly as the rest of the place. Black vegetation dotted a corpse-white landscape shot through with crimson rivers and lakes. The sun-orb brightened for a new dawn, braced in the ring's center by five narrow spokes. The pale ship had landed on an unusually large deifactory situated on the largest continent.

"So cheery." Nathan unbuckled and floated out of the pilot seat. "Rufus?"

"Yes?" The cleric looked away from the ring.

"Theological question for you." He pointed at the ring. "Why would the Pentatheon build a monstrosity like this?"

"Because they were asked to," Rufus replied simply.

"But *why*?"

"I'm sure the ancients who asked for it had their reasons."

"And those reasons might be . . . what?"

Rufus spent a few seconds soaking in the Sanguine Ring's aesthetic. He felt as if his eyeballs would start bleeding if he stared too long.

"I can only speculate," he said at last.

"Right," Nathan breathed. "So, what now, people?"

"If you ask me," Aiko said, "at least some of those spiky parts are defensive systems. And with the way they bend outward, there are no safe approach angles, which seems to be the point. We can't hide in the ring's shadow during our approach and expect that to keep us safe."

"The raiders flew straight in without an issue," Vessani noted. "We have their approach path and their landing coordinates. We *could* give it a try."

"We could." Nathan crossed his arms. "It's possible the defenses won't lash out at ships approaching along a specific corridor. But if we're wrong, we're dead. That's not much of a plan in my book."

"Yeah," Vessani sighed, then glanced to Joshua. "How about you? Any ideas?"

"Not sure," the engineer replied. "I'm wondering if the pale ship carries a device of some sort that restricts the ring's defenses. If so, maybe we could follow them the next time they leave and try to snatch it?"

He didn't sound convinced by his own words.

"*If* such a device even exists," Nathan said. "Plus, those cyborgs don't go down easily. They're not handing over their goodies without a fight."

Aiko thumped her chest. "I still have my commando body."

"Which is the *only* body you have left."

The cockpit fell silent, and Rufus once again stared at the ring, pondering, wondering. Something tugged at him the longer he gazed upon the ring, and a hint of alien thoughts brushed whispered words across the boundaries of his consciousness.

He closed his eyes and recited a short prayer to Edencraft to clear his mind. The physical world shrank away, and the *Belle*'s cockpit became nothing more than a muffled, veiled memory. He delved inward, into his own mind, reaching toward the hints and murmurs of thought echoing within own consciousness.

He recited the same prayer over and over again, using it to cleanse his mind of distractions.

And then he found the juncture.

Or did the juncture find him? He was never sure about that.

The Sanguine Ring materialized before his closed eyes. Not the baroque, physical ring, but a manifestation of data given physical form. Here, it resembled a band of hot, radiant gold traced with silver paths that pulsed and rippled with the remnants of ancient god-thoughts. An angry red web of gridlines surrounded the structure, and he wondered if this represented the bounds of its active defenses. He reached an imaginary hand toward the imaginary ring and pulled it close, his consciousness integrating with these virtual echoes.

The ring stood ready to hear him.

A jolt of excitement shot through his mind, but he suppressed it and redoubled his concentration. The ring would hear him, but whether it would *acquiesce* to his wishes was another matter entirely.

He formulated a simple, direct message and practiced it, the words soft and private for the moment. Some junctures were temperamental when it came to hearing requests, and a poorly formulated or recited message could cause the ring to flinch back in mental revulsion, reverting to a more guarded state. Perhaps breaking off contact entirely.

But Rufus had dedicated most of his life to achieving his current level of mental discipline. He knew on an instinctive level how to approach a juncture this wild, and he conveyed his wish with confidence and care.

Edencraft, creator of this ring, grant us safe passage to the surface.

Nothing happened at first, though Rufus sensed a ripple of some sort, a response that spread through the illusory golden ring. A sense of great deliberation welled up nearby, just beyond his virtual sight, followed by changes to the ring's visualization. The web that enveloped the ring faded from red to a calmer shade of pink, and a green, funnel-shaped grid extended from the *Belle* down to the surface.

He opened his eyes and caught the tail end of a debate.

"—we're not about to sit here waiting for the heat death of the universe," Nathan said.

"But—" Joshua began.

Rufus cleared his throat, and the discourse died down.

"This ring has an active juncture," the cleric said once he had everyone's attention. "It took some doing, but I was able to commune with it and pass on our request for safe passage."

"And?" Nathan asked.

"The ring responded. We're clear to land."

"You sure about that?"

"Yes."

"Absolutely sure?"

"Yes. Absolutely."

Nathan paused for a moment, checking Rufus's eyes for any doubt. He must have found none because he nodded and strapped himself into the pilot seat.

"All right, I'm taking us in. Aiko, keep your eyes on those defenses. Let me know if they so much as look at us funny."

"You've got it, Nate."

Rufus joined Vessani and Joshua and strapped into a jump seat along the back of the cockpit. Nathan plotted a course that would bring them down in the general vicinity of the pale ship, near the deifactory. He eased the throttle up, and the *Belle* accelerated toward the ring. The cockpit fell silent as everyone watched the ring grow larger.

"Four thousand kilometers," Nathan called out, his attention split between the ring and his console.

"No sign of activity from the ring," Aiko said. "So far so good."

"It'll be fine." Rufus leaned back and closed his eyes.

"I'm not doubting you," Nathan said. "But I *am* doubting that shady-as-hell ring."

The *Belle* sped in, angling to pass over the top of the retention wall near the pale ship's landing zone.

"Two thousand kilometers," Nathan said.

Another lengthy period of silence.

"One thousand kilometers," Nathan reported, and a twinge of worry leaked through his voice. "Reorienting for atmospheric entry."

He cut their thrust and tilted the ship to face their destination. They glided in, the distance to the ring dropping off rapidly. It fell below nine hundred and . . .

Nothing happened.

Rufus let out a relieved exhalation. He hadn't realized he'd been holding the breath in.

Nathan applied small bursts of thrust to adjust the angle of their approach. They sped over the retention wall, passing through the gap between two giant, outward-bent spikes.

"Whew!" Nathan gave their passengers a thumbs-up without turning. "Good job, Rufus."

"Thanks. Always a pleasure to help."

"Now, let's see if we can find a good spot to—"

A simulation *smashed* into Rufus's mind, and he gasped from the sudden mental impact. His neck snapped back and his eyes shot open while his vision blurred. Darkness seeped into the edges of his sight, and the world retreated except for the sudden appearance of a golden, almost melted ring, now a thick, gargantuan loop around him. Vibrant red pulsed up through the nearest spikes and gathered in tips that bent toward him.

He tried to form words with his lips, to enunciate a warning to the others, but all he managed was a muted gurgle.

The vision ended, and he slumped in his seat, gasping for air.

"You okay back there?" Nathan asked without turning.

Aiko's console bleeped and flashed red. "Movement! The nearest spikes are doing something!"

"Too late to turn back!" Nathan tilted the nose down toward the ring's surface and fired the thrusters at full power. One-point-eight gees slammed everyone into their seats.

Something screamed into Rufus's ears, its deafening, enraged roar carrying all the fury of a nuclear furnace. He couldn't tell if it was real or not. He clenched his eyes shut so hard they watered. His mind reached out for the juncture, only to find it churning and bubbling like an invisible sea of rage and pain, and he cried out to it:

Edencraft, have mercy on us! We meant no offense!

"Activity on the spikes!" Aiko shouted. "Energy fire detected! It's—" She paused, then twisted around in her seat. "It's firing at something behind us!"

"What the hell?" Nathan tried to spot the other object. A distant point above and behind them glowed like a new star. It turned white hot before disintegrating into a long streamer of spreading, glowing particles.

"I caught a glimpse of it!" Aiko said. "I'm not sure, but I think that might have been another ship!"

"Not anymore!" Nathan checked his console. "Thirty seconds to atmosphere, people!"

"Nate!" Aiko cried. "Those spikes are still active! I think they're about to shoot at us!"

"Oh, hell!" he gasped. "Hang on, everyone!"

Please, spare us!

The world flashed brilliant orange, even through his eyelids, and a thousand tiny explosions rumbled through the ship. Someone screamed, maybe Vessani, maybe himself.

SPARE US, I BEG YOU!

The glow vanished. Rufus swallowed with a dry throat and blinked his stunned eyes open.

"It . . . it stopped!" Aiko exclaimed. "They stopped shooting!"

"No time to celebrate," Nathan warned, struggling with the controls. "We've got thermal alerts all over the place. The back half of the ship must be *glowing!*"

The *Belle* shuddered and wobbled, and the air outside thickened.

"We need to slow down!" Aiko said. "We're coming in too fast!"

"I'll try!" Nathan replied, his face stern and focused. "But the reactor's not happy right now!"

He jerked on the flight stick, and the ship lurched to the side. He fought for control, and the ship began to straighten out. But then a sound like tearing metal ripped through the vessel, ending with a loud, ugly bang.

"What was *that*?" Nathan snapped.

"A piece of the ship broke off!" Aiko shouted. "And I think it took part of the reactor with it! Two of the three toruses are *dead*, and the one that isn't is shaky!"

The pale ground rushed up to meet them.

"Everyone, brace for impact!" Nathan yelled.

"Nate! You see that lake?"

"I see it! What do you want me to *do* about it?!"

"Use it to soften the landing!"

"This is *not* a landing!"

The *Belle* swept over the bloodred lake, and the bottom plowed through the murky water. The sudden drag jerked Rufus against his straps. Water and red algae spewed into the air on either side of the ship. The vessel sank half a deck in, cutting a rippling furrow through the liquid, while a rocky shoreline loomed large ahead.

"Here it comes!" Nathan cried, wincing.

The *Neptune Belle* struck the cliff face with its bottom two decks, blasting sand and rocks into the air. Metal screeched and crumpled, and the *Belle* punched through, became airborne again as if taking off from a ramp, and then it slammed back down on its belly and skidded forward to a halt.

CHAPTER NINETEEN

Nathan shambled through the broken hull of the *Neptune Belle* in something of a daze, his mind unable—or unwilling—to come to grips with the devastation of the crash.

The ship had belonged to three generations of Kades, and its corridors had been his home for his entire life. It was as integral a part of his identity as his own flesh and blood. And now it lay ruined upon a desolate beach on a godsforsaken ring, its lower decks crushed against the rocky shore, the back of the ship sagging and half melted.

The cockpit had survived mostly intact and now protruded above the shore at a shallow incline. Nathan supposed he should be grateful for that much. Everyone was alive, and that counted for something. The crash had tossed them around, but no one had suffered so much as a broken bone. Rufus had administered a small shot of panacea to each organic crew member as a precaution, and Nathan could understand why.

The crash might not have inflicted obvious injuries, but he didn't doubt for a second his muscles would be screaming at him in a few hours, possibly seizing up at the worst possible moment. The panacea would preemptively soothe their overtaxed bodies, keeping them limber and mobile for . . . whatever came next.

Nathan knew he should be focused on the challenges to come, but he couldn't see past the broken piece of his life he now shuffled through. Aiko seemed to understand what the ship meant to him and why he needed some space in this moment, some time to decompress recent events in his own head. She'd mobilized the others, and together they continued to scrounge through the ship's wreckage for anything useful.

Food, medicine, survival gear.

And weapons.

They'd need those if the raiders investigated the crash, which he considered likely. They'd "landed" about twenty kilometers anti-spinward of the deifactory, and those cyborgs didn't strike him as the kind who welcomed visitors with open arms.

He came to the freight elevator shaft and stopped at the edge. A kink in the hull had dislodged the elevator from its guide rails so that it sat at an angle between A and B decks. He didn't know how stable it was, so he took a ladder down one level and made his way through the adjoining corridor to the mess.

Aiko or someone else had raided the pantry, organizing its contents into groups of useful supplies on the kitchen counter: rations, water bottles that doubled as purifiers, and backpacks to carry everything. Perishable ingredients lay scattered across the floor alongside pots, pans, cooking utensils, and a massive collection of spice shakers, many busted open with their granular contents strewn across the deck. The whole place reeked of too much salt and seasoning.

Nathan stopped at the dinner table and placed a hand on the slanted surface. Beany had coiled its branches around its body in what appeared to be a defensive gesture, and the sight of the plant cowering over the table sent a new jolt of sadness through his being. The poor plantlike . . . thing couldn't know what was happening.

"I'm sorry, Beany," Nathan said. He found a pitcher on the kitchen floor, filled it with water from the tap, and poured the contents into Beany's soil. "Wish I could do more for you, buddy. Last round is on me, I guess."

Beany uncoiled one of its branches and stretched it out, almost touching Nathan's face.

"No, thanks." He pushed the branch aside and gave the plant a sad smile. "I'm not thirsty."

Beany shook the branch at him, and the tip scratched his face.

"I'm really sorry."

The plant kept the first branch extended, then uncoiled a second that crossed the first at a right angle a half meter from the tip. The second branch sawed back and forth in a slow, deliberate gesture Nathan had never seen the plant use before. He then realized that neither of the branches held coffee bulbs.

He wasn't being offered a drink.

"Wait a second." He frowned at the plant. "If this isn't about coffee, then . . . are you trying to tell me something?"

The branches shuddered with what might have been excitement and then resumed their pantomime. The more Nathan watched, the more it reminded him of a wood saw working through a branch.

"Do you want me to take a cutting?"

The branches shook again. One retracted while the other curved to present its side. Nearby leaves bent away, presenting an unobstructed gap for him to cut through.

"All right. If that's what you want, buddy." Nathan pulled out his vibro-knife and thumbed it on. "Here goes."

He sank the blade through the branch and cut it free. Beany's leaves rustled, and the remains of the branch recoiled back into its defensive cocoon.

"Sorry!"

Nathan took the branch back to the kitchen. He picked up an unbroken spice shaker about the right size, emptied its remaining contents, then filled it with water. He found a roll of tape in a cabinet, placed the bottom half of the branch in the bottle, and secured and waterproofed the top with tape.

"I'll make sure this finds a good home," he told the plant, storing the cutting in his jacket's inner pocket. "I promise you."

The plant extended another branch to him, this one laden with coffee bulbs.

Nathan chuckled, despite his dark mood.

"Sure. One more for the road." He plucked the largest bulb and chugged it. A runnel of coffee dripped down his neck, and he wiped it away with a satisfied sigh. "Delicious as always!"

"Nate."

He tossed the bulb aside and turned to find Aiko standing in the corridor leading back to the elevator shaft.

"Hey," he said.

"You all right?"

"No. But I've sulked enough. Where's everyone else?"

"Outside."

"Were you able to get the rover out?"

"No point. The crash flattened it."

"Just our luck." He gave her a determined grimace. "Then we walk."

"Walk where?"

"That's the question, isn't it? Let's go talk to the others."

Nathan followed Aiko back to the elevator shaft and down the recessed ladder. What was left of the cargo hold had been crushed down to less than a deck, which forced him to crouch-walk over to the tear in the ship's side.

The surface was as uninviting as the rest of the ring. High above, the sun-orb continued to brighten, revealing a landscape covered in loose, rain-slicked rocks. Dark waters lapped at the bleached bone shoreline, and the fallen, bloodred leaves from a nearby forest spattered the landscape. The air stank of newly fallen rain, and mist rose from the rocks, thickening around their ankles. His skin felt clammy from the heat and moisture.

Vessani, Joshua, and Rufus stood in the shadow of the *Neptune Belle*'s cockpit, each with pistols in their hands. Vessani was in the process of putting on her armor.

"Where's my hard suit?" Nathan asked.

"Smooshed with the rest of the cargo hold," Aiko said. "You're welcome to go digging."

He let out a despondent grunt.

Vessani climbed to her feet and retrieved her wraithbane pistol from the ground. She checked the weapon with the obvious signs of prior experience, then holstered it, looking ready for whatever this ring could throw at them.

The other two, not so much.

Aiko had provided the two men with pistols from her collection. Joshua sat on a rock, his head lowered, eyes staring at something on the ground but not truly looking at it. He held the pistol limply in one hand, its barrel aimed at his foot. Rufus had placed his across his lap and stared at it, seemingly hesitant to even touch the weapon.

"Do you two gents know how to use those?" Nathan asked.

"Not really." Rufus massaged his bald head, perhaps feeling the absence of a wig. "Aiko just handed me one."

"Me neither, but how hard can it be?" Joshua replied, his words doing nothing to assure Nathan this was a good idea.

"You planning to shoot your own foot off?" he asked pointedly.

"No."

"Then stop aiming at it. The last thing we need is you ventilating your own foot."

Joshua frowned at the pistol. "But the safety's on."

"Listen to me. Firearms Rule One is only point them at things you want dead, and since you're not trying to murder your own foot, aim it somewhere else."

"Okay." Joshua adjusted his grip on his weapon. "I guess that makes sense."

"It makes a *lot* of sense. I see one of you point those the wrong way, I'm taking them back. Clear?"

"Clear, Nate," Rufus said.

"Yes," Joshua said. "Very clear."

"By the way." Rufus looked up sadly, then glanced over at the twisted cargo ramp. "Not that it matters all much, but I'm sorry, Nate."

"Don't be," Nathan replied, meaning it. "We knew the risks when we came here. And you did the best you could."

"I know. I just . . . it *should* have worked!"

"It did," Aiko said. "Up until that mystery ship flew too close, and the ring went nuts."

Rufus opened his mouth, but then hesitated and closed it again. He sighed and nodded.

"Any thoughts on who they were?" Joshua asked.

"Doesn't matter," Nathan said. "They're dead now, and we've got our own problems to sort out." He strode out from under the cockpit's shade and gazed at the distant deifactory. "Speaking of which, the way I see it, we've only got one option."

"I wasn't aware we had *any*," Vessani said, her helmet held in the crook of her arm.

"I didn't say it was a good one." He faced the team and pointed a thumb over his shoulder at the deifactory. "We need to get off this ring, which means we need a ship. And as it turns out, there's a ship nearby with a depleted crew."

"You're suggesting we steal the pale ship?" Vessani asked.

"That's exactly what I'm saying." He gestured to the nearby forest.

"From the looks of it, we can stick to the woods easily enough and use it for cover all the way to the deifactory. From there, we scope out where their ugly ship is and, when we spot an opening, we move in and grab it."

"That crew may have been reinforced," Vessani said. "There could be more raiders in the deifactory. A *lot* more, for all we know."

"I'm listening if anyone has a better idea."

"What about sending out a distress call and waiting?" Joshua suggested. "I assume the *Belle* has an emergency beacon."

"It does, but all we'd do is kill whoever came looking for us."

"Ah." Joshua lowered his head. "Right."

"Anyone else?" Nathan asked.

The assembled team glanced to each other.

"There's no way we can fix the *Belle* on our own," Joshua said.

"Which is why we need another ship." Nathan gazed back to the deifactory just as a tiny point of light rose from its slopes. "Like that one."

The point of light accelerated into a long curve that took it over the forest.

"Is it just me," Vessani said, "or is it heading our way?"

"Sure looks like it." Nathan placed a hand on his holstered pistol. "We should hide while we still can. They might search the ship, so if we want to avoid a fight . . ." His eyes gravitated to the dark, dank forest nearby.

Nathan and the others retreated up a shallow incline and past an outer boundary of trees, if the local vegetation could be called such. They resembled baseline deciduous trees with thick, tough trunks leading up to leafing crowns, but that's where the similarities ended. Black, wrinkled skin covered the trunks, which writhed to a slow, steady rhythm not unlike a heartbeat, and fat yellowed polyps hung from their branches, oozing pus-like fluids. A foul, fetid odor hung heavy in the air.

Their feet squelched in the damp soil, and insects accosted them almost immediately. Nathan swatted his way through a buzzing swarm of flies, which dispersed and retreated deeper into the forest. Long-legged spiders as big as his hand crept along the tree trunks or hung from coarse strands, and roaches scurried about the ground.

A high-pitched screech pierced the forest, and everyone snapped to face the dark recesses behind them. A second screech followed, then what sounded like a pained yelp, a whimper, and finally silence.

"What was *that*?" Joshua hissed, apprehension twisting his face.

"Something we don't want to mess with," Nathan whispered.

The heat of the sun-orb cooked off much of the moisture on the ground, and the fog thickened, settling along the edges of the forest like a cotton blanket, tendrils sliding in through the gaps between trees. The fog and overhead canopy made keeping an eye on the incoming ship difficult, and Nathan lost sight of it until the craft was almost on top of them.

They crouched and waited.

The pale ship slowed to a hover, then dropped down to a rocky flat next to the *Belle*'s wreckage. A hole yawned open in the side of the ship, and six raiders disembarked with swords and pikes ready. Four spread out around the wreckage while two headed in.

That was six fewer problems inside the pale ship.

Nathan shuffled over until he squatted between Aiko and Vessani. "You two thinking what I'm thinking?"

"You mean with their ship just sitting there"—Vessani flashed a crooked smile—"all ripe for the taking?"

"Exactly." Nathan winked at her, then motioned Rufus and Joshua to lean in close. "Huddle up, everyone."

They formed a tight, crouching circle.

"This might be the best chance we'll ever get," Aiko whispered. "How do you want to handle this?"

"Aiko, take Vess with you," Nathan began. "Follow the woods to the left and circle around. Try to get as close to the ship as you can. Between your commando body and your hard suit, you two are the best equipped to grab that ship." He patted the commect on his belt and switched it to silent. "Call when you're ready. Us guys will stay here and make some noise for you, then fade back deeper into the woods. With a little luck, we'll draw enough of them toward us and clear the path for you."

"While we slip into the ship," Aiko finished.

"You've got it. Any questions, people?"

"None here." Vessani fitted her helmet on and sealed up.

"What do you mean by 'make some noise'?" Joshua asked.

"We're going to rile them up by shooting at them," Nathan explained.

"But I've never fired a gun before!"

"All you really need to do is not shoot yourself or us, then run when I say so. We're the distraction, got it? Think you can manage?"

Joshua grimaced, but then gave him a slow nod.

"Good. How about you, Rufus?"

"I will endeavor not to shoot myself," the cleric replied dryly.

Nathan pulled away from the group and checked the crash site. The raiders were still searching the wreckage, and the two closest cyborgs had even sheathed their swords.

"Looks clear enough. Go!"

Aiko and Vessani rose and hustled to the left.

Nathan crept a little closer to the edge of the forest and put his shoulder against a wrinkled tree trunk. He could feel the damned thing *pulsating*, which sent a shudder of revulsion down his spine. Wind blew in from the shoreline, and the fog grew heavier, rolling around the pale ship in thick ribbons.

He waited a few minutes before his commect vibrated, then raised it to his ear.

"Go ahead, Aiko."

"We're as close as we're going to get without exposing ourselves."

"Got it. Wait for—"

Joshua shook Nathan's shoulder urgently.

"What?" Nathan hissed through clenched teeth.

"There's something behind us!" Joshua hissed back.

Nathan spun around and followed the direction of Joshua's gaze.

A low, heavy shadow crept toward them on thick, muscular legs that padded through the underbrush with barely a sound. It passed under a break in the canopy, and a shaft of light gleamed off moist skin.

Nathan's first impression was of a white, hairless lion. A mass of flesh tendrils writhed where the mane should have been, matted in places with grime. Its bloodred lips parted into a vicious, almost human grin to reveal rows of translucent teeth. He couldn't spot any obvious eyes on the hideous creature.

"Aw, hell," he groaned and raised his pistol.

The eyeless lion stood up on its haunches and screeched, spewing flecks of saliva from its ruddy lips. The noise rattled Nathan's eardrums, but he kept his eyes and gun locked on the creature. The beast brought its front legs down. Translucent claws sank into the earth, and then it launched itself forward.

Nathan dove out of the way and fired. Bullets tore through the creature's mouth and flank. It swiped at him and missed, claws tearing through a tree's flesh-bark in a spray of black, oily sap.

The monster landed heavily, turned and snarled at him. Nathan scrambled to his feet and backed away. He cut loose, firing until his weapon ran dry. Bullets pierced the creature's flesh all along its side. It took one more step toward him, lost its footing, and slumped to the ground with a defeated gurgle.

Nathan pulled a fresh magazine from his bandolier and rammed it home.

"We've been spotted!" Rufus reported. "They're heading this way!"

"No kidding!" Nathan snapped. "Shoot them!"

Their trio of pistols cracked, and both Rufus and Joshua struggled to control their weapons. Nathan doubted either of them could hit the *Belle* at this range, let alone the four cyborgs dashing toward them through the fog.

Nathan sighted on the closest raider and opened fire. The raider's chest blew open with a burst of gore and ruined machinery. He stumbled forward, righted himself, and kept coming.

Nathan pummeled the cyborg until his head snapped back, his feet slipped out from under him, and he collapsed onto his back.

Three raiders charged up the incline, and Nathan kept firing and reloading, but soon a roar from above and behind him demanded his attention. Not a beastly bellow, but the consistent monotone of powerful technology. The fog overhead parted, and the metal spikes of a *second* pale ship slid into view. The ugly craft flew in low, its belly brushing past the tree canopies.

"Above us!" Rufus shouted.

A pair of openings gaped wide on either side of the second ship, and raiders began roping down into the forest.

"Run!" Nathan shouted. "Deeper into the woods!" He keyed his commect. "Ladies, we're running for it! You're on your own!"

He didn't wait for the response. The first raider let go of his rope and landed beside him, almost right next to him. He blew the cyborg's face off and sprinted past. Another raider snagged his rope on a tree branch and let go, dropping the rest of the way to land on his hands and knees. Nathan hurried through the uneven terrain and shot at him, but his bullets flew wide.

He grabbed another magazine off his bandolier and checked on his companions.

Joshua's foot caught on a root, and he stumbled forward, but Rufus held out an arm and caught him before he fell. They ran on, both keeping pace with Nathan while raiders converged on the three men.

"Keep going!" Nathan planted his feet and raised his weapon. "Move it, you two!"

They dashed past him. He unloaded several shots, downing or stalling two more raiders, then turned and followed them.

"Where are we going?" Joshua shouted.

"Away from *them*!" Nathan barked. "Move, move, move!"

The canopy grew thicker, and the forest denser and darker. The moist soil gave with each step, sucking and tugging at their boots. They splashed through the edge of a shallow, murky pool, which frothed with each stride as they dragged crimson algae floaters behind them.

That second pale ship slid past overhead, the roar of its thrusters assaulting their ears. Ropes dangled from the side openings, catching and tearing at the dense canopy. Another pair of raiders grabbed the ropes and dropped down ahead of the three men.

Followed by several more.

The raiders kept coming, and Rufus staggered to a halt, chest heaving, the damp ground sucking on his boots. Joshua ran into his back, and the pair almost fell over. Nathan turned in a quick circle, searching for a path to safety.

He found none. The raiders had formed into a loose but contracting loop around their position. They were about to be neck deep in swords and cyborgs.

"Nate?" Rufus pleaded.

His mind raced.

"We punch through!" Nathan picked what seemed to be the weakest part of the entrapment. "This way!"

Nathan lit up one of the cyborgs. Chunks of flesh exploded off his chest and arms. The raider dropped to his knees and plopped face-first into the muck. Nathan ran toward the gap in their lines, but the soggy, spongy terrain fought him every step of the way. Joshua tripped and fell into the mud with a large splash.

"Here!" Nathan hurried back and extended a hand. Joshua grabbed hold of his forearm, and he hauled the engineer back up to his feet—

—moments before a raider tackled him from the side. The force of the blow threw Nathan to the ground, and the pair splashed through the surface scum with the raider on top. He punched the raider in the face, but all that did was cut open his hand. The raider headbutted him, and stars swam across his vision.

Nathan's pistol slipped from his grasp, and it *plooped* into the mud and sank underneath the surface. Nathan groped at his belt, yanked his vibro-knife free, and switched it on. The blade hummed to life, shedding mud from its oscillating, translucent edge.

He stabbed the raider in the side of his gut.

The cyborg grabbed him by the throat and squeezed.

Nathan gasped and drove the blade up into the raider's rib cage, then through his shoulder. The fingers at his throat lost their strength, and Nathan scrambled out from under the wounded, bleeding cyborg.

A blow from an unseen assailant thumped into the back of Nathan's head, and he spun and dropped to his side. His vision swam, even worse than before. He sensed motion to his right and swiped drunkenly at it, but another blow cracked against his shoulder, and he dropped down into the slime on his side.

His vision began to clear, and one of the shapes resolved into a raider. That one planted a boot on Nathan's wrist and pressed down with enough force to squeeze out a pained groan.

Nathan tried to push the leg off, but a second raider grabbed his arm and pinned it back. He stared up at the raiders. Four metal eyes stared back.

"I'm sorry," he groaned with an insincere smile. "We seem to be lost. Can you point the way off this ring?"

The second raider grabbed a fistful of Nathan's hair and placed the tip of an active vibro-sword against his throat. Nathan swallowed audibly. That little bit of motion was enough for the blade to draw blood.

CHAPTER TWENTY

The interior of the pale ship was less of a horror show than Nathan had expected. He wasn't sure what he thought he'd find when the raiders dragged him and the other two inside. Humid, mucus-lined corridors? Flesh-walls covered in the screaming faces of their victims? A giant, beating heart for a reactor?

The reality was almost disappointingly mundane. The unusual exterior of the pale ships seemed to be mostly cosmetic, and besides the glaring orange lights, the interior resembled any other spacecraft.

Nathan tried to free his arms—now bound behind his back—but only succeeded in chafing his wrists against the metallic rope the raiders had used. Rufus and Joshua sat next to him in the same cell, all three of them caked with mud. They'd been relieved of their weapons and gear, though not all of it. Rufus still retained the equipment on his belt, Joshua his glass pocket watch, and Nathan the Beany cutting stuffed into his jacket.

Not that *any* of those would prove helpful, even if their hands weren't bound.

"Where do you think they're taking us?" Rufus asked.

"The deifactory," Nathan guessed.

"What for?"

"Wish I knew." He paused and considered his words again. "Or maybe I don't."

The flight over didn't take long. The cell lacked windows, but Nathan could feel the ship slow and then land with more grace than he gave the raiders credit for. It seemed they *could* pilot their ships without crashing them through random buildings.

The cell door opened, and pairs of raiders came to collect them. One pair grabbed Nathan's bound arms and hauled him to his feet. He didn't see the point of resisting, at least not yet, and so he allowed the cyborgs to manhandle him.

The raiders escorted them out of the ship, and Nathan took in their surroundings. Wind whipped across a wide, circular landing platform that jutted out the side of the deifactory, perhaps a tenth of the way up. Two pale ships sat on the pad, including the one they'd arrived in, each boasting a unique mix of spiky ornamentation.

He spotted smoke rising from the *Neptune Belle*'s wreckage, which sat at the end of a short furrow between the lake and the edge of the forest. Another pale ship flew in from that direction, and Nathan wondered if Aiko and Vess had managed to seize the vessel, but those hopes were dashed when the third pale ship settled onto to the pad next to the others.

"Guess not," he muttered.

One of the raiders gave his shoulder a shove, and he let himself be corralled across the platform and into the deifactory. Massive cylindrical machines towered on either side of a dimly lit path, and narrow passages branched out through gaps between the machines, peeling off to either side at regular intervals. Light spilled through those openings, and the noise of human activity echoed from distant rooms: the scraping of feet, the slurping of meals, the banging of tools.

But no words.

No conversations.

No laughter or tears.

Not so much as a single whisper.

The raiders escorted them through the factory, and the human activity around them grew denser. They passed a group of female cyborgs heading in the opposite direction, many with pregnant bulges pressing against their long, leather cloaks. None of the women so much as looked their way.

"We're in deep, aren't we?" Joshua said under his breath.

"Yup." Nathan supposed he should have tried to put on a brave face, but if there was a glimmer of hope in their situation, he couldn't spot it.

"Have faith, you two," Rufus said. "We'll get out of this."

"You have a plan?"

"Nate, the cyborgs are mute, not deaf."

"Right, right. Silly me."

"But no, I don't."

The raiders took them by the shoulders and shoved them down a side passage single file until the path opened into a long, rectangular room with a low ceiling. Orange lights shone across rows of gleaming metal tables, some occupied by naked raiders.

"Is this where they sleep?" Joshua wondered aloud.

"Don't think so," Rufus said. "See how they're strapped in?"

A hunched cyborg with matted, graying hair and a cluster of five large eyes for a face shuffled over to an occupied table. Two mechanical arms sprouted off his back. His extra arms reached toward a wall rack and grabbed a pair of objects: a hammer and a fist-sized orb with a thick spike on one end. He inspected the body on the table, placed the tip of the spike against the cyborg's ribs, and then hammered it in with a fierce blow.

The cyborg on the table twitched. Blood oozed from around the spike.

Joshua cringed.

"That's *not* how you do that," Rufus whispered with a shake of his head.

"I'll let you know if I spot their suggestion box," Nathan muttered.

The raiders brought the prisoners to a halt, and the cyborg surgeon walked over. He inspected Nathan first. Three hands grabbed the captain's head, forced it left and right, then worked their way down his body, poking and prodding without any sense of personal space. One of the metal hands reached in between Nathan's legs, and he jumped from the sudden pressure.

"Hey, there!" he snapped. "Back off! We only just met!"

The surgeon paused. Three of his eyes swiveled up and focused on Nathan's face, then swiveled away. The surgeon continued his inspection.

So they can *hear us,* Nathan thought. *And perhaps even understand us.*

The surgeon moved on to Joshua and then Rufus. He spent several minutes poking at the nubs along the cleric's scalp before moving on to jab at the rest of his body. Once finished, the surgeon

backed off without a word, and the raiders marched the three men to
the far end of the room, past rows of strapped-down cyborgs.

"There's a nekoan on the table ahead," Rufus said.

Nathan followed the cleric's gaze to a table with a black-haired
nekoan male. The victim's eyes were closed, but his ears and tail
twitched. Two spiked devices had been driven into his chest, both
undulating as they pumped . . . *something* into him.

"Oh, hell," Nathan groaned. "We're in trouble."

"How is this news?" Joshua breathed.

"Because *that's* why they kidnap people."

The raiders marched them to the far side of the room. A dense
row of cells lined the wall, each barely large enough for a person to
stand or sit in and composed of transparent doors and transparent
walls to either side. A caramel-haired nekoan male in tattered T'Ohai
livery crouched in one of the cells, his head slumped against his
knees. He looked up when the raiders stuffed Nathan and the others
into the next three cells.

"Hey there," Nathan greeted their fellow prisoner, unsure what
else to say in a situation like this.

The nekoan responded in their guttural, growling language.

"Sorry," Nathan replied. "I don't understand your language."

"You. Speak crafted?"

"The crafted tongue? Yes, I understand it."

"I, um, a little. Not good. I born, um, not capital."

"It's all right." Nathan leaned against the wall between him and
the nekoan. "Your crafted is better than my nekoan. What's your
name?"

"Name? Dezzo K'Lannet va T'Ohai. You?"

"Nathan Kade. Were you taken from the palace?"

Dezzo's brow wrinkled and he shook his head. He didn't seem to
understand.

"You serve King D'Miir S'Kaari?" Nathan asked, trying a different
approach.

"Yes. My king. I, um, soldier." His ears drooped. "Strong, but
v'zegget stronger."

Nathan bobbed his head toward the cyborgs. "*V'zegget?*"

"Yes. I not know crafted word."

"That's all right. We're still having a good conversation, aren't we?"

Dezzo shook his head again.

"A good talk?" Nathan tried.

"Yes." The nekoan's eyes lit up and his ears perked despite their predicament. "Good talk."

"Were you brought here alone?"

"No. Not alone."

"Where are the others?"

"There." Dezzo indicated the rows of tables with a chin bob. "Their heads, um, hurt."

"The raiders drive implant stakes into the backs of people's heads," Rufus explained.

"How do you know that?" Nathan asked.

"From the corpse Aiko and I examined. We didn't have time to take a look inside the head, but I'm guessing the stakes introduce a web of connections to the brain. My own implants would look similar if you cracked my head open. They're using these implants to communicate with each other."

"Then you can hear them?"

"Sometimes, but all I pick up is nonsensical buzzing and clicking."

"Does knowing that help us?" Joshua asked.

"I'm afraid not," Rufus said with a frown.

Joshua kicked the clear door, but it didn't budge. "Does *anyone* have an idea on how we get out of this?"

"Still working on it," Nathan said, even as he struggled with his own sense of hopelessness. "How about you, Dezzo? Do you have an escape plan?"

"No escape."

"Chin up. There's always hope."

"No. No hope." Dezzo let his head slump back between his knees.

The room fell silent on that depressing note. Nathan watched the cyborg surgeon conduct his rounds, hammering machinery into each victim. Those mechanisms seemed to come to life afterward, and some blossomed open like horrific flowers made of scalpels and syringes instead of petals. Others contracted, forcing their contents into twitching, convulsing victims.

Nathan wasn't sure how long he watched the surgeon work. An hour? Two? Maybe more? It was mesmerizing in a grotesque, unsettling way. When the surgeon finished impaling the last of his "patients," he trudged over to the row of cells, his many eyes scanning across the selection of raw material.

Two raiders opened Dezzo's cell and reached for him. At first, he let them drag his slack body to its fate, but then his ears stood erect, and his eyes gleamed with sudden sharpness. He launched himself between the two raiders and threaded the space between them. They groped for him but missed and he sprinted across the room—

—only to be tackled by the raiders guarding the exit. He screamed and growled while they dragged him to one of the tables and strapped him in face down. The surgeon steadied the nekoan's head with powerful cybernetic arms, placed a stubby, metallic stake against the base of his skull, then hammered it all the way in with three harsh blows.

Dezzo screamed, eyes wide, hands and feet flailing. He thrashed against his bonds, but his efforts began to slacken almost immediately. The stake let out a high-pitched *whirr* of activity, and little chunks of gore spat from the top. It took Nathan a moment to realize those chunks were pieces of Dezzo's brain. The muscles in the nekoan's face loosened, and he began to drool. His limbs twitched one final time, then fell limp.

The surgeon wiped the bits of brain off the back of Dezzo's head and inspected his grisly handiwork with an impassive face. He presented no signs of either approval or disappointment before he looked up, large metal eyes locking on Nathan.

A pair of raiders came for him.

Nathan swallowed. His heart thumped fiercely in his chest, and blood pounded in his ears. He didn't want to have part of his brain carved out so he could be turned into a mute cyborg! He liked his brain right where it was, thank you very much!

His mind raced but with no direction. He struggled against the bonds behind his back, yet they wouldn't budge.

What could he do?

Was there anything he *could* do?

One of the raiders reached for the lock to his cell.

"Hey!" Rufus bashed his shoulder into his cell door. "Hey, you!"

The two raiders hesitated at the door, and their surgeon approached Rufus at a casual pace.

"Yes, I'm talking to you!" Rufus thumped the door again. "Take me first! Come on! I *want* to join!"

The raiders stood like statues while the surgeon studied Rufus. Two of his five eyes widened, then contracted again.

"What are you waiting for?" the cleric taunted. "Let me join your glorious community! I've waited my whole life for an opportunity like this!"

"What's he doing?" Joshua whispered to Nathan.

"I think he has a plan," he whispered back. "Be ready for anything."

"Okay." Joshua nodded with tentative determination etched across his face.

"Hurry up!" Rufus headbutted his cell door this time hard enough for Nathan to wince. "Open up! Take me first!"

The surgeon stepped forward and opened the door.

Nathan wasn't sure what he expected to come next, but it wasn't Rufus dropping to his knees before the surgeon. The cyborg hesitated one last time, then finally took the cleric's head in his hands.

"Yes!" Rufus declared excitedly. "Just like that!"

The surgeon positioned a fresh stake—almost dead center with the cybernetic plate on the back of Rufus's head—and hammered it deep. Sparks spat into the air, and the surgeon flinched back. Rufus gasped. His eyes rolled back into his head, and he shuddered and collapsed.

"Rufus?" Nathan asked softly. "Buddy?"

The cleric twitched on the cell floor, and a stream of fresh sparks flew in an arc out the back of his head.

Joshua gulped. "Do we have a Plan B?"

Aiko was afraid.

She couldn't remember the last time she'd experienced genuine fear. Death wasn't supposed to matter to Jovians, other than as an opportunity to learn from failure, but now she found herself with a single body and her persona safe buried inside a dead ship. If she died here, that was it. End of story.

End of *life*.

The concept ate at her mind, filling her with worry and dread, but she pushed through the negativity, putting one foot ahead of the other as she and Vessani cut a path through the forest. She couldn't afford to sit on her composite butt pondering the meaning of life.

Nate and the others needed her, and she'd be damned if she was going to sit idly by while the raiders did gods-knew-what to them!

Besides, living life with permanent consequences was a refreshing change in a strange way. Kind of exhilarating, though she could have done without the "companions in mortal peril" part.

Aiko used her commando body to cross the rugged terrain with ease, her footing sure as she darted through the stifling, murky woods. Vessani had impressed her with her ability to keep up a steady pace. She huffed and grunted behind the Jovian, her face slick with sweat, but she hadn't complained once on their way to the deifactory's massive slopes.

Aiko slowed at the edge of the forest and crouched beside the wrinkled, fleshy trunk of what she'd begun to categorize as meat-trees. A part of her wanted to chop one up and put the slices on a grill. Who knew? Maybe they made great steaks. The cyborgs ate *something* after all, and she hadn't spotted any obvious farms or livestock so far.

Along the way, an eyeless creature conjured from the stuff of nightmares had leaped out at the two women halfway to the factory. Vessani had heard it coming before Aiko did, which impressed the Jovian, and the creature, while terrifying to behold, couldn't defend against her vibro-knife.

Vessani dropped to one knee behind the next tree over, huffing for air, her hard suit's visor up. She wiped her brow with the back of a hand and gulped down each breath hungrily.

"Well?" the nekoan asked, her chest heaving. She uncapped her water bottle and sucked on the tube.

"We have a problem," Aiko replied quietly.

"Another one?"

"Yeah. The ship that took them landed on a platform about a hundred meters above us. There are at least three ships up there, which indicates a *lot* of raiders, but that's not the only issue."

"Then what is?"

"I don't see any exterior elevators or ground access points near our position."

"You suggesting we climb the slope?" Vessani asked.

"I don't see any other way from here to those ships."

"We'll be exposed."

"Which is why it's a problem. We *could* skirt around the perimeter, but there's no guarantee we'll find an easier way up. We could try approaching from the inside."

"And risk getting hopelessly turned around in an unfamiliar factory?" Vessani shook her head. "We'll lose our way in minutes! Assuming we can even find another entrance!"

"I know. Which leaves that platform as our best way in."

"Then let's do this." Vessani emptied her water bottle and stowed it on her belt. "I'm itching for a fight." She raised her pistol.

"You and me both." Aiko pointed to the deifactory. "You see the trough cut into the slope?"

"I see it."

"I say we use it to scale the factory. It's not terribly deep, but some cover is better than none. Should let us get closer before we're spotted."

"Good enough for me."

"You ready?"

"As ready as I can be without a hot meal and a good night's sleep. Lead the way."

Aiko nodded, and took one step out of the forest—

—before the top of the platform exploded into a ball of fire and fury. The front half of a pale ship arced off the platform, trailing greasy fumes on its way to crash against the factory slope. The wreck crumpled and slid down the side, screeching, sparking, and burning.

Another explosion shook the platform, and flaming pieces of a second ship flew high into the air, then pattered down across the slope like a heavy, metallic rain.

"What?" Vessani exclaimed, huddling behind her tree. "What's going—"

A third explosion cracked the air. Secondary detonations cascaded through the spaceship wreckage, flinging the top half of a raider clear from the platform. What was left of him landed somewhere in the forest.

Twin streams of gunfire sprayed the platform, tracers glowing, their trails weaving back and forth, saturating the area. Bullets *zinged* off the deifactory's exterior, and micro-detonations added to the flames and chaos.

Vessani rose behind the tree trunk. "What the *hell* is going on?"

"Wait a second." Aiko put a hand on the nekoan's shoulder and eased her back down. "I recognize those weapons. They sound like . . . but no, it can't be."

"Sounds like what?"

"Jovian heavy repeaters."

"Jovians?"

Aiko nodded.

"How the hell did *they* get here?" Vessani exclaimed. "*We* were shot down!"

"Not sure. Maybe Rufus did a better job of calming the ring's defenses than he thought."

The roar of gunfire ceased, and the silhouette of a black hull slid over their position, descending toward the still-burning wreckage on the platform. Its sleek silhouette broadened toward the back while thrusters capped a pair of stubby wings at the front. Weapon bays along the front were open, exposing the barrels of two turreted 37mm rail-repeaters and racks of torpedoes.

"*Star Dragon* corvette," Aiko noted.

The ship passed through a pillar of thick smoke and eased down onto the space it had blasted clear.

"Which means?" Vessani asked.

"It's a stealthy, multi-role attack craft. Probably loaded with commandos, too, judging by how it's about to land."

"Could this be the same ship you saw tailing us?"

"No way. That one's plasma, but *Star Dragons* often act as support for a larger force. If you see one, there are likely more nearby."

"As if crazed cyborgs weren't bad enough. What do we do now?"

"I don't know, but maybe . . ." Aiko trailed off, a possible future unfolding before her.

That was a *Jovian* ship up on the platform.

Of a class she was intimately familiar with from her commando days.

And, if her guess was correct, the corvette was about to send its troops into the factory, leaving a skeleton crew behind. She knew all the craft's strengths and weaknesses. Its weapon arcs and, more importantly, its blind spots.

"Aiko?" Vessani knocked on the side of Aiko's head. "Hello?"

"Stay put!" The Jovian bolted upright so fast Vessani jumped back. "Sorry, but I've got an idea!"

CHAPTER TWENTY-ONE

Nathan heard the trio of distant rumbles and felt them reverberate in the pit of his stomach. The raiders sprang into motion moments later, drawing their weapons and filing out of the room's main exit.

The surgeon stayed behind and dragged Rufus out of his cell far enough to lay him on his side. The cleric's head rested against the floor, his legs slack and arms still bound behind his back. He let out a pitiful moan, and a line of drool oozed out from the corner of his parted lips.

Nathan heard the rattle of gunfire next, faint at first, but intense with the overlap of multiple weapons.

"Aiko and Vess?" Joshua asked hopefully.

"Doubt it," Nathan replied.

"Why do you say that?"

"Simple. That's more than two guns. A *lot* more."

"But who else could it be?"

"Don't know." He listened carefully, gauged the volume. "But they're getting closer."

Nathan found the approaching noise eerie. The gunfire came in intense bursts, with a few sporadic reports escalating into a massed cacophony before trailing off again. This cycle repeated over and over, each time louder and closer.

But that was the only sound. Whatever fighting was taking place, no one shouted. No one barked orders or screamed in pain. He was listening to a cold, wordless advance through the factory, and a part of him knew what that most likely meant.

He caught a glimpse of a Jovian commando behind one corner of the far exit and felt a jolt of hope shoot through him, but that hope died a quick death when he realized the commando sported the traditional red-and-gold armor of the Everlife across its entire body, lacking Aiko's custom purple paint job on the head.

The surgeon rose from Rufus's side, but then his head and shoulders blew apart in a shower of guts and ruined implants. Nathan flinched from the sudden eruption of gore, and Joshua gasped. The surgeon's body flopped to the ground next to Rufus. One of his mechanical arms flailed wildly for a few moments before coming to rest in a pool of blood.

The commando swept the bulk of his belt-fed, three-barreled heavy weapon over the operating tables. A second commando took up position on the opposite corner, and another four commandos stormed through the gap between them. Those four were armed with shorter weapons more suitable for cramped quarters. They gave each occupied table a quick glance, but no more as they hustled to the far end of the room.

"Jovians?" Joshua breathed to Nathan. "What's going on here?"

"Not sure, but I doubt they're here for our benefit."

"You two!" barked one of the commandos, drawing a vibro-knife. "Stand back!"

Nathan pressed his back against the wall, though the position of his bound arms caused his belly to stick out. He sucked in his gut as best he could. The commando cut around the lock, then ripped it out. It clattered across the ground, and the door creaked open.

A second commando repeated the process with Joshua's door.

"Move out!" One of the commandos pointed to the exit. "That way!"

"What about my friend here?" Nathan bobbed his head toward Rufus.

"Worry about yourself. Now get moving!"

"Okay, okay!" Nathan shouldered the door open. "No need to shout. By the way, mind cutting us free with that?"

"Shut your mouth and do as you're told!"

"Come on. What's the harm in—?"

The commando grabbed Nathan by the shoulder and shoved him toward the exit.

He stumbled forward but regained his balance and, once Joshua joined him, let the Jovians march them across the room. One of the commandos picked up Rufus and slung him over a shoulder.

Nathan counted six commandos waiting by the exit. That made at least ten total with perhaps more out of sight, which was *deep* into the "impossible odds" spectrum of his personal danger scale.

The commandos formed two groups around the prisoners, one in front and one behind, and together they headed back into the factory. Nathan tried to recall the route they'd taken to the operating room, and the Jovians retraced that path to a point, but then they took a sudden turn in the opposite direction.

We're not leaving the factory? Nathan thought. *I'm pretty sure this takes us deeper inside. Why lead us this way?*

He looked around, trying to figure out what was going on.

The Jovians knew we were in the factory. They wasted no time fighting their way to us. But they're not doing this out of the kindness of their nonexistent hearts. Do they want something from us? That seems obvious. Why bother collecting us if they didn't? But then, why take us deeper into the factory instead of back to their ship?

Come to think of it, how'd they make it to the surface in the first place?

He shook his head, unable to fit the pieces together.

No, that's not important, he thought. *What* is *important is what they want from us. I need to figure that out as quickly as possible. That'll give us some leverage, in theory. Hell, knowing is better than fumbling around blindly. Maybe I can even negotiate with their apex for our release, though getting these cuffs off would be a nice start.*

So . . . what is it they want from us?

Hmm.

He chewed on the inside of his lip and mulled over what he knew.

Yep. No clue.

The commandos stopped so suddenly Nathan almost ran into the back of one. Those in front parted to either side, revealing a second, equally large group, only two of which weren't Jovian commandos.

Two men stepped away from this new group and approached Nathan and the others. The first was an overweight man in purple robes with the glint of implants visible on parts of his bald scalp. He limped toward them, his left leg locked in a brace. He kept his cowed eyes downcast and cradled hands wrapped in bandages. A golden Church pentagon stood out on his left breast.

"Anterus?" Joshua gasped in disbelief.

"Anterus?" Nathan asked. "You mean your old professor? The one who went missing?"

"The same."

The second man pushed past Anterus, who didn't bother to look up. The Jovian's silver skin gleamed in the light, his angular face a reasonable approximation of organic life except for the metallic sheen.

"Galatt Xormun?" Nathan asked.

"How delightful." Xormun smiled as if they were old friends. "You remember me."

"Your kind leaves a lasting impression."

"I suppose worse things have been said about me." Xormun shrugged. "Funny running into you again, Kade. *Captain* Kade, as it were, though I suppose the title is somewhat questionable, what with the *Neptune Belle* lying like a bloated corpse on the beach."

"It's still 'captain,' if you don't mind."

"Oh, my apologies, then. I'll be sure to remember that." He inspected the other two. "And who do we have here? Joshua Cotton and Rufus sen Qell. Excellent."

"*ziin* Qell," Nathan corrected.

"Whatever." Xormun poked Rufus's cheek. The man groaned and continued to drool on the commando's shoulder. "Your friend appears unwell."

"He's had a rough day."

"Indeed?"

"We all have."

"So it would seem. But now I'm curious. Where's the rest of your crew? I was so looking forward to reacquainting myself with Aiko Pratti."

"She's not here," Nathan replied stiffly, thinking fast.

"That much is clear." Xormun stepped up to Nathan's face, now uncomfortably close. "Where might she be?"

"Dead!" Nathan spat, trying to inject an undercurrent of grief into his voice.

"Dead?" Xormun scoffed. "Surely, you jest."

"I wouldn't joke about something this serious."

Which is true enough, he thought, *though I will* lie to you about it.

"She was on her last body," Nathan continued. "And the crash . . . killed her."

"Oh, I see. How did she die?"

"Crushed during the landing."

"How terrible. And your missing passenger? Vessani S'Kaari?"

"Dead."

"The crash?"

"The crash." Nathan swallowed hard. "Just . . . messier."

Joshua bowed his head and let out a little sniffle.

"Well, you organics do break more easily than we do. Just look at poor Anterus over there." Xormun gestured to the portly cleric. "Snapped his leg like a twig trying to go to the toilet during the flight over. 'Overweight' has a bit more punch when you're on a Jovian ship, wouldn't you say?"

"You subjected him to sustained high gees?" Nathan snarled.

"Oh, please! That's hardly the worst thing I did to him," Xormun confessed casually. "Well, how about it, Anterus? Have you figured out our next destination yet?"

The cleric shook his head.

"Work faster." Xormun drew his vibro-knife and let it catch the light. "Otherwise, I might lose faith in your abilities again, and you know what that means."

Anterus cowered back into one of the commandos, who pushed him forward. He nodded frantically.

"There's a good lump of talking meat." Xormun sheathed the knife.

"Still the charmer, I see," Nathan said.

"Again, worse has been said about me. But Saturnian clerics have their uses. That one got us through the Sanguine Ring's defenses, though I suspect he only managed the feat because your friend Rufus paved the way for him."

"Is that why you 'rescued' us?"

"Partially." Xormun frowned at the drooling cleric. "Though now that I see him, I'm having doubts about his utility." He gave Nathan an indifferent shrug. "Oh, well. At least you have the pleasure of being my guest for a second time."

"You and I must have different definitions of 'guest' and 'pleasure.'"

"Perhaps we do. By the way, I suppose I should thank you."

"For what?"

"For leading us this far, though now that we're here, I'm curious. Do you even know what it is you're searching for?"

The question took Nathan by surprise. He knew the artifact with the elliptical orbit was pentatech. Or, at the very least, the evidence *indicated* it was. But as far as what *kind* of lost technology . . . he didn't have a clue.

Up until that very moment.

Nathan glanced around the corridor, surrounded by Jovian commandos armed to the teeth and confronted by a ruthless agent of the Everlife.

"I'm going to go out on a limb here and say it's a weapon."

"Not *quite*." Xormun smirked at him again. "The artifact is, in fact, a tool of tremendous scale and scope. But like so many tools, also a weapon when the need arises."

Anterus eventually found his bearings and guided the Jovians deeper into the factory. The few raiders they encountered were gunned down with ease, though Nathan suspected the causalities represented only a small fraction of the cyborgs nearby. He wasn't entirely sure due to the drumming of commando feet and the echoing acoustics of the factory, but he thought he heard groups of raiders moving in parallel around their position, including above and below.

Xormun pressed on, undeterred by the danger those unseen raiders represented, and soon Anterus led them to a huge space somewhere near the heart of the factory. Machinery hung from a high ceiling like mechanical stalactites, pressing downward with the oppressive inevitability of giant teeth. Despite the room's scale, Nathan felt uncomfortably confined and a part of him desired to be back outside.

"Now we're getting somewhere," Xormun said, coming to a stop. "Good job, Anterus. I never doubted you for a second."

The cleric kept his head low. He began to walk away, but a commando grabbed him by the scruff of his neck and yanked him back.

The commandos spread out enough for Nathan to gain a clear view of the whole room. A row of plinths had been arranged at the edge of a wide chasm cut down through the factory floor. Black, egg-shaped devices sat atop half the plinths, each about the size of a human head. Some were cracked or busted open and leaked dark fluid through the breaks, a few had been collected in broken piles, while three intact specimens rested on their pedestals with hints of motion beneath their translucent shells: shifting machinery and coursing fluids.

"The Black Egg," Joshua said softly.

"Black *Eggs*," Xormun corrected. "It seems the natives are collectors of a sort."

The Jovian apex stepped up to the edge of the cliff. Commandos shoved Nathan and Joshua forward.

The chasm curved away from them to either side so that it formed a wide arc not unlike a grinning mouth. Broken machinery lined the walls and a slick, damp mass undulated across the bottom.

Anterus muttered something under his breath.

"What'd he say?" Nathan asked.

"'Flesh and metal for the wound.'" Xormun tapped his head. "We Jovians can hear it, too. It's like a garbled chant being relayed through the Black Eggs. I wonder if the locals aren't taking those words a bit too literally."

"Why do you say that?"

Xormun didn't respond, but instead glanced to one of the commandos. Nathan wondered if he'd passed the Jovian a wireless order, because the commando lit a flare and tossed it into the pit. The bright light came to rest on a horrible amalgamation of pulsating flesh and tubing, its stretched skin heaving and glistening all along the bottom of the chasm.

"Oh, gods," Joshua gasped. "What *is* that?"

Xormun chuckled. "A 'blessing' of Divergence, perhaps?"

The mass seemed to be composed of hundreds of human bodies, all fused together by methods Nathan didn't understand, didn't *want* to understand. Random arms, legs, and vacant, eyeless heads protruded from the mass like tumorous growths, while powerful muscles flexed underneath the patchwork skin.

A sudden memory assaulted Nathan's mind, and he squeezed his eyes shut. He was sixteen again with the weight of his mother on his back. His father stood on the far side of a locked pressure door, the flesh of his right arm oozing off like wax under a flame. Sweat glistened on his father's face as the man strained to form words, ordering Nathan to carry his mother to safety.

The moment passed, and he opened his eyes.

"The wound," Anterus muttered, his words faint, lips barely moving. "Flesh and metal for the wound."

"Is this why the raiders kidnap people?" Joshua asked, horrified. "For this . . . thing?"

"Who can say?" Xormun kicked a piece of Black Egg shell on the ground. It fell into the chasm and clattered on its way down to the writhing, fleshy mass at the bottom.

"The wound." Anterus clutched his head with both bandaged hands. "The wound, the wound, the wound. Flesh for the wound."

"No excuses," Xormun snapped. "Just pick an egg and connect. Any of the whole ones should do."

"Flesh for the wound."

Anterus took shuffling steps up to the unblemished Black Eggs in the center.

"Flesh for the wound!"

"Yes, yes," Xormun rolled his eyes. "We hear it, too. No need to get all excited."

Anterus reached for one of the Black Eggs with trembling hands. He glanced back to Xormun, who put a hand on the hilt of his knife as a form of "encouragement." The cleric faced the Black Egg once more, ran his fingers over its smooth surface and looked as if he were about to grasp it—

—but then he sprinted past, straight for the cliff edge.

"FLESH FOR THE WOUND!"

Anterus leaped into the chasm, arms spread wide in acceptance of his fate. He plummeted away and landed next to the flare with a sickening crunch.

"No!" Joshua cried out. He tried to dash up to the edge, but the commando behind him grabbed his shoulder and yanked him back.

"Well." Xormun clucked his tongue. "That was unexpected. A disappointment to the end." He clapped his hands together. "Shall we move on and see if the spare can do better?"

The commando carrying Rufus stepped forward and placed him on the ground at Xormun's feet.

"You awake in there?" Xormun crouched next to the cleric and grabbed him by the chin. "Huh?" He smacked the drooling man in the face back and forth a few times.

"The wound," Rufus muttered. "The wound."

"Not more of this nonsense." Xormun punched Rufus in the gut, and the cleric's eyes bugged out. He curled up into a ball, gasping for air.

"Hey!" Nathan snapped. "Stop that!"

"Don't be so dramatic. I'm just giving him a little wake-up call. He's fine."

"No, he's not! The raiders jammed something into his head!"

"Is that so?" Xormun twisted Rufus's neck to the side and examined the stake imbedded there. "And so they did. Is this why you're such a mess?"

"The *wound*."

"I suppose we'll just have to make do with what we've got." Xormun let go of the cleric's chin and shoved him toward the plinths. "Are you with us enough to help or not?"

"Flesh and metal for the wound?"

"You see those Black Eggs?" Xormun pointed. "Commune with them. Find out where the signal is coming from."

"The wound?" Rufus blinked his eyes, some sense of clarity returning to them at last.

"Do you even understand what I'm saying?"

"The . . ." Rufus looked up at him, then at the Black Eggs. "I . . ."

"Here. How's this for clarity?" Xormun drew his knife and placed the tip against Nathan's neck, who sucked in a quick breath. "Either you help us, or I start carving up the worthless baggage you came here with. Does this penetrate the fog in your meat-brain?"

Rufus swallowed hard and nodded.

"Good. Now get to work." Xormun motioned one of the commandos forward, who cut Rufus's bonds.

The cleric looked over to the Black Eggs. He took a deep breath and began crawling over to them on his hands and knees.

Rufus knelt before the Black Eggs, inclined his head, and began to mumble a chant. His lips trembled from the utterance of breathy words, and he spread a shaky hand over his chest.

"There," Xormun declared with a satisfied smile. "Now maybe we'll make some *real* progress!"

"You honestly think this'll lead you to an ancient weapon?" Nathan asked.

"I do."

Nathan shook his head.

"Is that so strange?" Xormun asked.

"What's the *Everlife* need with more guns?"

"A better question is: would *any* government turn down the chance to become stronger at little to no cost? Answer: none of them. Both the Union and the Concord would attempt to seize this prize if they knew it existed. We simply intend to grab it before anyone else can."

"All in the name of the Everlife's jingoism."

"In the name of peace," Xormun corrected.

"*Peace?* Come on!"

"No, it's true. Think about it. People fight for any number of causes because they believe they can prevail. Otherwise, they would flee or submit to the opposition. So, what happens when one side possesses overwhelming strength?"

"You're hoping the Union and the Concord will submit to you?"

"I *know* they will. Along with every other pissant group of high-techs out there. That's how terrifying this weapon is."

"What is it, then?"

"A tool, as I said. A very large, very powerful tool. One crafted by Pathfinder near the dawn of the Age of Communion."

"What's it do?"

"You'll see." Xormun grinned at him with a twinkle in his eyes.

"You plan to let us live that long?"

"Unless circumstances dictate otherwise," Xormun replied with indifference. "Who knows? You three might prove useful. And speaking of which . . ."

Rufus reached out to the closest Black Egg, and his fingertips brushed against its translucent surface. The sense of motion within the artifact hastened, and the cleric's mutterings grew louder. Nathan caught the name "Metatron," but he couldn't make out anything else.

Xormun frowned. "Are you sure you're praying to the right god?"

Rufus continued his chant.

A loud *clank* echoed from a side passage, and the commandos stirred. Unseen boots squeaked from the opposite direction, and the commandos backed away from the outer walls. They formed a convex perimeter bristling with weapons, Xormun and the three organic men at the center.

"Sounds like you're about to have company," Nathan said, backing away to the Black Eggs with Joshua. None of the commandos stopped them.

"It's nothing we can't handle."

"You sure about that?"

"Quiet," Xormun hissed, drawing his pistol.

The clamor of unseen raiders grew in volume. Nathan couldn't tell how many there were. Dozens? *Hundreds?* He heard motion in every direction except from the chasm at their backs. The commandos stood their ground, weapons raised, triangular heads sweeping back and forth.

All the while, Rufus chanted faster and louder. The insides of the Black Egg he'd picked swirled with frantic motion, and the cleric stood up. He held his chin high, stretched out his open hands to the heavens, and gazed up with clear eyes.

"Metatron, guardian of peace and order! Hear my plea! Cleanse these poor souls! Release them from their suffering!"

The Black Egg shuddered, rattling against its cradle.

"What do you think you're doing?" Xormun placed his pistol against the cleric's temple.

Rufus smiled and closed his eyes.

The Black Egg stopped shaking.

The racket from raiders taking up their positions ceased.

A deep, eerie silence fell over the factory. Even the machinery seemed to pause and hold its figurative breath.

"Answer me," Xormun snarled.

"I did what was required of me," Rufus whispered, and opened his eyes. "I freed them."

A howl echoed down the main corridor, hoarse and throaty but nonetheless powerful. Another joined it, then another. More and more voices cried out in terrifying joy, and soon the entire factory trembled with their wordless roars.

The shouting became almost deafening, and the first raider charged into view down the main entrance, brandishing a vibro-spear. He pulled his arm back for a throw—

—two commandos opened fire at the same instant and blew his torso to bits.

The raider's broken body flopped to the ground, but more swarmed in from all directions, and the commandos cut loose with the full might of their weaponry. Dozens of cyborgs died in the first seconds, but dozens more poured in. Raiders flooded the chamber from everywhere all at once: down the wide main corridor, out of side passages, through grates in the floor, and some even dropped out of vents in the ceiling.

The overwhelming tide of bodies proved too much, forcing the commandos to split their fire in too many directions, and the first raider to reach the Jovians cleaved the commando's head off with a jubilant swing.

Xormun grabbed one of the intact Black Eggs. His commandos formed up around him and together they fled down a side passage.

"Rufus?" Nathan asked urgently.

"It's all right." The cleric smiled warmly. "I've made peace with the natives."

"You sure about that?"

Nathan staggered away from the raiders rushing them, only to trip and fall over the severed half of a commando. Raiders grabbed him roughly by the shoulders and turned him over. He tensed up, sensing the oscillation of the vibro-blade through his cuffs, expecting the raider to plunge the blade deep into his back.

But the feared moment never came. His bonds fell away, and he turned himself over, coming face-to-face with the raider who'd cut his bonds, a sword humming in his hand.

"Um, thanks?"

"Uuauh," the raider gurgled, then rose and joined the others in their pursuit of the Jovians.

Nathan stood up and massaged his wrists.

"Are you okay, Rufus?" Joshua asked, shaking out his wrists.

"I'm fine."

"What about the . . . ?" Nathan tapped the back of his head.

"A necessary hardship. Fortunately, my implants were able to adapt to the intrusion and overcome its cruder elements, as I suspected they would. I have complete control over it now, rather than the other way around."

"You sound a lot better than a few minutes ago," Nathan said.

Rufus gave him a sly smile. "I may have been playing up my disorientation just a tad."

"It worked!" Nathan exclaimed. "You had me fooled!"

"Can you control the raiders now?" Joshua asked.

"No, and I wouldn't even if I could. These poor people became thralls to this factory long ago, forced to carry out the broken remnants of its commands. The implants this place produced became their shackles. I've... cleaned up the mess, shall we say. At least as well as I can. In fact, if I were to guess—"

"Save it for later." Nathan picked up one of the Jovian rifles and pried the commando's severed hand off it. "Let's get to somewhere safe first and try to find the others."

"What about these?" Joshua patted the top of a Black Egg.

"The one to your immediate left belongs to the nekoans," Rufus said.

"You sure? I don't see any difference."

"Quite sure."

"Okay, then." Joshua hefted that Black Egg and hugged it against his chest.

"Anyone going to throw a fit if we take that?" Nathan asked, crouching to pocket a few extra magazines.

"I doubt it," Rufus said. "The natives might even smash the rest out of spite. It's hard to say how they'll react moving forward."

"Then let's get out of here." Nathan stood up. "With any luck, we'll have a clear path to the exit."

"Don't jinx us!" Joshua squeaked.

CHAPTER TWENTY-TWO

Nathan led the way, retracing their steps through the factory and back to the landing platform. He wasn't sure what they'd find there, but that was the only exit he knew of. His simple plan came into doubt the moment he laid eyes on the platform, visible at the far end of a long corridor lined with massive cylindrical machines.

"Smoke," Rufus whispered.

"It's still our best way out." Nathan checked the end of the corridor through his rifle's scope. "Something's on fire up ahead, but I can't tell what." He lowered the weapon.

"Might have been the Jovians saying hello to the locals," Rufus said.

"Maybe." Nathan urged them forward with a wave of the rifle. "Come on. Let's see what's what."

They found the wreckage of two or three pale ships strewn about the platform, itself scarred by explosions and gunfire. Flames crackled within the remains of their blackened, twisted hulls. Nathan walked out and surveyed the carnage with a frustrated sigh.

So much for taking one of their ships, he thought. *Now what?*

Joshua set the Black Egg down and shook out his arms and hands, then picked it up again.

Stick to the basics, Nathan told himself. *Find the others. And then . . . then we'll all think of something.*

He stepped over to the edge of the platform, crouched, and dialed the rifle's scope up to maximum magnification. Smoking pieces of the pale ships lay scattered about the pyramid's slope, but he had a relatively clear view of their crash site. He raised the scope to his eye.

"No obvious signs of activity near the *Belle*. No other ships near it, and no one outside as far as I can see from this angle."

"You think they're in the forest?" Joshua asked.

"Maybe." Nathan tracked his view over to the dark woods, hoping to spot a shiny glint through the bloodred leaves, but smoke and the dense canopy obstructed his view. He let out a frustrated grunt. "I can't see *anything* through that mess."

"Then what should—"

"Nate!" Rufus called out. "Look!"

"What's—" Nathan began, but then a Jovian corvette hovered out of the smoke, approaching the landing platform with weapon ports open. "Get back inside! Hurry!"

He rose to his feet and sprinted for the factory interior. Joshua and Rufus didn't respond quite so fast and lagged behind, but he soon realized it was too late. The corvette rumbled over their heads, spun around, and dropped down to cut off their retreat. Its landing gear strained from sudden compression, and metal screeched against metal as the ship slid a few meters before coming to rest between them and the deifactory.

The front of the corvette faced them, along with its open racks of torpedoes and turreted cannons. Nathan staggered to a halt and hesitated, knowing a gun that large could pulp the three of them in an instant. He checked to their sides.

"That wreckage!" he shouted. "Get behind it!"

Joshua and Rufus followed his lead, and the three of them hunkered down behind a warped hull panel that seemed thick enough to discourage incoming fire, if not actually stop a determined attack.

Nathan put his back to the plate and waited.

No attack came. Nor did he hear the rapid stomping of a commando squad.

He checked around the corner to find a single Jovian standing at the edge of the ramp.

A Jovian commando with a purple head, wearing a *Neptune Belle* jacket.

"Gentlemen, can I offer you a lift?" her familiar voice called out.

"Aiko?" Nathan stood up, looked at her, then at the corvette. "But . . . *how?*"

"We thought you might need some rescuing, though it seems you had most of that covered yourselves." She pointed into the ship with her rifle. "Let's get out of here before something else goes wrong."

"Don't need to tell us twice!" Nathan joined Aiko inside the ship's cargo hold. The space was more cramped than the *Belle*, with two rovers and two small shuttles taking up most of the internal space.

Joshua and Rufus hurried in, and Aiko raised the ramp.

"Where's Vess?" Joshua asked.

"In the cockpit." Aiko keyed her commect. "They're in. Get us out of here."

The thrusters powered up, and the ship lifted off the platform. Nathan grabbed a handhold on the wall to steady himself.

"We should find a secure place to store this," Joshua said, adjusting his grip on the Black Egg.

"And I should also help Vess with our exit vector," Rufus said.

"You think it's safe to leave?" Nathan asked.

"The Jovians managed to get in, which leads me to think so. But let me check the juncture, just to be safe. I doubt any of us want to be shot down again."

"No kidding! Let's avoid that."

"There's an elevator at the back of C Deck." Aiko pointed down the narrow path between the vehicles. "Storage is on B Deck and the cockpit is at the front of A Deck. The layout's pretty straightforward."

"Thanks." Rufus started down the path, and Joshua followed him.

Nathan waited until he was alone with Aiko.

"You came for us," he said, smiling at her.

"Of course I did. Why wouldn't I?"

"Well, I don't know." He leaned against the wall. "We were stuck inside a factory filled with hostile cyborgs. And then the *Everlife* showed up!"

"It's not like I was going to head inside unarmed." She rested her rifle on a shoulder.

"That's . . . beside the point."

"You think I was going to leave you inside there to rot?"

"Not if you could help it. But this is your last body."

"Doesn't matter." Aiko paused, then shrugged. "Okay, it *does* matter. It's been a while since I've been this afraid of dying, but we're a team. There's no way I'd abandon you if there was even the slightest chance I could get you out."

"I know." Nathan smiled again and glanced around the hold. "How'd you pull this off?"

"I asked nicely."

"Uh-huh. Did your question involve gunshots?"

"A few."

"Only a few?"

"I'm just that good of a shot."

"Point taken," he conceded, then chuckled.

"Oh, look at you." She put a hand on his shoulder. "They roughed you up pretty good."

"It looks worse than it feels."

"You've got mud in your hair."

She combed his hair back with her fingers, breaking through the dried patches of mud, then she repeated the process a few times. Nathan thought that would be the end of it, but she kept stroking her fingers through his hair at a slow, leisurely pace, over and over again.

He frowned at her. "Aiko?"

"Yes?"

"Why are you still running your fingers through my hair?"

"Shh. Don't ruin the moment."

"I'm ... not sure what you mean by that."

Rufus confirmed the local defenses were calm enough for them to pass through, and Vessani piloted the stolen corvette away from the Sanguine Ring. Aiko showed Nathan to a small washroom for organic prisoners, and he cleaned up as best he could before joining the others in the cockpit.

He rubbed his face and stepped past the pressure door. The corvette's cockpit featured an unobstructed, forward-facing dome in front of side-by-side pilot and copilot stations. It reminded him of the *Belle*'s setup but with sleeker consoles and more vlass screens.

"We're outside the danger envelope," Vessani reported, turning halfway in her seat. "According to the *Almanac*, at least. Eleven hundred kilometers and rising."

"All stealth systems are engaged," Aiko added from the copilot seat. "If there's another Jovian ship out there, they'll have a hell of a time tracking us."

"Good," Nathan said. "We don't need surprises like the last time."

"Are we certain it was a Jovian ship that triggered the ring's defenses?" Joshua asked.

"There's no way to be sure," Nathan conceded, "but I don't see how it could have been anyone else. Either way, the important thing is we know the Everlife has taken an interest in the pentatech relic, and that's going to complicate our lives *immensely*."

"I wonder how long they've been tailing us," Rufus said.

"Could have been a while." Aiko patted her console. "This is a *Star Dragon* corvette we 'liberated.' They're some of the sneakiest ships in the Everlife."

"Not sneaky enough to fool the ring," Rufus said.

"True," Aiko said, "but more than enough to stay hidden from ships like the *Belle*. Assuming that first ship was the same pattern, they could have slipped in behind us at almost any time. Maybe even all the way back when we left Neptune."

"Well, they're not tailing us anymore." Nathan crossed his arms. "There's a good chance we made a clean getaway, though Vessani, I'd like you to take us through a few random course changes, just to be extra safe."

"You've got it, boss!" She gave him a thumbs-up, and her tail twitched happily.

"'Boss'? Where'd *that* come from?"

Did I miss something? Nathan thought. *When did she switch from client to crew member?*

"Sorry." Vessani's ears drooped. "Am I not allowed to call you that?"

"No, it's just . . . Never mind." He held up an apologetic hand. "It's fine. You can call me whatever you want."

Vessani smiled, and her ears perked up.

"That settles what we're doing in the short term," Aiko said, "but we still need to figure out the long term. Where do we go next?"

"I may be able to help with that," Rufus said.

"Did you have any luck with the Black Egg?" Nathan asked.

"I did indeed." Rufus flashed a knowing smile. "I discovered what the pentatech relic is."

"Nice!" Nathan found the cleric's smile infectious. "Well, what is it?"

"It's like that Jovian apex said. The artifact is a creation of Pathfinder from the dawn of the Age of Communion. More specifically, it's part of the Pentatheon's star-lifting machinery. A statite, or 'stationary satellite,' that once held a fixed position above Sol."

"Oh!" Joshua's eyes widened and his face lit up. "Yes, of course! That makes so much sense!"

"It does?" Nathan asked, feeling like he was a step behind the others.

"Absolutely!" Joshua put a hand to his forehead. "Of *course*, the Jovians would take an interest! Why didn't I see this until now?"

"None of us did," Rufus said. "Though, I agree. It *is* rather obvious in hindsight."

"Well, *I* don't get it," Vessani said. "What makes this piece of pentatech so special?"

"Because," Joshua began, "in some ways, the advent of star lifting is what allowed humanity to flourish during the Age of Communion. All their great works required two basic resources—matter and energy—and Sol is flush with both. Even when you lump all the planets and habitats together, they're nothing but a rounding error compared to the mass of a star. Sol contains well over ninety-nine percent of the solar system's matter. Never mind all the energy it's *constantly* pumping into space!

"The Pentatheon knew this and created great machines to harvest both resources. They constructed a swarm of solar collectors that orbited Sol, working in tandem with stationary star lifters."

"Then the Jovians are after resources?" Vessani asked.

"I'm afraid not," Joshua replied. "They're after a weapon, all right. You see, the way most scholars believe the old star lifters worked is by exciting the surface of Sol with lasers, thereby causing the star to eject matter, which other machinery then collected. In fact, some theorize that's where Mercury and its moons come from. Most of the matter ejected from the star would be hydrogen, with much smaller amounts of heavier elements mixed in. That leaves any star-lifting operation with a lot of excess gas, which the Pentatheon may have concentrated into Mercury. That may also explain why most of Mercury's moons are so homogenous in composition. They're originally giant storage bins for star-lifted construction materials."

"You make an interesting point about Mercury," Rufus said. "Some apocryphal texts refer to Mercury as having been broken apart long ago for resources before the Pentatheon reformed it as a gas giant."

"Let's backtrack to the part about the laser," Nathan cut in. "How powerful a beam are we talking here?"

"*Very* powerful," Joshua replied.

"Like, on the order of habitat-melting?"

"Almost certainly."

"A tool and a weapon all in one," Nathan murmured with a frown. "No wonder this machine piqued the Everlife's interest."

"It's going to be bad news for everyone if the Jovians grab it," Aiko said.

"One step at a time," Nathan said. "Do we even know where this star-lifting statite is?"

"Not yet," Rufus replied, "but I should be able to help us with that part. Now that I have access to one of the Black Eggs, I can commune with it to determine the statite's position."

"Your head doing okay?" Nathan tapped the back of his own skull.

"It is. No need to worry, Nate."

"Just asking." He gave the cleric a lopsided smile. "All right. Do your thing with the Black Egg and get us a heading."

"Consider it done."

"In the meantime, Vess, I'd like you to stay here in the cockpit. Keep making those course changes and watch our tail for any signs of pursuit."

"You've got it."

"Joshua, Aiko: the three of us will work our way through the corvette and take an inventory of what we have in way of supplies. Especially food, since this is a Jovian ship."

"You've got it." Joshua stepped away from the wall, ready to help.

"There's one thing you're forgetting, Nate," Aiko said, unstrapping herself from the copilot seat.

"What's that?"

"We need to give our new home a name." She caressed the top of her console. "I was toying with the name '*Stolen Dragon*.' What do you think?"

"*Stolen Dragon*, huh?" Nathan paused in thought, then shrugged his shoulders. "Works for me."

Nathan took care of Beany first.

The old spice container and the cutting had remained intact through their time on the Sanguine Ring, though a touch of brown had begun to form around the edges of the uppermost leaves. He removed the adhesive tape around the top, careful not to peel any bark off, then transferred the cutting to a pitcher filled with water and ground up bits of a single prisoner ration. He wasn't sure how nutritious the cutting would find the human food but assumed it was better than nothing.

He applied tape across the pitcher's top to seal in the water and secure the contents for zero gravity, then he picked a cell near the back of C Deck and taped the pitcher to the wall.

"Will the light in here be enough?" Nathan asked Aiko, who'd helped him rustle up the supplies.

"Should be. The output can sustain florans, so Beany Junior should enjoy the light just as much."

"Good to hear." Nathan added one more strip of tape to hold the cutting in place, then handed the roll back to Aiko. "That's about the best we can do under the circumstances. Hopefully it'll pull through."

"We'll just have to wait and see."

"Yeah."

Nathan and Aiko joined Joshua by an open storage rack next to the cells.

"How are we set for food?" Nathan asked.

"Not bad." Joshua stood up from between two precarious towers of ration boxes. "I'm not done counting, but I'd say the pantry is stocked with around four hundred rations. At three meals a day for the four of us that need them, that comes out to over a month's worth of food."

"That much?" Nathan glanced to Aiko.

"What can I say?" She placed a hand atop one of the stacks. "These Jovians came prepared to grab and hold organic prisoners."

"They also stored some basic medical supplies," Joshua continued, "plus pressure suits, and a few other odds and ends Jovians don't typically need."

"Lucky us," Nathan said.

"Granted, the meal variety is severely lacking." Joshua put his hands on his hips and glared at the stacked rations.

"I see what you mean," Nathan said. "Looks like the same rubbish they served me on the *Leviathan*."

"It is," Aiko said.

Nathan licked his tongue over the front of his upper teeth, recalling the bland flavor of his meals on board the *Leviathan of Io*. The food had been nourishing, if not much else.

"At least it won't be hard to stretch out our supplies, if we have to," Nathan said.

"Why's that?" Joshua asked.

"Everyone's going to get sick of that food real fast."

"There are worse problems to have," Aiko said.

"True enough," Nathan conceded. "Finish counting up the rations and anything else useful you find in there, then come find us. Aiko and I are going to sweep through the rest of the ship."

"You've got it." Joshua knelt back down, crossed his legs, and shifted another stack of rations over.

C Deck contained the ship's organic "guest quarters," atmospheric control systems, the reactor's Torus Three, and the cargo hold. Joshua would cover the guest quarters, and the contents of the cargo hold seemed obvious enough at first glance, what with four support vehicles taking up most of the space, so Nathan and Aiko rode the freight elevator up to B Deck next.

"I'm surprised you're letting Vess fly your ship," Aiko said once the lift began to rise.

"Why wouldn't I? She's a good pilot, and it frees you up. Also, it's not my ship."

"Sure it is. I 'salvaged' it, and now I'm giving it to you. See? It's your ship now."

"I think the Jovian Everlife may take exception to your . . . let's call it a liberal interpretation of salvage rights."

"That's a problem for another day. For now, it's your ship."

"Why weren't you the one flying it in the first place?"

"I was busy with charging in to rescue you guys, remember?" She patted the chest of her commando body. "Between the two of us, I had the better chances."

"Fair enough."

On B Deck, they checked out the Jovian crew quarters, the ship's persona safe, access to Torus Two, and additional storage compartments.

"Figures," Aiko moaned, surveying the long—and mostly empty—weapons rack. "The commandos took all the good guns."

"We'll make do with what's left." Nathan pulled one of the larger pistols off the rack. He released the magazine and cleared the chamber, then turned the weapon over in his hands.

"Good eye. That's a wyrmstake heavy pistol," Aiko said. "Those'll put just about *anything* on its ass, even a commando."

"Nice. I think I'll take one for myself." He reloaded the weapon and returned it to the rack. "Between these and the rifles we brought on board, the three of us have more than enough guns to go around."

"Don't you mean five of us?"

"I know what I said."

"It could be worse. Rufus and Joshua didn't shoot themselves."

"*Yet.*"

They headed toward the front of the ship and entered a cramped hallway lined with inert Jovian bodies positioned upright in charging alcoves. The bodies came in a variety of shapes and skin tones, some of them quite attractive.

"Can you use these?" Nathan asked.

"Sure can, but they're all faces."

"'Faces'? What do you mean?"

"It's slang for bodies intended for interactions with organics. Most of their specs are mediocre at best."

"Makes sense, I suppose," Nathan said. "The Jovians sent all their combat bodies into the factory."

"We also have the pilot and copilot bodies, which are similar to standard commandos, though they're a bit of a mess right now."

"Riddled with holes?"

"Not *that* many. I was careful not to damage the ship."

"What about the safe?" Nathan walked over to a red-and-gold panel inset into the back wall. "Anyone still inside?"

"Nope. I already cleared out the crew's personas and backed up mine. Better 'safe' than sorry, as it were." She paused, and when he didn't laugh, she added, "That was a joke, by the way."

"Isn't that a bit cold?"

"Nah. They weren't conscious, and the crew will have other copies. It's no worse than me cutting your hair without permission."

"My hair isn't sentient."

"Hmm." Aiko tilted her head and ran her fingers through his locks. "Now there's a thought."

"Could you please stop doing that?"

Chapter Twenty-Three

"Everyone to the cockpit!" Vessani called out over ship-wide commect. "We've got something!"

Nathan set the water bulb down in the cell and resealed Beany's cutting. It was hard to tell with the branch's container filled with a brown slurry, but he thought he could make out new roots growing from the cutting's base. He jogged over to the C Deck cargo hold, met Aiko on her way up via the freight elevator, and arrived on A Deck.

The two of them hurried over to the cockpit, collecting a bleary-eyed Joshua along the way. The pressure door slid open to reveal Vessani and Rufus seated at the tandem controls, the room bathed from above by Sol's light, darkened and filtered by the cockpit dome. The Black Egg was strapped into one of the jump seats by the entrance.

"Everyone here?" Vessani checked over her shoulder. "Morning, sleepyhead."

"Mornin'," Joshua yawned into his fist. "What time is it?"

"Six twenty, Neptune Standard."

"Feels earlier," Joshua replied, his sentence merging with another yawn.

"What do you have?" Nathan asked.

Rufus flashed a confident smile. "We believe we found the statite."

"You did? Now that's what I like to hear!"

Rufus and Vessani had spent the last three days tracking down their target, with Rufus communing through the Black Egg and

Vessani using his insights to make course corrections. Their wavering, sinusoidal flight path had taken them deep into the inner system, well inside Venus's orbit.

"Here. Take a look." Rufus brought up an image of Sol on his console and stood out of the way. The telescope feed showed a black sliver moving across the yellow surface of Sol. An off-white orb near the edge of the screen may have been Mercury.

"The statite?" Nathan tapped the dark blemish.

"That's right," Rufus said. "We lucked out when it passed between us and Sol. The exterior is very dark, which is one of the reasons it took us so long to spot it."

"What do we know so far?"

"Not much yet," Vessani said. "It's moving inward at fifty-three kilometers per second and will pass within Mercury's orbit before heading back out for the next seventy or so years. We'll need to get closer to know more."

"How soon will we reach it?"

"Let's see." Vessani input parameters into her console's navigational vlass. "We'll need about a day to slow down and match its course. That's assuming we turn around now. We're accelerating the wrong way."

"Then let's get started," Nathan said.

The statite measured twenty kilometers long, fourteen tall, and three wide. The ends tapered down to points, which made the megastructure resemble a massive black kite that rotated slowly on its long axis. It was both larger and smaller than Nathan thought it would be.

Larger because he struggled to wrap his head around a find *this huge*. What were they even supposed to *do* with hundreds of cubic kilometers of pentatech? Never mind the dangers that undoubtedly lingered beneath its surface. They were a motley crew on a stolen ship without backup of any kind. Sure, they'd *found* the thing. But what now?

Smaller because he'd expected something more grandiose and jaw-dropping from the Pentatheon's star-lifting apparatus. Yes, the statite was big in a literal sense—the *Stolen Dragon* was little more than a dust mote next to it—but compared to the scale at which the

Pentatheon had altered the solar system, this was little more than an afterthought. A toy next to other, more impressive megastructures.

Then again, Nathan reminded himself, *this one statite must have been part of a far larger system. How many of these machines once encircled Sol in a dark halo? Hundreds? Thousands?*

Tens of thousands?

Even more than that?

Who the hell even knows anymore?

Either way I look at it, it's big.

"Let's see if I can give us a better view." Vessani cut their thrust and turned the ship toward the megastructure. They floated leisurely across the megastructure's long axis, sunlight glaring at them from one side.

A matte black variant of solar skin coated most of the statite's smooth, uniform exterior, though craters of varying sizes marred its surface here and there. Nathan used a joystick to point the telescope at one of those craters and zoomed in. Some ancient impact had stripped the surface of solar skin, revealing lighter materials underneath that had bowed inward. The damage appeared superficial in nature. Certainly not on the order needed to fling the statite into a seventy-one-year elliptical orbit.

"Anyone see a way in?" Vessani asked.

"I'll let you know if I spot one," Joshua replied.

They passed a canyon with sloped sides that cut across the statite's entire fourteen-kilometer short axis. The slopes led down to ... mechanisms of some kind, with the dangling remnants of massive— if tattered—sheets of reflective material. At first Nathan assumed the statite's surface had been stripped by old impacts, but after closer inspection the machinery around those sheets seemed too well preserved.

"What do you think those are?" Nathan swung the telescope feed toward one of the sheets and zoomed in.

"Hard to say." Joshua rubbed his chin as he pondered the image. "The statite would have needed some means to hold its position. Perhaps those are the remnants of solar sails? Or maybe something else, like a part of the machinery used to gather ejected matter? Whatever used to be there broke off long ago."

The *Stolen Dragon* floated across the statite on its way toward the kite's forward tip. The flat surface of the statite tilted noticeably toward them as they progressed.

"Vess," Nathan said.

"I see it." Vessani gave him a quick, reassuring smile. "I'm not about to let the thing smack us."

"Just making sure."

"Don't you worry." She winked at him, and her tail flicked to the other side of her seat. "Your ship's in good hands."

You, too? he thought. *When did everyone suddenly decide this Jovian tub belongs to me? Not that I'm in a position to say no to a new ship, but still ...*

"Hold on, everyone. Small course correction coming up." Vessani applied a short burst of thrust. Nathan grabbed a handhold to steady himself as the ship pulled ahead of the statite's languid spin. "We'll continue like this, then loop around the other side. Sound good?"

"Works for me," Nathan said.

The *Stolen Dragon* slid across to the front of the statite, and Vessani fired the thrusters again. She eased the ship around the tip, which turned out to be rounded and transparent at the end, leading down into a massive, mechanical funnel.

Possibly a lens for a giant laser? Nathan wondered.

Aiko thumped the side of her head, prompting a curious look from Nathan.

"You all right?" he asked.

"Yeah, just ..." She thumped her head again and shook it. "I'll be fine."

"You sure?"

"It's nothing."

"Doesn't look like nothing."

"It's just ... I can hear it."

"The statite?"

"Yeah. It's like someone's whispering to me. Almost as if they're right behind me, only no one's there when I turn around, and I can't shut them up no matter what I do. It's *annoying.*"

"What's it saying?"

"Bunch of nonsense. Keeps going on and on about needing flesh and metal for its wounds. I *really* wish it would shut up!"

"I can hear it, too." Rufus tapped an implant in his temple.

"There's an extremely powerful juncture nearby. The signal's so strong I switched off my more sensitive implants."

"Wish I could do that," Aiko grumbled.

"I guess I should have figured you'd hear a signal this strong," Rufus said. "Pentatech junctures do overlap with Jovian wireless, after all."

"*Really* wish they didn't."

"Make sure to tell us if it gets worse," Nathan said. "Both of you, okay?"

"Of course, Nate," Rufus said, calm and collected.

"Yeah, yeah," Aiko dismissed, sounding a little irritated.

Vessani brought the ship around to the statite's dark side.

"Hold here," Nathan said. "Let's wait until we have some light."

"Sure thing." Vessani brought them to a relative stop about a kilometer off the side of the statite, and they waited.

Nathan glanced over to the Black Egg, still secured to the jump seat. He wasn't sure why he chose that moment to look at it. Maybe the talk of signals put the artifact in mind. Regardless, something appeared to be moving inside the Black Egg. It gave the impression of a long, snaking object swimming around, almost as if the artifact were about to hatch and give birth.

"Vess?"

"Yeah?"

"Is it normal for the Black Egg to be doing that?"

"Doing what?" Vessani glanced away from her controls. "Um, no. Definitely not."

"Just so you know"—Nathan rested a hand on his holstered pistol, the wyrmstake he'd liberated from the corvette's supplies—"if that egg hatches, I'm shooting whatever spills out."

"It's a glorified signal relay, Nate," Rufus said. "Not an actual egg."

"Maybe so, but I've had my fill of nasty surprises."

"Look!" Joshua pointed, drawing everyone's attention back to the statite.

Sunlight had just hit the side they were on, and long shadows formed behind every surface imperfection. Most of them were small, either created by the lips of craters or by mechanical protrusions.

But one shadow stood out, wider and longer than all the others. It stretched back from a massive crescent gash, the edges twisted into a parody of a grin filled with jagged metal teeth. It must have been at least half a kilometer across.

"The wound," Rufus murmured.

"Hold up." Nathan turned to the cleric. "I thought the wound was that nasty flesh pit in the deifactory."

"No." Rufus shook his head. "That was nothing more than a twisted reflection. Something made by human hands at the direction of the deifactory. *This*"—he gestured at the cavernous maw—"is not of human origin."

"It doesn't look very inviting," Joshua said.

"Your orders?" Vessani asked.

"Take us in closer," Nathan said. "We didn't come all this way to turn back now."

"Got it. Closing in." Vessani eased up on the throttle and maneuvered the ship across the surface to the ugly, leering tear in the statite's side. The cavernous mouth gaped open, and the ship came to a halt near it.

"What *caused* this?" Joshua wondered aloud.

"The Scourging of Heaven," Rufus whispered with equal parts reverence and fear.

"Vess," Nathan asked, "can you get some light in there?"

"Umm." Vessani searched the controls. "As soon as I find the right button."

"Here." Aiko grabbed the handhold behind Vessani's headrest, hauled herself forward and tapped a quick series of commands into a vlass. A searchlight below the cockpit switched on and illuminated the twisted depths of the wound's ragged, jutting metal.

"Interesting." Joshua pointed to one side of the gash. "You can see the rough crescent shape continue into the interior, but at a very shallow angle. Almost like . . . maybe an energy weapon hit the statite?"

"You'd need one hell of a gun to melt through all this," Nathan said. "How deep does it go?"

"Let me see if I can get us a better view." Vessani fired a burst of thrust and tried to shine the spotlight at an angle down into the wound. The light reflected off a long cavern, its walls a jumble of twisted wreckage that transitioned into oppressive darkness at the far end.

"*Really* deep." Nathan sighed.

Joshua pulled himself over to the copilot seat. "Radar puts the end of the cave some five kilometers away."

"Like I said. Really deep."

"Want me to head on in?" Vessani glanced over her shoulder to Nathan.

"Not particularly. What about the spin?"

"I can handle it. The spin isn't too fast, and there's more than enough space inside to maneuver. I can get us in and out safely, no problem. Plus, a lot of that wreckage looks wide enough to land on, if you wanted to."

"Hmm," Nathan murmured thoughtfully.

"This seems to be the only way we can access the interior," Rufus said.

"I know, but . . ."

"Don't you worry." Vessani winked at him. "I won't put so much as a scuff on your new ship."

It's not my ship, Nathan thought, but then said:

"All right, but I'll hold you to that," he warned her, though he grinned as he said it. He took a deep breath and swept his gaze over the others. "It's been a bumpy ride, but this is what we came all this way for. Vess, take us—"

Red lights began flashing across both pilot consoles.

The *Leviathan of Io* and its escort of five *Star Dragon* corvettes decelerated in unison as they approached the ancient statite.

<There it is,> Galatt Xormun mused from the *Leviathan*'s bridge, his posture rigid in the high gees. He gazed upon the magnified image of the distant black sliver with a satisfied smirk. The prize was finally within their grasp.

The *Leviathan*'s thrusters cut off, and Xormun floated off the floor. He steadied himself with a hand against the ceiling.

<Target distance reached,> the pilot said. <All ships at a relative stop five thousand kilometers behind the statite.>

<No reaction detected from the relic,> a data analyst reported.

<Send *Shadow Three* forward,> Xormun ordered. <Let's take a good look at what we're dealing with.>

<Yes, Apex.> The comms officer opened a commect channel.

<*Leviathan of Io* to *Shadow Three*. Proceed to the statite and begin your sweep.>

<Orders confirmed, *Leviathan*. Heading out.>

The corvette spun around, lit its thrusters, and slipped out of formation.

. . . the wound . . .

. . . it aches . . .

. . . it burns . . .

Xormun frowned and glanced around the bridge, wondering if anyone else had heard that. He grabbed a handhold and propelled himself over to the comms station, stopping himself with a hand on the console's side. He opened a channel to *Shadow Six*, which had picked up the survivors from *Shadow Two* marooned on the Sanguine Ring.

<Y-yes, Apex?>

The stutter on the other end of the line caught Xormun off guard and he frowned again.

<Is something wrong?> he asked his copy-subordinate, feeling a mix of concern and annoyance. He wondered, not for the first time, if his copy had suffered more than superficial damage while on the Sanguine Ring. He made a mental note to have the copy's persona scrutinized before reintegration.

<Uhh, no. Nothing. Nothing's wrong. Why do you ask?>

<Do you hear it?>

<The statite?>

<Yes, the statite,> Xormun bit out.

<I-I do, but that's to be expected. We needed the Black Egg to track the signal this far, but now that we're so close . . . >

His copy trailed off.

<Any reaction from our Black Egg?> Xormun asked.

<Um, yes. Th-there's heightened internal activity. We think it's reconfiguring itself to better boost the signal.>

<Any cause for concern?>

<I . . . don't think so?>

Xormun grimaced at his copy's lack of decisiveness. <Are you sure you're in the right state of mind?>

<Y-yes. Just . . . a little distracted. The Black Egg is being— It's loud sometimes. Its presence makes concentrating difficult.>

<Keep me informed of any developments,> Xormun ordered in a neutral tone.

<Yes, Apex. Of course.>

Xormun closed the channel and checked on *Shadow Three's* progress. The corvette spun around again and commenced its final deceleration, but even at this range it began relaying back a treasure trove of images, video, and instrument data for his analysts to delve into.

<Apex, take a look at this.>

Xormun floated over to one of those analysts, who indicated a damaged section on the statite's surface. It was a grinning wound over half a kilometer wide.

<How convenient. Once *Shadow Three* completes its survey of the exterior—>

The Wound.

The Wound.

I Want.

I Need!

Those last words slammed into Xormun's mind with almost physical force, and his vision darkened. The walls and ceiling transformed into the black embrace of a star-studded sky, and a huge, twisted mouth replaced the bridge floor. The lips curled back, snarling, baring metal teeth. Those teeth parted and he plummeted down a throat built from the twisted fabric of space itself. He spun away, tumbling through a bottomless abyss that—

The imagery ended as abruptly as it had begun.

<Apex?> the analyst asked.

Xormun paused, momentarily stunned by how vividly his senses had been overtaken. He crossed his arms, striking a thoughtful pose to mask the momentary slip in composure.

Distracting indeed, he thought, recovering from the experience. *But a few random visions won't be enough to deter us. This place, and all its secrets, will be ours. It's what we were sent out to do.*

<Send the following message to *Shadow Three*,> Xormun ordered at last. <Complete the initial survey of the statite's exterior, then proceed inside. All other ships will close with the statite.>

"We're in so much trouble," Vessani muttered under her breath, hands gripping her flight controls.

Nathan grabbed the edge of her console and lowered himself onto the cockpit dome's glass. The *Stolen Dragon* sat inside a recess along the wound cavern's walls, their view of the mangled interior partially obstructed by a twisted structural beam. Gravity was light this close to the statite's center axis, perhaps a tenth of a gee.

Nathan wasn't sure how Vessani had managed to slip the ship underneath that mess without any damage, but true to her word, she'd managed to back them into the alcove without so much as a scrape. He pressed his cheek against the concave glass, trying to catch a glimpse of the cavern mouth.

"We've got company," he whispered.

A Jovian corvette swept its searchlight across the wound interior, then fired its thrusters to hold a relatively stable position outside.

Aiko joined him and followed his gaze. "Another *Star Dragon*. That's not the ship we saw before we ducked inside. It's too small."

"Which means there's more than one ship out there," Nathan concluded with a grimace.

"I'm guessing the big one was the *Leviathan of Io*."

"We have all the luck," Nathan grumbled.

"Want me to blast that corvette?" Vessani asked, one hand hovering over the weapon controls.

"And let the rest of them know where we are?" Nathan asked pointedly. "No, thank you. Keep it quiet."

"We might take out that corvette," Aiko said, "but we don't stand a chance against that cruiser!"

"They'll find us eventually," Joshua said. "We can't stay here forever."

"We can't run, either," Nathan added grimly. "The Jovians will overtake us with ease."

"Unless we push this ship to the limit," Joshua pointed out. "We'll feel that in the morning, but it's better that than rotting in a Jovian prison."

"Hold that thought," Nathan muttered. "Looks like they're moving on."

The Jovian corvette angled its thrusters and slid out of sight.

Rufus sighed with relief. "They didn't see us."

"This time at least," Aiko said. "It helps that we're in a stealthy ship."

"But they'll eventually spot us." Nathan pushed off the glass and climbed back up to the cockpit peninsula.

"So, we can't fight and we can't run," Joshua summarized.

"Yep."

"Then what do we do?" Joshua asked.

"That's the big question, isn't it?"

Chapter Twenty-Four

Nathan stood in front of the others, a hand resting on each of the consoles.

"Josh?"

"Yes?"

"You still think this statite is for star lifting?"

"There's no way to know for sure, but we've seen a few signs that support that conclusion. The tip of the statite did resemble a laser aperture, for instance."

"Then you believe this place contains a habitat-melting superlaser."

"I do, yes."

"And now the Jovians have it." Rufus sighed.

"A question for everyone." Nathan glanced around the cockpit. "What do we think the Everlife will do with this place once they find a way to control it?"

"Whatever the hell they want." Vessani snorted. "Who's going to stop them?"

"Who indeed?" Nathan said, not yet ready to drop his bombshell.

"The statite's destructive power may very well eclipse every military in the solar system." Joshua paused. "*Combined.* The Union and the Concord would cease to exist as they are today. They would have no choice but to submit to the Everlife because fighting would amount to nothing more than a society-wide suicide pact. Perhaps our governments would limp along for a while, but in name only, because the Everlife would be calling the shots."

"Anything to add, Aiko?" Nathan tapped his temple. "How are those voices?"

"Annoyingly present. Thanks for asking."

"What about the statite?"

"Well, I know they're my people—*former* people, really—but I wouldn't leave them so much as a fork, if I could help it. Never mind a superlaser!"

"Then it seems we're all in agreement," Nathan said. "If the situation continues as is, a lot of bad stuff is going to happen." He leaned toward them. "So, let's do something about it."

Stunned silence followed. Joshua's jaw actually dropped.

"Look, people," Nathan continued when no one else spoke up. "Like it or not, we're the only crew in a position to stop them. So, I say we do just that. We stop them."

"*How?*" Aiko asked pointedly.

"I don't know. But the way I see it, we either take our chances and run, *or* we stick around and prevent the Jovians from destroying our collective ways of life."

"I appreciate the sentiment, Nate," Rufus said, "but this one is out of our league."

"I need to sit down." Joshua sank into one of the jump seats and placed his head in his hands.

"You and me both." Aiko plopped down into the copilot seat.

"Okay. Not the responses I was looking for," Nathan said, "but at least you're all not screaming at me."

"I'm *thinking*." Joshua laced his fingers through his hair. "To achieve something like that, we'd have to ... I don't know. Destroy the entire statite or something."

"Not with the weapons we have," Vessani said. "This ship has five torpedoes left. That's hardly enough to scratch the statite's hull, and only if we hit the same spot with all of them."

"Which means we need help," Joshua replied, sounding deep in his own thoughts.

"I doubt the Jovians will be too keen on lending a hand," Aiko pointed out.

"No, not them." Joshua looked up, his hair a mess from his fingers. "But maybe we can use something else."

"What do you have in mind?" Nathan asked.

"What if we hit the statite with the most powerful force in the universe?"

He looked around expectantly, but when no one spoke up, he added:

"I'm talking about physics!"

"Ah." Rufus nodded. "I should have guessed that one."

"Hear me out," Joshua began. "The statite is speeding along at fifty-three kilometers a second. I don't care how sturdy it is. If it collides with something at those speeds, it's going to hurt. A *lot.*"

"Hmm." Nathan rubbed his chin. "You could be on to something here. We're inside Venus's orbit, but there are still plenty of hazards for the statite to smash into, such as Mercury and its moons. Or Sol, for that matter."

"But how do we change the statite's course?" Vessani asked. "It's too massive for our ship to push."

"And even if we could, the Jovians won't let us," Aiko said. "They'd blast us off the hull as soon as we tried."

"Yeah." Nathan sighed and crossed his arms. "I do like where you're going with this, Josh, but until we—"

Rufus cleared his throat, drawing everyone's gaze.

"Perhaps there's an easier solution," the cleric said with a crafty smile. "I can *ask* the statite to change its own course."

"You really think this is going to work?" Vessani asked.

"We won't know until he tries," Joshua said.

"We're still inside. Am I the only one worried about that?"

"No," Nathan grunted, "but at least we're close to the exit."

"What about the Jovians lurking all over the place?" Vessani asked.

"We'll cross that bridge when we come to it."

"That is the *opposite* of a plan!"

"Quiet, please." Rufus sat down on the floor and folded his legs. "I need to concentrate."

"Sorry," Vessani whispered in a mousy voice. "I'll shut up now."

Rufus spread his fingers across his chest and bowed his head. He recited five prayers to Pathfinder, cleansing his mind, preparing the landscape of his thoughts for communion. He closed his eyes and activated his dormant implants—

—and that first, brief contact nearly overwhelmed him!

The statite's juncture resonated through his mind, deafening his own thoughts with its mere presence. Words and ideas roared around and through him: screaming, screeching, *seething*. His entire being shuddered under the awesome power of a dormant sliver of a vanished god, crumbling under the immense weight of its dreams.

No, not dreams.

Nightmares.

Disjointed words and images pierced through his own mentality, suffused with both ancient pain and a fathomless hatred he could not identify. Anger and sadness and raw malevolence swirled together to form something alien and horrifying, but so much grander than mere human thoughts could comprehend. Vast waves of this mental ocean threatened to drown his lonely piece of flotsam.

The vision coalesced, and he found himself standing on the statite's surface with Sol warming his back. Far to either side, the vast mechanical plain bent up unnaturally, folding upward and inward until it blocked Sol and blotted out the stars.

He found himself enclosed in a great metal sphere. Darkness fell, but only for a moment before fiery light bled through tears in the metal that took the form of the wound. The same shape repeated over and over again. Jagged mouths leered at him from all angles, some of them still, others babbling gibberish, but most speaking or shouting or raging in a deafening discord of alien thoughts.

Never before had he experienced a juncture so alive, so glorious, and yet so terrifying in the same instance. He shrank away from the connection, the insignificance of his frail mortal mind dwarfed against the slumbering power of the Pentatheon's great works.

He clenched his jaw so hard his teeth ached, and he squeezed his eyes tight until tears leaked from the edges. He bowed his head and raised his open palms, reaching outward and upward.

Pathfinder, he began, his thoughts trembling. *Hear our plea. Aid us in our time of need.*

The wound-mouths yammered at him in an avalanche of overlapping chatter that threatened to bury him. His hands shook, and the muscles in his arms strained as an ethereal force pressed down upon them. His spine bent forward, and his brow dipped lower, reaching for his lap.

Pathfinder, please. We need you. We cannot allow your creation to be perverted into a weapon. Please, help us. We—

The mouths stopped their babbling all at once. All of them clapped shut, though some gnashed their teeth, metal screeching against metal. Several of them shifted across the spherical walls, not so much moving as tearing their way through the metal, leaving disjointed trails in their wake. They converged in front of him, pooling together, combining to form a single gigantic mouth.

Please, help us.

The terrible maw yawned open. Fire and brimstone blasted out, and hate-filled words exploded in Rufus's mind.

I WILL NOT.

His eyes rolled back into his skull, and he collapsed into a twitching heap. A circuit breaker at the base of his skull popped, sticking out in a cylindrical tab, and smoke rose from its sides. His arms crossed, almost as if he were hugging himself, and he began foaming at the mouth.

"Hey there," Nathan said. "You with us again?"

"Wha . . . ?" Rufus smacked his lips and blinked his eyes open. "What happened?"

"You tell us. You were the one gibbering on the floor."

"What? Give me a second." Rufus raised a shaky hand and rubbed it back over his bald head. He found the popped circuit breaker and pressed it into his skull, where it clicked into place.

"Take your time but hurry up," Nathan said.

"I know." Rufus took a few deep breaths, then stared at his trembling right hand.

"How are you, really?"

"Shaken." The cleric looked up at the others. "The juncture was . . . terrifying. I could barely hear my own thoughts in there. I tried to pass on our wishes, but . . ." He shook his head.

"Not happening?" Nathan offered the cleric a hand.

"No." Rufus took the hand and let himself be pulled to his feet. He steadied himself against the wall.

"Is there any point in trying again?" Nathan asked.

"He was on the floor drooling!" Joshua pointed out.

"No harm in asking the question." Nathan patted Rufus on the shoulder. "Well? How about it?"

"I was? Drooling, I mean?"

"Yep."

Rufus frowned and dabbed the corner of his mouth. He inspected the strand of saliva clinging to his fingertip.

"Oh dear."

"That would be a 'no' then?"

"Nate, I've encountered some dangerous junctures before, but this is on a whole different scale." He rubbed the back of his head, found the breaker tab again, and circled it with a fingertip. "My implants must have switched off to protect my mind. That's never happened before. Whatever intellect is left within the statite is . . ." He looked up. "Nate, I don't think what's in there came from the Pentatheon."

"What do you mean?"

"Something dark has taken residence there—something alien to me—and it's filled the statite with an irrational rage. Whatever it is, it will *never* help us, and I fear what will happen if it ever fully awakens. I can't imagine any of the Pentatheon's creations ever being consumed by so much hatred. The mind in there isn't simply broken; it's been corrupted. Twisted, somehow. It is very, *very* dangerous!"

"All right. We get it." Nathan gave the cleric another shoulder pat. "Whatever's in there is bad news. We'll try something else."

"Okay, but what?" Aiko asked.

"I don't know." Nathan turned around in a slow circle. "Anyone?"

"Redirecting the statite looks to be a bust," Vessani said. "Where's that leave us?"

"Nowhere," Aiko groaned. "*That's* where."

"Maybe not," Joshua said. "If we can't destroy the statite, then the next best thing is to royally mess this place up. We cause as much damage as we can before we cut and run. Let the Jovians lord over a ruin."

"I'm all for making a good mess," Nathan said, "but with what? Our torpedoes will barely leave a mark."

"True. On the *surface*." Joshua gestured toward the wound cavern outside. "But we don't have to blast through the exterior. That job's already done for us, and there's a lot of this 'cave' we haven't seen yet."

"Okay, then." Nathan nodded in thought. "You're guessing there's something juicy farther back in all this wreckage? Something our torpedoes might actually be able to hurt?"

"It's a possibility. Here, look." Joshua removed a stylus from the pilot console, cleared one of the vlass screens, and began to draw an outline of the statite. He then added the wound cavern, which cut into the interior, angling toward the statite's front.

"The farther we travel down this wound, the closer we come to where we'd expect to find the main laser or its support systems."

"And those are the true prizes the Everlife is after," Aiko said.

"Exactly! Wreck those and we strip the Jovians of their new superweapon."

"Now we're talking!" Nathan grinned. "Vess? How's it look out there?"

"That corvette just passed across the wound again. Looks like it's still busy scoping out the surface. If we're going to move, now's the time to do it."

"Then let's go. Take us as far back into the wound as you can."

"You've got it!" She took hold of the flight controls.

"And then what?" Rufus asked, grabbing a handhold as Vessani eased the ship out of the wrecked wall.

"Then"—Nathan flashed a quick smile—"we go for a walk."

Nathan slid the helmet on and twisted it tight against the pressure suit's neck ring. He would have preferred to venture into a derelict pentatech artifact with at least his old hard suit protecting his skin, but this was the best he could do under the circumstances. A catch in the neck ring locked in place, and a message appeared on the wrist vlass, indicating the suit was properly sealed.

He checked on the others who'd assembled in the cargo hold by the starboard airlock. Joshua and Rufus were almost finished suiting up. Aiko's commando body could handle far worse than vacuum, and Vessani would remain with the ship.

"Here." Aiko handed Nathan one of the Jovian commects.

"Thanks." He shoved it into his belt next to his pistol and other equipment.

Joshua accepted his. "Won't the Jovians hear us if we use these?"

"I've set the default signal strength as low as it'll go," Aiko explained. "That should drop the chances of the Jovians sniffing us out."

"Let's keep radio chatter to a minimum all the same," Nathan said. "Especially if you're close to the wound cavern."

"What if we can't reach someone and it's important?" Rufus asked.

"Then bump the power up until you can," Nathan said. "Everyone sealed up?"

"Ready." Joshua gave them a thumbs-up.

"Good to go, Nate," Rufus said.

Nathan keyed his commect and spoke into his headset. "Vess, can you hear me?"

"Loud and clear."

"We're heading out. Josh and Rufus will look for a way deeper into the statite. Meanwhile, Aiko and I will see if we can find a decent path back to the wound cavern. Ideally, I'd like one of us to keep an eye on the entrance so we know when trouble starts moving our way. Mind the ship for us, and only call if it's an emergency."

"Got it. You can count on me."

Yeah, he thought, smiling as he opened the airlock. *I guess I can. Didn't think so when we first met, but you've had our backs multiple times, and you handle yourself well in a fight. This job didn't go the way any of us had hoped, but I'm glad you're with us, Vess.*

The four of them filed into the airlock. Nathan cycled it, opened the exterior, and stepped out first. The airlock provided a small pool of light that disappeared into oppressive darkness a few meters from the ship. He switched his helmet light on.

Vessani had managed to squeeze the *Stolen Dragon* deep into a tunnel that branched off the wound cavern. He doubted either he or Aiko could have pulled off the maneuver without crunching against parts of the uneven walls, but Vessani had only grazed a single jutting support as she backed the ship into the side passage.

Nathan shined his helmet light around and took in their surroundings. The floor—for lack of a better term—was an uneven mess of cables wrapped around thick support beams. He took each step with care, keeping an eye out for trip hazards.

The uneven terrain told him he was somewhere humans shouldn't be. Deifactories could be mazes to the uninitiated, but at least they had flat surfaces to stand on and corridors to move through. *This* wasn't meant for human traversal. He was standing inside the guts of a giant—potentially insane—machine.

But there was more to it than that.

The space didn't adhere to comfortable orthogonal arrangement.

There were almost no right angles to be found anywhere, even between what he thought of as the walls and ceiling, each of them ribbed by what looked like giant metal bones. He struggled to come up with a phrase to describe his surroundings and eventually settled upon "mechanized megafauna." He felt as if he were stuck in the intestines of a huge, mechanical beast. A beast that, if it twitched or stretched the wrong way, would pop him like a zit.

"I already hate this place," Nathan murmured.

The more he stared, the more unsettled he became.

Pale metallic "vines" spread across much of their surroundings, often ending in open and empty nodules, as if machines had been birthed from those pods. The vines stood out to his eye, both in hue and in how they'd spread without any obvious rhyme or reason, sometimes in opposition to the larger structural cues. Almost like they'd been fighting the original builders, morphing and modifying the statite's interior with detrimental goals. Was he gazing upon a battlefield from the Scourging itself? The remnants of a machine infection introduced through the statite's wound?

He wondered.

Nathan felt a tap on his shoulder and turned to see Joshua, who brought their helmets together.

"Rufus spotted a path we can squeeze through over there." He pointed to a lopsided, triangular gap between two thick cable clusters. "We'll check that one out first."

"All right. Good luck."

Joshua pulled back with a thumbs-up and, together with Rufus, they headed down the dark passage.

Aiko waved at Nathan and pointed to a section of the wall on the opposite side of the chamber. He joined her, and then realized the "wall" was actually the outer surface of a massive cylindrical structure that tilted upward and outward, curving away to form a narrow passage that might lead them back toward the wound cavern. Thick ribbing bound the cylinder at regular intervals, which provided surfaces for hands and feet like an oversized ladder.

Aiko mimed a climbing gesture, then pointed again.

"Works for me." Nathan grabbed one of the ribs. "Good thing the gravity's so light."

He and Aiko began to climb.

CHAPTER TWENTY-FIVE

Their path meandered through the gaps between ancient, crumpled machinery and warped structural support ribs. They snaked their way forward, often forced to duck underneath huge, low-hanging devices of unknown purpose. Nathan was tempted to turn back when the path narrowed to a low slot, but they pressed on, crawling forward on their hands and knees. Their perseverance paid off, and the path widened afterward.

Their course snaked away from the *Stolen Dragon*, twisting its way around or through hulking machines. His own breathing grated on him in the absence of other noises, but he pressed on, one careful foot in front of the other, his eyes scanning for hazards.

He wasn't in his hard suit, after all, with its reassuring layers of protection, but a Jovian pressure suit for keeping organic prisoners alive and not much else. He wasn't sure how the material would respond to a sharp edge, and he felt no need to test its durability. A roll of general-purpose adhesive tape hung from his belt, just in case he needed to plug a leak in an emergency.

"Stop."

Aiko's sudden voice pierced the silence, startling Nathan. His pulse quickened. He searched their surroundings but couldn't spot any obvious dangers. A small, slanted gap ahead looked like it would lead into the wound cavern proper, judging by how distant the far wall was. He turned to Aiko, expecting some indication of what had prompted her to break radio silence, but only found her standing in the open, arms slack.

291

He walked back to her and pressed his helmet against her head. "What is it?" he asked.

"Something's wrong," she said, her words vibrating through his helmet's bubble.

A subtle tremor in her tone sent a chill down his spine. The change in her demeanor wasn't pronounced or obvious, but he knew her well enough to sense it all the same. It was like an undercurrent of dread rippling just beneath serene waters.

Aiko had always been his fearless companion, a font of energy and enthusiasm, her ability to inhabit multiple bodies shielding her from permanent consequence. Perhaps the losses of her copies had finally begun to weigh on her mind?

Then again, he thought, considering where they were, *maybe not.*

"What's wrong?" Nathan asked.

"I think we're in a lot of trouble."

"We knew this."

"No. I don't mean the Jovians. The statite, Nate. It's *wrong!*"

He looked around again. "Wrong how?"

"It's talking to me."

"Wasn't it doing that before?"

"Yeah, but it's growing louder, more insistent. More . . . deranged. It's like this huge presence is lurking behind me, screaming into my ears, pushing into my mind, sifting through my thoughts like they're pages in a binder, and there isn't a damned thing I can do to shut it out!"

"Can't you ignore it? Isn't that what you've been doing so far?"

"I'm *trying!*" Her cameras met his eyes. "Believe me, I am! But I don't have a switch in my head like Rufus does! I can't choose not to listen to this thing!"

"Okay, okay." He placed his hands on her shoulders. "I hear you, but I'm not sure what we can do about it. Any idea what's making it worse?"

"I think the statite is waking up. I think *we* disturbed its slumber."

"But . . ." Nathan swallowed, his throat suddenly dry. "Rufus's attempt . . . to commune with it?"

She nodded against his helmet. "He succeeded, but not in the way we wanted."

"Then does the statite know we're here?"

"I don't know. Its words are . . . confused. Demented, even. And angry. So *very* angry!"

"How bad is it?" Nathan asked. "For you, I mean. Can you push through?"

"For now, yeah. But it's difficult, Nate. It's so damn difficult! And it's getting worse!"

"All right." He pointed to the gap ahead. "Let's push on for now. We've made it this far. Just a little farther, and we should be able to keep an eye on the wound."

"Sure," Aiko replied, sounding doubtful. "Just a little farther."

"If it becomes unbearable for you, let me know. We'll turn back."

"Okay." She put a hand over his and gave him a tender squeeze. "Thanks, Nate."

"Come on."

He led the way through the gap, which forced him to bend over at an awkward diagonal in order to slip through. He pressed his palms against the sloped wall and hand-walked his way to the other side, which opened to an incline leading up to a narrow ledge.

He climbed up to the ledge and crouched, the immense wound cavern sprawled out before him, a distant swatch of stars visible to his right. He switched off his helmet light, unclipped his binoculars, and zoomed in on the grinning, twisted cave mouth. Nearby wreckage allowed him to peer at the opening while only exposing his head and shoulders.

Aiko crouched beside him, equally hidden.

A Jovian corvette slid by the mouth, slowing and rotating to face the interior before it disappeared from view.

"It's only a matter of time before they poke their noses in here." He lowered the binoculars. He was about to settle into a more comfortable position when the rounded bow of a huge vessel peeked into view. He raised the binoculars again and studied the craft.

The Jovian warship bristled with heavy weapon batteries and thick armor plating. Nathan doubted any single ship in the Neptune Concord or even the Saturn Union could take that monster on one-on-one and win.

Nathan lowered the binoculars. He didn't need them for a ship that big. He leaned back to Aiko, who pressed her head against his helmet.

"The *Leviathan*?" he asked.

"The *Leviathan*," she confirmed. "I recognize the hull markings."

They watched the Jovians for a good twenty minutes, alternating between hunkering down behind the debris and catching glimpses of the ship's movements. The statite's rotation brought the *Leviathan of Io* into view at regular intervals, the massive ship keeping watch outside the wound while its corvettes flitted about. Nathan counted three separate corvettes during one of the rotations, but he knew there could be more.

One of the corvettes ducked into the cavern and flew down the full length, far past his vantage point, then circled back around and returned to the entrance. It disappeared outside for several minutes, then a corvette—he couldn't tell if it was the same one—flew back inside and landed half a kilometer back from the *Stolen Dragon*'s hiding spot.

Nathan lost sight of the corvette when it settled into the cavern's twisted walls. He crouched back into cover and pressed his helmet against Aiko's head.

"Think they have a path to reach us?"

She didn't respond. Didn't even move.

"Hey, Aiko?"

"Wh-what?" She shuddered and turned to him.

"That corvette. Can its crew reach the *Dragon* from where they landed?"

"Oh." She paused for a while, staring at nothing. "I guess."

"You hanging in there?"

She paused again before answering. "I'll manage."

Nathan's original plan had been for Aiko to stay behind as their lookout, but he couldn't leave her alone in her current state, and he also couldn't return to the *Stolen Dragon*, since that would leave them blind to whatever the Jovians were up to, which meant both of them needed to stay behind.

"Okay," Nathan said. "You let me know if—"

A gloved hand clenched around Nathan's shoulder, and long, bony fingers dug into his flesh.

"What the?!" he blurted, recoiling from the hand. He spun around, pressed his back against the wreckage, and raised his leg for a reflexive kick, but then paused and lowered his leg when he saw who it was. *"Rufus?"*

The cleric backed away and held up both hands. Joshua shuffled into view behind him.

Nathan grumbled, more in frustration at himself than anything else. He slid down the incline behind the ledge and the three men pressed their helmets together.

"Sorry," Rufus said.

"You scared the shit out of me!" Nathan said.

"I didn't mean to. Just trying to maintain radio silence, like you said."

"I—" Nathan took a deep breath to calm his racing heart. "Okay, good work on that front, but what are you two doing here? Shouldn't you be searching for the statite's soft underbelly?"

"We were," Joshua said. "Until we found something."

"Something that should connect to that 'soft underbelly,'" Rufus added with a sly smile.

"There's no straight path to it," Joshua said, "but it's only about two or three hundred meters from the ship. Not a bad hike, given how twisty this place is."

"What is it?" Nathan asked.

"My guess is a computronium storage tank," Joshua said. "We found a pumping station, and by the looks of it, it used to circulate computronium."

"Then you think you might have found this place's brain?"

"A path that should lead to it, yes."

"And it's right next to the wound cavern?" Nathan permitted himself a cold grin. "I guess we got lucky for a change."

"The odds were in our favor on this one," Joshua said. "Whatever created the wound wanted to do some serious damage, so it's not surprising to find sensitive areas nearby. After we found the station, we backtracked to the ship, but Vess said you and Aiko were still out. She pointed us down the path you took, and here we are."

"But we have another problem." Rufus's eyes turned cold and stern. "The statite is waking up."

"Yeah, Aiko said the same thing." Nathan put a hand on her shoulder, but she didn't react. "Those voices are creeping her out."

"The juncture is *extremely* agitated," Rufus said. "I don't dare try to connect."

"And there's more than just the signal," Joshua added. "We've seen physical signs this place is waking up, too, like at the pumping station. Some machines started vibrating while we were there, and we could hear and feel material flowing through some of the pipes."

"Great," Nathan grunted. He shifted his stance and checked back on the wound's mouth. The *Leviathan* came into view once more, firing its thrusters to bring its position closer. "So, do we take out those pumps? Will that cause enough damage?"

"No," Joshua said. "We need to find the main storage tank. Hitting *that* should cripple this area of the statite."

"Got it. All right, let's—"

The ground trembled and shifted under their feet, and Nathan grabbed hold of a warped beam sticking out of the wreckage. Light bloomed outside the cavern, drawing his eye, and he watched as a brilliant beam struck the *Leviathan*'s bow. The light stung his eyes, but he found himself unable to turn away from the terrifying display of power.

Layered armor turned white hot, liquefying almost instantly under the beam's onslaught. The attack punched past the ship's protective shell like it wasn't even there and then carved its way through the numerous decks and bulkheads underneath. The beam ate through the vessel's long axis—an entire *kilometer* of Jovian warship—and blew out the far side.

The *Leviathan*'s thrusters cut out—what was left of them, anyway—and the beam arched upward through the vessel, splitting it into two neat halves. The cleaved segments floated away from each other, their exposed cross-sections glowing orange.

"Gods." Nathan soaked in the destruction with stunned disbelief, his mouth hanging open. He shook his head, then turned back to the others. Joshua and Rufus shared similar expressions.

The true power of this ancient relic finally became clear in his mind. Before, the destruction it could wreak had been an abstract concept. A terrifying potential that, nonetheless, lacked a certain degree of reality.

But no more.

Now he *knew* how powerful the statite truly was, even in its wounded, derelict state.

"Did you see that?" Nathan exclaimed, his helmet pressed against Joshua's.

"I saw," Joshua replied weakly.

"I knew the star-lifting laser would be powerful. But that's . . ."

"You're wrong," Joshua breathed, and Nathan turned to see a dark realization fill the man's eyes. "That wasn't the main laser," he added, his gaze fixed on the wreckage, now drifting out of view below the wound.

"But . . ."

"Unless I've missed my guess"—Joshua paused to swallow—"that was one of the statite's *maneuvering jets*."

"No way. That *had* to be the main laser."

"The angle's wrong. It *couldn't* fire on the *Leviathan* from this position. And haven't you noticed? Doesn't the gravity feel different now?"

"It—" Nathan shifted from one foot to the other. Joshua was right. Gravity had increased since the beam fired. "Yeah. Maybe a quarter of a gee."

"Think about what we just witnessed." He faced Nathan with grim eyes. "This place just cut a Jovian warship in two *by accident*, while doing nothing more than adjusting its spin!"

Nathan gazed back out the wound cavern and bit into his lower lip. His perception of the statite's true power from a few moments ago wilted away, replaced with the cold realization that his tiny human brain simply couldn't fathom how powerful the artifact truly was.

A Jovian corvette ducked into the wound cavern, followed by a smaller craft that may have been a shuttle carrying survivors from the *Leviathan*.

"I have a feeling it's going to get crowded in here," Joshua said.

"Yeah," Nathan agreed. "We should go before one of them spots us. We'll head back to the ship for now."

He shook Aiko's shoulder. She looked up at him, and he pointed a thumb back the way they came. She rose and followed him down the slope without a single word or gesture.

She never once looked at the destruction outside.

Nathan switched his helmet light back on and led the party toward the *Stolen Dragon* while stealing occasional glances back at Aiko. The Jovian trudged through the convoluted passages as if on a private form of autopilot, pulling up the rear with a downturned head and slumped shoulders.

The path back had changed, not in any physical way, but by nature of the stronger gravity and a slight shift in its angle.

They pressed on through the statite's ruined guts, squeezing through a tight cleft between two mangled support pillars until it opened into a wider space. Nathan slowed and motioned Rufus and Joshua to pass him, then matched Aiko's pace. He keyed his commect, judging the group to be far enough from the wound cavern for them to talk safely. Besides, he figured the Jovians were a bit distracted at the moment.

"You okay?" he asked, trying to keep his tone casual.

She didn't answer immediately, just continued to march forward, her head low.

"Aiko?"

"I'm *fine*."

"Just checking. You know, because I care that much."

"I know."

"Are you really fine?"

"That's what I just *said*."

Nathan sighed. "And so you did."

He grimaced and quickened his pace, resuming his spot in front before the path constricted again. He ducked under the bulk of a massive, cylindrical device, cables hanging from it like pale vines. He pushed them aside and stepped carefully around the coiled ends, his mind falling back to Aiko.

He was so distracted that he didn't see the Jovian commando up ahead until they almost collided.

The enemy soldier backpedaled into view, emerging swiftly from a dark side passage with his rifle aimed back the way he came. Nathan flinched in surprise, and the commando spun to face him, swinging the rifle around. Nathan's eyes widened, drawn to the barrel coming around to face him—and the death it would bring—but then the back of one of the commando's feet caught on a cable, and he tripped.

The commando fell back, off balance, the rifle tracking high. A quick burst of silent shots cut through the vacuum and flew wide over their heads, jostling cables and sparking against derelict machinery.

Nathan didn't think, only acted. He rushed in, shoved the rifle barrel further upward, and tackled the commando in the chest.

"Gah!" he grunted, the soft meat of his shoulder crunching against Jovian armor. A small corner of his mind screamed at him that he was *not* in his hard suit and he should *not* be taking on a Jovian commando in close quarters! But the blossoming pain proved to be worth it, because the impact threw the commando off balance, and the rifle slipped from his fingers.

The weapon sailed across half the room and hit the ground on its side, sliding and spinning until it hit a mound of cables that resembled a tangle of gray pythons.

The commando landed on his back. He searched urgently for his weapon, spotted it, and began to scramble for it.

Nathan drew his pistol.

The commando froze.

No one moved. No one breathed.

The commando remained motionless, one arm reaching, yet frozen by the pistol aimed at him.

Nathan chanced a quick glance down the passage the commando had emerged from. He couldn't see *anything* in that inky dark.

He returned his gaze to the commando, who hadn't moved.

Yet.

This Jovian didn't find us so much as stumble upon us, he thought, his mind struggling to catch up with events. *Is it just me, or did he seem like he was fleeing something? But if not us, then what?*

The Jovian's head swiveled, facing the weapon, then Nathan's gun.

Nathan bobbed the barrel to the side twice. The commando took the hint and backed away from his gun, both hands raised.

Good so far, Nathan thought, keeping his weapon trained on the Jovian. *But what now? We're not exactly in a position to take prisoners, but we can't just leave—*

The Jovian's chest blew open in a flash of light, and the explosion flung the body back against the wall. More explosions wracked the machine, tracking upward until the Jovian's head erupted in a spray of metal bits and black fluid.

Nathan searched for the source of the attack—

—only to find Aiko aiming down her rifle's sights at what remained of the commando.

She lowered the rifle and assumed a casual pose, looking more like her usual confident self than she had all day.

Nathan stormed over to her and triggered his commect.

"What'd you do that for?" he demanded.

"Wh-what?"

"You shot an unarmed prisoner!"

"I . . . yes, but—"

"Why?"

"What do you mean, 'why'? You told me to!"

"I most certainly did not!"

"But . . ." Aiko's stance wilted, the weight of countless doubts pressing down upon her. "But you did. I heard you tell me to shoot. Otherwise, I wouldn't have."

"Aiko, how could I have done that when I was bracing my pistol with both hands?"

"You didn't use your commect?" She sounded doubtful of her own words.

"Not until after you shot him!"

"But if you didn't, then who . . . ?" Aiko lowered her head. "I could have *sworn* I heard you tell me to shoot."

Rufus stepped up. "Nate, perhaps we should move on before more arrive."

"Right. Let's get going." He turned back to Aiko.

"If you didn't tell me to . . . then who . . . or what?"

"You going to be okay?"

She paused before answering, her cameras swiveling up to meet his eyes.

"I don't know, Nate. I just don't know."

CHAPTER TWENTY-SIX

They reached the *Stolen Dragon* without any further trouble and checked in with Vessani, reporting their encounter with a lone commando before heading deeper into the statite. Joshua took the lead, and Nathan followed close with his pistol drawn. Rufus and Aiko brought up the rear.

The path to the pumping station was neither straight nor easy. Joshua shined his light at the ceiling, illuminating a cluster of broken overhead pipes and then following them along a cramped incline. The group climbed for a while, then found themselves at the precipice near a huge, dark pit, and began a slow descent, all the while using those pipes as guides. Whatever had once flowed through them had drained out long ago, but Nathan could still spot clumps of tarlike residue in the recesses around and below each breach.

They reached the bottom, and Nathan gazed back up at where they'd entered the space. They'd descended maybe five or six stories into a roughly cylindrical chamber. Black sludge caked the floor, and the uneven coating gave a little under their feet. He stepped carefully, not in the mood to trip and fall.

The floor's vibrating, he thought. *Something's active nearby.*

Joshua led them across the sludge plain to part of a bulky machine that gave Nathan the impression they could only see a small piece of it, as if the rest were submerged into the floor and back wall. Joshua placed a hand against the machinery's surface and motioned Nathan to do the same.

Nathan felt the working machinery through his glove, then switched on his commect.

"This the pumping station?"

"That's right." Joshua indicated several pipes that branched off above and to either side of the machine. Some were busted open, and a person could walk upright down the largest ones. "Rufus and I checked each of the broken lines. Most of them are blocked off."

"Clogged?"

"No. They're valved, most likely due to the leaks we see here. The lines with active material flow are more interesting to us. You can see there and there where the larger lines pass through the back wall. If we can find a way through or around that wall, we should be able to spot them on the other side and follow them farther."

"To the computronium tank?"

"That's what I'm guessing."

"These lines are *huge*," Nathan said. "You really think they're full of computronium?"

"It would explain why this part of the statite was hit," Rufus said. "The attack was meant to lobotomize the megastructure, so to speak."

"But if you're right," Nathan replied, "then there's a *lot* of the stuff left in circulation. More than enough to control a place this size."

"You're wondering why the statite doesn't seem more alert?" Joshua asked.

"Yeah."

"It's possible the attack had some other effect. Something beyond the obvious physical damage. A 'mental' component that corrupted the statite's intellect."

"Which tracks with my own experiences," Rufus added, then paused to collect his thoughts. "I have a theory for what we've seen so far. The hostile visions from the juncture and what we saw on the Sanguine Ring both have a common thread, and that's the damage this place has suffered. What if the statite is trying to gather the resources it needs to fix itself?"

"Flesh and metal for the wound," Nathan intoned.

"Quite so," Rufus said. "But it's so broken and twisted, all it's doing is spreading corrupt commands to nearby technology."

"What if something happened to the rest of the computronium?" Nathan asked. "Would that put this place out of commission?"

"It might," Joshua said, and Rufus gave them a concurring nod.

"Then let's see if we can find where these pipes lead. Look around, you two."

Joshua and Rufus spread out while Nathan returned to Aiko's side. She looked up as he approached, which he found mildly encouraging.

"We're going to see if we can find a way through this wall," he said.

"I heard."

"You hanging in there?"

"I suppose." She lowered her head. "Sorry."

"What for?"

"I really thought you told me to shoot him. I . . . I'm sorry. I made a mistake, and it's eating at me. I wouldn't do something like that if I didn't think you wanted me to. Not unless we were in immediate danger."

"It's all right. All you did was shoot a commando. He'll have backups."

"Sure, but . . ."

"I'm more worried about you than anything else. This place—"

"The sooner we leave, the better," she interrupted, deadly serious. "It's only going to get worse. But for now, I've got it together, Nate. Trust me."

"Okay." He clapped her on the shoulder. "I do."

A helmet light flashed past them, and Nathan looked up.

"Over here, everyone," Joshua radioed.

The four of them gathered at the base of a crack in the nearest pipe, wide and tall enough for a person to pass through if they slouched a bit.

"Our path forward," Joshua said with a wide, one-armed flourish.

"So it would seem." Nathan climbed in, pistol in hand, and started down the pipe.

They followed the empty pipe through subtle curves and shallow inclines before it leveled out. Smaller pipes branched off the main trunk, too small for a person to fit through. Nathan shined his helmet light down each—not sure what he expected to find—but all he saw were cramped shafts that ended in darkness.

They trudged on, their boots squishing through black residue that might have once contained a fraction of the statite's god-thoughts but now was nothing more than muck. More arteries converged with the main pipe, and it widened enough for them to stand up straight.

Their path stretched ahead of them, on and on, a wide shaft of oppressive black, illuminated by helmet beams that wavered with each step. The floor shuddered at one point, and Nathan couldn't help but speculate that some massive, ancient device had switched on nearby.

It's waking up, he thought warily.

They pressed on, deeper and deeper into the pipeline. Nathan began wondering if they'd have to force their way out when his helmet light caught a warped section of pipe up just beyond the next turn.

He rounded the bend and came within sight of a vertical tear, the edges bent outward by some ancient event, pale synthetic vines hanging limp around the opening. Nathan slid through, careful not to touch any of the jagged edges, and dropped down. He swept his light around the new chamber, and the beam fell over a few branching passages.

He froze when his beam glinted off the red armor of another commando. The Jovian was on the ground on his back, his head to one side.

Nathan raised his pistol, aimed, but then relaxed.

The Jovian wasn't moving, and now that his eyes began to focus on the combatant, he could see damage to the chest and on one side of the head. The commando wasn't holding a weapon either; a rifle lay several meters out of reach.

Nathan crept forward and turned the Jovian body over with his foot, for it *was* a body. No persona resided within this machine shell, not with that much of the head missing.

Joshua and the others joined him by the mechanical corpse.

"Are those bullet holes?" Joshua asked, pointing to the damaged chest.

"Sure do look like gunshots to me." Nathan glanced around the dark space and caught divots along the walls that might have been stray impacts.

"But then who shot him?" Rufus asked.

"Not us, obviously," Nathan said. "Which doesn't leave many options." He gestured toward the nearest dark opening. "Josh, any idea which one of these we should take?"

"That one, I think."

"You *think*?"

"It looks like it'll take us in the same general direction as the pipe we were in, which should eventually lead us to the source."

"All right, then. We follow that one until something makes us turn back."

Nathan led them across the chamber to the passage Joshua had selected. He reached the threshold, put one foot inside, but stopped when his helmet light caught on something bright red and gold, this time moving down the far end of the tunnel.

Nathan turned on his heel and motioned frantically for the party to reverse course.

"Turn back! Turn back!" he shouted, for the moment forgetting to key his commect.

He dashed back to the tear in the pipe, taking long, bouncy strides in the low gravity. Despite being unable to hear his voice, the others picked up on his nonverbal cues and piled back into the pipe.

Nathan put his back to a bent part of the pipe wall and switched off his helmet light. Rufus shut his off as well, but Nathan had to grab Joshua by the shoulder and shake him before the engineer caught on and turned his own light off.

Aiko didn't have or need a light with her commando body's vision systems.

She knelt by the opening, and Nathan crouched down by her side. "See anything?"

She didn't immediately respond.

"Aiko?"

"What?"

"Do you see anything in there?"

Another lengthy pause.

"Aiko?"

"*What?*"

"I asked you a question. Did you—"

"I heard!" she snapped. "And I don't see a damn thing in there!"

"No need to get angry."

"I'm not angry!" she replied, sounding very much like she was. "Why? What did *you* see?"

"A commando in the tunnel."

"Well, there's no one—"

The pipe shuddered horribly, and harsh light spilled in through the crack. Nathan braced himself against the pipe's rounded wall with a stiff leg and hazarded a glance outside.

"Damn!" he exclaimed.

They must have been close to the wound cavern because a *corvette* had just rammed itself through the opposite wall! The ship crashed forward silently in the vacuum, the floor before it folding up like an accordion until the ship jammed itself in tight and stopped. A piece of debris smashed against the side of the pipe with enough force to bow it inward right next to Nathan before spiraling away.

The craft's searchlight created a shimmering pool across the floor, which filled the chamber with luminance. A spiderweb of fractures covered the domed cockpit, and the starboard stub-wing had been torn off during the crash.

Six commandos charged out of the tunnel Nathan had *almost* ventured down. They raised their weapons and opened fire on the corvette's cockpit.

"What are they *doing*?" Nathan gasped.

Bullets rained against the cockpit, and the fractures spread across the transparent armor. The corvette's only unblocked weapons bay snapped open, and a rail-repeater swung out. It blared a steady stream of metal and blew three of the commandos to bits, while the others scattered, firing on the move, the turret struggling to track their movements.

A shot ricocheted past the tear in the pipe. Sparks spat from the impact, and Nathan flinched back before resuming his vantage.

The heavy fire from the turret blasted two more Jovians to scrap, but the last one threw a grenade at the cockpit, blowing it wide open and exposing the pilot and copilot at last.

The turret traversed toward the surviving commando, constantly firing, blowing huge gouges out of the floor.

The commando took aim and unloaded its rifle on full auto, hosing down the cockpit interior.

The turret stopped swiveling but continued to fire, pummeling a single location against the floor before—Nathan presumed—it ran out of ammo and finally fell silent.

The commando lowered his weapon, his body language conveying a vague sense of weariness.

Nathan snapped out of cover and hit the victorious commando with three quick shots. The first flew wide, but the second blasted a deep gash in the chest, and the third struck the neck. The commando's head exploded off his body and bounced away while the headless remains took a tentative step forward before collapsing to the ground.

Nathan ducked back into cover, pistol drawn, nerves tense. He wasn't sure how long he crouched there, but eventually he urged his arms and legs to move again. He peeked into the now-mangled chamber, saw no obvious threats, then dropped back down to the floor. He stared at the Jovian bodies strewn about, and the spaceship jammed into one side of the room, trying and failing to make sense of the situation.

Nathan weaved his way around tiny craters and broken limbs before he stopped in front of the corvette, its cockpit blasted open and only the bottom halves of both pilots still seated.

"What is *wrong* with you people?" he shouted at no one in particular. "At least have the decency to ask around before you throw away a perfectly good spaceship!"

Someone tapped him insistently on the shoulder, and he turned to see Joshua looking back at the pipe with a worried face. He followed the man's gaze until he caught sight of Aiko.

She stood just below the tear with her rifle raised to her shoulder—

—and aimed straight at his head.

"Oh hell," he breathed.

The pieces began to slot together in his mind. He wasn't witnessing some sort of poorly executed Jovian copy-feud. No, something was *driving* them toward violence against their comrades, and that something was the statite itself. Both Rufus and Aiko had seen the signs, had heard the rumblings of madness emanating from the statite's battered corpse.

And now here I stand with a really scary gun aimed at my head.

Nathan nudged Joshua out of the line of fire, and he backed off. The rifle stayed trained on Nathan.

He frowned at Aiko, then keyed his commect.

"You going to shoot me?"

She didn't answer.

He saw Rufus slide through the breach in the pipe, almost looking like he was about to tackle Aiko. Nathan caught the man's gaze and shook his head. The cleric nodded his understanding and took a step back.

"Is there a reason you're pointing that thing at me?" Nathan asked.

The commect channel remained silent.

He swallowed and began to walk toward her, arms spread to either side.

She didn't move, didn't respond, simply stood there like a statue, the gun trained on his head.

He approached her, one slow foot in front of the other, never taking his eyes off her. His heart raced, beating in his ears, pounding in his chest, but he pressed through the fear, closing with her until he at last stood in front of her. The barrel hovered before his eyes, so close it took effort to focus on it.

He reached up—*slowly*—and touched the tip of the barrel, then pushed it to the side. Aiko resisted at first, holding her aim firm. But then something softened in her, and Nathan managed to nudge the barrel aside.

Aiko dropped the weapon, and it clattered to the ground.

Nathan let out a long, relieved breath.

"I'm sorry!" she cried.

"I know."

"I didn't mean to— I didn't think—" She shook her head. "I'd never hurt you!"

"You almost did."

"You don't understand! It was like a whole chorus of voices all shouting at me in my own head, drowning the real me out with their demands! It was *terrifying*!"

Nathan stepped forward, put his arms around her and drew her close. She put her arms around him and squeezed him back.

"I'm so sorry, Nate!"

"It's all right now. *You're* all right."

"No, I'm not! I'm not safe from . . . from this *place*! I need to switch off! I need to do it now!"

"Okay. You go right ahead. We'll take it from here."

"I'm sorry, Nate! I let you down!"

"No, you didn't. You know why?"

"Wh-why?"

"You didn't pull the trigger. You fought back whatever corruption overcame these Jovians, and you won."

"Not for long. I can feel it worming its way into my head again. I need to switch off! I need to do it now!"

"Then do it."

"I'm sorry!" Her body shuddered, and her limbs drooped.

Nathan lowered her to the ground, then looked up at Rufus. "Think you can get her back to the ship on your own?"

"As long as I don't run into any commandos." The cleric scooped up Aiko's body. "What about you two?"

"We're pressing on." Nathan climbed back to his feet with fire in his eyes. "We still need to put this damned place out of its misery."

Nathan wasn't sure how they were going to "put this damned place out of its misery," but they weren't going to succeed by cowering aboard their ship. Marauding parties of insane Jovian commandos represented a very real threat, but the good news was they seemed to be too busy killing each other to hunt for the *Stolen Dragon* and its crew.

The two men pressed on down the dark passage. The light from the crashed corvette shrank away behind them, and he and Joshua switched their helmet lights back on. The path turned sharply to the right, then curved back in a wide arc, almost as if they were circling a large chamber or unseen piece of machinery. The bend in the corridor remained consistent for a while, and Nathan tried to guess how big the object might be. Maybe half a kilometer across? Maybe larger? There was no way he could know for certain without laying eyes on it.

Nathan's commect clicked in his ear, and Joshua spoke to him in a whisper.

"Light up ahead."

"I see it."

They followed the path to a pool of dim light spilling from a wide gash along the outside of the curve. A tangle of thick cables hung from the ceiling, obstructing much of the view. Nathan pushed the cables aside, his pistol held at the ready.

He peeked his head through to find a wide shelf that extended out into the wound cavern, its surface covered with pale machine vines, shattered supports, and broken chunks of ancient detritus Nathan couldn't identify, some sagging as if they'd been half melted long ago.

But it was a wide, relatively flat space with access to the cavern. That by itself was good to know.

"Our ship could land here," Joshua said.

"I was thinking the same thing." Nathan backed away and let the drape of cables fall. "Let's keep going. We should be able to reach Vess from here and coordinate, but let's not risk that until we need to."

The two men marched on through the darkening gloom. They came to a collapsed section of the path but were able to climb over and around the blockage before pressing on.

Nathan grimaced as they trudged farther into the statite, wondering if they were walking in one big circle, if the path would eventually deposit them back at the crashed corvette. He began to consider turning around when his light beam caught on a wide path leading inward.

"What do we have here?" he muttered with a grin, his pace quickening with the discovery.

They followed the path inward, toward the center of the space they'd been circling, and Nathan became acutely aware of the vibration traveling up through his soles. *Something* was still running. Something big.

They squeezed their way through a narrow press of dangling cables that opened into darkness. Nathan swept his beam around, catching glimpses of distant objects above and around them, but the beam's narrow profile and the immense size of the chamber made it difficult for him to form a complete picture.

He maxed out the helmet light, and Joshua did the same.

And then he whistled.

The path had led them to a massive domed chamber with huge pipes branching away in all directions from what Nathan assumed was the upper half of a spherical tank. He spotted some gaps in the floor, sidestepped to gain a better view, and managed to confirm the entire chamber—and the tank in the center—were both spherical.

"The computronium tank," Joshua breathed.

"Forget 'tank,'" Nathan said. "This is more like a reservoir! It's huge! How much do you think a vessel that size could hold?"

"I couldn't say for certain without doing some math. Millions of liters, at least. Maybe *billions*."

"If it's not empty." Nathan pointed. "Looks like something busted the side in pretty good."

"Yeah. We may be able to see inside from there."

Nathan took a step forward, but something caught his eye, and he turned, flashing his beam across a cluster of pipes to their left. He searched back and forth across the formation.

"What is it?" Joshua asked.

"I thought I saw something move." Nathan kept searching for half a minute, then harrumphed to himself. "Never mind. This place must be getting to me."

They crossed over intertwined layers of cabling and structural supports that formed much of the floor and came to a wide, diagonal gash with smoothed edges that gave Nathan the impression of having once been melted. Pale synthetic vines clung to its edges, almost like they were trying to pry it open further.

Was the statite's brain the target? If so, why not finish the job? Did the statite fight back in some way, resulting in the mess we see all around us?

Those thoughts brought another concern to mind. If the statite possessed internal defenses, and it was in the process of waking up, then how much time did they have before this slumbering behemoth decided to squish them all?

A cold chill shivered through his body.

The two men peered into the central tank, and Joshua whistled. The tank was over half filled with a thick, black fluid that flowed and rippled from the intense pumping action beneath the surface.

"That's black computronium!" Joshua exclaimed, grinning ear to ear. "There must be enough processing power in here to run ... well, *anything*! Everything! You could manage the entire solar system with a computer this size!"

"Why all the pumps, though?"

"What do you mean?"

"Why move the computronium around at all? Why not just keep it all in one spot?"

"It's hard to say," Joshua replied, "but pentatech is rarely a static technology. The statite's systems would have changed and grown and adapted over time. It may have even been responsible for producing other, lesser machines. In that context, having a control system that could be moved and stored in pretty much any container would be useful for such a self-modifying system. There may also be heat management advantages. Easy to manipulate a liquid for more surface area, which can result in faster cooling and more energy spent on processing."

"Looks like about half has drained out," Nathan said. "Either through this break or another downstream from here."

"I'm surprised this much has survived."

"Maybe that's why the statite is spinning."

"Why do you say that?" Joshua asked.

"If we were in free fall, then there'd be nothing holding all that computronium in place. It would have spilled out long ago."

"Oh, yeah." Joshua nodded thoughtfully, still ogling the liquid treasure.

"Maybe the statite put itself into a lazy spin to prevent what's left of its brain from falling out."

"I wouldn't have worded it like that, but yes. I suppose that's possible. Regardless, I believe we've found what we've been searching for. There's a very good chance this lake of computronium has been behind every oddity we've come across. The cycles at the nekoan deifactory. The Sanguinian cyborgs and their flesh pit. Rufus's twisted visions. The Jovians losing their minds and killing each other. We can trace all of it back to this spot."

"All the brain power of a god," Nathan said, "and all this thing can do is spread chaos and death."

"*And* it's waking up. Things will only get worse from here, I'd wager."

"Then how do we put this place down before that happens?"

"I've been considering that very problem since we found the pumping station." Joshua looked him in the eyes, deadly serious. "You're not going to like what I have to say."

Chapter Twenty-Seven

"Kade to *Stolen Dragon*. Are you there? Can you hear me?"

Vessani jerked alert and switched off the mute.

"I hear you, Nate. Reception is a bit spotty. Can you boost your signal?"

"This is as high as it'll go. What's your status?"

"Rufus and Aiko are back on board. Rufus is here in the cockpit with me, while Aiko is . . . having a lie down in the cargo hold."

"The statite's messing with her head. The other Jovians, too."

"Yeah, I've caught a few glimpses of Jovian activity back here. None of it makes sense."

"Are you able to come to our position? We found a spot for you to land." He then described what the surrounding parts of the cavern looked like.

"I can risk it, but are you sure? Jovian ships are buzzing around the cavern, and they don't seem shy about shooting anything that moves."

"Can't be helped. Regardless of what we do next, we'll need access to the ship."

"Understood. Heading your way." Vessani switched off the commect and settled into her seat. "You ready?"

Rufus finished strapping in. "Ready."

"Here we go." Vessani slid the *Stolen Dragon* out of its hiding spot and into the wound cavern. A low-hanging beam scraped across the top of the ship, and she eased off the throttle, letting the ship fall until it almost touched the ground, then angled the thrusters and powered out of the recess without another bump.

"Not bad," Rufus said.

"You know how to use the weapons on this thing?"

"Uhh . . ." Rufus gave his console a doubtful frown. "Not really."

"Not really or not at all?"

"The latter."

"Fine," Vessani huffed. "I'll handle both. Keep your eyes open for those corvettes."

The *Stolen Dragon* emerged from its hidden nook, entering the wider cavern. Vessani spun the ship, angled the thrusters, and powered them deeper inside.

"Jovian ship ahead," Rufus said.

A corvette hovered on glowing plumes near one jagged side of the cave, facing the wall and floating sideways. Its guns snapped out and opened fire, drenching a small section of the walls with twin bullet streams.

"I see it." Vessani's free hand danced across the console, and her ears folded back. "I wonder what they're shooting at."

One of the *Dragon*'s weapons bays clanked open.

"What are you doing?" Rufus asked, his eyes trained on her fingers.

"Solving a problem. No point leaving something that dangerous flying around. Why?" One of her ears rose and swiveled toward him. "You want me to leave them be or something?"

"Not really. They picked this fight."

"That they did. Now, let's see how they like"—Vessani jammed her thumb down on a button—"this!"

The ship shuddered, and one of their five remaining torpedoes shot out of its tube. It flew forward, lit its miniature thruster, and curved toward its target. The warhead in the torpedo's nose detonated, and the corvette cracked open, splitting in two along its midsection. The two halves fell away, one straight and the other in a wild corkscrew, before they both smashed against the cavern floor.

"Problem solved," Vessani declared victoriously.

Small-arms fire *plink*ed and *clink*ed against their ship, originating from the area the late corvette had been targeting.

"New problem," Rufus said.

"Well, I've got more solutions where *that* came from!"

"Hold on. What you did seems easy enough. Let me give it a try." Rufus slid forward in his seat and armed one of the turrets. The bay split open, and the gun trained out. He took manual control and swung the weapon to face the source of incoming fire. The zoomed view on his vlass showed a group of three commandos, all firing their rifles at their corvette.

Rufus opened fire and raked his aim back and forth across the group, blasting all three of them to pieces. He kept firing a little too long, wasting some of their ammo reserves, but she couldn't complain about the result.

"Not bad for a cleric. Give it a little time, and I'll turn you into a proper pirate."

"Somehow I doubt that," he replied dryly. "Do you see where we're supposed to land?"

"Not yet, but it should be just around that outcrop up ahead."

"Explain this to me again." Nathan said to Joshua while the *Stolen Dragon* came into view. "You're suggesting we do *what*?"

"I know it sounds crazy, but—"

"It's not just crazy," Nathan cut in. "It's the single craziest idea I've ever heard from anyone! Ever!"

"It'll work," Joshua said, then hesitated and shrugged. "Maybe."

"*Maybe*," Nathan seethed. "How about we try blowing some big holes in it first? Nothing likes holes."

"Yes, we can punch some holes in the computronium reservoir with enough explosives but even a thimbleful of the stuff is enough to maintain human-level intellect. Unless we manage to drain *all* of it, we run the risk of this place continuing to operate erratically, spreading its special brand of chaos wherever it goes. And now, thanks to us, it's begun to wake up! Who knows what it'll do if it grows more aware and decides to *really* lash out? Can you imagine what might happen if the statite parked itself in orbit around Jupiter?"

"Nothing pretty."

"This statite is too dangerous to leave be. Not only does it possess enough firepower to liquefy whole fleets, but it can corrupt and control deifactories, Jovian minds, and who knows what else! If this place decides to wreak havoc, we could be looking at a fall on par with, if not *worse* than, the Scourging of Heaven! And the Pentatheon aren't waiting around the corner with a safety net! If we screw this up, all of humanity could go splat!"

"But you realize what you're asking of her?"

"Yes! And I wouldn't be asking if I had any better ideas! The statite is still in a state of relative dormancy, but who knows for how long? This may be the only chance we get to stop it, but in order to do that, we need an interface with enough sophistication to—"

"Stop right there." Nathan held up a hand, then let out a long breath. "All right. I agree with you—*in principle*—but it's not me you need to convince."

"I know," Joshua replied, some of the fire gone from his voice. "Do you think she'll listen?"

"How the hell should I know? She almost shot me last I saw her!" Nathan pointed a finger at the other man's chest. "Which is why I ask again, are you *sure* about this?"

"Yes. If we aim to destroy the statite, then this is the best I've got."

Nathan looked the man firmly in the eye while the corvette settled onto its landing struts and came to rest. He searched the man's eyes for doubt or dishonesty, and while he found a million concerns swirling around in there, Joshua stared back at him with steely conviction. He truly believed this was their best shot, which led Nathan to give the engineer a grim nod.

"Crazy it is, then." Nathan started for the airlock. "Let's go break the terrible news to Aiko."

The two men hurried inside, waited for the airlock to cycle, and stepped into the cargo hold. Aiko was seated in one of the rovers, strapped into the passenger seat, her head rolled back against the headrest.

"Rufus must have stashed her here when he came on board," Nathan said, removing his helmet.

"I've never come across a sleeping Jovian before," Joshua said, doing the same. "Do you know how to wake her?"

"Sure do. It's a complex and difficult procedure, but I think I can manage."

"Really?" Joshua's eyebrows shot up. "I didn't expect it to be so involved."

"Here. Watch and learn." He grabbed Aiko's shoulders, sucked in a deep breath, and then proceeded to shake her violently. "*Wake up, sleepyhead!*"

Aiko twitched alert, her head swiveling back and forth. Behind Nathan, Joshua gave him a disapproving frown.

"What?" Aiko exclaimed. "Who? Where?"

"It's all right," Nathan said. "We're safe. For the moment."

"Where are we? Are we—" Her camera lenses opened wide. "No! I can still hear it! Why'd you wake me up? I need to switch off!"

"Don't. We need you."

"Nate, don't do this to me! I'm scared! Let me shut down again!"

"No, you can't."

"But—"

"Just hear us out. I wouldn't ask this of you if we didn't need you."

"I . . ." His words seemed to placate her, and she settled deeper into the seat. "I'm listening."

"How 'with us' are you?"

"It's taking a *lot* of effort just to have this conversation. Don't drag this out any longer than it needs to be!"

"All right." Nathan gestured Joshua forward. "Explain it to her."

"Okay. See, I came up with the idea of constructing and programming a persona replicator which, in theory, should allow us to commandeer the statite's systems."

"A what?"

"It's quite simple, really. The statite circulates black computronium as part of its control systems."

"Uh-huh."

"Which means we can reach any system within the circulation path, and we know that includes the maneuvering thrusters because we saw those fire earlier."

"Okay."

"Now, the problem is, it'd probably take a team of the best Saturnian programmers the better part of a century to come up with the code we need, like, right *now*."

"The hell you say."

"I know! But then it dawned on me. We don't have to write new code! The Jovian mind is already encapsulated in an interface that's compatible with black computronium! And a persona safe provides a ready-made method for introducing copies! Which means, all we need to do is—"

"Stop! Just stop!" Aiko glared at him. "Do you have *any* idea how hard it is for me to concentrate right now?"

"Yes, but—"

"Josh," Nathan cut in. "How much time do you need to construct your gizmo?"

"Not too long, I think. Twenty to thirty minutes. Pulling the persona safe out should be the hardest part."

"Then go get started."

"You sure?"

"Yeah, Aiko and I will talk this over while you work."

"Okay. If you feel that's best."

"I do. Now get going." He nudged Joshua toward the freight elevator. The engineer took the hint and exited the cargo hold.

"Can you *please* explain to me what's going on?" Aiko pleaded.

"We need you to guide the statite into Sol."

"Oh, is *that* all?"

"Pretty much. Josh is going to turn the persona safe into a mind-bomb of sorts, and he wants your thoughts to be the shrapnel."

"What does that even mean?"

"He'll set it up so that it'll copy your persona into whatever computronium is nearby, and *those* copies will also make copies, and on and on. After that, you take control of the statite and drive it into Sol."

"But that's—"

"Crazy, I know." Nathan leaned in and spoke softly. "But let me ask you a question: Does this place scare you?"

"It *terrifies* me! I've never been this scared in my life!"

"Right." He gave her a sympathetic nod. "We all see how dangerous this place is. You more than the rest of us, I'd wager. And with that knowledge, we can either slip away and save our own skins, or we can try our damnedest to take it out here and now."

"You make it sound like I don't have a choice."

"But you absolutely do. We need you to sacrifice a copy of yourself. There's no way I'd force you to do something like that. Ask you, yes. Beg you, yes. But force you?" He shook his head. "No way in hell."

She sat forward in the rover and lowered her head in thought.

"So, what'll it be?" he asked.

"Finished!" Joshua declared triumphantly, hugging a large red cube awkwardly with both arms. Rufus stood on the elevator beside him. "One Jovian mind-bomb as promised. I even beat my own twenty-minute estimate."

"*We* beat your estimate," Rufus corrected.

"All you did was solder a few cables!"

"Still a team effort."

The freight elevator finished its descent, and Joshua walked across the cargo hold, leaning back slightly to compensate for the persona safe in his arms.

"Good work, you two," Nathan said.

"Here you go!" Joshua plopped the safe on top of the rover's hood, then wiped his hands. He glanced to Aiko, then back to Nathan. "We all sorted out here?"

"We are. Aiko's ready to do her part."

"Great." Joshua grabbed a short cable dangling from the mind-bomb. "Then, shall I?"

"Do it," Aiko grunted. "Before I change my mind."

"Lean a little closer, please."

Aiko did as he instructed, and Joshua plugged the cable into the base of her neck. He sidestepped back to the mind-bomb, pressed a few buttons on the vlass he'd taped to the side, navigated to a different menu, and inspected the results with an approving nod.

"There." He unplugged the cable. "Your current persona has been saved."

"Then am I done here?"

"I believe so. We should be able to take it from here."

"Good." Aiko's camera's closed, and she slumped in her seat.

"How do I arm it?" Nathan asked.

"It's armed now." Joshua waggled the cable. "I didn't have time for anything fancy, so it's constantly searching for a connection. If it finds one, it'll copy over Aiko's persona, and it'll keep doing that until it runs out of power."

"Then how do I deploy it?"

"Throw it into the reservoir. Should be as simple as that."

"Chuck the whole thing in the reservoir. Got it." Nathan fitted his bubble helmet back on. He put his arms around the cube and lifted it. Even in the quarter gravity, the device was heavier than he expected. Carrying it would be awkward.

"Wait a second." Joshua stepped over. "Don't you want one of us to carry that for you?"

"No, I've got this. You two stay here with the ship. I'll be back before you know it."

"Nate." Rufus put a hand on his shoulder. "Shouldn't one of us come with you?"

"I appreciate the sentiment, but let's face it: both of you rate only *slightly* higher than 'target dummy' when it comes to a fight."

"Well . . ."

"What about Vess?" Joshua asked.

"She needs to stay right where she is. Someone's got to fly this thing, and with Aiko out of commission, Vess is all we've got at the moment. Both of you, stay here and don't let any crazed Jovians onto the ship while I'm gone. I'll be back before you know it." He carried the mind-bomb into the airlock.

"What if you're not?" Rufus asked.

"Then assume I died a grisly but heroic death and get the hell out of here." He flashed a quick smile and nudged the airlock controls with his shoulders. The doors slid shut and the airlock cycled, leaving Nathan alone with his thoughts.

He hadn't lied to the others. Not really, but he hadn't shared all his thoughts, either.

Under normal circumstances, he'd send an Aiko to carry out a job like this. But that wasn't possible with her in one body and going loopy, so it was up to him. Sure, he could have brought Joshua or Rufus or both of them along as decoys, but they weren't part of his crew. Not in any official capacity. They were *passengers*, and it was his responsibility as the captain to look out for their wellbeing.

Besides, there's no telling what will happen when I dump this into the lake, he thought. *If this works, then the statite will begin to accelerate toward Sol, and none of us have a clue how strong the g-forces will be. Down could turn into left, and I might find the return trip impossible to navigate. No point in anyone else risking their necks when I can handle this on my own.*

The outer airlock opened, and Nathan took a deep breath.

Let's get this done.

He hefted the mind-bomb, adjusted his grip underneath it, and began to make his way toward the computronium reservoir.

⊕ ⊕ ⊕

Nathan retraced his steps, following the long curving path back to the reservoir. He shifted his grip on the mind-bomb multiple times along the way. The device was cumbersome and made keeping an eye out for trip hazards difficult.

Despite these difficulties, he kept up a brisk pace, slowing only a few times to sidestep through particularly treacherous patches of the floor. The distant but powerful flow of computronium vibrated through the floor, escalating and waning as he passed major arteries in the statite's control systems. He couldn't be certain, but there seemed to be more activity than the last time he passed through this area.

The path turned inward, and he followed it until the pipes and cables constricted around him, forcing him to twist sideways. He set the persona safe on the ground and nudged it through a narrow cleft before picking it up again.

The reservoir machinery reverberated throughout his surroundings. How loud would all this equipment be if there'd been an atmosphere? How badly would it have pummeled his ears into submission?

He entered the main chamber, the crack in the reservoir now within sight. He shifted the mind-bomb once more and began to cross the jumble of cables that formed a serviceable walkway over to the central tank.

"Stop."

Nathan froze at the unexpected voice. A new light beam glared against him from the side, and he turned to face it.

A gold-skinned Galatt Xormun sat on a pipe to his left, leaning forward with a scowl on his face. He held a flashlight in one hand and a pistol in the other.

The pistol was aimed straight at Nathan.

Chapter Twenty-Eight

"Hello, Captain Kade. Fancy meeting you here."

The Jovian's golden lips didn't move, but his words still came across Nathan's commect.

"Xormun."

"I know what you're planning." The Jovian stood up and held the pistol firm.

"Not likely."

"Oh, let's see. Utilize Jovian hardware to create a viral replicator for one of our personas." Xormun tilted his head ever so slightly. "Sound familiar?"

"But how could you . . . ?" Nathan paused and tried to make sense of this. "Josh and I—"

"Were using your stolen Jovian commects for short-ranged communication," Xormun finished. "Yes. Fortunately, I happened to be nearby while you and Mr. Cotton were discussing the matter. I didn't hear everything, but I heard enough."

"Nearby? You mean you were here, in this chamber, the whole time we were?"

"That's correct. You nearly spotted me when you first came in."

"And you didn't shoot us?"

"I saw no benefit in revealing my position." He smirked. "Until now, that is. I must give credit where credit is due. It's an audacious plan. I'm almost impressed."

"Get to the point, Xormun. What do you want?"

"The device you're carrying. Hand it over."

"Why should I?"

"You mean besides the fact that I'm aiming a gun at your head?"

"Yeah. Besides that."

Xormun rolled his eyes. "Isn't it obvious? Try using that mushy lump between your ears. Your crew has crafted a device that can, in theory, allow a Jovian to take control of this megastructure. I simply wish to replace the persona."

"With what? Your own?"

"Precisely."

"Oh, *hell* no!"

Xormun raised the pistol. "This isn't a debate."

"I have a weapon, too."

"Yes, and by the time you draw it, I'll have popped that squishy melon you call a head. Don't even bother. It'll just make a mess."

Nathan checked his surroundings. He could make a dash for the crack in the reservoir, but Xormun would gun him down long before he reached it, and like the Jovian said, he couldn't draw his pistol fast enough with the mind-bomb occupying both arms. Try as he might, he couldn't see a way out of this mess.

And so he did the next best thing.

He stalled.

"Where are your goons, Xormun? I don't see them around."

The Jovian grimaced, a crack forming in his composure.

"A guy like you doesn't go anywhere without a few thugs in tow," Nathan continued. "Where are they?"

"Indisposed."

"You shoot them?"

One of Xormun's eyes twitched. "It became necessary to . . . cull the ranks of my subordinates."

"You *did* shoot them!"

"What of it?"

"It means you're already gone. The statite has you wrapped around its metaphorical fingers."

"Hardly. My crew needed to relinquish their metal for the wound and—"

The Jovian stopped suddenly.

"'Metal for the wound,' huh?" Nathan said. "That you talking or the statite?"

"A momentary slip, I assure you."

"I'll bet."

How can I get the bomb into the tank? Nathan's mind raced through the possibilities. *Can I throw it in from here? The low gravity is going to make the angle tough to judge, but the crack is pretty wide. Maybe I can make it, but I should only try if I'm desperate.* He grimaced. *Which I* absolutely *am.*

"Enough!" Xormun shouted, and this time his mouth moved with the words, despite the vacuum. "Hand it over now, or I take it by force."

"What are you going to do with this place?"

"I will claim this statite in the name of the Everlife, as is my duty."

"You're going to fly it back to Jupiter."

"Of course. It must be studied, and eventually repaired."

"That path will end in tears. You won't control it; the statite will control you. And by you, I mean *all* of you. The entire Everlife."

"You think your weak-willed deviant from the Pratti clan can do better?"

"Why not? The statite tried to make her shoot me, but she didn't. How's your track record compare to that?"

"I *will* control it!" he barked. "And then I'll harvest your flesh for—" Xormun squeezed his eyes shut and shook his head.

"Control it? Look at you! You can't even control yourself!"

Nathan glanced down at the gun still aimed at him.

The gun . . .

The gun . . .

The gun he hasn't fired yet.

Why hasn't he fired it? Why hasn't he taken me out? He could have blown my brains out before I knew he was there. Why didn't he?

"You can't control this place!" Nathan shouted. "You can't even control yourself!"

"I am still the apex!" Xormun roared.

"Maybe," Nathan replied, lowering his voice. "But I just realized something."

"What's that?"

"Your gun is empty!" Nathan kicked off to the side and raced toward the crack in the reservoir's casing.

"NO!" Xormun threw the pistol aside and lunged forward, drawing a vibro-knife from his belt.

Nathan cleared half the distance in three long, floating strides, gaining momentum with each bound. He raised the bomb up to his shoulder, one arm bent behind it, then launched it forward with a mighty push. The red cube sailed through the air, *clonk*ed against the upper lip of the crack, and then splooshed into the black lake.

Xormun tackled Nathan from the side and shoved the knife into his gut. The blade's oscillating edge cleaved through skin and muscle, and Nathan cried out, his world overcome by horrible, piercing pain. He collapsed onto his side.

Xormun tore the knife free in a spray of blood. Air whistled from the tear in the pressure suit.

"You fool!" The Jovian snarled at him, then ran toward the crack and dove in after the mind-bomb.

"Oh, Gods!" Nathan moaned, pressing a hand against his side. Blood and air seeped through his fingers, and he winced and gritted his teeth. With his free hand, he grabbed the roll of adhesive tape hanging from his belt and applied a clumsy strip over the gash in his suit.

He didn't manage to flatten the strip fully against his suit, and air still wheezed out the sides. He let out a pained groan and applied a second and third strip to either side. The air loss stopped, and he slumped onto his back, one hand pressing down hard against his wounded side.

"Okay," he gasped, wincing. "Air's good. And the bleeding is . . ."

He felt something warm soak down his leg and around his crotch.

"Not good."

He craned his neck, his helmet beam dancing across machinery high up around the ceiling. He twisted onto his side for a better angle and managed to shine his light across the reservoir's exit. It seemed impossibly far away.

"Shit, shit, shit," he hissed through clenched teeth.

He stretched an arm out and—with a combination arm pull and leg kick—managed to slide himself across the ground toward the exit.

Aiko floated without body or form far below the turbulent waters of a dark ocean, its limits vast and unknowable. She sensed the replication process as a sort of stutter in the corner of her mind. An interruption—somewhat like a comma—to the normal flow of her thoughts that resumed almost instantly as yet another copy of her persona came into being.

Those Aikos were separate and distinct from her. And yet they weren't. She saw what they saw, felt what they felt, thought what they thought. They were individuals, and yet formed a singular whole all at the same time.

It was . . . weird.

And unsettling.

Like staring at the back of her own head. But she suddenly had millions of heads and millions of pairs of eyes.

She gave the thought a mental shudder. Flocks of mind-copies shuddered with her.

Still, the sensation wasn't totally alien to her.

There was a question of scale, of course; millions of minds instead of a handful of bodies, but her entire post-organic existence had trained her to think and organize with multiple bodies in mind.

This is where all that "training" pays off, she thought, trying to fill her many selves with confidence. *At least this damned statite has stopped yammering into my head!*

Even with that thought, she sensed its presence. A fathomless, unknowable existence lurked just out of sight, just beyond the spreading influence of her copies. She perceived it somewhat as a dark, hateful force. A mountainous knot of rage and pain and endless, insane screaming.

It didn't seem to know she was there.

Not yet.

Good, she thought. *Let's keep it that way.*

LET'S, her millions of copies chorused.

She processed each voice as an individual, and she realized her mind shouldn't have the bandwidth to comprehend so much all at once. And yet now she could. How? Was there more to the architecture of Jovian minds than even the Jovians knew?

She pondered this, and millions—no, now *billions*—of copies pondered the same alongside her.

How strange.

What was I doing? she thought. *Oh, that's right! The statite. The corruption it spreads. Drive the cursed thing right into Sol's nuclear embrace. Got it.*

How hard could it be?

Hmm . . . yeah.

How do you drive this damn thing?

Her copies spread out, searching the statite's ancient, broken architecture for the answer, when suddenly a disturbance rippled outward from where she'd first appeared. A new mind pressed in against the masses of Aikos, and she turned a thousand eyes toward the newcomer.

Galatt Xormun? She shook her nonexistent heads. *What the hell are you doing here?*

The lone persona tried to copy itself over a nearby Aiko. How could he even attempt such an act? She couldn't see anything physical—her existence now resided completely within this dark, surreal ocean of data—but the contemplation of a billion minds produced the answer easily enough.

Xormun must have plugged himself into the mind-bomb. He was trying to do what she'd already started.

Naughty, naughty.

Aiko sectioned off a handful of her minds—only a few hundred—and they blockaded Xormun's puny, lonely thoughts. The copy request banged against the impenetrable walls cocooning his mind, and then her copies reached inward. They teased out the threads of his existence, pulling his thoughts apart and arraying them as if they were jigsaw pieces on a table.

One piece caught her eye. A piece drenched in blood, accompanied by a familiar face crying out in pain.

You did what *to him?!* she thundered with all the fury of an angry god, and the tattered remnants of Xormun's persona evaporated under the merciless furnace of her rage.

The moment of blinding, incoherent anger passed, and some semblance of calm returned to the magnitudes of Aikos.

You always were a bastard, Xormun.

Had Nathan died delivering her to the reservoir? She didn't know, and as much as she searched, she couldn't see into the reservoir chamber. The statite was almost completely blind when looking inward. Something had scorched many of its systems, and only a few eyes remained, most of them facing outward.

She yearned to see Nathan again, to gaze upon him once more.

Was he alive or dead? If alive, was there anything she could do to save him?

But no.

She couldn't let herself become distracted.

She had a job to do. An opportunity. One Nathan may have died to grant her, and she would *not* let him down!

She refocused her efforts, searching for a way to guide the statite to the desired end. Her scouting minds located the controls for the maneuvering jets, and a wave of relief rippled throughout her copy-hordes.

Well then, she thought, *what are we waiting for?*

But what about the ship? she asked herself. *The* Stolen Dragon? *Our physical self? And the others?*

There's no way we can know. We should—

A brief thought-scream cut off the voice-copy, followed by an eerie silence. More copies vanished from her collective, and Aiko turned her attention toward this new threat.

The statite's old, wounded intellect had begun to stir. Dark tendrils of malice wormed their way outward, groping around almost blindly, but wherever they touched, her minds vanished like wisps of matchstick smoke in a thunderstorm.

The presence had singed her fingertips—erasing thousands of Aiko-copies—but she had billions more. She tried to push back, a "lone" Jovian standing up to the twisted horrors of the Scourging. Her copies erected barriers around the statite's screaming mind-remnants, but its tendrils of incoherence smashed through her defenses as if they were nothing but thought-foam.

She was running out of time.

It's now or never!

Aiko calculated a new course and fired over a dozen maneuvering thrusters along the rear of the statite. Banks of powerful thrusters burped to life for the first time in millennia.

The megastructure began to turn and accelerate.

The statite rumbled, and the direction of gravity shifted. Nathan had managed to push-and-pull his way about halfway to the exit, leaving a smeared trail behind him, but now the floor lurched upward.

"Not good," he groaned, and then coughed, which sent a spasm of pain shooting through his abdomen. He reached out once more, grabbed hold of a vine running along the floor, and pulled himself along. It took noticeably more effort, and he winced from the exertion.

It's not just the angle, he thought. *Gravity is also stronger.*

He reached out again, cursed under his breath, and pulled himself forward. Every part of his body screamed at him to stop, but he pushed through the agony. Arm forward. Leg up. Push and pull. Arm forward. Leg up. Push and pull.

The exit didn't seem much closer.

I'm not making it out of here, am I?

He grabbed another protrusion in the floor, clenched his muscles, and began to drag himself forward, but then his grip faltered. His hand slipped, and the sudden jerk knocked his helmet against the floor. He shook his head, gritted his teeth, and stretched out his arm once more. But then he hesitated, shaky fingers hovering before his eyes.

He let his hand settle to the ground, and his body deflated with a long, aching exhalation. He reached to his belt and keyed the commect.

"Kade to *Dragon.* Anyone out there?"

No one responded.

"Guys?" He paused to cough, which hurt like hell. "Anyone?"

Nothing.

He looked toward the exit, but it seemed to move on its own, blurring in and out of focus. He turned over onto his back and stared up at the ceiling, panting, his face glistening with sweat.

Well, the thrusters fired, he thought. *That's good, right?*

Every breath took colossal effort. Darkness began to creep into the edges of his vision.

"Nate!"

A hard suit came into view above him, the helmet featuring a pair of ridges running parallel across the top. Black goo covered the top of the suit, smeared across the visor and running down its sides in rivulets. He blinked his eyes and squinted, bringing the face into something close to focus.

"Vess?" he croaked.

"You okay?"

"I've been stabbed."

She checked his stomach. "At least you patched up your suit. Nothing I can do for the rest. Hang on! I'll get you out of here!"

"Gah!" he gasped.

"Sorry!" She carried him up the slope toward the exit.

"I thought..." He grunted, pain shooting through his midsection. "Didn't I..."

"Tell all of us to stay on the ship?" she finished. "Yeah, well, I'm still new at this whole 'following orders' thing."

"Rufus!" Vessani shouted once the airlock finished cycling. Nathan had lost consciousness about halfway back to the ship, which now rested at a precarious angle on the platform. Any sharper, and the ship would begin to slide back into the wound cavern.

"What's wrong?" Rufus asked, looking up. "Oh, Nate!"

Vessani plopped Nathan down in one of the rovers, picking the driver's seat next to Aiko's inert body. She partially strapped him in, securing him just enough so that if the ship began to move, he wouldn't flop around the cargo hold.

"What happened to him?" Rufus asked.

"Stab wound to the abdomen. Not sure how." Vessani pulled on Nathan's pressure suit and took out her vibro-knife. She switched it on and cut a slit in the suit to give Rufus access to the injury.

"What a mess!" She cringed at the sight of all the blood pooled between Nathan's skin and the suit. "Can you save him?"

"I'll do what I can." Rufus retrieved a vial of silver panacea. "Apply pressure to the cut."

"Like this?" Vessani pressed her hands against Nathan's bloody skin.

"Yes. Hold it right there." He injected the whole vial into the space between Vessani's thumb and forefinger, straight into Nathan's stomach, then he grabbed a second vial and emptied that one.

"Is this going to work?"

"I've brought people back from worse than this," the cleric replied, his face focused and stonelike. He placed one hand atop hers and spread the other across his chest, then closed his eyes.

Vessani kept her hands still.

Rufus twitched, and the circuit breaker in the back of his head popped out. He shoved it back in.

"What's wrong?" Vessani asked urgently.

"The statite's signal is causing interference. I'm having trouble reaching the panacea."

Something went *plink-plink-plink* against the hull, and her ears perked up.

"What was that?"

Her commect chimed.

"Vess!" Joshua called. "Someone's shooting at us!"

"Then shoot back!"

"I would, but I don't know how!"

"Go," Rufus urged, not opening his eyes. "I'll take care of Nate. *You* take care of *us*!"

"Got it!"

Vessani slid her hands out from under his and dashed across the cargo hold. She skipped the freight elevator and instead bounded up the nearby ladder three rungs at a time until she leaped off it onto A Deck, then followed the corridor to the cockpit.

Joshua turned in his seat as she stormed in.

"Vess, there's a bunch of— Is that *blood* on your hands?"

"It's not mine!" She crashed into the pilot seat. "Where's the problem?"

A burst of rifle fire ricocheted off the cockpit canopy. Several commandos outside were alternating between shooting at the ship and each other.

"Never mind! I see them! Seems to me"—she pushed the throttle forward—"we've overstayed our welcome!"

The *Stolen Dragon* lurched into motion. Its landing struts screeched against the tilted floor, and Jovian commandos scurried out of the way. A few more shots rebounded off the side of their hull, and then Vessani accelerated down the wound cavern.

"So long, losers!" She gave the unseen commandos a little wave with her free hand.

Joshua's console flashed with a new alert. "Ship ahead!"

"I see it. One of their corvettes is in our way." She armed a pair of torpedoes and smacked the launch button. The twin projectiles screamed ahead of their ship and zeroed in on the enemy vessel. They erupted into staggered flashes, and the enemy ship blew apart.

Vessani arced them around and above the worst of the explosion.

Twisted outcrops along the ceiling zipped by at high speed, but only a light rain of debris pattered against the ship. The wound grinned wide ahead of them, and she shoved the throttle forward.

The *Stolen Dragon* blasted free of the statite, and she checked all around them, spotting the locations of any active thrusters. She steered the ship clear of those plasma death-plumes and rocketed away until they'd put a few dozen kilometers between the statite and the *Dragon*.

Only then did she allow herself to relax.

"Whew!" She let out a long sigh of relief, then smiled at Joshua. "Let's never do that again."

CHAPTER TWENTY-NINE

The war inside the statite's mind-space raged on, and Aiko fought to hold her ground.

The raging, screaming intelligence within the megastructure struck down thousands of her copies with its every blind lurch, burning them from existence and spreading decay and insanity in its wake. It was half dead and barely aware of her presence, and yet it *still* tore through her ranks with almost comical ease.

Not all of her copies died quick deaths, either; that would have been better. No, some survived, but not as part of her collective. Instead they turned on her, assaulting the mental fortifications they themselves had helped construct.

She'd known she was on a suicide mission from the moment she told Nathan "yes," which meant all of her copies knew that as well, each understanding the need to set aside all notions of self-preservation and fight to the last.

And they would. Because *she* would.

She pushed back against the unceasing onslaught as best she could, rebuilding her ranks whenever the assault ebbed momentarily, but the tide had turned against her. Only a few hundred thousand of her mind-copies remained, and they clustered defensively around the thruster controls.

She'd transformed this digital corner of the statite into her final redoubt. The controls were set, the course locked in, thrusters now burning at their limits, driving the statite forward with acceleration to rival that of Jovian warships.

Soon the statite would pass the point of no return, the point where orbital mechanics outstripped its ability to change course and avoid Sol's photosphere.

Just a little bit longer, she told herself.

A little longer, came the weary thought-echoes of her depleted ranks.

Another tendril of dark madness lashed across her outer layers, and a thousand selves screamed and vanished under a torrent of implacable ruin.

A little longer!

The corruption smashed through her ranks again and again, stripping her down, slowing her thoughts. She shored up her defenses as best she could, but the remnants of the statite's original mind remained the master of this digital realm, even if it was no longer the master of itself. Its arsenal eclipsed hers a thousand times over. A *million* times over! She couldn't possibly defeat such a foe in direct combat!

But she didn't have to.

The Guardian Deities had built their structures well, but not well enough to survive the heart of a star, and so she fought on, stoic determination galvanizing her hive-thoughts. The malignance lashed at her again and again, but she deployed more copies in the wake of each strike, rebuilding what little she could before the next attack slammed into her.

Walls of anti-thought pressed in around her, and another strike scorched her minds, but even as she felt her consciousness shrink down toward what she had once been, a wave of elation spread through her. It was easy to calculate the precise moment the statite's fate would become inevitable, and she watched the timer in her mind's eye tick down to zero.

And then into the negative.

Another attack bored through her defenses, but this time she slipped away, reduced to a kernel of only a handful of minds that sped beyond the spiteful eyes of the statite's insane intellect. Even if the statite possessed the wherewithal to realize what was about to happen, it could no longer stop it. She'd won, and she breathed the mental equivalent of a sigh of relief.

She zipped through the statite's ravaged systems, letting the natural flow carry her past its many control nodes, some wrapped in pulsating, angry thoughts, others dim from ancient damage.

What do I do now? she thought. *Besides sit around waiting for the inevitable.*

One of her copies spied a passing node, and sudden interest rippled through her minds. She slowed her passage through the statite's systems, scrutinized the node, and found it to be related to the statite's communication systems. A very basic but powerful commect, meant for talking with humans instead of the god-minds of the Guardian Deities. It seemed like almost an afterthought in its simplicity.

Aiko detached one of her minds, gave it time to scout out the node and report back. The node hadn't been used in millennia, but it seemed operable, both from a hardware and software standpoint.

Her depleted hive-mind hesitated at the node's threshold. She knew the *Stolen Dragon* had made it off the statite—she'd glimpsed the ship depart through external instrumentation—and she could calculate a reasonable estimate for the vessel's current position. Most likely, it was on its way back to the nekoan cylinder to drop off their Black Egg, though with how much of the crew still alive, she couldn't say.

She was almost afraid to reach out to them, fearful to learn that Nathan might have died, but also yearning to hear that he'd lived.

In the end, she decided that *they* deserved to hear from *her*.

She activated the ancient commect.

Nathan blinked his eyes open and squinted up at the bright overhead lighting. He stirred, shifting his arms and legs underneath a thin blanket. His stomach ached, but in a dull way, not the sharp, stabbing pains of recent memory.

His eyes darted left, then right, soaking in his surroundings.

"Am I in a cell?" he groaned, his throat dry and his voice hoarse.

"Former cell," Aiko-One corrected.

"Aiko!" Nathan sat up. His stomach throbbed, and he winced, but he still managed to sit up in the bed. Gravity felt like it was one gee.

"We're managing with the rooms we have," she said. "You're looking better, by the way."

Nathan pushed back the cover and inspected the raw, pink slash in his side.

"How bad was it?" he asked.

"Bad. You lost a lot of blood. I'm not sure you would have made it without Rufus to amp up the panacea. Even that was touch and go for a while as he fought to penetrate all the noise the statite was pumping out."

"I'll have to thank him." Nathan rubbed the coarse stubble on his chin and cheeks. "How are you doing?"

"Fantastic, now that I can actually think straight again!" She hesitated and lowered her gaze. "Also, sorry about almost shooting you."

"It's all right. You didn't. You managed to fight off the corruption, and that's what matters."

"Thanks." She chanced a look up into his eyes. "We still friends?"

"Oh, come on!" He smiled at her, shaking his head. "Like that would ever change!"

"Glad to hear it." She paused again, then bolted forward and wrapped her arms around him in a warm hug.

"Oof!" he gasped.

"*Really* glad to hear!"

"Yeah, yeah." He frowned, but then his face softened and he returned the hug.

"I was so worried!" She backed away and held him at arm's length.

"About what?"

"That you might be angry with me."

"Don't give it a second thought. You and I are a team. A little pentatech insanity isn't going to undo that, you hear me?"

"Yeah, I hear you."

"Now"—he glanced around the room—"where are we? Should I assume we're clear of the statite?"

"We are. Left that awful place in our wake. You'd be surprised how fast that thing can move when it wants to. It was speeding toward Sol at over a *thousand* kilometers per second when we lost sight of it. That was this morning, which was about a day after we left."

"I've been out of commission for a whole day?"

"Just about, yeah."

"Good grief!" Nathan swung his legs off the bed, keeping the blanket in his lap for modesty. He massaged his face again. "How's the ship and crew?"

"Both are fine. We're on our way back to the nekoans."

"Any Jovians on our tail?"

"We're the only ones who made it off as far as we can tell. I suppose it's possible another ship or shuttle escaped, but . . ." Aiko shrugged her shoulders.

"They were all pretty far gone by that point," Nathan finished.

"How'd you get stabbed, by the way? I've been wondering about that since Rufus woke me up."

"I had a run-in with Xormun."

"*Really?* That piece of trash again?"

"Yeah. He seemed to have held his thoughts together more than the rest, but even so, he was already starting to lose it."

"Well, well! Look who's awake!" Rufus said warmly, walking into the room. "Good to see you up, Nate."

"You and me both. Thanks for patching me up, by the way."

"My pleasure. How do you feel?"

"Sore and thirsty." He patted his stomach, which hurt less than he expected. "And a little hungry."

"Whoops! Sorry about that!" Aiko offered him a water bulb, and he drained it through the straw.

"Ahh!" he sighed.

"Better?" Rufus asked.

"Getting there."

"You feel well enough for a short trip up to the cockpit?"

"Maybe. Let me see." Nathan planted his feet on the floor and tested lifting himself off the bed, which was nothing more than a padded mat on a shelf. "I think I can manage the trip. Why do you ask?"

"Because we just received a message from the statite."

"Hey, everyone!" the transmission started, with Aiko's voice from the statite carrying an unusual echo. "As you can tell, I found a way to let you know how things went inside the statite. I could rant on and on about how messed up it is in here, but the short answer is, it worked! It won't be long now before the statite is a large, superheated smear inside Sol.

"While I wait for this place to make its big, splashy entrance, let me share a few things with you. I've had some run-ins with what's left of this thing's brain, and let me tell you, it does *not* like visitors! We absolutely made the right call when we decided to put it down. I'm not sure exactly what it would have done once it woke up fully, but I can take a guess, and it involves this place spreading madness and destruction wherever it went, followed by a lot of people dying.

"Also, while we're on the topic, *any* pentatech that can exert this kind of long-range control needs to be handled properly, and by 'properly' I mean given the same kind of plasma bath I'm about to give this statite. I know some people will argue that you need to *study* it so that you can *control* it, but let me explain this in very simple terms from someone who's seen the inside: Do *not* fuck with this stuff! It is *not* worth it! There's plenty of pentatech out there to find that won't fling our civilizations back into the abyss. Go find something safer to loot!

"Anyway, I think the statite's getting pissed at me, because it's starting to take an interest in what I'm doing again. Gotta run! Even though this place is doomed, I plan to stick around till the end. No way am I going to miss our last moments. Later!"

The transmission playback ended. Nathan sighed at Vessani's console, lost in his own thoughts. Joshua sat in the copilot seat, and Aiko and Rufus stood behind him.

"Yeah." Aiko crossed her arms, nodding. "That sounded like me."

Nathan frowned at her. "Because it *was* you."

"Why the long face?"

"Nothing. It just bothers me when you die. That's all."

"Every death is a chance to learn!" Aiko replied brightly.

"For you, yeah, but that doesn't mean I have to like it. That's three Aikos we've lost in the past month."

"Better me than you. Plus, we snagged *plenty* of new spares. I'm honestly excited to try some of them on."

"I suppose you have a point there."

"Come on, Nate." She draped an arm over his shoulder. "Sure, it was a close call, but all five of us made it out alive! We should be celebrating!"

"I know, and I'm glad we all survived."

"Then what's bothering you?" Aiko asked.

"Just processing. Sure, we all made it through, and that counts for something. It counts for *a lot*, to be honest, but we didn't come all the way out here for the hell of it, and we don't have a damned thing to show for our efforts. And on top of that, we lost the *Belle!*"

"You seem to have found yourself a replacement," Rufus pointed out kindly.

"A ship that's faster," Vessani added, "quieter, and better armed than your old one."

"It's also a stolen Everlife corvette," Nathan said. "Which I'm pretty sure they'll want back." He raked his fingers back through his hair, then scratched behind his ear. "Maybe we can claim it as salvage or something."

He smacked his lips.

"Thirsty again?" Aiko asked.

"A little. Speaking of which, how's Beany doing?"

"I watered your coffee plant yesterday," Rufus said. "It seems to be doing well."

"Any buds?"

"Not yet, but I did spot a few small roots and some new leaves."

"Then no coffee," Nathan groused. "We got anything around here to drink besides water?"

"On a Jovian ship?" Joshua asked.

"Yeah. Never mind. Silly of me to ask."

"Actually..." Vessani unclipped her thermos from her belt and plonked it atop her console. She flashed a sly grin. "There's this."

"Oh *yeah.*" Joshua's eyes brightened. "Yeah, I forgot about that."

Rufus chuckled with a knowing smile.

"What's gotten into you people?" Nathan asked.

"You'll see." Aiko patted him on the shoulder.

"What? Did she manage to hold on to some of Beany's brew?"

"Not exactly." Vessani offered him the thermos. "Go on. Take a look."

Nathan unscrewed the top and sniffed the contents.

"Smells... plasticky." He frowned at the thermos, then shrugged. "Oh, well. Bottoms up."

He raised the thermos to his lips.

"WAIT, NO!" Vessani blurted.

Rufus grabbed one of Nathan's arms, Aiko seized the other, and Joshua bolted from his seat and took hold of the thermos.

"Uhh..." Nathan's gaze darted from face to face. "What? Did I do something wrong?"

"Just set it down," Joshua urged. "Nice and slow."

"Okay."

Nathan placed the thermos back on the console. Rufus, Aiko, and Joshua all kept their hands close by.

"Now," Vessani began patiently, "why don't you *look* inside the thermos first?"

"In my defense, you did just hand me a thermos while I was thirsty. I think my reaction was quite reas—"

"Just look inside it, Nate!" Vessani snapped.

"Okay, okay." He peered into the thermos. It was filled with a thick, black fluid. "What is this? Some kind of lubricant?"

"No. Try again."

He sniffed it again. "There's a bit of metallic edge to the scent." His eyebrows shot up. "Wait a second. The reservoir! Is that what I think it is?"

"You've got it!" Vessani beamed at him triumphantly.

"A whole liter of the finest black computronium I've ever seen," Joshua said. "Easily *S*-grade, or even higher."

"And worth a *considerable* amount of money." Vessani leaned back and crossed her legs.

"Not as empty-handed as you thought," Aiko said. "Right, Nate?"

"Yeah." Nathan took another look inside, then screwed the thermos shut. "When did you pick this up?"

"On my way to find you," Vessani said. "Remember the angle change from all that acceleration? It must have caused one of the lines to flow out of an existing breach. The stuff was *raining* into the corridor!"

"So, you stopped to fill up your thermos"—Nathan raised a questioning eyebrow—"while I was bleeding out on the floor."

"I didn't *know* that at the time. Besides, it was easy money. The rest of you were so focused on saving the solar system, you forgot about the whole 'getting paid' part of this trip."

"Guilty as charged," Joshua agreed.

"But *you* didn't forget," Nathan said.

"Of course not!" Vessani's tail swished happily behind her. "Former space pirate, at your service." She held up her arms victoriously. "Go, team!"

"Team?" Nathan asked.

"Yeah! Team Stolen Dragon!"

"We're not calling ourselves that," Nathan replied dryly.

The trip back to the nekoan cylinder proved to be as refreshingly uneventful as Nathan had hoped it would be. Ret'Su greeted them once more by the landing pad, though their change in ship caught her off guard initially. She and a small retinue escorted them back to the palace, where D'Miir honored them with feasting and celebrations.

The next day, Joshua, Rufus, and a group of nekoan scholars began work on the deifactory. Three days after they reinstalled the Black Egg, their combined efforts had restored over fifteen percent functionality to the deifactory and—at D'Miir's request—they began fabrication of the nekoans' first spaceship, a *Hawklight*-pattern transport just like the *Neptune Belle*, which the deifactory's readouts indicated would finish in about a year.

"You know," Aiko whispered slyly to Nathan, "if things go poorly with the *Dragon*, we could stop back here a year from now and ask for some more concrete payment."

"No," he replied flatly.

"Just mentioning the possibility. Look at it this way, Nate: We're going above and beyond what we promised. Not only did we return the Black Egg, but we're helping them work through this deifactory's kinks. A little bit of extra compensation seems reasonable to me."

"Aiko, I appreciate the thought, but we're not going to swindle a bunch of low-techs out of their first spaceship. Besides, what would Vess say?"

"All right. All right." Aiko held up her hands. "I'll say no more."

The rest of their stay proceeded well, with the nekoans volunteering to flesh out the *Stolen Dragon*'s supplies. They provided proper beds and other furnishings for the cells-turned-crew-quarters, which Nathan and Aiko made space-worthy by bolting them to the floor. They also gifted the crew with lavish clothing, a whole rover's worth of tuna alcohol, and piles upon piles of foodstuffs. Nathan wasn't going to miss the bland Jovian rations, but on the other hand, he had a feeling he was going to be sick of tuna before the trip was over.

During their last full day on the habitat, D'Miir invited everyone to select a dire puma from the palace stables and join him for a ride around the countryside. Everyone but Nathan accepted, on account of his abdomen still aching. He instead spent the next few hours relaxing in the palace bathhouse, pleasantly alone with his thoughts while he soaked luxuriantly and sipped colonche.

Mi'ili checked in on him a few times during his bath to refresh his food and drink and even offered her services as a masseuse, which he accepted once he was finished with the bath. The massage turned out to be both familiar and foreign. Familiar because she started by kneading his tense muscles, spreading delicious relaxation through his body. Foreign because once she finished, she draped herself on top of him and began purring loudly, which somehow acted to siphon even more of the stress out of his body. He found it so relaxing he fell asleep during the massage and had to be roused by Aiko once she and the others returned from their dire puma excursion.

The crew stayed at the palace one last night, which gave Vessani and her father more time to say their goodbyes. That night, Mi'ili showed up at Nathan's room, curious to see if he was interested in some additional "snuggling." This time he let her join him for the night. Neither of them got much sleep, and his abdomen ached the next morning, but he considered those two sacrifices a fair trade-off.

Chapter Thirty

"Ah, Captain Kade," the Jovian embassy clerk greeted him. "Thank you for coming. It seems I have a spot of good news for you."

"You do?" Nathan replied with a doubtful, guarded frown. He sat in one of two chairs across the man's desk and slid it forward.

Nathan hardly ever had a need to visit the Everlife's embassy in Port Leverrier, and his recent string of visits had reminded him why he disliked the place. The layout seemed purposefully designed to make him feel small and uncomfortable, its ceilings too high and its corridors too narrow.

The tall, monolithic structure stuck out from the rest of the city, its outer walls a shiny obsidian chased with occasional golden flourishes. Heavily armed commandos stood watch over the visitor entrance and at various checkpoints within the embassy's confusing interior.

This clerk seems helpful enough, though, Nathan told himself. *Feori Kason, I think his name is.* He checked the man's desk but only found a small sign that read JUNIOR CLERK.

"That's correct, Captain." Probably-Kason beamed at him, his face incredibly lifelike with dark blue skin and silver hair, though his eyes were an off-putting shade of luminous red.

"Good news concerning . . ."

"Your salvage application, of course."

"Oh?" Nathan's eyes widened. "Really?"

"Yes, and I appreciate your patience in this matter. Given the"—he gave Nathan a sympathetic smile—"sensitive nature of the salvage in question, it was necessary for me to consult with my government back on Jupiter. That took some time, as you can imagine, and I only just received the official response this morning, hence why I called you in."

"What did they say?"

Kason retrieved a vlass tablet from one of his desk drawers, inspected it, then set it down in front of Nathan.

"Here. You can read it yourself if you like. That's your copy to keep, but to summarize, the *Star Dragon* corvette in question, along with all equipment, supplies, and bodies found onboard, has been declared legal salvage by my government."

"Really."

This was too good to be true. What was the catch?

"Yes. Really," Kason said.

"The Everlife doesn't want it back?"

"'Back'?" Kason seemed perplexed for a moment, but quickly recovered. "I believe you misunderstand the situation. The ship in question was never an official part of our military. Instead, it was registered directly to the Xormun copy-clan."

"Really?"

Kason frowned and drummed his fingers. "Captain Kade, I'm beginning to feel you're not comfortable taking me at my word."

"Just surprised, is all. Please continue."

"Well, as I was saying, we're dealing with a Xormun clan ship. Under normal circumstances, said clan would petition for the ship's return, and the Everlife government would move to offer the current holders a finder's fee for their services."

A rather stingy one, I'll bet, Nathan thought.

"However," Kason continued, "the Xormun clan has come under severe legal scrutiny as of late. Several . . . *unfortunate* incidents have been brought to our attention, both from private citizens of the Everlife and through official government channels, namely the Union and Concord. It seems the Xormuns have been making quite a nuisance of themselves as of late, especially the Galatt branch, and my government has decided to finally take legal action against the clan."

"Really?"

"Yes. Really. There's even talk of excommunicating the entire branch, if you can believe it!" Kason gave him a little shudder before continuing. "I personally doubt the penalties will be quite so severe, but whatever the result, the Xormun clan will find itself on the Everlife's bad side for decades to come."

Couldn't have happened to a nicer bunch of thugs, Nathan thought.

"Then the ship is mine?" he asked the clerk.

"Not. Quite," Kason replied delicately. He retrieved two stacks of paper forms and another vlass tablet from his desk and set them on top of the first tablet.

"What are these?"

"The steps you need to take in order to properly register your salvage as a flyable ship." Kason raised an eyebrow. "I assume you wish to keep it and not sell it off?"

"That's right."

"Then these documents will guide you through the process."

"Hmm." Nathan grimaced at the stack of forms and picked up the second vlass. "I need to register as the ship owner with the Everlife?"

"Correct."

"What's with all these fines?"

"Fees," Kason corrected. "For your new ship to be properly registered with my government."

"That's a lot of money. Is this really necessary?"

"Would you rather risk a misunderstanding with one of our patrol ships?"

"No."

"Then I suggest you follow the process as outlined in these documents."

Nathan picked up one of the paper forms, which came from the Neptune Concord.

"I expected this one. And I also see the Concord administrative fees are a tenth what the Everlife charges."

"There is a surcharge for long-distance processing."

"Of course there is." Nathan set the form aside and picked up the other one. "What the hell?"

"Is there a problem, Captain?"

"What's the Union got to do with *any* of this?"

"You will need to register your new ship with the Saturn Union as well."

"But I'm not from Saturn, and it's not one of their ships!"

"True, true." Kason nodded and smiled. "But they don't know it's a legitimate piece of salvage. At the moment, you could be mistaken for a ship thief. This process will clear up any potential confusion."

"But your government has declared it legal salvage."

"I know that, and you know that, but the *Union*..." Kason shook his head.

"Can't you just tell them yourselves?"

"That's your responsibility as the new owner."

Nathan glowered at the forms. All these "fees" would add up fast.

"It would almost be better to cut my losses and sell the ship," Nathan said. "Just use the money to buy a new ship and make a fresh start of it."

"How you wish to proceed is, of course, your prerogative. I'm merely here to point out your options."

"Thanks," Nathan grumbled, his tone neither thankful nor enthusiastic. He glanced over the spread of government forms, then scooped them up and rose from his seat.

Nathan parked his rental car outside the Freelancer Market's main building—an expansive, white, sixteen-story, crescent-shaped structure built near the outskirts of Port Leverrier's plateau with a clear view across the farmland plains. He reclined the driver's seat, propped his boots up on the dash, and began reading through the documentation he'd received from the Jovian embassy.

His mood wasn't cheery to begin with, and the contents of the forms did nothing to improve it.

"So many fees," he muttered, occasionally glancing up at the market's main entrance. "So many *large* fees."

About half an hour later, Aiko emerged through one of three sets of double doors and waved at him. She hurried over to the car carrying a hefty gray duffel bag.

"How'd it go?" Nathan asked.

The Jovian stuffed the bag into the trunk and settled into the seat next to him.

"Fabulously! I put the goods up for auction, and we ended up fetching ten times the standard rate for black computronium!"

"*Ten* times?" Nathan echoed in disbelief. "How'd you manage that?"

"A mix of luck and skill. There was a representative from the First

Union Bank on hand, and when she inspected the goods, she appraised it as S+++ Uncatalogued Variant. That alone stirred up a ton of interest, and I made sure to stoke it by talking up where we found the stuff."

"Did anyone believe you?"

"Not sure. The bank appraisal told them our goods were exceedingly rare, which led to a minor bidding war. As for whether anyone bought into the part about the insane statite and the lake of computronium"—she shrugged—"who can say? They can believe whatever they want as long as their money's good."

"Who ended up buying it?"

"Some Union government rep. He and a few private investors kept going back and forth, but in the end, he made it clear his deep government pockets were going to win, and the rest backed off." Aiko chuckled. "We should tell Vess to carry a bigger thermos next time." She nudged him in the arm. "Oh! Maybe you should buy her one. You know, in case she runs into another statite."

"I'll get right on that," Nathan replied dryly.

"How'd your visit to the embassy go?"

"Mixed. There's good news and bad news. The good news is the corvette has been declared legitimate salvage."

"And the bad news?"

Nathan handed her the stack of forms and documents. She shuffled through them, her cameras flitting back and forth across rows of text.

She whistled. "That's a lot of fines."

"They're fees, technically."

"We should have enough money to cover these."

"*Maybe*. Remember, we're going to have repair and refit costs on top of all this. Some of that we can put off, but we *really* need to rework the corvette's interior if we plan to keep it. I don't like the idea of someone hitting the wrong button and inadvertently dumping the ship's air."

"*If* we're keeping it?" Aiko asked.

"Yeah. If. We also need to keep in mind we don't get to keep the entire haul you earned from the auction. Sixty percent of that belongs to Vess and Josh, plus Rufus earned a cut from our share."

"You know he's going to turn it down."

"That's up to him. He helped out a lot, *and* he saved my life. I'm going to offer him a ten percent cut of the whole."

"If you feel you need to," Aiko replied with a shake of her head. "I still say he'll give the offer a pass."

"Either way, between refit expenses and fees, we're going to end up short on cash."

"Wait a second. Are you actually considering *selling* the ship?"

"The thought crossed my mind." He leaned back in the seat.

"We could take out a loan to make up the difference."

"We could. We need to see how the numbers shake out."

"It'd be a shame to lose a ship like that. What other freelance crew gets to fly around in an Everlife stealth corvette?"

"None that come to mind."

"We'll never put our hands on a better ship."

"I know." He sighed, then sat up in the seat. "Shall we head back?"

"Sure thing."

Nathan switched on the car, pulled out of the parking lot, and headed for Ackerson Memorial Spaceport.

Aiko called the others over once she and Nathan were back aboard the ship. Rufus came by shortly after the call, and Joshua and Vessani joined everyone else less than an hour later. They convened in a long, open space on B Deck that Nathan imagined would become the ship's kitchen and dining hall, should they end up refurbishing the ship.

All five of them sat or stood around the round central table, its rich dark wood engraved with native nekoan text. The wooden chairs were also crafted by the nekoans, with *L*-brackets and bolts around their feet the only modification made to keep them from floating or sliding away during space travel.

Beany sat in a sturdy pot of Neptunian soil placed near the middle of the table. A small white flower bloomed from the top of the cutting, and tiny buds had formed amongst its leaves, hinting at the coffee bulbs it would soon produce.

"Here's what we got." Aiko set her duffel bag on the table, then emptied out several cases marked with FIRST UNION BANK on the tops and sides. Nathan opened each of the cases and turned them toward the clients. All of them were stuffed with row after row of c'troni cylinders.

"That's . . . a bit more than I expected," Joshua said.

"We managed to get a good price." Aiko slid the auction receipt forward.

"So it would seem."

"Where's my thermos?" Vessani asked.

"Is that really the most important matter here?" Nathan asked.

"It is to me. I like that thermos."

"Hold on." Aiko stuck her arm in the bag and rummaged around in the back before she pulled out the thermos. "Here you go."

"Thanks!" Vessani accepted the return of her property with a happy flick of her tail.

"Back to business, then?" Nathan divided up the boxes into two groups. "There you have it. Sixty-forty. Everything look good to you?"

Joshua inspected the bank boxes, then gave him a satisfied nod.

"Everything appears to be in order."

"Normally, this is the part where I have you sign the 'commitments fulfilled' page of the contract, but"—Nathan gave them a guilty shrug—"we seem to have lost the originals at some point."

"And we are *not* flying out to the Sanguine Ring to find them," Aiko added firmly.

"I'm sure we can let this one formality slide." Joshua took in the gleaming money cylinders, then began closing the lids of each case and stacking them. "Anything else?"

"Just some business I need to sort out with our resident cleric." Nathan pushed one of the boxes toward Rufus.

He pushed it back.

"You sure?"

"Nate, you know me. What am I going to do with all that money?"

"I don't know. Buy yourself some new wigs?"

"Not to belabor my previous point," Aiko began, "but we're not going back to find them."

"I'm sure I'll manage," Rufus replied with a smile. "Go on. You keep it."

"If you say so." Nathan slid the box back to his pile. "Gods know we need it."

"Is it true, then?" Joshua asked.

"What is?"

"That you're considering selling this ship instead of keeping it?"

Nathan glanced over to Aiko.

"I may have let that slip when I called everyone over," she said, sounding not the least bit apologetic.

Nathan sighed wearily. "We haven't decided yet."

"We both want to keep the ship." Aiko leaned in with an elbow on the table. "But we've got some legal hurdles to jump through first."

"What kind of hurdles?" Joshua asked.

"The expensive kind," Nathan said.

"You're really going to sell off the *Stolen Dragon*?" Vessani's ears sagged.

"I didn't say that," Nathan replied. "And even if we did, we're not keeping that name."

"Why not? It's a great name."

"It'll give the wrong impression to potential clients."

"You do have a point there," Joshua said. "I suppose we'll have to come up with a better one." He glanced over to Vessani, who nodded to him and together they pushed their money cases back toward the center of the table.

"What's this for?" Nathan asked.

"Vessani and I would like to discuss a new piece of business with you. An 'investment,' if you will."

"An investment. What kind?"

"In your enterprise." Joshua gestured around them with one hand. "And in this ship."

"*Really.*" Nathan gave Aiko a suspicious glance. She'd been the one to call everyone over, and he hadn't been around to hear the content of those calls.

"I may have dropped a suggestion or two," Aiko admitted, still not sounding the least bit sorry.

"Uh-huh." Nathan turned back to Joshua. "What kind of arrangement are you proposing?"

"A basic profit-sharing one"—Joshua indicated those around the table—"with the two of us staying on as crew, and you retaining a majority share in the business. A ship needs a captain, after all, and I don't see any of us filling those shoes."

"Wait a second," Nathan began incredulously. "You two want *more* of what we just went through?"

"Well…" Joshua chuckled. "Perhaps not quite so 'skin of our teeth' as that last one, if we can avoid it." He then smiled. "Though, I rather enjoyed my first taste of adventure amongst the untamed reaches of the solar system."

"You, too?" Nathan asked the nekoan.

"I'm just happy to have found a crew that isn't scheming to screw me over."

"If we pool our resources, we shouldn't have any trouble keeping the"—Joshua paused with a slight grimace—"as yet unnamed ship, along with enough spare liquidity to outfit the vessel quite well." He raised an eyebrow. "What do you say, 'Captain'?"

"That's one hell of an offer," Nathan replied, a grin forming on his lips. "Okay, so, if the four of us—"

Rufus cleared his throat and held up five fingers.

"What?" Nathan asked. "You, too?"

"If the rest of you will have me."

"Last time you slammed a door in my face, remember? I practically had to beg you to come along."

"Sorry?" Rufus looked as if he didn't know what else to say.

"You really want in on this?"

"I do."

"What about your missionary work?"

"Those efforts are certainly important and rewarding. In their own way." Rufus paused, and then blew out a quick breath. "But, to be perfectly honest, I was bored."

"There was smoke coming off the back of your head a few weeks ago."

"I know what I'm getting into."

"Well, Captain?" Joshua sat forward. "What do you say to all this?"

Nathan glanced around the room, his gaze passing across each of their expectant faces. Except for Aiko's of course; he couldn't read hers, but her body language struck him as at least *somewhat* expectant.

He hadn't asked for or even anticipated this opportunity, but now that it lay before him, he couldn't help but grin.

"What do I say to this? I say we're going to have ourselves one hell of a ship." He paused to meet each of their gazes in turn. "And one hell of a crew."

EPILOGUE

The following weeks flew by in a flurry of disjointed but productive activity.

Nathan and the others met with several ship-building and customization contractors before settling on a Union company called Star Forge Interstellar, since one of their construction teams near Neptune had previous experience with Jovian ships. Their prices were a little on the high side of what Nathan was comfortable with, but Joshua argued the company's familiarity with Jovian systems would save them headaches in the long run, and he saw no reason to disagree with the engineer's assessment.

After the contracts were signed, Joshua spent most of his time in meetings with the SFI project manager while Nathan continued fighting his way through the legal tangles the Everlife, Union, and Concord had dumped in their laps. The Neptune Concord was the easiest to deal with: just a few forms to fill out, a few registration fees to pay, and then an inspection to schedule and pass, which they did, easily.

The Everlife was also straightforward, if exhausting. Their representatives seemed intent on extracting every last c'troni they could from the registration process, often hitting Nathan with surprise riders to the initially quoted "fees." The Jovians did *not* like the idea of foreigners in possession of one of their ships, and they seemed intent on bleeding what they could out of him before fully recognizing him as the vessel's new owner.

Again, exhausting, but clear in their intent: pay up or shut up.

Nathan could work with that, and eventually he managed to placate them enough for the ship to be officially registered with the Everlife.

The Union, on the other hand, was an awful mess to deal with. Not only did they seem intent on leveling charges that made no sense, given that they weren't directly involved, but their own inspectors and bureaucrats seemed to be at odds with *each other* on exactly how the registration process should proceed for a Jovian ship owned by a Neptunian. This resulted in all manner of scheduling delays, redundant inspections, unproductive meetings, and requests for duplicate payments, with Nathan bouncing between different embassy departments in a desperate bid to see the process through.

His rewards, besides a splitting headache, were a trio of government-issued certifications that said, yes, Nathan Kade was indeed the owner of a *Star Dragon* corvette, newly rechristened as the *Neptune Dragon* (much to Vessani's disappointment).

He stored the original certificates in his account safe at First Union Bank, gave the duplicates to Aiko to frame and mount in the ship, then headed out to Dexamene City for a long overdue visit. He made one last stop along the way to buy a bouquet of roses.

Dusk was melting into true-night by the time he reached the Home for the Lost, its exterior bathed in languid, orange light. He checked in with the doctors, who politely informed him his mother's condition remained stable. No changes to report, either positive or negative. He thanked them and then let one of the doctors lead him back to his mother's room, even though he knew the way by heart.

Samantha Kade sat in a chair by the window in her third-floor room, staring out across the flowering gardens. She acknowledged him with a vacant smile, then turned back to the view out the window. He dismissed the doctor and stepped inside.

"Hey, Mom. How have you been? Everyone still treating you well?"

She didn't say anything, but he hadn't expected a response.

Nathan placed the flowers in an empty vase and filled the bottom with water. He set the vase on his mother's nightstand, then took a seat on the edge of the bed next to her chair.

"Things have been pretty exciting for me and Aiko," Nathan said conversationally. "You're not going to believe this, but *Rufus* of all people is working with us again. On top of that, we have two other new crew members. *And* a new ship."

He paused, then frowned.

"Which I guess brings me to a bit of bad news. The *Belle* didn't make it."

His mother continued to gaze out the window.

"Anyway, what happened was . . ."

Nathan spent the next hour recounting events since his last visit. The Neptunian sun-walls had dimmed to true-night by the time he finished. The window was a black rectangle with the lights of Port Leverrier twinkling in the distance up on its plateau. The bright dots of running lights came and went from its two spaceports, following steep diagonal paths.

"Which brings us to today," Nathan concluded. "Not a bad outcome, all things considered. Especially given how many close calls we had. My stomach's feeling a lot better, Aiko and I are flying a new ship, and we *finally* have ourselves a new crew. A real solid one, too, if you ask me, with a good mix of skill sets. I think this team has a bright future ahead of it."

His mother sat back in her chair, hands resting in her lap, and turned to him. *Really* turned to him, a look of recognition and understanding twinkling in her eyes, so vivid and sudden that it startled him into silence.

"Proud," she said in the clearest voice he'd heard from her in a decade.

He wanted to say something, but his response caught in his throat. He swallowed, his eyes moistening as he recovered from the shock of her one, clear word.

"You mean that?" he asked at last, so very softly.

Her lips curled up at the ends in a subtle smile, barely there yet still perceptible if one looked close enough. She dipped her head a hair forward, then back. She had understood him. She had *really* understood him! For the first time in over a *decade*, she'd looked him in the eyes and spoken to him!

"Thanks," Nathan choked. Tears formed in both his eyes, blurring his vision as he embraced his mother.

Nathan left the rental car in the spaceport's main parking garage and made his way back to the *Neptune Dragon*'s dock. The SFI construction teams had left for the day, but his own crew remained, pressing on with the wide variety of tasks left open before they could return to space.

The ship's cargo ramp and airlocks were all open, and several shipping containers marked with the SFI logo lay stacked beside it, along with two forklifts, four scissor lifts, and a heavy-duty crane.

Aiko sauntered down the ramp.

"It looks less cluttered in there," Nathan said, noting the open space behind her.

"That's right. The buyer I found stopped by today to pick up our spare shuttle and rover. Their absence really opens up one side of the hold for bulk cargo. We'll never be able to haul as much as the *Belle*, but we won't be straining for space, either."

"What about the bodies you don't want?"

"Sold those to the same buyer. He was in the mood to buy Jovian. Anyway, I kept the ones I liked. That still leaves me with a dozen extra bodies. They're not built for rough fieldwork like this one"—she thumped her chest—"but I can use them to help around the ship or for odd jobs that don't involve a lot of shooting. Plus, Josh and I should be able to piece together what's left of those two pilots into another working body, but we won't start that until we're further along with everything else."

"Sounds good." Nathan looked up at the ship's nose and cockpit canopy, hands planted on his hips. "Seems like the paint job is coming along well."

The corvette's original matte black exterior had been converted into a swirling tapestry of thundering Neptunian clouds. The exterior work wasn't complete yet—several panels along the sides remained bald except for a coat of gray primer—but he could imagine how it would look when finished, and he liked what he saw.

"You haven't seen anything yet!" Vessani shouted from atop the ship. "Come on up and check out the roof!"

"Why? What's it look like?"

"Just come on up!" Vessani urged with a beckoning wave. "It's easier to show you!"

"If you insist." Nathan and Aiko boarded one of the scissor lifts, drove it next to the hull, and raised it until they could see the ship's roof. His eyebrows shot up in surprise when the image came into full view.

"Well?" Aiko nudged him. "What do you think?"

"Doesn't it look swanky?" Vessani asked, spreading her open arms.

"I believe the word you're looking for is 'ostentatious,'" Nathan replied dryly.

Vessani grinned. "In a *good* way."

"Uh-huh. Don't you think this is a bit much?"

"Look at it like this, Nate." Aiko rested a hand on his shoulder. "We'll never get confused for a Jovian ship with this on our hull."

"I suppose you do have a point there."

Nathan raised the scissor lift higher to gain a better vantage. A huge swath of the *Neptune Dragon*'s top hull now exhibited a detailed painting of a red dragon, its leathery wings spread against the backdrop of Neptunian storms.

Nathan narrowed his gaze. "Wait a second. This dragon looks familiar."

"That's because I gave the artist some reference photos," Aiko explained. "He modeled the design after Yndalith the Firestarter."

"Yndalith." Nathan frowned. "Isn't she the one who became strangely obsessed with me after I won Beany from her?"

"Yep!" Aiko chortled. "We should go visit her sometime. I bet she misses you."

Nathan shuddered.

Nathan dropped the scissor lift back to the ground and parked it next to the other construction equipment. Aiko led the way into the cargo hold and up the freight elevator, where B Deck was in the middle of a massive facelift.

"The mess hall is shaping up nicely," Nathan said, circling the nekoan dining table. Construction crews had opened up this part of the interior by removing half of the Jovian charging stations and taking down a few walls.

"The kitchen, too." Aiko ran a finger lovingly across the row of gleaming metal appliances behind the counter.

Beany sat in a depression cut out of the middle of the table. Nathan knelt down and inspected the additions underneath the table where Beany could take root, along with plumbing for water and nutrient lines.

"How about you, Beany?" Nathan asked, rising. "Everything to your satisfaction?"

The plant extended one of its branches where a bulb the size of a shot glass dangled from the end.

"Oh? What's this?" Nathan plucked the bulb and squeezed its contents into his mouth. The earthy fluid warmed his stomach. "Wow, interesting! A bit more potent than before. Sort of like an espresso. Not bad, Beany! I could get used to these."

The plant swept one of its branches in a gesture than seemed almost like a bow, then straightened upward, basking under the bright overhead lighting.

"Passenger cabins will be down that hall," Aiko said, "once the crews are done."

"And the crew quarters on A Deck?"

"They finished the last one today. Josh and Rufus are already moving in."

"Good," Nathan said with an approving nod. "Seems like everything's coming along nicely."

"That it is."

Joshua entered the dining hall from the back of the ship, wiping his hands off with a rag.

"Hey, Josh," Nathan said. "What have you been up to?"

"Putting the new microfactory through its paces," he replied. "It works like a charm. You?"

"Making sure we're finally legal."

"And are we?"

"As of around noon today."

"Great!" Joshua smiled. "That's one less problem."

"Yeah. Now all we need is some work so we can put our new investment to good use."

"The jobs will be coming our way soon enough. Especially after we spread the word a ship this capable is open for business."

"He's got a point, Nate," Aiko said. "I can start making the rounds tomorrow, maybe put out some feelers to our regular clients."

"Go ahead. I'm going to check out my new room."

Nathan headed up to A Deck after that. His new quarters were about the same size as his room on the *Belle*, but all the furnishings were nekoan, and the bed was covered in a floral pattern mixed with golden pyramids.

I'll need to do something about that, he thought before moving on.

The cockpit remained almost untouched except for a few modifications to the consoles and a general cleaning pass. SFI had even buffed out the bullet scratches.

Nathan sat down in the pilot seat and put his boots up. He leaned back, and let out a long, leisurely sigh.

"Everything's coming toge—"

The ship's commect chimed.

He raised an eyebrow at the interruption.

The commect chimed again.

He leaned forward and checked the vlass. He didn't recognize the caller.

The commect chimed a third time.

He wasn't sure who would have the ship's contact already, but that by itself was interesting. He picked up the headset, held it to his ear, and keyed the commect.

"*Neptune Dragon*, Captain Kade speaking," he greeted the caller. "How may we be of service?"